MAKING THE CALL

AMANDA SHELLEY

Visit my website at
www.amandashelley.com

CONTENTS

ABOUT THE BOOK

Dani

As a bestselling romance author, most assume my life's glamorous, filled with combustible chemistry, and most of all, romance. Ha! I can only wish. With a deadline looming, I've escaped to my family's cabin on Anderson Island to free myself from distractions. My plan's great, until a man, who could pass as a cover model on one of my books, comes to my rescue. Is there chemistry? Sure. Is he everything I'd look for in a guy? Absolutely. But will my career be at risk if I give into my desire?

Luke

For a player, women line up outside the locker room. For coaches, we're lucky to get in the game. As the youngest coach in the league, I live, eat, breathe, and even sleep football. To gear up for this season, I return to my home on Anderson Island for a much-needed break. When Dani literally crashes into my life, my mind's suddenly on the sexy brunette with a sailor's mouth, rather than my team's next play. She has me dusting off another playbook entirely, making me wonder, did I make the right call?

CONNECT WITH AMANDA SHELLEY

Want to be the first to know about upcoming sales and new releases? Make sure you sign up for my newsletter as well as connect with me on social media and your favorite retail store.

Website:
www.amandashelley.com

Newsletter:
https://bit.ly/3iyENe6

Facebook:
https://www.facebook.com/authoramandashelley/

Instagram:
https://www.instagram.com/authoramandashelley/

Twitter:

https://twitter.com/AmandShelley

Reader's Group:
https://www.facebook.com/groups/AmandasArmyofReaders/

Amazon:
http://amazon.com/author/amandashelley

Goodreads:
https://www.goodreads.com/author/show/
19713563.Amanda_Shelley

Book Bub:
https://www.bookbub.com/profile/amanda-shelley

AUTHOR'S NOTE

I intentionally made up the names of these professional football teams. Not wanting to get into licensing issues, I chose to create a world I hope you will enjoy. I know this may bother some, but hopefully you will see that this is to focus on the story, not on the accuracy of football. I'm an avid fan of football and often will be found supporting my favorite teams during the season.

LUKE

FOR PLAYERS, GIRLS ARE A DIME A DOZEN; THE COACHES, NOT SO much. I must keep my eye on the game. I've worked for this my entire life. I played college ball and was even offered a pro contract. But when a misguided tackle ended my career by blowing out my knee, I changed gears, switched my focus and spent the last six years working my ass off. I became the assistant coach to one of the best in the nation. My entire life's been devoted to learning what I can to help make my dream a reality. When Ray Carson chose to retire due to health reasons, my name was at the top of the list as his replacement. I never actually thought I'd be starting this next season as the head coach for the Rainier Renegades, a team I've always wanted to be a part of my entire life. But, in a matter of weeks, that's what's happening.

I'll never forget the day I walked into the owner's office. I rushed in to be early, unprepared to find everyone already waiting. I'd thought we were meeting to discuss the plans for summer camp. Little did I know they had something else in mind. Thank God, I'd been sitting down when I received my life-changing news.

"Hey, Luke," Mike Townsend greets, shaking my hand as I enter his office and gestures to the large conference table where I find both Tony Marcelli, our team's GM, and Ray Carson, the head coach, already sitting. "Why don't you have a seat. I have some things I'd like to discuss with you."

Instantly, my gut churns. Being under the impression we're meeting to discuss the summer camp training schedule and the logistics of getting everyone to camp, the expectant looks on each of their faces makes me think otherwise.

"Okay," I slowly draw out. "Aren't we meeting to discuss training camp?" I look from person to person already seated at the table, seeking clarification. But all of their faces remain stoic, giving nothing away. *The sorry fuckers. Couldn't they at least give me a heads-up as to what was coming?*

"We'll get to that," Mike bellows out as he takes a seat at the head of the table. He rubs a thick hand through his short, graying hair and rolls his chair forward to lean his elbows on the table. Okay, this is serious.

I take in a deep breath wondering where he's going with this. "All right."

I'm surprised to find Ray is the next to speak. "Son, you know I had a valve replaced last spring after the championship game, right?"

"How could I not? You nearly gave me a friggin' heart attack right alongside you, when I found you that day," I tease in return. Ray Carson has been my hero since I was a kid. To work with him has been a dream come true. I've followed his career since he took over for the Renegades. When I began coaching, he took me under his wings and showed me what it takes to coach a team to be champions.

Ray's gravelly voice begins an explanation, "Well," he draws in a long breath, "I thought I'd try to make it through another season, but my wife has other ideas. She wants to travel and make the most of the time we have left together." Ray looks a little sheepish, which is completely out of character for him.

"You're not going anywhere soon, Ray," I eagerly remind him. "Your doctor gave you the green light months ago, and I know you work out, so you're healthy. You have years left in you," I argue to refute his response.

"Well, I have a couple of championship rings, and more money than I could ever spend. Who knows how much time we all have left? I could be hit by a bus tomorrow, you never know," Ray states with a shrug. "You know I'm a hard-ass on the field, but when Vivian wants something, she's ruthless. I'm smart enough to give her what she wants."

Mike clears his throat. "That being said, I wanted to tell you how much we appreciated you stepping up to fill in for things last spring, while he was recovering."

"It was nothing any of you wouldn't do," I respond automatically. "Just doing my job."

"Well," Tony Marcelli interjects, "it didn't go unnoticed."

"What would you say to being the youngest head coach in the league?" Mike's deep voice suddenly fills the room.

The fuck? Did he really just say that? No fucking way. I. Am. Speechless. As my mama would say, I could catch flies with my mouth. Now that my jaw's dropped to the floor, I may need a

3

shovel to pick it up. *Fuck... and CPR to catch my breath.* Crickets could be heard from miles away; the room is that silent as they await my response.

"Luke?" Mike says as he places his arm on my shoulder, breaking me from my trance.

"Excuse me?" I manage to get out. *There's no fucking way he just offered me the head coach position. I'm only twenty-nine years old. I won't even turn thirty until August.*

"What do you say, Luke? Do you want to be the youngest head coach in the league?"

"Seriously?" Apparently, I say it aloud.

The room fills with laughter from everyone. "I think you shocked the shit out of him, Mikey," Ray bellows out. "The boy doesn't know what to do with himself."

"I'm as serious as a heart attack," Mike says again. "No offense, Ray."

"None taken."

"Wow. That would be an honor." I finally manage to get my wits about me. "I thought it would be years before Ray retires. I love the Renegades."

"We know you do, Luke," Tony Marcelli states. "We've been thinking about this for the past few weeks, and you're the only one we want to lead this team. You stand out above the rest."

I take in another deep breath. This is certainly humbling. "Thank you for even considering me."

"Do you not want this?" Ray asks in disbelief.

"Hell, no! I want this. I'm just thinking aloud, what an honor it is to be considered in the first place. There's no way I'd pass up this offer!"

I stand and gratefully shake everyone's hand. I receive

congratulations and slaps on the back as I make my way around the room. This is the job of a lifetime. I know I can do just as good of a job as Ray. I know the members of the team, and the inner workings of the Renegades, better than anyone else in the running.

"Glad to keep you around," Tony states to me as I shake his hand. "I'll have my secretary send you a new contract, and we can hash out the details later."

After another round of congratulatory handshakes that morning, we do discuss the logistics of training camp as well as some of the added responsibilities required of me in the coming weeks, since Ray will leave before camp begins. Ray had a lot more responsibilities than I did over the past few years, but I know I can handle it.

Since that meeting, my life hasn't been the same. The weeks have flown by in a blur. I'm up well before six each day. I work out on my own, eat breakfast then meet with the team by seven. I have meetings all day, work with the team during practices, and plan for the next day with my coaching staff before returning home late at night.

I prefer to get away from it all when I go out to my house on Anderson Island, but since becoming head coach, I've stayed in town more often. There's a ferry that gets me to Steilacoom, just before six thirty a.m., but I've been too tired to make the forty-five-minute commute.

Thankfully, this year's training camp went by without any major complications. Our practice schedule was rigorous, and the team feels in good shape, just coming off the championship win last season. Most of our team consists of returning players, with only a few rookies we'll test out in the pre-season games as well as some pivotal trades pushed through to help strengthen our O-line and special teams. Our hard work will pay off this fall, once the season officially starts.

To give everyone a break after our grueling schedule during summer training camp, the team has five days off before we come back at full force to gear up for the season. Many players will use this time to be with their families. It's an unspoken rule that each will continue their workout regimen on their downtime, but they don't have to be at our practice facilities for the next five days. Most of the members of our team are superstitious as fuck, so I'm sure they'll continue whatever gets them into their 'zone' as a professional athlete.

Myself, I'm looking forward to spending some time away from it all. I've been working my ass off around the clock to ensure nothing gets dropped through the cracks as the season begins. I know I need to prove myself not only to my team, but to the entire league, as I'm the youngest to ever do this. There's been a lot of hype and speculation, but I know the Rainier Renegades are ready, and I'll be there to ensure they keep the steady momentum we've built these past six years since I began working for the team.

I'm not spending the entire five days out at my home on Anderson Island, but I'll happily spend the majority of my time there. Sure, I'll review film from last season for the teams we're playing in the upcoming weeks. Since everything's digital nowadays, I can do it from the comforts of my couch, just as well as my office at the stadium. But I'll also spend time enjoying the remaining days of summer in the Pacific Northwest. There are a few projects I want to complete while I'm home, since I'll have free time to finally get around to them. The team's charity auction at the local children's hospital is the Saturday before we report back, so I must head back earlier than I'd hoped.

I pull off the ferry from Steilacoom just after four in the afternoon, and I quickly make my way to my home on the northeast side of the island. I love the land I purchased when I first was hired by the Renegades. I have a phenomenal view of the Sound as well as Mt. Rainier on clear days. I can hear the breeze as well as the water lapping against the shore when I sleep with my windows open at night. Sure, I have central air with my heat pump, but living in Washington, you don't need AC that many days of the year. Being on Anderson Island, it's nice to relax and take a break from the hustle and bustle of the city. The back side of my property is lined with trees, so I'm secluded while I'm here, which is a perk. Privacy is something I never thought was a luxury until I took this head coaching position, and my name was thrown into the limelight.

Anderson Island is the home to approximately a thousand residents. Most homes are vacation homes, so during the summer, the population raises to nearly four thousand. The island itself is just under eight square miles. It has a few restaurants and some stores if you need the basics, but if you want an item from a box store, you'll have to go to the mainland.

Thankfully, I have Evelyn, a woman who lives in the apartment above my detached garage, do my shopping and errands for me. Her young grandchildren live on the island full-time and when her husband passed away a few years back, she was looking for a part-time job close to her daughter so she could help her. I was looking for a housekeeper at the time and with my needs being flexible, it worked out for both of us. I don't have time to shop or clean for that matter and living on a remote island, it's necessary to keep things stocked up if I plan to spend any amount of time here.

Within a few minutes of exiting the ferry, I pull into the garage attached to my home and park my Mercedes next to my Jeep. I quickly unload the few things I brought with me and change into a pair of cargo shorts and a black t-shirt from back in my college days. Pulling a beer from the fridge, I prepare my dinner. I'm pleased to find Evelyn has the fixings for steak, corn on the cob, and a baked potato. Not wanting to waste time, I head to my back deck overlooking Puget Sound as well as Mt. Rainier in the distance to turn on the barbeque. Within fifteen minutes, I'm enjoying a delicious meal in complete solitude. I can already tell this is going to be just the break I needed before the season starts.

2

LUKE

I MAY BE ON VACATION, BUT MY BODY'S TRAINED TO WAKE UP before the sun each day. I manage to sleep in until six, but beyond that, I might as well be wasting the day away. I get up, change into some shorts and a t-shirt, put my running shoes on, and begin to stretch. I don't have a state-of-the-art gym out here, but I do have the open road. Well, I do have a weight bench and a few free weights in a spare bedroom, but not much more than that.

I'm out the door within minutes, making my way across the island in no time. Since it's not a big island, I have a route planned that takes me along the outskirts, maximizing the amount of pavement, so I can get a good run in. The sun's bright in the sky, and the weather's warm. As I run, I take in the stillness of the island, since its inhabitants are still enjoying their Wednesday morning from the warmth of their beds. I make my way up and over hills, sharing my morning with the few deer and the birds chirping in the distance. I have one earbud in, and my favorite playlist beats out a rhythm I easily keep pace with.

Rounding the last bend, my heart clenches in my chest as I witness a bad accident. Ahead of me, a bicyclist flies over their handlebars at the bottom of the hill. They go ass over end and skid across the pavement, to an abrupt stop. *Fuck, that had to hurt.* From the looks of it, they must've hit the large pothole on the side of the road. Their tire's now bent and twisted in an unusual shape. *Damn, they had to be cruising down this hill.* I pick up my pace to see if I can be of any assistance.

The closer I get, the more I realize it's a woman who's fallen off her bike. Thank fuck, she's wearing a helmet since her head bounced across the pavement a few times. By the time I arrive at the scene, she's sitting up inspecting the gravel embedded into her knees, palms, and elbows. *Christ, that looks awful.* Her curly brown hair spills out from her helmet, and her back is to me as I approach.

"Are you okay?" I ask, so I don't scare her.

"I'll live, but I don't think my bike will." She glances to me then winces as she pulls a large pebble from the palm of her hand. She points in the direction of her bike, and I can confirm for myself, it won't be in working order anytime soon. "Do you have a phone I can borrow? I seem to have lost mine in the wreck." I look around the area but have no luck spotting a phone. She takes off her helmet, and her brown hair springs free. It distracts me for a moment because she suddenly takes out her ponytail, shaking her locks free. God, even with dirt in it, it's beautiful. Her curly hair comes to life with each movement, catching hints of auburn in the sunlight. It's almost mesmerizing, but eventually, I remember my manners.

"Um, I live just two driveways down. Would you like come to my place to clean up, or maybe I can call someone for you? I left my phone at home this morning, so I'll have to go home either way before I can help you." I walk over to her and hold out a hand. "Do you think you can walk?"

"It'll just be easier if I come with you." She lets out a groan as pain radiates across her face. I immediately reach out to assist her into a standing position.

"Are you sure you're okay?" I ask as I steady her. She immediately begins hobbling as weight is put onto her feet. "Here, let me help you."

As if on instinct, I reach behind her back and under her knees to pick her up. Standing at her full height, she comes only up to my shoulders. She's a slender woman with curves in all the right places. If I had to guess, I'd say she's around my age, and she can't weigh more than 140 pounds. I can easily carry her to my house and get her fixed up in no time.

"Wha... What are you doing?" she stammers as I walk in the direction of my home.

"I'm taking you to my place to get you cleaned up. Then I'll come back for your phone and bike, to take you wherever you need to go," I say as I reach the entrance to my driveway.

"But I don't even know you. You could be an axe murderer for all I know."

I can't help the grin spreading across my face. She's adorable as she attempts to get stern and pin me with her ocean-blue eyes. There's a girlish presence about her, but her body tells me she's fully a woman. The short riding shorts she's wearing have crept up her thighs, and I can tell she works out regularly by the firmness of her beautiful body. Her loose tank has risen as well, revealing a toned abdomen. *She's definitely all woman.*

"Well, I'm Luke. I'm pretty sure if I were an axe murderer, the community would've found me out by now. It's a small island. I can promise you, I have nothing but good intentions. I'll let you sit out on my back deck and tend to your wounds without making you step foot in my house. I have a housekeeper, who lives in the apartment above the garage over there. So, if you'd like to have someone present, I'll gladly wake her if it'll make you feel more comfortable."

Heat creeps up her face, making it turn slightly red. *She is adorable.* "I don't think that'll be necessary. Besides, you didn't have to help. You could have just left me on the side of the road," she says as she shakes her head to hide her embarrassment. Her hair brushes my bare chest, and my senses go on overdrive. *Calm the fuck down, Luke. She's injured, and you're only helping her out.*

"What kind of company do you keep, if you think I'd just leave you out alongside the narrow road with no shoulder?" I ask incredulously.

"It was a figure of speech," she deadpans, her eyes narrowing.

"Just checking," I reply, not knowing what to say. I walk up the steps to my back deck and set her down on a lounge chair.

"Wow, you have an amazing view," she whispers as I set her down.

"It's incredible," I say before I open the French doors to go inside. "I have a first aid kit, I'll be right back."

I rush upstairs to my bathroom and return only a few minutes later to find the mysterious woman on my porch beginning to pick out rocks from her palms. *She sure is stubborn.* "Here, let me help." I open the kit and look for a pair of tweezers. She appears to just have major road rash, but I should look things over as I help her clean her wounds. She may need a trip to the mainland to an urgent care clinic if anything needs stitches.

We spend the next few minutes cleaning out her gashes. It's just as I expected, only road rash. It'll hurt like hell for a few days, but she doesn't have any major injuries. She does her best to control her winces as I clean out each area. I try to distract her with conversation, though I'm not sure how effective it is.

"So, do you have a name?" I ask as I go through a particularly gnarled piece of skin on her knee.

Embarrassment floods her features. Her face flushes with color, and her ocean-blue eyes are suddenly hidden beneath her long lashes. "Uh, it's Dani?" she states, making it sound like a question and causing me to narrow my eyes at her. Before I can say anything, she continues, "It's short for Danika."

"Well, Dani..." I draw in a deep breath as I attack a stubborn piece of debris from her left knee. "What brings you barreling down the road this early in the morning?"

"I was trying to wake up by getting a workout in. I stayed up late last night working on a project, and I need to get into the zone, so I can continue today." A look of apprehension flickers across her face, as if she's revealed too much.

Not sure if I should pry further into what she's revealed, or let it go, I stick with a safe line of conversation. "Well, let's get you cleaned up so you can get back to it."

Dani lets out a groan, and I'm unsure if it's in frustration or from pain. "There's no way I'm going to be able to work today," she says as she shakes her head in disgust. *Well, at least she solved that mystery. Her project must be important.*

"Why is that?" I ask, genuinely interested in her answer. There's a look of determination that I don't find on many others. It's as if she's internally kicking herself for getting injured, and I'm not entirely sure why. It was obviously an accident.

Letting out a huff of breath that washes over my chest like a live wire sending electric pulses throughout my body, she states dejectedly, "I have a deadline in the next few weeks that I need to meet. There's no way I can work on my computer, when I can barely use my hands. God, I was just getting ahead, too. Nancy's going to kill me."

"Is Nancy your boss? I'm sure she'll understand," I offer, trying to show sympathy.

"No, she's my editor."

Before either of us can say anything else, Dani's distracted by the hydrogen peroxide I pour onto her knee, and she instantly gasps. "Fuck! Give a girl some warning. That shit hurts like a sonofabitch!" She lets out a low hiss, then lowers her voice as "DAMN! FUUUCK! SHIT!!!" come out in a slur of words. She takes in a deep breath and holds it, while I press on the cloth to take the sting away. I can't help my smile when I realize this sexy woman could curse a sailor out of a bar with that mouth of hers. She'd definitely give the boys in my locker room a run for their money and would certainly make them stand up and listen. I nearly lose it when she suddenly turns tomato red and covers her face with her hands. "I am so sorry," she mumbles from behind her splayed-out fingers.

"No worries, Dani. I didn't mean to hurt you." I can't help when the corners of my lips tip up. "I'm honestly quite impressed you weren't cussing up a storm when I arrived on the scene. I watched you go airborne and skid across the pavement." I can't help but cringe at the image that replays in my mind.

"God, this is so embarrassing." She shakes her head and refuses to make eye contact.

I reach my hand under her chin and guide it to make her look at me. "Dani, you have nothing to worry about. Seriously. I just want you to be okay."

When our eyes lock, I'm not sure what comes over me, but I find myself sucking in a breath to steady myself. *What the fuck was that? Focus, Luke. This isn't the time. She doesn't seem to be like a girl who is into one-night stands, and that's all the fuckin' time you have these days. And let's face it, you don't even have time for that.* I shake my head and regain control of myself. *Sort of.*

"I know," she whispers. "I do appreciate your help. Please know that."

I release my hold on her chin and try to focus on getting her left elbow clean. It only has a bit of debris in it, so it cleans up quickly. When the last of her battered body is bandaged up the best it can be, I offer her some ibuprofen to reduce the swelling and pain. I quickly make my way into my kitchen for a glass of water and the bottle of pills. Upon my return, she quickly gulps it down and rests back on the lounge chair I had placed her in.

"Would you like to sit here for a bit while I fetch your bike and look for your phone? Here, put your number into mine, so I can search for it easier." I reach my arm over, handing her my phone.

Without any hesitation, she dials her number. When she places it back in my hand, I notice she's already pressed send and hung up. "I'll be right back," I say to her as I hop off my porch and jog down my driveway.

3

DANI

"THIS CAN'T BE HAPPENING TO ME," I MOAN ALOUD. *THIS ISN'T real. What else could it be? Not only do I crash and burn of epic proportions, but I must do it in front of Ian Somerhalder's doppelganger? Of course, 'just Luke' is likely taller than Ian and much better built, if that's even possible. He freaking picked me up as if I were a toddler and carried me all the way up his driveway. He's lucky I was too injured to think about his sculpted hot body or the way his scent was masculine and uniquely him. Damn, even covered in sweat, the man's smell could be bottled and sold on the black market for billions.*

When my face cradled against his bare chest, I couldn't help but notice the small tattoo across his right pec. It was an ornate balance scale. On the trays hanging from each side of the scale were the words 'ability' and 'choice." Choice was made to appear heavier. *I wonder what it means?* On his inner bicep on his right arm, he also had an amazing design of Mount Rainier with a few trees in the foreground. Both of his tattoos would have been completely hidden, if only he had put a shirt on.

He's gone only seconds, or I'm just too distracted to notice his absence, when his deep voice pulls me out of my reverie. "You're in luck. I found your phone about twenty feet away from your bike. It must have gone flying when you went airborne. Thankfully, no damage was done to it, that I can see."

"Thanks again," I offer as I reach out for my phone to tuck it into my shorts pocket.

He leans my now-dilapidated bike against the railing to the deck, then he comes to sit in the chair next to me. I start to stand, but Luke stops me when he says, "Why don't you take it easy for a few minutes. I was just about to make breakfast. Would you care to join me? Or, if you'd rather, I'll take you home." He suddenly stops and looks everywhere but at me, then he stammers a little, "Uh. That's if you want my help." He looks toward the pocket I placed my phone inside.

"I might be persuaded to stay for breakfast," I say with a teasing tone.

"Great. Want to stay out here while I whip something up?" His lips turn up like he wants to smile but is holding back. The gleam in his eyes gives it away, too.

"Um," I hesitate. My manners say to get up and go inside, but my body protests otherwise. "Would you mind if I stayed out here? I'm only *slightly* stinging at the moment and if I don't move, I might be able to imagine this never happened."

Luke lets out a soft chuckle and shakes his head slightly. "Not at all. I have the makings for omelets. Would you like one?"

"Sure, sounds good."

"Be right back." He walks a few steps toward his door before stopping to ask, "Are you allergic to anything?"

"Nope. I'm good with anything."

"Be right back."

Wow! A man with his looks, that's kind, helps those in need, and can cook? I must have woken up in an alternate reality. The last man who cooked for me was my college boyfriend... and that ended years ago. Since then, I've been so busy on my own, I haven't made time for anything serious.

When was the last time I even had a meal with someone who wasn't family or there for business? Hell. I have no idea. I need to get out of the worlds I create and live in the real one for a while. Though, if I'm being perfectly fair, Luke does seem like a character I'd write about, rather than someone I'd meet in real life. I could only be so lucky...

I *am* lucky though, if I'm being honest. I've taken something I enjoy and found a way to make a living out of it. As an English major, I've always loved literature and everything about it. I'm an avid reader and nine times out of ten, can be found with my nose in a book. In fact, once as a child, I was on vacation and as a punishment, my parents threatened to take my books away if I didn't come out and enjoy some time with my three brothers. I still laugh at the memory. But through the years, books are still a huge part of my life.

When I was struggling to make ends meet and wanted to prove I could do it on my own in college, a friend of mine suggested I self-publish a story I had written, "just for fun." I didn't think anything would ever come of it, but that one choice became the starting point to a career I thoroughly enjoy today.

When I published the first book in a romance trilogy, I was able to make enough money to cover the cost of publishing the entire trilogy, but not much else. It wasn't until I had written my fourth book, that people took notice. To my surprise, my hard work paid off. It actually made some of the top sellers lists and paved the way for the career I have today. By the time I graduated from college, I no longer wanted to work for anyone else. I have a steady flow of income as long as I continue to keep up a rigorous schedule and publish books in a timely manner.

It's not to say I'm all work and no play, but the last three years have kept me busy. My ex didn't understand why writing was so important to me, so we parted ways long before graduation. Not wanting distractions or having to explain why when I'm "In the zone," I might not be able to keep track of time or even shower regularly. I try to vacation or at least take a break a few times a year, so I can keep my mind fresh, but once the publishing cycle starts, I'm constantly working on one project or another. Speaking of which, what should I do about my characters in my current book...

Just as I begin to zone out, thinking about how to get my characters out of the predicament they're currently in, Luke interrupts my thoughts with his sexy deep timbre, "Hey, Dani, what would you like to drink? I have orange juice, coffee, milk, or water."

"Uh..." *How long have I been spacing out?* "I'll have orange juice. Thanks."

"Sure thing." I hear from inside the house. "I'll just grab it and come out."

As Luke enters the deck, I attempt to stand and help him, but he stops me. "No need to get up. I got it."

He flashes a brilliant smile as he hands me a tray with my entire meal resting on it. "Oh, you deliver, too. I'll have to keep that in mind."

Luke rolls his eyes and shakes his head. "Don't be too impressed. This and barbeque are about all I enjoy cooking."

The delicious aroma hits me before I can say anything. My stomach beats me to voicing my appreciation with an audible rumble. *Great. I can't catch any breaks when it comes to this man.* I do manage to stifle my embarrassment by saying, "Thanks, it smells amazing."

The crinkle around his deep-blue eyes and the twitch at the corners of his lips are the only hints he finds me amusing. I'm not sure if this is a good thing, but I make the best of it by taking a quick bite to occupy my mouth before I embarrass myself further.

Luke sits down in a chair next to me and takes a bite from his own plate. We spend the next few moments enjoying the food and the indescribable view of Puget Sound before us. I could spend days out here and never get enough.

"So," Luke clears his throat then says as he points to my plate, "what do you think?"

"Um..." I cover my mouth as I finish chewing. "This is delicious. Thank you." There's the perfect combination of eggs, cheese, bacon, and fresh mushrooms. *Holy shit. The man can cook.*

"Glad you like it."

"So, do you live on the island full-time or are you just here for vacation?" I can't help but ask. This home is beautiful, and it's obviously well cared for. There's no way he's only here for a vacation.

"I try to get out here as often as I can, but I have a loft in Tacoma as well," he admits. "What about you, are you a full-time resident?"

"I'll be out here as much as I can for the next year or so. I have some commitments off the island, but I hope to consider this home when I'm not traveling for those." Other than the signings I've committed to attend around the country, I intend to get as much writing done as I can. Being at my family's cabin will limit my distractions and hopefully keep me meeting my deadlines.

"Which part of the island are you staying?" Luke asks after he finishes his last bite of food.

"The east end of Florence Lake. It won't take long to get there."

"Ha. Nothing on this island takes long to get to," Luke teases.

"You're right about that. I've spent many summers out here as a kid and now that I live here full-time, I realize just how small the island is."

"You sound like you're not enjoying it," Luke surmises.

I shake my head, he has it all wrong. "No! Not at all. I love it here. It's why when my grandparents decided to stay in town full-time, I jumped at the chance to stay at their home here on the island. Most of my brothers are still in school, and Derek wasn't interested. Besides, this is just the place I need for limited distractions."

"Distractions?" Luke prompts.

"Well, as I started to tell you before, I'm on a tight deadline." I flex my hands open and shut. It shouldn't take too long to be back to normal. Nancy shouldn't get her panties in too much of a twist if I take a day or so off. Being the ambitious person I am, I have a book releasing every eight to twelve weeks for the next year. Thankfully, I already have the next four written, and they're off to the editors, but it still puts a lot of pressure on me to perform. I don't want to disappoint my readers.

"Oh," he hesitates for a moment then asks, "you mentioned your editor earlier, what do you write?"

Here it is, the one question that will either get me looks of admiration, or like I've lost my mind. Win or lose, I own it. I love my job and wouldn't have it any other way. "Contemporary romance." I hold my breath as I scrutinize his response.

"So, how long have you been writing?" *Huh, that's not what I was expecting.* His face looks as if he's genuinely interested.

I blurt out, "All my life," before I can fully answer the question he's probably asking. I add, "Well, I've only been published for the past four years."

"Wow, that's impressive." Once again, his response is genuine. Most guys I meet don't know how to respond when I tell them what I do for a living. They either get flirty and offer to enact any romance scene I write, or they scoff and act like I don't have a real job.

"Thanks," I say suddenly, feeling a bit shy. "I'm just lucky to get to do something I love."

A huge grin spreads across his face. "I can completely relate to that. I just started my dream job as well."

"It's a lot of pressure to keep things up," I admit for the first time to anyone.

"Well, you must be pretty good if you're able to make a living from it," he offers.

"Well, since I self-publish, I cover the costs of publishing and have enough to live on afterward, so I can't complain." It's true. I've done well for myself over the past few years. From the start, I made a point to go wide and market myself on all platforms; making the top sellers list a few times hasn't hurt either.

His eyebrows knit together slightly, and he contemplates something. "Would I know any of your work?"

"Do you read romance?" I ask, once again caught off guard by his question. This is something I usually get from women, not men. *Not that I'm gender typing.*

"Uh... Can't say I've read much." He looks a little disappointed to admit, then if I'm not mistaken, his cheeks turn a shade darker. "I've... Uh... Only read what I had to in college and watched a few movies... that were once books."

I let out a sound that's a cross between a sigh and a snort. *I know, very unbecoming of me.* "Well, then it's safe to say you likely haven't read my work. I haven't been around long enough to be considered a classic, and I'm certainly not famous enough to have a book made into a movie. An audio version, yes, but nothing on the big screen. I'm afraid you'll have to wait a bit longer for that, but don't hold your breath. It may never happen."

He suddenly stiffens. "It's not that I don't read." He leans forward in his seat to make sure he has my attention. "I read all the time, when I'm not reviewing film, it's how I spend most of my flights, actually."

"So... You're more of a movie buff, I get it. It's totally acceptable even." I try to tease at the end, but I'm not sure if it's received as I intend. *Crap. I didn't mean to offend him by saying he didn't read.*

"I... I... Just usually read mysteries or suspense... Even quite a bit of biographies." He scrunches up his nose and pulls a face. It's the most adorable thing I've ever seen on a man, as sexy as him, do. I can tell he's about to deliver me news I might not like to hear. *God, what's he going to tell me next?* "Well, I can't say I actually read a lot of romance. It's not really my thing... You know..." He trails off and lets me come to my own conclusion.

The look on his face trying to explain that he isn't into romance is downright hysterical. I outright belly laugh. I can't help it. He's so concerned he might've offended me. I end up doubling over, gasping for air. There may or may not be some snorting involved, but I won't admit to anything. Just as I'm going into convulsions, he joins me. *God, his laugh is beautiful. It brightens his entire features and makes him even sexier, if that's possible.*

After a few moments, when we've both calmed down, I ask, "So, romance isn't your thing?"

He shakes his head and tries to keep his composure. "Nope. Can't say that it is. I'm not opposed to it, but I can't say I've read much."

"Well, you can't be perfect. At least I can say you now have at least one flaw I'm aware of," I tease then realize what I just said aloud. *Shit. What's wrong with me?*

"Dani, I'm far from perfect." He shakes his head as he rolls his eyes. "Trust me."

"Good to know," I respond automatically. *I really need to shut up.*

We spend the next few minutes talking about some of our favorite authors. He likes Tom Clancy, Dan Brown, and a few others I enjoy reading as well. We talk about our favorite books as kids, too. His were the Hardy Boys and the Box Car Children, while mine were Sweet Valley High and Nancy Drew. Thank God, we both love Harry Potter, or I might not be able to talk with him about books much longer. By the time we're done, we've shared quite a few laughs and gone down many memory lanes.

Eventually, we talk about life on the island and how much we enjoy it. At some point, Luke and I both get up and clear our plates into his kitchen. Thankfully, the ibuprofen's kicked in, and I'm beginning to feel better. The inside of Luke's home is stunning. It has an open floor plan, with hardwood floors throughout and granite countertops in the kitchen. There's a breakfast nook in a bay window that overlooks the Sound, and a countertop with four barstools opening to a large living room. As I look around the living room, I notice there's a larger than life television mounted on the wall with a large, dark-brown, leather sectional and matching recliner. This is the epitome of a bachelor pad, but with class and comfort mixed into it. The walls have still-life photos of things that can be found here in the Pacific Northwest. These images include Mt. Rainier, the Seattle City

Center, an aerial view of a football stadium, and Puget Sound itself.

Minutes seem to fly into over two hours. When I look at my watch, I'm shocked. "Wow! I'd better get going. I have a conference call to make with my editor in less than an hour."

"No problem. Let me just load your bike onto my bike rack, and we'll be on our way," Luke offers.

"Are you sure you don't mind?" I ask, not wanting to put him out any further. "I'm feeling better. I can just walk if you're busy."

"Dani," Luke says in the sternest voice I have heard yet, "if I didn't want to help, I wouldn't have offered." A grin spreads across his face. "Besides, I've enjoyed getting to know you. It's not every day you meet an author, you know."

"Oh, Geez." I shake my head in disbelief. I know he's joking, but I've never had it put that way. It seems ridiculous. "Authors are a dime a dozen. I'm nothing special." My attempt at playing modest is awkward at best. "I've enjoyed getting to know you better, too, Luke."

We walk out the front door, and he leads me to his garage. In it is a Jeep Wrangler and a sleek charcoal-gray Mercedes. Luke sure does seem to have fancy tastes. His garage is neat and orderly. There are a few mountain bikes hanging from the rafters as well as a couple of kayaks along one side. He must love the outdoors. Now that I think about it, we never did get around to discussing what he does for a living, but I think I'll wait for another time to ask that question. We seemed to get along well today, and I don't want to spoil anything.

He attaches a bike rack within minutes to the back of his Jeep and seconds later, my bike is loaded. He assists me into his lifted Jeep, and we are soon on our way to my place. I can't think of a time when I have enjoyed myself more in the company of a stranger. We make idle small talk as I direct him to my home. When we arrive at my place, he unloads my bike and puts it in my garage, next to my trusty Honda. My garage is nothing like his, as it has some of my grandparents' things being stored in it, until they can come out and continue going through everything.

"Thank you so much for your help today. I don't know what I would've done without you."

"It was my pleasure, Dani. I'm glad to have met you." His deep voice sends shivers through my body. He fidgets with the keys in his hands, suddenly for the first time looking awkward and out of place. It's like he's nervous or something.

"Maybe we'll see each other around?" I offer, not really wanting him to leave. *What the hell are you doing, Dani? You can't afford distractions. You came out to the island to keep your deadlines.*

"That sounds good. It was really nice to meet you today."

He starts to turn toward his Jeep but stops and shocks the hell out of me. "So... If I were to read one of your books, what name would I look for? You never told me your last name."

4

LUKE

"Uh, it's Fallon." Dani suddenly looks sheepish. "But you won't find my books under that name. My pen name's Charlotte Ann."

I raise an eyebrow, looking for further clarification. "Okay..." I await her explanation.

"There's a lot of crazies out there. Other than my family and close friends, I don't tell a lot of people my real name. It's easier that way."

Boy, do I know about the crazies. This is the first woman in forever to know me as just Luke. I haven't mentioned what I do for a living, because it's so refreshing to just be myself and not worry about any expectations she may have about me. Besides, I never know if the women I meet, who also happen to be fans, want to be with me or the man who coaches the Renegades. Even as an assistant coach, I've always had wanna-be WAGs, trying to go through me to get to the players. Dani seems different, she doesn't appear to want to be wife or girlfriend

29

material to members of the team, but I'm not pressing my luck. Besides, the season's just starting, and I hardly have time for more right now.

There's something about her that I don't want to let go of though, and I can't explain it. Perhaps that's why I asked her where I could find her books. *Who the fuck knows what I was thinking?* All I know is that I couldn't let her go, without trying to get to know her more.

"Well, your secret's safe with me, Dani," I assure her. Anonymity's priceless in the world we live in. It's part of the reason I chose to live on this island for the past six years. For the most part, I'd met most of my neighbors when I first started working for the Renegades. Now they think nothing of it. Occasionally, someone will mention how we did on our last game, but they're not fame chasers and respect my privacy, which I appreciate.

"Thanks." She pulls in her bottom lip and slightly appears shy. Her phone suddenly rings, and she shakes her head. "I have to take this and knowing it's Nancy, it'll be a while." She answers the call with a "Hey, Nancy. Can you hold on a sec?" She then looks in my direction and whispers, "Thanks again for your help and the ride home. Hopefully we'll run into each other under better circumstances next time."

"It's no problem. I'll let you get to your call." I gesture to the phone she's covering with one hand. "I'm sure I'll see you around." With that, I make my way back to my Jeep, back out of her driveway to head back to my place.

The entire ride home, I replay our easy conversations from earlier. Dani seems genuine. She has a strong head on her shoulders and is following her dreams. If I had time for anyone, she would be someone who'd pique my interest. *Who am I kidding? When was the last time I even thought twice about someone in any way? Obviously, she's piqued my interest, but with the season just getting started, I don't have time to start anything near what she deserves.*

When I park my Jeep in the garage, my thoughts are still on Dani. I pull out my phone and suddenly find myself looking at bike repair shops. I easily recall the model of her bike and before I have time to think twice about it, I'm ordering a new wheel for her. With a simple phone call, I'm talking with the manager of the store and convince them to deliver it to the ferry terminal later this afternoon. I'll just hop a ride over as a passenger and pick it up in Steilacoom. Sure, it'll take an hour out of my day, but it also means I'll see Dani again.

To pass the time until the ferry arrives, I spend the day tinkering out in my garage. My pet project these days when I'm not working, is restoring a '66 Mustang convertible. I bought it on a whim from an older woman who lived here on the island. Her husband purchased it in the early seventies and kept it in one of their outbuildings after it stopped working, nearly thirty years ago. She didn't even realize it was still on their property until he died, and she had to go through his things to downsize and move off the island.

Knowing that money was an issue for her, I paid a reasonable price and had it moved to my garage. I've had it for a few years and am slowly rebuilding the engine. It's in good shape, hardly any rust, and only some minor body work needs to be done. I would have had it up and running instantly if I'd sent it to a shop, but there's something to be said about doing things for yourself. Unfortunately, my time's been limited, and I've hardly had the chance to work on it, due to my chaotic schedule. But I hope to finish up the engine this week while I'm off. Then all I'll have to do is some minor dent repair and send it to a shop to be repainted its original color, nightmist blue. Who knows, by the end of the season, I might have it finished.

Time flies while I'm in the shop working. Though my mind drifts to Dani often, I manage to get a bit done. Evelyn hears me tinkering and stops in to say hello. She catches me up on her grandkids as well as things that have been going on around the island, while I've been gone at camp these past few weeks. She asks if there's anything I need at the store to put on her shopping list, as she's going to head to the mainland tomorrow to do her weekly shopping. I make my request of a few things, but nothing out of the ordinary.

By five p.m., I find myself on the ferry as a passenger to the mainland. It's a thirty-minute ride and only takes me a few minutes to find the delivery guy for the wheel I ordered. I reward him with a generous tip before making my way back to the line of passengers to get on the ferry once again. Within the hour, I find myself back in my Jeep that I left at the ferry terminal. As I try to decide which way to go, I realize I'm left with a dilemma. *How the hell am I going to give this to her? Do I just show up and act like it is no big deal, or should I wait a day or two to deliver it?* Sure, I've been busy all day, but if I'm being honest, Dani hasn't been far from my mind. Hell, I have no business taking any interest in her, not with the season just getting underway, but I can pass this off as a Good Samaritan, right?

Without allowing myself time to think about it more, I pull out my phone and bring up her contact information. When given the option to call or text, I immediately press the green button. Before I know it, there's ringing coming from the line. A flash of adrenaline courses through me, that I haven't experienced in years. I take a deep breath and steady myself. *Christ, it's not like I haven't called a girl before? What the hell is wrong with me?*

After three agonizing rings, I hear the line pick up, then a slight thud before a nearly breathless, "Hello?"

"Hey there," I open without thought again. *What am I, back in college?*

"Luke?" she asks in a clarifying tone.

"Yeah, it's me." *Real smooth, dumbass. Get to the point or at least stop sounding like an idiot.* "Um, I'm just checking on you to see how you're doing?"

"Oh." There's silence on the line for a moment, that seems to last for an eternity. Dani clears her throat. "I'm doing okay."

"Are you sure? You took one hell of a hit this morning," I say in disbelief, knowing she must be hurting to some extent.

"I'm a little rough for wear, but not as bad as I thought it might be," she sheepishly admits. Then after a pause, her voice sounds stronger on the other end of the line. "I'm getting better though. I've stayed on top of the ibuprofen as best as I could since this morning."

"That's good to hear," I say, more relieved than I would've thought for just meeting someone.

"Yeah, Nancy's relieved. I won't be down for too long. Thankfully I'm in the middle of edits this week and not having

33

to finish a manuscript. There's a lot more reading than typing at this point."

Ah, her editor. "When's your next deadline?" My curiosity gets the best of me.

"I have three weeks to fully complete the edits and have it ready for release date. My cover reveal is later this week, and I must spend time in book groups promoting my upcoming release as well as in my own reader's group. Now that I can afford it, I at least can hire a promo company to help deliver ARCs, as well as everything else needed for release date, so that's one less thing on my plate," she says in a blur. Once she stops, there's an audible huff as if she's overwhelmed by her list of things to do.

I follow most of what she says, but some things aren't clear. "ARCs?"

"Advance Review Copies to blogs and people who will promote me by leaving reviews on the retail sites."

"Oh." I'm still not completely following her, and thankfully she continues, so I start to understand.

"Yeah. If I send out ARCs, people will read my book and review it before release day. Then hopefully when release day arrives, they'll post their reviews, and I'll get further promotion from the various retailers themselves." She lets out a sigh, sounding exhausted.

"There's obviously a lot more than I ever thought that goes into publishing a book. I thought only publishing companies or something like that, leave reviews posted on the book jackets," I say without thinking.

"Not really. If I'm lucky, someone big in the book world will take it upon themselves to promote my book, but mostly it's through the average consumer, bloggers, and my fans that I get promoted by word of mouth to new readers. Sure, I can market to specific audiences, which I do. But how I've made it so far, is through my fan base. I'm honored the people who like my work take the time to promote it to their friends, making my fan base grow."

"That's impressive." I had no idea what went into getting a book onto shelves. "I guess I just take for granted, the authors I like publish books, and I pick them up when I need something to read." I can't say I've ever paid attention to when books are released, except for the Harry Potter series. *Who didn't pay attention to those?*

"Sorry, I've been in edit mode all afternoon. You'll have to forgive me. It makes me a little obsessive." She lets out a light laugh, and I feel a shiver run through my body. It's a warm summer evening, so the weather has nothing to do with it.

I grin in response. "It's no problem. It's nice to see how passionate you are about what you do." A horn from the ferry blasts as it takes off, and I recall what I had originally called for. "So, Um... You haven't fixed your bike yet, have you?"

"Uhhh, I have no idea where the nearest bike shop is, let alone the time this week to take care of it." She makes a sound as if she's laughing at me in private. *Obviously, she's been busy, and I now sound like a moron. Great.*

"Well, would you mind if I stop by and fix it for you?" *Yeah, that doesn't sound stalkerish or anything. What the fuck was I thinking getting that part for her today? She didn't ask or need my help, yet here I am ready to do it anyway.*

"I guess?" she says in what I can presume is shock.

"If you're busy, I can swing by another time," I offer as a

way of letting her off the hook if she doesn't want to be bothered by me today.

"No. Today's fine." There's a pause. "What time is it?" Another moment of silence. "Geez, it's almost seven. I haven't eaten since I left your house today. Have you eaten dinner?"

"No, not yet," I admit. Then I realize I dropped her off before ten today, and we ate somewhere around eight... I think. I ate lunch, and I'm already hungry. She must be starved.

"Wanna come over, and I'll treat you to dinner at the cafe near the lake? It'll be my way of thanking you for your help this morning. I'd offer to cook for you, but I'm not sure what I have around here. I need to make a trip to the grocery store." She lets out a light chortle. "Sorry, when I'm in the zone, the world around me ceases to exist."

"Obviously." I shake my head, knowing what it's like to be in the zone. "I'll be at your place in a few minutes. I'm not sure what time the diner closes, but if we're too late, I know somewhere we can go." I've got plenty of food to fix at my place.

Living on such a small island, I pull into her driveway within ten minutes. I'm greeted by an even more beautiful Dani than I remember. She's now wearing her hair in a top knot, which would be messy on anyone else but is gorgeous on her. She's changed into a loose blue tank with a fitted green one underneath and a pair of khaki shorts that are perfectly molded to her. Her knees are still covered in bandages, as well as her elbows, but she still looks amazing and nearly takes my breath away.

"Hey," she says as she greets me. "Give me a second, and I'll grab my purse."

"No problem," I say as I wait on her front walk. "I'll drive, since I'm blocking you in," I tell her when she reaches the door and locks it behind her.

"Sounds good," she says as I escort her to her side of my Jeep and help her in. It's lifted, and I use this as an excuse to stand behind her, ready to assist in any way I can. Dani's a champ and doesn't require assistance, so once she's in, I simply close the door and make my way to the driver's side.

I bought this Jeep when I was still in college. It's not flashy and doesn't stand out in this community, so it's what I drive while I'm here. I can't help the grin that spreads across my face when I remember how excited I was to buy it new, as a junior in college. I'd saved up and worked my ass off to get this on my own. Of course, I had it paid off as soon as I got my signing bonus when I was drafted into the league.

"So... What have you been up to today?" Dani asks as I put the car in reverse and leave her driveway.

"Well, after you left, I worked on a project in my garage for a bit then I ran some errands," I reply, keeping my answer vague. No need to tell her what I did to get the wheel for her.

She angles her body toward me in the seat. "What kind of project?" she probes with genuine interest.

"Well, when I get the time, I'm restoring a '66 Mustang."

"Have you been working on it long?"

Unfortunately, a lot longer than I would like to admit. "Yeah, a couple of years."

We pull into the cafe and realize it's about to close in the next twenty minutes. "Uh, do you want to try going in or would you like to try some place else?" I ask, not caring either way. I have plenty to eat at my house, or we can go get something from the grocery store if she'd prefer to go home and fix something there.

Dani bites on her lower lip and contemplates her answer as she looks at the sign reading the hours of operation for the cafe. "I used to work as a waitress, and I hated when people showed up close to closing... Maybe we can have a raincheck?" She tacks on at the end.

"Well, since you said you haven't eaten since breakfast," I eye her dubiously, "what do you say I either take you to the grocery store or we go back to my place and eat?"

"Luke," she draws out my name into more than three syllables. "I don't want to put you out. I'm supposed to be thanking *you*, not taking advantage of you... Again." The look on Dani's face is priceless. I know she wants to even the score between us, not feel at a disadvantage.

"I wouldn't have offered if I didn't want to. My housekeeper keeps my place stocked, so it's really no imposition." I can tell she's about to protest, but I continue before she says another word, "I'll admit I'm best at barbeque, so if you're up for it, we can make dinner together, and I'll bring you home afterward."

"Will I get to see your Mustang? I love classic cars," Dani hedges.

"Sure. She still has a lot of work left to do, but I'll show you the progress I'm making," I say as I pull out of the parking lot. Within minutes, we're in my driveway.

Once inside, we make our way to the kitchen. I notice Dani takes her time as she takes in my home even more than earlier today. I'm sure her injuries made her preoccupied earlier, but I find myself enjoying her reaction to the view of both Puget Sound, Mt. Rainier, and the Olympic mountains from my living room. Her eyes are wide, but she doesn't give any of her other thoughts away. I pop out to the deck to turn on the grill while she admires the view.

Within minutes, I settle into the kitchen and pull steak, mushrooms, asparagus, and baked potatoes to fix for dinner. I quickly prepare the potatoes and slice the mushrooms. By the time Dani makes it to the island, I've already begun chopping the asparagus to steam.

"What can I do to help?" Dani asks cheerfully. "You seem very efficient in the kitchen. Lots of practice?"

"Well, I have to eat," I say nonchalantly. "If I didn't cook for myself, I'd either have to go out for every meal, or starve. Being nearly thirty, and on the road a lot, I'd prefer a home-cooked meal." I point to the barstool at the counter and gesture for her to have a seat.

"You travel for work?" Damn, she picked up on that. I walk out to the grill to start the steak. Dani follows, eagerly awaiting my response.

I might as well be honest with her. "Yeah," I admit as I return to the kitchen. I place the chopped vegetables into two different pans, one to steam, the other to sauté. "I'll be traveling a lot of the next few months." I open the fridge and pull out a beer for myself, and offer one to her. "Beer?"

"Sure." I quickly pull out an opener and hand her one, after popping the top. She takes a long pull on her beer and instantly has my full attention. *What is it about women who aren't pretentious and are able to relax and enjoy a beer now and then?* "Ahhh," she sighs after her first drink. "I haven't had this

39

in forever. It's my favorite." I smile, knowing that most don't know Irish Death, or like the dark ale from Ironhorse Brewery in Ellensburg.

"It seems we have something in common." I set the burners on low and head out to the barbeque on the deck, checking on the progress. When I return, Dani's sitting at a barstool at the kitchen island.

"Are you sure I can't help you with anything?" Her ocean-blue eyes widen with disbelief that I'm doing everything.

I shake my head. "Naw, I got this. Have a seat and relax. Dinner will be ready before you know it."

"You sure know how to spoil me," she teases, and the smile on her face is infectious. "So, where do you travel?"

"I get to travel all over the country," I admit. Not that I want to hide what I do for a living, but that usually tends to have certain expectations. I'm enjoying her company and don't really want it to change.

"That has to be interesting," she assumes. "Where's your favorite place to go?"

"I don't get to see many sights, but when I'm not working, I've enjoyed going to New York and Boston. All of New England is actually a great place to visit."

"Those are some great places." She takes another pull on her beer before she continues, "I've always loved going to New York. I've gone there a few times but recently have only gone for work and didn't get to see much either."

"Another thing we have in common." I spend a lot of time in airports but don't get to see much of the cities I travel to. "I see more of the stadiums as well as hotels, than landmarks."

Dani cocks an eyebrow over her searing-blue eye and

prompts, "Stadiums?" as she leans in on an elbow, resting her chin on her palm.

"I... Uh... Work for the Rainier Renegades. Lots of travel with the team," I finally admit.

Nothing. No recognition whatsoever. Just a deer in the headlights look. *Does she live under a rock? Or does she just not follow sports? Maybe I should give her a hint.* "Football?"

"I've heard of it. You play?" Her eyes go wide with disbelief as she pulls her chin in and looks me up and down with care.

"I used to." It's been so long since I've had to explain this. "But not anymore."

"Oh," Dani whispers as she pulls her brows together, contemplating. "Why not?"

"Blew out my knee," I admit as I tap on my left knee.

She looks at me in disbelief. "But you were running this morning. You didn't seem like there was anything wrong with you."

"I'm about ninety-five percent recovered, but it won't last on the field." I plate the vegetables and motion for her to follow me out to the deck again with a plate in each hand. Once outside, I flip the steak once more, realizing they're not done. "How do you like your steak?"

"Medium, please," Dani states. "So... Now you work for the Renegades?"

"Yep." I realize one steak is done and pull it off and place it on her plate. Then I cover the grill to give the other a few more minutes.

"Wow, that has to be exciting. I'll admit I'm not one to really watch football, but I've lived here all my life and know the Renegades are a good team. Didn't you guys do really well last season?"

I laugh. I can't help it. "Yeah, we sure did." We're the World Champs, but I'm not one to brag. It's refreshing to meet someone who doesn't seem to care about the team at all. She's definitely not a wannabe WAG or jersey chaser. It's humbling to meet someone who has no idea what I do for a living.

"What?" she asks incredulously, with one hand punched into her hip as if she knows there's something I'm not telling her. The curly brown knot on the top of her head bobs as her head cocks to the side.

Trying to remain humble, I lose my smile and state, "We actually were league champs last season, so I'd say we did *really* well." I scrutinize her reaction. She must be joking. Who didn't know we won?

She seems genuine when she bites her lower lip. Her features flush the slightest shade of red, but I notice. "I... Uh... Know what it means to be league champs. But I have to admit..." She looks away to avoid my eyes before she whispers, "I never pay attention to who wins."

"Well, we can't have everything in common," I say, trying to make light of the situation, while holding in my laughter. She's fucking adorable. I've never been more interested in a non-fan before. I mean, it's not really a big deal if she likes football. Well, it's my life... but not the end of the world. I shake my head in disbelief and pull the last steak off the grill.

"Want to eat inside or here on the deck?" There's a light breeze coming from the Sound and still an hour or so until sunset.

"Let's go inside and eat at the table. Easier to cut steak that

way. I've already been enough of a mess around you today."
She smiles and shakes her head as she walks toward the
screen door.

"Inside it is then." I hold the door open for her, and she
makes her way to the dining room table. I can't remember the
last time it was used. I set my plate down and retrieve
silverware and our beers.

As she slices off a piece of steak and places it in her mouth,
Dani lets out an almost inaudible sigh, which as quiet as it is,
still sets something indescribable off inside me. Before I take a
bite of my own, I can't help but ask, "Good?" The savory flavor
bursts in my mouth, and I fully comprehend why a moan
escaped from her just now. *Not bad, if I say so myself.*

She finishes chewing, and a beautiful smile flashes across
her face. "This is sooo good. I had no idea I was this hungry."
She takes a sip of her beer and reaches for her napkin. "You'd
better watch yourself..."

"Why's that?" I play along.

"When the diner's closed, I might just show up like a lost
stray begging for food." The saucy look crossing her face has
me wishing she'd make good on her threat.

I roll my eyes as I shake my head in embarrassment.
"Seriously, don't be too impressed. This is all I can cook,
besides breakfast. You'd tire of it quickly, I'm sure."

She takes another bite, and her appreciation is evident on
her face. "I'm not so sure about that. This is fantastic."

Not knowing what else to say, I fill my mouth with more
food. We eat for a while in comfortable silence. I can't help but
notice as the sun illuminates her beautiful face. She has a light
dusting of freckles across the bridge of her nose, and the dark-

auburn streaks shine throughout the messy bun she wears as well. Dani is mesmerizing. I could sit and look at her all evening.

Eventually, I notice she's lost in thought, completely unaware of her surroundings as she takes in the view from my nearby window. She takes me off guard when she gasps. Her eyebrows knit together, and she cocks her head as if she's uncertain of something. I try to follow her line of sight, but I have no idea what holds her attention.

Within seconds, she confuses me even more when she suddenly scoots back her chair, abruptly stands, and mumbles something like, "Damn, that might work..."

What the hell is she talking about? I watch with interest as she darts across the room, going directly for her purse. "Dani?" I question, wanting to make sure she's okay. *Did I do something to offend her?*

"Just a sec..." she whispers. She digs around in her medium-sized brown leather purse. It isn't that big. What's she looking for? She pulls out her phone and immediately types something, but it beeps, showing it's almost dead. The flash of frustration on her face is evident. I can't be certain, but I think I hear a curse escape her mouth from across the room as she digs into her purse again. A loud groan can be heard when all she pulls out is a pen.

"Need something?" I offer, trying to be of help.

"Paper," she pleads, obviously in a rush. "My phone's dead, and I forgot the notebook I always carry."

Seeing her desperation, I immediately need to relieve her unneeded stress. I quickly get up and walk to my home office. I return with a brand-new notebook, the kind I always write in while watching film. It's nothing fancy, but the look of pure relief flowing from every essence of her being says it'll more than do.

"Thank you," she whispers as she takes it back to the table to sit next to her now-forgotten food. It's adorable how she immediately pulls one foot up to the chair, making her knee stand out from the table. She scrunches around the pad of paper with complete concentration, encasing the knee that's between her and the table as if she's Gollum seeking his precious ring. Words fly onto the page as she bites on her lower lip in concentration.

Her creative process is phenomenal to watch. She completely tunes out the world around her as she immerses herself into the one she creates in her mind. Not knowing what else to do, I return to my seat and finish the rest of my meal. After filling eight to ten pages, Dani lets out a deep breath and finally makes eye contact with me.

A blush creeps over her as she realizes I'm still in the room with her. I'm not sure what to make of it. But her sudden embarrassment's amusing. It's as if she actually forgot I was even here. *Talk about humbling.* I have lost track of time as I watch her, so I'm not put out by it at all.

"Hey there," I say as a smile spreads across my face. "Welcome back."

5

DANI

ONE MINUTE I'M ENJOYING A WONDERFUL DINNER WITH THE intriguing man before me, the next I'm completely struck with an idea for a new book to write. I don't really know what happened. I was looking out at Puget Sound, enjoying the view, and the next thing I know, an entire plot came to life. I had to write it down because I knew that if I let it go, I'd never capture it the same way. My freaking phone was dead and to top it off, I left my trusted notebook for such emergencies at home. Leave it to Luke to swoop in and save the day, again. Geesh, this man sure has a knack for doing things like this. But in all honesty, it made my day to simply be supplied with silence and enough paper to complete my thoughts.

I'm not actually sure what brings me back. Maybe it's the fact I finished my outline, or that I sensed someone staring at me. Either way, once I come out of my revelry, I'm completely mortified. Luke just witnessed me in my "zone," and seems to think little of it. *How embarrassing. He must think I'm the rudest person ever!* When we make eye contact, my face instantly flushes with heat. Usually only my immediate family and close friends experience this side of me.

"Hey there," Luke says as he welcomes me back with a goofy grin that's entirely too sexy. "Welcome back."

"Ohmigod." I cover my face with my hands as I speak through them, "I'm so sorry. I have no idea what came over me. You must think I'm the worst guest ever."

"No." He shakes his head in disbelief. "I don't think that at all." He's quiet for a moment. "Did you get everything you need to write onto paper? Or do you need more time?"

I roll my eyes. *How is this man so understanding?* Chris, my ex, used to get so upset when I'd zone out. As I scrutinize Luke's face, he almost seems amused, which confuses me.

"What?" I blurt out, not understanding his reaction.

He shakes his head. "Nothing."

Liar. "No, it's something. Spill it," I demand, not wanting to let it go. I have three brothers. I can tell when they're holding back. I was a better interrogator than my mom, when it came to finding out what they were up to.

His lower lip jets out, and he shakes his head in disagreement. "It really is nothing, Dani."

"Why are you smiling at me? Do you think I've lost all my marbles? Or are you just trying to be polite because I've outstayed my welcome, and you can't wait to be rid of me?"

"Not at all, on either account. I actually found it rather entertaining. You were so tuned into what you were doing, I couldn't help but wonder what you're writing about, that's all."

Now that's unexpected. "Well, it's still rough, but I think I just found a new story to write. It'll be a stand-alone to begin

47

with, possibly turning into a new series." I pull my lower lip in as I contemplate how I can make it happen.

"What's the premise?" Luke encourages as he points to my plate of uneaten food. "Why don't you finish your meal and tell me more about it."

Looking at the plate of food, I realize I've literally just dropped everything, including my fork and was locked into my zone. I'm horrid company. He seems genuinely interested in what I have to say, but I can't help but feel a little chagrin about showing him this side of me so soon. He hardly knows me, and here I am being completely self-absorbed. When I gaze into his eyes once more, I don't see judgement or discontent though. All I see are expressive deep-blue eyes penetrating my defenses. Suddenly, I feel the urge to share what I just experienced with him.

I begin by explaining the method to my madness. He listens with interest as I describe this natural high that occurs when I get into the zone. I go further into detail by telling him it doesn't matter how tired I become; when I'm there, I can stay in it for hours, just feeding on the enthusiasm I experience.

As I finish, I notice Luke still seems receptive, so I explain how my zoning out contained a story about a runaway girl living on a remote island. She travels by boat each day to get to school, so people won't find her. She's faked her address, so she can attend one of the better schools of the area and graduate on time for her senior year. She'll eventually meet a boy who she'll become involved with. He'll become her best friend and help her through her difficult time, but ultimately, she'll be the one to save herself from a terrible situation. They'll have to part ways because she gets a scholarship to college. She can't turn it down. As adults, they'll reunite. I haven't worked out the details obviously, but they'll have life circumstances bring them back together by chance. Eventually, they pick up where they left off, as friends as well as admit that their feelings for one another have never left.

"Wow," Luke says in disbelief after I finish my lengthy explanation. "You got all that from staring out my window and taking a few minutes to jot it down? Is that how you get your ideas for all the stories you write?"

I wish. I sigh and let out a deep breath. "No. I never know when inspiration will hit. I haven't felt something so strong in such a long time. I just had to write it down. Sorry for being such a dork." I shake my head in disbelief of my ability to block everything out. *Sometimes it's not always a good trait to have.* "When I get the chance to sit down and write this story completely, hopefully I'll still feel just as passionate about it, or I may have no connection to it at all. If my characters 'speak' to me, I'll write the story. If not, I'll move in the direction of other characters who are speaking to me at the time." I shrug, hoping what I have just said makes sense to Luke.

"How many books do you have plotted out like this?"

I look to the ceiling and tap my chin as I contemplate just how many I have. Honestly, I have no idea, so I mentally tick them off on my fingers. "Probably about ten to twelve."

Luke nods his head, seeming impressed. "Do you have to commit to them in any order?"

I take a deep breath, trying to figure out where to begin. "Hmm... Well... Thankfully, I've been writing a series that doesn't seem to be coming to an end anytime soon. I need to keep writing those stories on a regular basis to keep my fans happy, but I can add other projects now and then, and they're usually just as excited. I don't really have an order per se, but I kind of have one worked out in my head, which characters I want to work on next, based on who I've introduced in the previous book."

Luke's quiet for a moment when I finish. I still can't believe he's genuinely intrigued by what I'm saying. He runs a hand through his inky black hair, and his deep blue eyes shine with interest. Upon further inspection, I notice his face is covered with a sexy five o'clock shadow. Since I've gotten to know him throughout the day, he's even more intriguing. I can't even remember the last time someone who wasn't in the book world took interest in what I do for a living. *Well, I'd probably have to interact with people outside the book world or my family to give that last statement a fair assessment.*

I'm not really sure how long I've been staring at him because he catches me off guard when he asks, "How long does it typically take you to write an entire book?"

I sigh as I shrug. "Depends."

"On?" Luke prompts with interest.

"Time, how well the characters speak to me, how much research is required to make it authentic, random things like that. I've written a full-length novel in just a few weeks, but sometimes it has taken months to write a simple novella. It all depends on life and the circumstances around it." I shrug, knowing I didn't give him an exact answer.

Luke smiles in understanding as he says, "That makes sense." The features on his face change to a more serious tone when he adds, "I seriously had no idea what went into writing a book. I've simply picked them up for pleasure and enjoyed them throughout the years. You've certainly enlightened me this evening. Thank you."

Without another word, he stands and picks up our plates to clear the table, now that I've finished. Crap, did I just bore him to death, and he's just being polite? Surely, I haven't read him wrong. I feel so comfortable around him, and he honestly seemed genuine in his probing. I watch him effortlessly rinse our plates and put what remaining dishes we used into the dishwasher, unable to speak my mind, for fear of finding out I've been reading him completely wrong.

Thankfully, he puts me out of my misery when he asks, "So, what do you want to do next?" He gestures to the dark, inviting sectional in the living room. "Do you mind hanging out in here for a while?"

"Sure!" I squeal out a little too high, causing him to eye me skeptically.

He doesn't have to say anything, his raised eyebrow has me instantly spilling my thoughts, "I'm not sure if I just bored you to death, and you're wishing I'd take the hint and leave."

Laughter erupts from him, making my stomach clench, leaving me unsure how to respond. "Seriously, what kind of people do you hang out with, Dani?" He takes a deep breath to steady himself, while I stare at him, wondering what he finds so comical. "One thing you'll learn about me is I hardly say anything I don't mean." He shakes his head as if trying to clear his thoughts. "I find you very intriguing. There's something about you that I want to know more about. I may sound like a desperate fool, but I haven't stopped thinking about you all day. Why else would I have used the ruse of fixing your bike to see you again?"

Shocked he's revealing his hand so soon, I toy with him a little. "A ruse? You mean... You didn't actually get a new tire? Didn't you just tell me, you don't say anything you don't mean?" I eye him quizzically, eagerly awaiting his response.

"Oh, I got the tire. Trust me." He shakes his head, realizing his mistake. Another smile transforms his face as he walks into his living room and sits down on the large sectional. He pats the couch. "Have a seat."

I sit down a respectable distance away from him. Not too far, not too close. I slip my sandals off and pull my feet up to tuck them under me as I face him, while leaning against the 'L' of the sectional. The leather is cool and smooth as I settle in. This is the kind of couch that's not only fashionable, but entirely functional. I could sit like this for hours. Give me my computer, and he might have to get court orders to evict me. I let out what I'm sure is an audible sigh, but as I seek further comfort, I simply don't care. Between my wreck this morning as well as hours spent hunched over my computer, I hadn't realized how tight and stiff my body had become until this very moment. Add in a full belly from a wonderful dinner, and I don't think I could want for anything else.

"You okay, Dani?" Luke asks.

I can't help it. A gigantic yawn escapes my mouth. "Yeah. I'm fine. I just found the most comfortable place in the world, don't mind me." I can't help but snuggle into the couch a little further, so I can rest my head on the back of it. I'm shameless, I know. "Where on earth did you get this couch? I want one."

A deep chortle comes from Luke. "I have no idea. My sister's a decorator." He runs a hand over his chin, and his eyes seem a bit mischievous. When I scrutinize him further to prompt him to continue, he adds, "I just asked that it be comfortable. I didn't care what it looked like."

This makes me take a closer look at his home, giving me a whole new insight on his life. I love the simplistic and comfortable home he has here. I notice the color scheme of his home blends perfectly. There are a few personal photos of what I assume are his family around as well, as some photos of the mountains found around Washington. "So... You didn't choose any of this?"

"Nope." He lets the p, pop at the end. "Marie was not only my sister but one of my closest friends growing up. She probably knows me best of all. She works in New York City as a decorator, I figured, if I didn't like it, I could always change it." He looks around his home, and a smirk forms on his gorgeous face. "I did have to get rid of the 'foo-foo' things she had as knickknacks. There's no way I need or want anything that has no function other than to collect dust."

I can't help but roll my eyes. *Typical guy.* And of course, Luke catches me and voices my thoughts, "I know... Typical guy... Right. Well... I want a home, not a magazine layout. If it's not functional, it doesn't belong here."

"Did you grow up around here?"

"Uh... I'm from Tennessee, just outside of Nashville."

"That's certainly a long way from home. How'd you end up in Washington?"

He scratches the beginnings of scruff on his strong, angular chin. I'm not sure if I'm reading him right, but the briefest hint of relief flashes over his features before he schools them. "Well, there's not much to tell. I played for Stanford and managed to get myself drafted. You already know how I blew out my knee and ended up working for the Renegades, so that's what brought me here."

"Do you see your family often?" I can't help but wonder. I can't imagine being far from my family.

"Well, my sister lives in New York, and my parents still live in the same home I grew up in. I travel to see them when I can, and it helps they're willing to meet me at games as well as travel here in the off season, too."

I can't help but be in awe of the man before me. Sure, he's probably the epitome of a bachelor, but I can tell he's a family man, too. "It's amazing to have a family that supports you." He and I have yet another thing in common. I don't know where I'd be without my family's support.

"It sure is." His deep voice rumbles directly into my heart, causing it to wobble a little. The sexy turn of his lips into a smile has me licking mine. I'm not sure how long I'm captivated by him because his expression changes, and I'm caught staring at his arched eyebrow. *Crap. He must have said something, and I missed it.*

Luke clears his throat and asks, "So, are you?" *Am I what? Thankfully, he fills me in quickly on what I've missed.* "...close to your family."

Whew! Relief washes through me. I can easily answer this line of questioning. "Yes... I'm incredibly close. In fact, my parents are coming out to the island in a couple of weeks to spend their vacation with me. We're going to do some kayaking and other things around the island while they're here."

"Do you see them often?"

"We all live here in Washington, most within a few hours of here."

"It sounds like you have a big family."

"Well, if you consider being one of four kids a big family, then yes. Mom and Dad still run the hardware store in my hometown. My older brother Derek lives in Tacoma, Damien's a senior at the University of Washington, in Seattle, and Davis is a sophomore at Gonzaga."

Luke's brows knit together for a moment then they smooth as he asks, "Do all of you have names that start with D?"

I can't help the chortle that escapes. "Ha... Yes... Well, except for my dad. His name's Trent. My mom's name is Daisy, and Dad insisted we all have names that follow in her footsteps. They're kind of weird like that."

"Where do they run a hardware store?" Luke's deep-blue eyes scrutinize me as he waits for more information.

"On the outskirts of Cashmere, near Leavenworth. Dad runs the store, and Mom does the bookkeeping. I think they're a little sad no one wants to run the family business, but it's not like they plan to retire anytime soon. Neither are even fifty, since they had Derek when they were twenty-one."

"Wow, your parents are young. Mine are almost sixty. Both could retire if they wanted but still work because they enjoy it." Luke's about to say something more, but his phone rings, interrupting us. He glances at the screen before an apology crosses his features. "Sorry, I have to take this."

I shrug it off and nod that it's more than okay to take the call.

"This is Luke." I hear a male voice on the other end say something, and Luke's expression transforms from comfort and ease to hardened lines as he becomes strictly business. "You gotta be kidding me. Surely, it's a joke." Something's said

55

on the other end of the line, and he responds with, "I have it in my office." He glances over to me then says, "Hold on a sec," to the person on the other line. Then he whispers to me, "I'm so sorry. I have to handle something in my office. It shouldn't be long."

I nod once again that it's fine. Whoever's on the other end of the line, must have a serious problem to be calling at this time in the evening. Luke gets up and walks out of the room. His muscles strain with tension, and his voice is tight as his sentences are clipped. From the tone in his voice, I can tell whatever news he's just received, he's not happy.

As I look around the empty room, I see the notebook Luke gave me, calling from my purse. I retrieve it and return to the most comfortable couch I've ever had the privilege of sitting on, and nestle in. I read over my notes and add a few details here and there and even figure out a few plot twists. When I get stuck on what I think the main character should do next, I let my head fall back and relax further into the couch while I contemplate the scene playing through my mind. Maybe if I close my eyes and concentrate, it'll come to me.

6

LUKE

I WANT TO RIP MY HAIR OUT BY THE STUPIDITY OF SOME OF MY players. Yes, they're rich. Yes, they're famous. They should know better than to make spectacles of themselves in the eyes of the public. If they think they can have a weekend adventure that ends in a quickie trip to Vegas, with an impromptu marriage and the world won't know about it, they deserve every ounce of pressure the press puts on them.

Thank God for Tanya, the head of the Rainier Renegades' PR. She's already ahead of the story and found the dipshit who decided this week was the time to spring an elopement with his girlfriend into the mix was a fabulous idea. It wouldn't have been a big deal. Except he happened to be drunk off his ass and now thinks he *regrets* his decision. Don't you think you should know these things *before* getting married? Campbell Beck has been around this game long enough to know better.

According to Tanya, Beck's new wife, Hillary, appears to be the epitome of a Jersey Chaser and is in their relationship for her fifteen minutes of fame. Her first post on social media this evening after tying the knot was a picture of the two of them in a rather precarious position, which left little to the imagination of what they were up to. The caption read, "Look who's officially off the market." The next photo was of a wedding ring.

Regretfully, this situation forced me to leave Dani, so I could get to a computer where I have access to social media. I refuse to have it on my phone, since it would light up like the Fourth of July, on a minute-by-minute basis. By the time I'm brought up to speed and give my two cents for what should happen from the team's standpoint, forty minutes have passed. I'll meet with Beck, his agent, and lawyer first thing Monday morning, when we return from our scheduled break. I can't believe the shit show Beck's created. If he weren't one of my star players and a man I genuinely respect, I'd call him right now and rip him a new one.

For now, as I hang up the phone, all I can do is shake my head in disbelief. Closing down my computer, I take a moment to put things into perspective. I can't imagine getting so involved with a woman that I'd run off to Vegas and wind up married before the night's through. Beck usually has a good head on his shoulders, and his sponsors for endorsements are typically wholesome. *What the hell was he thinking?*

Hopefully, by the time we meet, he'll have his shit together, and I won't have to pull his head out of his ass for him. We have a season to win, and distractions aren't something we can afford. The Rainier Renegades have tremendous talent. I hope to bring us another record-breaking season.

I make my way out to the living room and find it's now

dark. The sun's completely set, and I wonder where Dani might be. Christ. I hope she hasn't taken it upon herself to walk home. There isn't much traffic on the island, but the thought of her walking home alone in the dark puts me on edge. I need to find her and make sure she's safe.

I frantically walk to the kitchen, flip on the lights, and look for my keys I'd placed on the counter. I swipe them up in a split second and turn to leave out the back door. Just as I'm walking out, I sense movement from the couch, stopping me in my tracks.

I slowly turn to face whatever caught my attention. My senses are on overload and my nerves frazzled. A mixture of emotions hit me at once. My stomach drops as my heart races. I'm stuck in place, yet I'm drawn in that direction. I take in a deep breath and slowly release it, as relief washes over me. I can't believe the sight before my eyes.

There, nestled on my couch, is the sexiest woman I've ever laid my eyes on. She's absolutely adorable lying there fast asleep, curled into the cushions, completely content. The notebook she's holding teeters on the edge of falling off the couch as she sleeps soundly, unaware of my presence.

I walk to the couch and pick up the notebook. Glancing down, it's obvious she's made use of her time while I was on the phone. She's further into plotting her story and now has possible names and events she wants to incorporate into her new book. I can't help but be impressed by her process.

Not wanting to completely invade her privacy, I place the notebook on the coffee table and turn to look at Dani. She's so peaceful and from the looks of it, in need of some rest. The bandages on her elbows and knees remind me of the events from this morning. Not only that, but she worked for quite a while on her latest book as well. She must be exhausted to have fallen asleep so soundly.

Should I wake her? Or let her sleep? There's a blanket draped on the corner of the couch I could cover her with. I reach to get it but stop myself. *How the fuck did you get yourself into this mess, Leighton?* And why are you so indecisive? You make a thousand decisions every day, why the hell can't you make this one? Stress from my earlier conversation with Tanya comes pouring out. As I look at Dani once more, I realize this is nowhere near a fucking mess. It's simply a beautiful woman sleeping on my couch.

Somehow, Dani's presence alone calms me. Without another second of hesitation, I reach over and cover her with a blanket. Maybe she'll wake up from the movement? Nope. She hunkers down and snuggles further into the couch, with the cutest little sigh I've ever heard. I can't help the audible breath that releases from me at the same time.

I walk to my kitchen and hesitate. What the hell should I do now? I can't sit in the same room and watch her like a creeper, but I don't want to leave her alone either. An idea pops into my head with the perfect solution as I quickly retreat to my office.

I pull out my laptop, grab a notebook, and return to the living room, to watch game footage, on mute. I'd been meaning to work on this today but got distracted by my Mustang... And let's face it. Dani might've had something to do with it. I bring everything to the living room and make myself comfortable on the other side of the sectional.

It takes a few minutes to get settled. Dani's sunken deeper

into the couch in my absence. As she takes a deep breath and releases it in a breathy sigh, I can't help but smile. *If* I had time for dating, she'd be the exact girl I'd choose. She's smart, sexy, and easy to hang out with. She doesn't have any pretenses, and I'll admit, it's a perk she doesn't have a clue as to who I am, other than just being Luke. God... it's refreshing to meet someone who just wants to get to know me, for me. When's the last time someone wanted to get to know me, without wanting something from my career? Hell. I can't even remember.

When she moves her hand to curl the blanket under her chin, I force myself to look away and get to work. She's beautiful, but I've creeped long enough, and I don't want to give her the wrong impression, should she wake up.

Before I know it, I've managed to watch an entire game— with no commercials. As I watch, I'm impressed by some of our plays. I manage to come up with a few new ones for our offensive line in our upcoming game against Carolina. I take note that our defensive ends left a gap between themselves and our corner back a few times, causing their fullback to break through our line. This can't happen again. I'll address this before we play them again.

I'm deep into the footage when I hear, "Ohmigod. What the hell's wrong with me?" burst out of Dani as she bolts off the couch, scaring the shit out of me. My heart races and instantly, I jump into action.

"What's wrong?" I dump my laptop on the couch as I stand to assist her. "What do you need?" The words fly out of my mouth before she can turn to look at me.

She freezes, mid-rant, her back to me. I swear I hear, "Fuck. This cannot be happening..." My instinct is to reach out and console her, but before I can move, Dani whispers, "Please tell me he's not standing right behind me."

"Who don't you want it to be?" I ask, unsure of what to do.

Dani lets out a strong huff. Slowly, she turns to face me. Her face flushed, and a cringe stretches across her features, as if she couldn't be more mortified. Her eyes flit everywhere but at me. What the hell is wrong with her?

"Dani? Are you okay?" Still no eye contact. "Dani?" I ask again to get her attention on me.

"I'm the worst *fucking* house guest... Ever. I fall asleep, then freak the fuck out when I wake up. I swear, things like this only happen in the books I write, not real life. I need to get out more, if this is how I behave when it finally happens. Or... Maybe it's best I just stay a hermit and stuck in my books. I'm not fit for company... I certainly don't have the social graces to even stay awake..." She looks to my couch, as if it's the scene of her apparent crime, and sighs. Then her eyes bore into me as she juts out her chin with resolve. "It's not my fault. Really. You have the most comfortable couch I've ever been on, and I entirely blame *it,* for making me fall asleep."

"If you say so..." comes out as a strangled laugh. I know I shouldn't make fun of her, so I attempt to contain it to a smile. She's adorable as she rants. Her wild curly hair flops, and her ocean-blue eyes darken. I'm fairly certain, this outburst is more from embarrassment than her actual personality.

"Ohmigod... You... You..." she mutters as I take a step toward her.

"Dani..." I plead to calm her down. She has nothing to be this upset over.

She frantically looks around as she mutters, "I need to get out of here... I need to leave..."

"Dani." My tone's serious, and she stops to pay attention.

Her eyes immediately lock onto mine. We stare at one another for a few heartbeats in silence.

I reach out to touch her arm. "You've done nothing to freak out about."

"B... But I... I... just..." She points to the couch and whips her head between the couch and me, as if she's giving me an explanation. "You've just seen me..."

I slide my hand up her arm and reach out and grasp her shoulder. When she still won't look me in the eye, I take my other hand, guiding it lightly under her chin to ensure I have her complete attention. Once her beautiful blue eyes lock with mine again, I assure her, "Dani. You've had an incredibly long day. I'm the one who left you alone for way longer than I anticipated. I'm the one who should be apologizing. It's no problem you fell asleep."

"But... You must think..."

I cut her off, without giving my words much thought, "I think... You're one of the sexiest, most genuine people I've met in some time."

"You... You think I'm sexy?"

"I haven't been able to get you off my mind all day," I practically growl, both in wanting to get the truth out there and to chastise myself. I don't have time for a relationship like she deserves.

"You can't be serious," she says shaking her head in disbelief.

With her chin still resting on my hand, I tip it toward me

again. She needs to know there's nothing to be this worked up about. "I'm serious."

"I've been nothing but a hot mess all day," she barely whispers.

She may have been hot but nothing close to a mess. To prove my point, I do what hasn't been far from my thoughts all day. One hand slides to her neck as the other falls to the small of her back. I lower my head to brush my lips against hers. Damn. Her taste's addictive. One kiss isn't enough. Using my hand at her neck, I guide her as I deepen our kiss, and she willingly reciprocates.

The spark we've been flirting with throughout the day ignites into an inferno of flames. I take a breath to steady myself before I kiss her once again.

HOLY FUCKING SHIT. What's this woman doing to me?

7

DANI

ONE MINUTE I'M FREAKING OUT FROM EMBARRASSMENT, THE next I'm consumed in the hottest kiss I've ever personally experienced. Damn. This man can kiss. Luke holds the perfect amount of pressure as he guides me to deepen our kiss. Of course, I willingly oblige. I haven't been kissed senseless like this in... well... ever.

On instinct, my hands wrap around his neck as he pulls me up his body, by simply placing a hand under my ass and standing to his full height. Naturally, as if we've been doing this for years, I wrap my legs around his waist and kiss him for all I'm worth.

It could be minutes, hours, or years. Time ceases to exist in this moment. All I'm aware of is Luke's mouth claiming mine. An electric current pulses through my veins, centering in my core. On instinct, I pull myself closer. I need more of this man. He's the perfect combination of hot, sinful desire, mixed with the kind of thoughtfulness I thought only belonged in fiction.

He takes a few steps from where we're standing and places me on the counter, which separates the living room from the kitchen. Instinctually, I let my fingers trace his sexy, stubbled jawline as my mouth devours him. I run my hands through his hair and can't help the moan that escapes when he kisses down my neck. God, he feels amazing.

Luke's hand hasn't left the base of my neck, but the other's found the hem of my shirt and has moved it slightly, so that it sits at my hipbone before skimming along the waistband of my pants. At this moment, he could ask me for *anything,* and I'd gladly hand it over. As long as he doesn't stop the sensation that's building inside me. *Can I actually come from a kiss alone?*

I feel the moment he slows things down and lessens the intensity of our kiss. I can't help myself when I nearly cry out, "Oh, Luke... Please... Don't stop."

"Are you... sure?" he gasps out between breaths. His eyes find mine, and they lock in place. So much is said between us, without muttering a syllable. I can tell he's just as affected by this as me. His eyes blaze with desire as his lips curl into the hint of a smile. His inky black hair's a disheveled mess, from my hands running freely through them. He couldn't look sexier if he tried.

It's then I remember we've just met, and embarrassment spreads over me for being so caught up in the moment. The moment I doubt myself, he cocks an eyebrow in my direction, letting me know he senses my hesitation.

Shit. I don't want whatever this is to end. So, I make a split-second decision to come clean with him. I take a deep breath and let the truth pour out. "It felt so good to get caught up in the moment."

I gulp down my nervousness and continue with this unexpected boldness he's built in me. "I guess what I'm saying... Is... I've enjoyed kissing you," I nearly spit out at the end.

A sly smile pulls at the corners of his delicious mouth for a few heartbeats before he speaks his mind, "I've enjoyed it, too, Dani. Trust me. But..." He takes a breath and looks to the ceiling, breaking our eye contact. Oh, shit. The proverbial but. He's going to stop this. My stomach clenches, and my body already feels withdrawals from our desire. When his eyes return to mine, they pin me in place, and I can hardly breathe from the intensity of his gaze. He lets out a deep breath. "Christ. I feel this, too." He runs a hand through his hair then continues, "I don't want to lead you on and other than these next few days, I'm hardly ever around the island during the season. After this week, my schedule's back on the game twenty-four-seven."

"Wh... What are you saying?" I say before I can stop myself.

Luke runs a hand through his thick hair as he returns his eyes to the ceiling. "Shit, I don't know," he mumbles just loud enough to hear as he shakes his head. It's as if he's at war with himself.

Okay... this is unexpected. What the hell am I supposed to say? Thankfully, I don't have to.

"Dani." The sexiest tone imaginable comes from his lips. His deep husky timbre sends shivers up my spine and leaves me pulsing in places I've forgotten existed until Luke. "I don't want to push you too far tonight. After all, we've just met.

What would you say to me taking you home tonight and continuing this again tomorrow evening?"

"Tomorrow?" He wants to continue this tomorrow evening? Didn't he just say he doesn't have time? I'm confused.

His eyes pierce me, and it's as if I can see entirely into his soul. "Dani," this time it has just as much force as before, "I clearly saw you hesitate."

At a loss for things to say, my mouth hangs open. He's right. I had second thoughts. There's no way this can go anywhere, but why not let myself get caught up in the moment for once. "Why tomorrow?"

His sexy grin melts my insecurities. "Because I haven't been able to get my mind off you all day, and even though the timing sucks, I'd love to spend more time with you." His blue eyes darken, and a few crinkles form around them when his sexy smile fills his face.

Who can resist that? "Okay."

He wraps his arms around my waist and pulls me in for another kiss. It's just as electric, but it's kept in control. When he pulls back, I can't help but shake my head at his request as he waggles his eyebrows. "Are you opposed to goodnight kisses?"

As soon as Luke drives away, I can't help but trace my swollen lips with my fingers. The man can kiss. I seriously thought I might combust on the spot when he walked me to my door. I wanted so desperately to invite him in, but he never allowed an opportunity to present itself.

After kissing me senseless, he simply whispered, "Tomorrow?"

I nodded, and the sexiest smile imaginable spread across his face as he turned to walk to his Jeep.

I start my nightly routine of getting ready for bed, though it takes longer than usual, as thoughts of this evening replay on a loop. *Did I really just meet Luke today?* Crawling into bed, still soaring on the high from being with Luke, I toss and turn in an attempt to get comfortable. Gaahh... I'm too keyed up to sleep. I punch my pillow and flip it to the cold side. Still, sleep evades me. When I can't take it any longer, I toss back the covers in defeat and make my way to my living room.

I pull out my laptop as I curl up on my couch. I should edit my current book, but my epiphany from earlier returns with a vengeance. I open a new document and furiously type the opening scenes of the story I developed at Luke's. Words flow as I lose myself to my characters.

Being in "the zone" completely consumes me. I don't surface until the first rays of light shine through my window. When I glance at the clock, I'm shocked to see it's six a.m. I stretch my stiff fingers and set my laptop aside. My body protests as I stand, having been in one position for so long. I make my way to my bed and crash instantly.

I resurface later that afternoon to find I've missed a few calls from my mom and editor. Those are expected. What has my heart picking up its beat, is a simple text from Luke.

Luke: Hey, Dani.

About an hour later, it's followed up with another text.

Luke: Let me know when you're free. Looking forward to seeing you later.

Shit! This last text was from forty minutes ago. Not wanting to let him think I'm too preoccupied, I quickly reply.

Me: Sorry. Got caught in the zone last night. Pulled an all-nighter. Just getting up now. What do you have in mind?

Luke: Dinner at my place?

Just the thought alone has my stomach rumbling.

Me: I could be persuaded into that.

Luke: You'd be amazed at my power of persuasion.

My pulse quickens as a smile spreads across my face. *He won't have to do much to persuade me, especially if he kisses me again like last night.* The thought alone has me brushing my fingertips along my lips.

Me: I still must get some words in. What time do you want me?

There's a long pause, and I take a moment to reread my words. *Shit!* There are so many ways he could take that.

Luke: You're welcome anytime. In fact, why don't you come over and write on my deck?

Before I can respond, another text comes through.

Luke: I hear my couch is comfortable, if you'd rather be inside.

Me: Ha-ha. Very funny.

I'm sure he has better things to do than have me come over and write. But the thought of being in 'the zone' last night makes me seriously consider it.

Me: But I did get in the "zone" last night.

I'm about to add more when my phone rings.

"Seriously, Dani." His deep, sexy timbre rings through my ears. "If you're busy, we can get together later this evening."

"No... I'm considering your offer. I haven't been in the zone like that in ages. I just feel rude coming over to your house to work. You have no idea how consumed I can be when the mood strikes."

Luke chuckles as he responds, "Oh, I think I might have an idea. But seriously. I have some work I need to do, then I'll cook dinner. You're welcome anytime."

Can I really do this? I don't really have time for distractions. But he didn't mind last night when I checked out on him... hmmm. Then I remember that kiss and all the words that flowed through the night.

"Okay. I'll take a shower and head over to your place."

I arrive at Luke's to find him on his deck typing away at his laptop. I've never thought much about forearms, but watching him type as I walk toward him has an effect on me I never saw coming. My mouth waters, and my heart races in excitement, making me quicken my steps to fill the distance between us.

He sets his laptop aside and stands to greet me as an inviting smile spreads across his face. "Hey, Dani." When I walk closer, he kisses me on the cheek. "Glad you could make it," he says breathlessly as he pulls away. The masculine scent of his cologne, mixed with a smell that's entirely Luke, overwhelms my senses, and I sigh as he steps back.

"Thanks for inviting me," I whisper quietly as I momentarily get lost in his deep blue eyes.

Luke breaks my concentration when he points to my courier bag and asks, "I see you came to work. Can I get you anything to drink or snack on? I have soda, beer, and wine, and was just about to pull out some pepperoni sticks from Stewarts, out in Yelm."

My stomach rumbles at the thought of finally getting food today. "Sure, sounds great."

As he turns to walk toward the door, he asks, "So, what did you work on that kept you up all night?"

"I started to edit, but the story that came to me last night during dinner wouldn't stop running through my mind, so I let it out. I managed to write nearly ten thousand words."

"Wow, I can't imagine writing that many words. Ten-page papers in college were long enough for me. What were those? Three thousand words?"

I chuckle as he shakes his head in disbelief. "I think they were something like that... But last night was a good night for me. I was so in the 'zone,' I hardly was aware of time passing. I get like that from time to time..."

Luke opens the fridge, then looks over his shoulder. "That has to feel incredible to be in the zone like that, for that extent of time. I can only imagine it from an athlete's standpoint, but I'm sure the rush of endorphins is enormous." He pokes around for a second, pulls out a package of pepperoni and a bottle of water, then asks, "What can I get you to drink?"

Knowing I need to concentrate and could use come caffeine, I go with, "Soda is fine." He pops the top and hands it to me. "Thanks."

We walk back out to the deck and once again, I'm in awe of his view. The sun glistens off the water and the ferry to Tacoma off in the distance. The breeze coming off Puget Sound is refreshing on this warmer than usual day for late July. The plot I formed while staring at the water from his kitchen table last night continues rolling through my brain like a freight train, but I manage to contain myself. Barely. *What is it about this place?* Luke gestures for me to sit in the inviting furniture he has placed in the shade. There's a small table between us that I set my drink down on before settling into the chaise lawn furniture.

"What are you working on?" I gesture to the laptop at the end of his lounger that he'd set aside when I arrived.

Luke settles into his chair and places his computer on his lap. "Just returning some emails. I might be on vacation, but they come in by the dozens every hour, it seems."

"Ugg... Email is the best and worst thing ever invented. I love the convenience, but if you step away, it can get out of hand when you return. I love being out here on the island. It forces me to unplug from time to time and just get away from it all." I pull out my laptop from my bag. "You sure you won't mind if I write?"

"Not at all. Unfortunately, I'm unable to completely unplug. I have work to do myself."

"Well, don't let me stop you." I gesture to his laptop as I start up my own.

As Luke types the chorded muscles in his forearm distract me from any productive thought. I pretend to read what's on my screen for a few minutes, but truth be told, my thoughts are entirely on him and each move he makes.

Of course, he's able settle in and begin typing furiously in response to an email, whereas my mind drifts to last night. Thankfully, the piercing shrill of his phone breaks my daydream, and he answers "This is Luke... Just a sec, I have that in my office." He looks to me in an apologetic shrug as he sets his laptop aside and stands.

He glances at me and I whisper, "It's no problem." I can't help but watch his muscular form retreat into the house. There's something about a man in a taut black t-shirt with defined muscles that makes my eyes stick like magnets. Throw in some well-fitted dark-green shorts and... *Damn...* was he a Calvin Klein model in his past life?

I'm not sure how long I stare in his direction before I get a grip and return to reality. Shaking my thoughts of Luke away, I dive into the scene I started early this morning. I make a few tweaks as I read but for the most part, I'm inspired to write more. When I get to the point where all that's left is a blinking curser, my fingers fly across the keys like a runaway freight train. Scenes come together, characters click, and plot twists form.

I'm brought out of my revelry by a tap on my arm, which scares the shit out of me, causing me to jump.

"Dani?" Luke's gravelly voice questions. "You okay? I didn't mean to startle you... I started talking from the door and thought you'd heard me."

Holy shit, I was out of it. I take a deep breath to steady my heartbeat, while shaking my head to clear my thoughts. "Sorry... Guess I didn't hear you."

Luke lets out a light laugh. "You can say that again. I came out to tell you dinner will be ready soon. I started cooking while I was on the phone. It's nearly six, are you okay with me putting the steaks on?"

My stomach audibly answers before I have a chance to speak the words, causing Luke's eyes to dance with entertainment. "Okay, then... I'll get right on that." The upward turn of his lips as he turns to walk into the house instantly causes me to heat from embarrassment.

"Wait..." I call out.

He turns his deep blue eyes in my direction.

"Can... Can I help you with anything?"

Luke shakes his head before assuring me, "Not this time. I got it. Get back to your book. I kind of feel bad for disturbing you. You were pretty intense before I startled you. I hope I didn't make you lose your train of thought."

Who is this man? Any other guy I've dated would have blown me off by now for being so engrossed in my own head. When he waits for me to respond, I quickly find my words. "No... I have things handled. I'm not sure what it is about this place, but if I keep at it, I'll likely have this book done in record time."

75

"That's incredible. How many words have you written since I went inside?"

I look to the bottom of my screen and my eyes widen. "Um... Almost fifteen-hundred... About five pages or so." It's not much in the grand scheme of things, but not bad for an hour's worth of work either.

"You're a *beast!*" His deep voice rumbles.

Pride shines through me as I appreciate his praise. I try to play it off, but this is a great day for writing. "Eh... Today's a good day."

Luke rolls his eyes, "Whatever you say, Dani. I'm still impressed. I'll be back out with the steaks in a minute." With that, he turns to walk back into his beautiful home, and I'm left in awe of his incredible backside, once again.

8

LUKE

FROM THE MOMENT I DROPPED DANI OFF LAST NIGHT, I HAVEN'T been able to get her off my mind. Sure, I got some work done earlier before she arrived, but I've been quite distracted. I felt like a school boy, calling up his first date when I texted her earlier in the day. Then when she didn't respond, I figured I wouldn't see her until later tonight, if at all. When she showed up on my deck in a loose tank, cutoff shorts, and flip-flops, it was all I could do not to pick up where we left off last night. Her curly hair is barely contained in one of those messy knot things on the top of her head. She's nothing like the WAG wannabes that linger around the locker room. In fact, I don't think I've ever met anyone like Dani. She's a breath of fresh air and as she clucks away on her computer, she couldn't look sexier if she tried.

If I weren't gearing up for the biggest season of my life, she's someone I'd consider seeing where this thing between us goes. Christ. I have no idea why last night keeps playing on my mind like a fucking loop. I didn't even fuck her. I haven't just made out with someone in years... yet, just our kisses alone, have me coming back for more.

What the fuck is wrong with you, Leighton? Get it together.

I pull the steaks off the grill and bring them into the house to plate them. I'm just about to bring them back outside when Dani walks inside.

"Mind if we sit at the table? I promise not to zone out again. I've made good progress and doubt another epiphany will strike."

"If it does... I won't hold it against you," I tease. By now, she's close enough that her delicious scent envelops my senses. It's a mixture of vanilla, amber, and something I can't recognize. Not that I care. My mouth waters, and it has nothing to do with the steaks in front of me.

True to her word, she doesn't zone out during our meal. Instead, we talk about how she's always lived in Washington. She tells me how she got started with writing while attending college at Gonzaga.

She also shares that her grandparents lived on this island for over thirty years. They moved out to their summer home once their kids graduated from high school. Her grandfather worked for the United States Postal Service and was assigned to the island. When her grandparents decided they wanted to be snowbirds and spend their winters in warmer weather, they passed down the family home to her mother and father.

Apparently, Dani had been renting a place in Spokane since college. She came to visit for a vacation and was productive with her writing. When her grandparents moved off the island, she stayed. She's been here since last winter and wouldn't have it any other way. She's fallen in love with the island life.

We laugh about our shared love for Anderson Island. I tell her how I came out to visit a teammate for a week away from the city and found this place almost by mistake. We were staying at a vacation rental on the other side of the island but went for a run one morning, and I saw the realtor sign. "The rest, as they say, is history," I explain.

"You certainly found a gem in this place," Dani says as she takes her plate to the kitchen and loads our dishes into the dishwasher.

I follow her to the kitchen and stand beside her as we effortlessly clean up from dinner. We finish in minutes, and I can't help myself when I reach out to brush a piece of her wild hair away from her eyes.

When I touch her, the electric current that pulsed between us last night returns with a vengeance. As if it has a mind of its own, my hand rests at the base of her neck. We stare at one another for an endless moment as I lose myself in her ocean-blue eyes. In this moment, I can't think of a single reason why I should stop whatever is going on between us.

As if there's a magnetic pull, I lean down and brush my lips against hers. She eagerly accepts this kiss and returns it by opening her mouth and sweeping her tongue against my lower lip. I deepen the kiss, and she returns it for all she's worth.

Dani's arms wrap around my neck as she presses her body against mine. One hand runs through my hair as the other holds tight to my shoulders. Her rich amber and vanilla scent has my senses in overdrive. I reach down and pull her body to my height by placing her on my kitchen counter. Her legs

79

wrap around my waist and fuck if I don't want to take her right here. I pull back, breathless and panting. Christ. I'm nearly defenseless against this woman. I'm acting like a randy teenager, and I need to slow things down, or it'll be over before we start.

"Dani," I whisper breathlessly.

"Luke..." she pants. Then her eyes lock on mine. "Please don't stop," she pleads. Like last night, she makes her needs clear. But this time, there's no hesitation. Her fingers trace my lips as a smile forms on hers. "I haven't felt like this in years."

"Me neither." I have better control over my breathing, but that's only from years of being a professional athlete, not my lack of wanting her. *Christ, Luke, what are you waiting for?*

"Then..." She kisses me softly. "What's," another kiss. "Holding... You back?"

My voice is deeper than I intend and much more urgent. "I want you far more than I should," I admit then return my mouth to hers for another mind-numbing kiss.

"I... want you, too." She pulls back to catch her breath. "We're both adults, what's stopping you?" Her blue eyes are dark with lust and pierce through to my soul. I couldn't deny her if I tried, but I need to make my intentions clear. I owe her that much.

"I really like you, Dani," I start.

The smile that spreads across her face is illuminating. "I really like you, too, Luke."

"No... I mean... You're the kind of girl I'd love to start something with. But right now is the worst possible time in my life for something like that. Like I said last night, I'm only here for a few days. Then once the season starts, I'll hardly be around. That doesn't seem fair to you..."

"Luke... when I say I've never felt anything like this, I'm serious. I'd rather have a few amazing days together with you, than to always wonder what if..."

Is she saying what I think she's saying? "Dani, I'm not really into one-night stands," I warn. Because let's face it. I was over that type of thing years ago. The connection I feel to her is different, and I don't want her to think it's less than it is for me.

Her face flushes a beautiful shade of pink. "We have that in common as well. I haven't had one since college, before my last boyfriend."

Wait. I cock my head to the side to see if I've heard her correctly. *She hasn't had a boyfriend since college and doesn't do one-night stands...*

As if she can read my mind, she interrupts my thoughts, "You're right. I haven't had sex in a few years." She shakes her head and rolls her eyes as if she can't believe she's told me that tidbit of information. "I'm not one to sleep around. But I can't deny the connection we have. You feel this, too?" She points between us. "I'm not the only one, am I?" Self-doubt fills her features as I take in what she's saying.

God, I want her. But I don't want to hurt her either. "But I'm only on the island until Saturday..." My voice trails off.

"What do you say to making the most of the few days we have together?" She raises an eyebrow as a challenge.

Holy fuck! I think this woman is either perfect for me, or will be the death of me. Oh, but what a way to go...

9

DANI

LUKE'S MOUTH CRASHES ONTO MINE. WHEN I GASP IN SURPRISE, his tongue darts out to dance with mine. The way he completely dominates my senses has my body slipping into overdrive. Electricity courses through my veins, pulsing toward my core, igniting a need I've never experienced. With each heartbeat, I'm closer to coming apart, and all he's done is kiss me.

Without breaking our connection, he suggests, "Bedroom?"

I nod fervently as I grip onto his body with my legs. I reconnect our mouths with a heat-searing kiss, getting completely lost in all that is Luke. Before I know it, I'm placed on an enormous king-sized bed. I'm so consumed with getting closer to him, I hardly notice how we arrived. I rip at his clothes, and he pulls back to break our kiss. He reaches behind his back and pulls his t-shirt over his head in the sexiest of ways. I practically drool when I see his sculpted muscles and beautiful tattoos on full display.

His smile is wide as he sees my appreciation for his body. "See something you like?" he teases. His blue eyes dance with pleasure as he looks me over with care.

Without any hesitation, I reach for the hem of my tank top and pull it over my head. He groans in appreciation. "You are so beautiful," he says, making me feel bold.

I reach for his face, and we fall back on the bed. His arms press against the mattress by my sides, making it dip as we get caught up in another breathtaking kiss. After all too short of time, he breaks our kiss. Slowly, he kisses down my jaw to my ear, where he practically growls, "You are so fucking incredible, Dani." His fingers skim against my ribs and trace along the fabric of my bra.

When his eyes lock with mine, he silently asks for permission to continue. I nod and devour the moment as he unclasps my bra with one hand and runs his stubbled jaw along my sensitive flesh until he pulls a taut nipple into his mouth. He massages one breast, while teasing the other with his tongue. My nerves light on fire. Heat flashes through me, and I can't help but arch toward him as I moan out in pleasure.

I've never come from just a simple touch, but with Luke, it might be entirely possible. Heat pools between my legs, and I squirm with need. "More, Luke... More..."

He reaches between my legs and presses against my mound through my shorts. This isn't enough. I need more...

"Oh... God... Luke..."

He senses my need and skims his warm fingers between my thighs. He traces the hem of my shorts and slides a finger up to the edge of my underwear as his mouth switches to my other breast to give it his full attention. Instinctually, my hips buck up, and I finally feel him push the fabric aside. "Yes…" I urge.

"You want more?" His sexy voice teases as he pulls back to examine my face.

Both of his hands go to the fly of my shorts. And he waits for my words.

I nod as I reach to assist him. "Yes…" comes out as a hoarse whisper.

He pulls back and focuses on my shorts. Within seconds, they're pulled down my body and thrown to the floor. I need his mouth on mine, so I pull him back to me. He braces his body on one elbow as he settles his torso to the side of my legs. With his free hand, he traces my breasts, plays with my nipples, and has me squirming with need. Just when I think I can't take anymore, he breaks our kiss and makes his way down my body. He once again stops at each breast as his hand explores the apex of my thighs, and his fingers glide along the edge of my panties.

Luke drives me mad. I don't think I've ever wanted a man more than I want him right now. When I can't take it any longer, I take his hand and press it against my dripping-wet core. Thank God, he takes the hint and moves the fabric aside to use his magical fingers against me. As if he hasn't a worry in the world, he slowly traces his fingers from my clit to my center. Back and forth. Back and forth. I moan and gasp my appreciation as he bites down on my nipple as he simultaneously presses against the spot that lights me on fire. He works his thumb in a slow circle around my clit as a finger enters me in a magical motion that has me soaring higher and higher. Just when I don't think it can get any better, he adds another finger into the mix. Energy sparks from the base of my spine. My body bucks, and I fly higher than I've ever experienced as wave after wave of orgasmic bliss takes over. Luke's right there with me, through it all, enjoying every moment with me.

As I come down, he kisses me softly on the lips. When he pulls back, he brushes my hair from my face, and a sexy smile greets me as my eyes open. "Hey there," he whispers.

"Hey," I whisper back, and I can't help the euphoria coursing through me. I reach up to trace his lips with my fingers, then run them along his sexy jawline. Luke's eyes drink me in, and I drown in their depths.

As if my fingers have a mind of their own, they trace down his chiseled chest, and a sly grin spreads across his beautiful lips. When I reach the waistband of his shorts, he groans. I trace the outline of his erection through his shorts, and the sensual moan that escapes his body only enhances my arousal.

I need this man inside of me.

As if he can read my mind, he quickly pulls back from my body to stand at the end of the bed. My mouth dries as I watch him quickly rid himself of his shorts and what I think are blue boxer briefs. A devilish grin forms as he watches me wetting my lips. *Oh, my! Is it possible to combust on the spot?*

His eyes bore into mine, and I feel my temperature rise. I squirm on the bed as I watch his thick cock bob as if it wants to greet me personally. My core clenches, and I groan in anticipation. Holy shit. I might have to take matters into my own hand if he doesn't pick up the pace. I prop myself on my elbows to get a better view, and his eyes dart to the bathroom behind us.

"Condom," he announces to the room then pivots on a dime to walk into the bathroom. Even from the back, Luke's utter perfection. His glutes remind me of carved marble as they flex with each stride. He disappears for a matter of seconds and returns with a strip of condoms and a look of determination that sets my heart racing.

In anticipation, I sit up to get my hands on his beautiful body. His lips crash onto mine, and I get lost in everything but him. He kisses my entire body with a mixture of tender and fervent motions. I. Can't. Get. Enough. If I combust on the spot, it'll be entirely his fault. Each nip, suck, and lick take my body higher than I've ever imagined. He finds erogenous zones I never knew existed. I let my head fall back and just enjoy all that is Luke. When he finally sinks into me, his eyes lock onto mine for a powerful still moment. When I can't wait any longer, I rock my hips into him, and he moves in a way that rapidly ignites each nerve ending I have. I have no idea how long we keep up this pace, but without warning, white heat explodes through my body starting at the base of my spine and flexes through my toes. Even my scalp feels the electric current pulsing between us. All I can do is cling to him as if my life depends on it, as I experience wave after wave of my orgasm build.

"I'm so close," I moan as I tighten my grip. Luke pumps into me not even two more times, and his body becomes rigid, causing my core to clamp around him and convulse.

"Christ, Dani!" he roars as pulse after pulse rocks our

bodies, and his cock empties into the condom. His arms wrap around me tight, and he buries his head into the crease of my neck.

When our bodies settle, he pulls back and kisses me tenderly. I feel his cock move, which sends aftershocks through my body. "You are so beautiful," Luke whispers between kisses.

Eventually, I feel him slip out of me. His face fills with regret, as he explains, "Gotta take care of this condom. Be right back." He kisses me once more, and I can't help but sigh as I take in his muscular form from the back.

I hear the water turn on, and Luke returns with a wet towel as well as a dry one. Before I can do anything, he presses a warm cloth to me, and I can't help the spasms of aftershocks that zing through me. I miss his cock already, so I reach out to stroke it in my hand. It quickly becomes the perfect combination of steel hard and silky smooth. As my thumb traces his crown, he shakes his head. "You just might be the death of me."

I wake up as the sun starts to shine, to the form of a man under me. I can't help the smile that forms on my face. I lost track of how many orgasms we shared throughout the night. Luke's arms cradle me as my head rests on his chest and my leg is thrown over his thigh. *A girl could get used to his.*

Instinctually, I trace the planes of his chest and feel the light dusting of hair slip under my fingers. Without any sign of movement, I'm startled when his sexy morning voice rumbles against my face, "I need sustenance, woman, if you're going to start that up again."

I can't help but laugh. "Okay. Okay. What are you making me today?" I tease. "Our last breakfast is pretty hard to beat."

He glides his hand along my back, making me shiver. "I might have something up my sleeve," he quips.

Unfortunately, eating means having to move. As I pull myself off him, I'm gloriously sore. My muscles ache in places I'd forgotten existed. What did this man do to me?

Luke walks in all his naked glory to his dresser and pulls out a pair of boxers and t-shirt. With a wink, he tosses the t-shirt to me and slips on the boxers. I pull his soft cotton shirt over my head, and I can't help but inhale slowly as his scent washes over me. The shirt hangs to mid-thigh and although I wish I had a clean pair of underwear, I have little intention of wearing clothes for long. This will have to do.

Soon my mouth waters from the savory flavors lofting through the room. Though watching Luke's sexy body as he maneuvers his way through making an omelet for us to share might have something to do with it. I force myself to keep from ogling by keeping a steady flow of conversation.

"So... Where'd you learn to cook so well?" I ask after I take the first delicious bite. I hadn't known how hungry I was until I started eating. *Damn. This man can cook.* I quickly take another bite as I await his answer.

Luke rolls his eyes. "Well... Don't get your hopes up. You've basically experienced my culinary expertise."

"Hmmm," I moan as I finish another savory bite. "Do you make house calls?" I tease.

"Ha..." He chuckles and looks out the window. "I'm usually

well into my workout by this time of the day. I can't say I've had much time for house calls."

As I take in his sculpted form and remember yesterday morning. "Is running typically your thing?"

"I've kept to a strict regimen for as long as I can remember." He's quiet for a moment then adds, "Hell, I don't even know when I started training rigorously."

"What do you mean?"

"Well, I guess as far back as middle school, when I dreamed of playing professionally, I've taken my training seriously. My coach had us meeting up for optional workouts each morning before school."

"How long did you play professionally?" I might not be into sports, but after spending time with Luke, it's obvious it's been a big part of his life.

"Just one season. But I've coached for the past six, and I have the philosophy of never asking my players to do something I won't do myself."

That's impressive. He must be a great coach. "That's honorable."

In response, he shrugs it off as if it's not a big deal. Interesting. It appears Luke may be an athlete, but not one who's overly cocky. Just add one more thing to the growing list of qualities I like about him.

Crap. I'm not supposed to be making a list. Remember... this is casual. I repeat as I busy myself with eating until he breaks the silence.

"So, what are your plans today?" When I look up from my plate, I can't help but be captured by his deep-blue eyes. For a second, I think this might be a hint that I should get going. Yet, on further inspection, I see he's genuinely interested.

"My days consist of working on edits or my next book." Disappointment passes through his features, and I quickly add, "What are yours?"

He lets out a low sigh. "Well... I should probably get some work done, too. But... would you want to take a ride on the Sound? I'd like to take my boat out and would love the company."

I look to my computer bag I'd left in the living room. Knowing there's a shit ton of work I have to do, I compromise with myself. "What if..." *How much would I need to do to stay on track?* "What if we work for a bit this morning, then go out later this afternoon."

A knowing grin spreads across Luke's face. "I think I can manage that." Luke's voice is deeper than before, and his eyes darken. He looks me over from head to toe before adding, "Do you want to work here?"

I look down to the t-shirt I'm wearing and shake my head. "Eventually, I'll need a change of clothes..." His hungry stare has me stopping in my tracks, and I'm certain it has nothing to do with the food.

"I'm sure that can be arranged." His voice is rough as he stands and reaches out for my hand. When his fingers grasp mine, electric currents pulse through me.

Suddenly, I have no intentions of working on anything but him.

LUKE

As I wake the next morning, my hand instinctually reaches out to pull Dani closer. She's completely content using me as a body pillow and for the first time in my life, I have no place I'd rather be. I know the timing is shit, but I've never had a woman I connected with on so many levels.

Not wanting to disturb her, I let my thoughts wander through our past few days. Even in silence, we're comfortable around one another. I can't believe how focused she is when she's writing. Yesterday, we spent the morning, after breakfast, in bed. But diligent as she is, Dani managed to get us both to focus on the jobs we needed to do before spending the evening cruising across the Sound, on my thirty-five-foot American tug.

Watching Dani in a pair of denim cut-offs and a navy tank sprawled across the top deck was a sight to be seen. We'd stopped for a late dinner at one of my favorite restaurants on our way back. I love going to Budd Bay Café because I'm hardly ever recognized, or if I am, no one makes a spectacle of me. Besides, with our casual attire, we fit right in.

When Dani starts to stir, my fingers trace invisible circles along her spine. She has the most beautiful blue eyes that lock with mine when they finally flutter open.

"Mornin'." Her deep, raspy tone has my body standing up to take notice.

"Good morning. Sleep well?"

She stretches as a yawn escapes. She couldn't look more beautiful in this moment if she tried. Her curly brown locks spring out in every direction as if they have a life of their own. Her plump pink lips are swollen from our night together. Her radiant glow that shows *'I've just been fucked,'* makes my pride soar, knowing I'm the one who's done this to her. When she lets out a light moan, my mind instantly returns to last night. Christ, she's gorgeous.

As she settles her head back onto my chest, I feel content, and my body settles slightly. Continuing to rub my fingertips along her back, an unexpected question flies from my mouth before I've given myself permission to ask, "Do you have plans tomorrow evening?"

"Uh..." Her wheels visibly spin as she contemplates her plans. "Saturday... hmmm... my brothers are supposed to be in town. Why? What's up?"

Damn, she has plans. I can't ask her to ditch her family. "It's nothing." God, I wish I hadn't made commitments to attend the team's charity auction. But being the head coach means duty calls. I know we're supposed to keep this casual and take it one day at a time, but I don't want my time with her to end.

I realize she has an eyebrow cocked in my direction, waiting for more explanation. Obviously, I've left something out. *Damn. Maybe I should hire her to keep the team on track.*

"It must be something..." she continues, eyeing me inquisitively.

After a few moments of silence, I realize she's not giving up. "I don't want my time with you to end," I admit honestly. "I was hoping to convince you to go to this thing for work."

Her expressive face shows she doesn't buy my half-explained answer. "And what exactly is a *thing* for work?" Flies out of her upturned lips, causing me to smile in return. *Damn, I love her quick mouth.* It stirs things in me I long ago forgot.

"Well..." How do I tell her I wanted her to drop everything for a black-tie affair and not disclose my status of head coach? I love being just Luke with her and not having any expectations. I can't remember the last time someone liked me for just me.

"Well..." she repeats with a crooked grin.

"There's this charity auction I have to attend," I start slowly, hoping I don't have to explain much more.

Her eyebrows raise to her forehead. "A charity auction... As in... You're being auctioned?" Her voice raises at the end, and her eyes are as round as saucers.

"Oh, God, no!" I say in a fit of laughter. "Who the hell would bid on me?" I say in disbelief. "No..." I state emphatically. "Besides, this isn't that type of auction. Trust me."

She eyes me suspiciously. "You honestly don't think anyone would bid on you?"

"Why would they when there are actual pro-athletes at their disposal?"

Dani rolls her eyes as she shakes her head. "I'm sure you could bring in some large bills at that type of auction. Have you looked in the mirror, Luke?"

"Oh, please... Don't be ridiculous. Besides, in a room full of players, I'm the last one anyone would look twice at." Maybe when I was playing, that would've been a different story, but I don't nearly have that kind of clout anymore.

"Oh, trust me, Luke. Women look twice at you."

"Whatever you say, Dani..." I pull her close, pretending to snuggle, but instead, I tickle her.

Laughter fills the room, and her thoughts of a bachelor auction are soon forgotten.

As we make breakfast later that morning, Dani's hips sway to the music she's set up on her phone. She's waiting to flip the pancakes in front of my stove, as I slice fruit into a bowl. Instead of it being weird or awkward, it feels right to have her here in my home with me. It's right then, I realize I don't want my time with Dani to end. I know we said we'd keep this casual, but this feels anything but. With the season starting, I'll have zero time for a relationship. I know it isn't even fair to ask, but the thought of walking away and never seeing Dani again guts me. I almost drop the knife at the mere thought. Holy shit! How does someone I just met days ago have this effect on me. Yeah, the sex has been amazing, but with Dani, it's more than that.

I watch her dance some more and realize I can't keep these thoughts to myself. I need to put it out there, but how do I approach this, when she's the one who suggested we just make the most of our days together? Shit. I'm usually the one who likes to keep things low key. What if that's all she really wants? *Can I let this be just a fling?*

Christ, Leighton, get it together. Just man up and have a conversation, for crying out loud. It's not like you're a prepubescent asking a girl out for the first time. I will myself to come up with the words to tell her how I feel. But each time she dips and sways, my tongue gets tied, and I find myself at a loss for words. *What the hell is wrong with me?*

She plates the pancakes and pours more batter into the pan. She flits around my kitchen like she belongs here. As I watch her, I become more aware that this isn't just a casual vacation hook-up. I don't want to come on too strong, and I have no idea where this might lead, but I do know there's no way I can leave tomorrow morning and not plan to see her again. As I watch her load up the last of the pancakes onto a plate, I know my time with her is limited today, and I hope when I bring up the conversation, she feels the same.

When she turns around, I'm caught staring. A blush quickly fills her features, and her beauty radiates. "What?" she asks defensively. "Do I have something on my face?"

"No," I answer honestly. "You've never looked more beautiful." My words cause her face to pinken more. I've told her how beautiful she is several times since we've met, but for some reason, she's shy at this moment.

"Oh," she whispers. Then she seems to regain her

confidence. "Well, breakfast is ready. Want to eat at the bar or at the table?"

"The bar's fine with me," I suggest as I pull a stool out for her to sit.

Dani sets into making her pancake with butter and powdered sugar, while I go to the fridge and pull out the maple syrup for myself. I've learned yesterday she doesn't care for syrup, and I loved teasing her about it throughout the day. *Who doesn't like real maple syrup?*

"Mmm..." she moans, making me think of our time in bed together. "These taste great." She'd added fresh blueberries into the batter, and they smell delicious. I quickly cut off a bite and confirm.

"You're right, these are delicious! I haven't had real blueberry pancakes in forever," I say as I finish chewing another large bite.

We eat for a few moments in silence. I watch her as she eats, and something in my chest squeezes. "I've had an amazing week with you, Dani."

She stops chewing, and her eyes fly to mine. Her features are no longer casual as if a wall has formed between us. *Shit! Did I say something wrong?* She swallows her food, then states, "I have, too." She opens her mouth to say more but instead, goes back to eating. *Okay, that's not what I was expecting.*

My throat tightens, and a lump the size of a grapefruit forms. I take a drink of orange juice and when she still hasn't looked at me, I clear my throat to get her attention. I'm met with wide, apprehensive blue eyes, causing my heart to nearly beat out of my chest. *Have I been reading this wrong?*

"I know we said we'd keep this casual..." I start, but I stop when I see her pull in her lower lip and chew on it.

"Okay..." she draws out into three syllables but doesn't say more. It's as if she's waiting for me to continue and won't allow herself to speak because she tucks that lower lip into her teeth again.

Jesus, Leighton. Get it together. You've asked a girl out before, why are you stalling now? I take a deep breath and prepare myself for the possibility of being shot down. "I know the timing is shit, and with the season starting, I have no idea how much time I'll be on the island, but would you be willing to see me again... After today, that is..." God, am I fifteen? Why am I stuttering like a fool?

Dani's mouth drops into a perfect O, giving me zero indication of her feelings.

Is she shocked? Happy? For fuck's sake, say something already. It's not like it's that hard of a question to answer. I'm just about to say something when her eyes light up like the Fourth of July. She's smiling but shakes her head no.

What. The actual. Fuck. I don't think I could get a bigger mixed message than the one she's sending me now.

"So... I'm not the only one who's been feeling this?" she asks in a small voice.

"Christ, no," I nearly burst out. "I have no idea what," I point between the two of us, "*this* is, but I have no intention of letting it go." I reach out and caress her face as she leans into me with relief filling her features.

"Thank God," she whispers nearly to herself. "I thought I was going crazy, if this was only in my head."

For clarification, I force myself to ask, "So, you're not opposed to seeing me again?"

I can't help the goofy grin that forms on my face. Her expression says it all. "We are definitely on the same page. I absolutely want to see you again."

Relief washes through me and tension I didn't know I'd been holding onto, leaves my body immediately. I have no idea how I'm going to make this work, but I will make time to see Dani again.

11

DANI

LUKE TELLING ME HE WANTS TO KEEP SEEING ME, HAS ME ON
cloud nine. My heart plummets to my stomach, when he
brought up the subject. I'd been dreading this conversation
and going insane, wondering how I could walk away
unscathed at the end of this week. I tried to convince myself I
could have a fling and not get attached. But that went right out
the window as I got to know him better.

Let's face it. I'm not the casual type. I never have been.
That's why I've chosen to be single, rather than attempt any
form of casual relationship. With Luke, I desperately wanted
to be the type who could just let things happen, so I could
simply enjoy this experience with him. But I just don't have it
in me. I know he says he'll be busy for the next few months,
but at least he wants to see me again. I'm not a stage nine
clinger or anything, but if I'm being honest, I'm not one-night
stand material either. Well, I guess we've had more than one

night together, but we both agreed to an expiration date at the end of the week.

Since today is his last full day on the island, I need to make the most of it with him. As we finish breakfast, I ask, "Do you have anything pressing you need to do before leaving tomorrow?"

Luke's eyes light up with delight, and a smirk flits across his features. "What do you have in mind?"

"Well... for starters, let's clean up from breakfast. Then we could either go out on that magnificent boat of yours or at the very least, spend the day doing something other than work."

"I could be up for that." Luke's voice fills with mischief. "Especially if it involves you wearing those cut-off shorts." He waggles his eyebrows, and I can't help but laugh. When I calm down, he adds more serious, "We could pack a bag and return in the morning if you want. I won't catch the ferry until early afternoon. The charity auction isn't until seven. Though I left my tux at my loft in town."

The thought of Luke in a tux nearly has me salivating. The man is hot wearing nothing but a smile. The thought of him dressed up has me wishing I could attend. I'm sure he would look sexy as sin decked out in a well-fitted tux. But my brothers are due in around noon, and since Davis only has a short break from his summer classes at Gonzaga, I don't want to miss this time with him.

"Dani?" Luke asks, breaking me from my thoughts. "If you... Uh... don't want to stay on the boat, we can come home tonight."

I shake my head, realizing he's misinterpreted my silence. My face heats, knowing he's caught me fantasizing about him.

He eyes me suspiciously and begins to say something when I interrupt, "No..." I shake my head once again to clear my thoughts. "I was just imagining you in a tux," I whisper.

Luke rolls his eyes and dismissively states, "If you've seen one man in a tux, you've seen us all."

Somehow, I highly doubt that. But I try to pass it off. "As long as we're back before noon, I wouldn't be opposed to staying on the boat. My brothers have tickets for the one o'clock ferry."

"We can make that happen." Luke smiles as he pulls me in for a kiss.

Before we can get carried away, I regretfully break the kiss. "I'd better run home and grab a few things. I'll be back as soon as I can. Need me to grab anything at the store?"

"No. I'll pack some food from here and be ready to go when you return." He kisses me quickly once more before pulling back and pushing me toward my things by the door. "Go... Or we'll never leave," he teases.

We end up going to Orcas Island. It's a beautiful day on the water. Luke and I just kept wanting to go a bit further. We enjoy the sights on Puget Sound, and the weather couldn't be better.

I'm mesmerized when I spot a pod of Orca whales. Three are traveling together between the islands. Their surfacing catches me by surprise. We follow them from a safe distance for quite some time, just as we get outside Seattle. Luke's amused by my reaction and probably followed their path longer than necessary, just to appease me. Which makes me like him a bit more. I have no idea how long we watch them play with one another before diving deep into Puget Sound once again.

When we get near Orcas Island, Luke suggests anchoring for the night near a cove out of the way. Not having done this before, I simply agree and enjoy my time with him.

As we stand on the deck to take in the beauty that is around us after dinner, I feel Luke's arms snake around my body and pull me closer to him. I'd been lost in thought and didn't hear him approach.

"Hey." His deep, sexy voice pulls me out of my trance. "What's going on in that brilliant head of yours?"

"Just taking it all in. Wishing we didn't have to go back tomorrow."

Luke lets out a quick breath. "You're telling me. I can't tell you how refreshing it's been to take a break from everything."

Remembering my looming deadline and the odd hours I've been keeping, I can't help but agree. "I know," I whisper as he nuzzles my neck as his body presses against my back. Tingles explode up my spine from his closeness. Instinctively, I spin to loop my arms around his neck. My breath catches as I take in his gorgeous smile.

"You have no idea what it's like during the season. Don't get me wrong. I love my job and can't wait for the start of the season, but I haven't had a vacation like this in so long. I almost wish it wasn't ending. I really like you, Dani, but..." *Oh, shit, here it comes. The proverbial but. I knew this was too good to be true.* "I...Uh... Must warn you, Dani, my schedule's insane for the next five months or so... And if we make it to the post season, I won't be available to come to the island much."

"Okaaaay..." I drag out, wondering where he's going with this.

"Would you be opposed to visiting Tacoma from time to time?" His sincerity slays me. His piercing blue eyes reveal there's a lot riding on my answer.

"I'm sure that could be arranged," I tease.

Relief washes through him, and I reach up on my toes to kiss his worries off his face. Time ceases to exist as he thoroughly kisses my worries away as well. When he breaks the kiss, I'm breathless and admittedly panting slightly. *Holy shit, have I turned into a horny teenager?*

His deep-blue eyes lock with mine as he regains steady breathing. *At least I have the same effect on him.* "Seriously, Dani. You need to know for the first time, in a very long time, I want something more than a temporary fling."

"Had many of them, have you?" I tease, not knowing what else to say. *Fuck! I don't want to know the answer to that. Shit. Shit. Shit. Me and my big mouth.* I sputter as quick as my mouth can, and his lips part and cringe. "Don't..." I place a finger to his lips. "Don't answer that. I don't want to know the answer."

A sexy grin forms at the edge of his lips, making my knees go weak. "There's not much to tell."

I eye him suspiciously, and he shakes his head dismissively. "Seriously. I've spent the better part of my teens, college, and professional career working to get where I am now. When I was younger, I couldn't lose focus on the game. My carrot was the playing professionally. If it didn't better my chances of reaching that goal, I didn't have time for it."

He shakes his head as he shrugs adding more, "There was also the bit of never knowing if anyone was dating me for me.

Somewhere in the back of my mind, I always wondered if they were trying to ride my coattails to an easy future. So, I avoided the Jersey Chasers as best as I could. Beyond that, there simply wasn't time. I don't mean to sound callus or conceited, but that's just how it's been."

Taking his words into consideration, I remain silent as I roll them over in my brain. For as private as he's been this week, this is the most I've gotten out of him. It's a lot to take. "I can see that..." I whisper almost to myself.

He places both of his hands on my shoulders and waits for me to make eye contact again before continuing. The sincerity in his eyes reach the depths of his soul. I know with every fiber of my being he's telling me the truth. I can't help but ask, "Why me? What's changed?" He still seems as busy as ever, if he says the next six months will be crazy and chaotic.

"You're the first person to see me for me... if that makes sense."

It's like he's taking my thoughts and voicing them aloud. "I haven't felt this type of connection... ever," I admit. "At first, I thought it was just our incredible sex and off the charts chemistry. But as I've gotten to know you this week, I know there's more, too. My schedule is also crazy and chaotic. I have to write when the inspiration hits. I keep odd hours and zone out when my characters talk to me."

He chuckles at that last moment. "That's a sight to be seen. I wish I could focus as intensely as you."

"Yeah, well, even my own family wants to disown me when it happens. You'll tire of it soon enough..." I tease.

Instead of the playful banter I've come to enjoy with Luke, I see his features tighten and a seriousness return to his deep-blue eyes. "That's just it, Dani. I don't think I will. I have no fucking clue as to how I can make this work between us, with our time and geographical constraints. But I want to try. I'm just as devoted to my job as you are, and that might become problematic. So... I give you fair warning, if I slip up and become a complete shithead as a boyfriend, please talk to me first before kicking me to the curb. I'm charting new territory here and might need some assistance."

I smirk as I poke my finger into his well-defined chest. Damn, the man has muscles for days. "I think I can work with that."

Luke pulls me in for another kiss, and I know we'll figure it out somehow.

Saying goodbye to Luke was harder than I expect. Hell, I've only known the man a week, but as I pull out of his driveway to go home, my stomach feels as if there are lead weights sinking in it. Who knows when I'll see Luke next, but he's promised to text and call throughout the week.

Luke's auction is tonight, and the season's in full swing, starting Monday. Apparently, he flies to Dallas on Thursday and returns Monday, since the team has a Sunday afternoon game. Having never followed football, I'm clueless about his schedule in the coming months. If I recall, growing up in a house full of fanatic fans, there's multiple games a week. *How will I ever get this straight?*

As I plop down on my couch, I let out a heavy sigh. Being with Luke is like riding a euphoric high and now that he's gone, my exhaustion catches up with me. Nights of limited sleep will do that. Not that I'm complaining. I'd happily relive those moments over and over again. I allow myself to replay a few memories of my short time with Luke. *He really is something.*

When my phone buzzes with an incoming text, I pull myself out of my revelry.

Christ on a cracker. I need to get my shit together and focus. My brothers will be here any minute, as they're due on the next ferry.

I dig through my purse to find my phone. When I unlock the screen, there's a picture of the island from the ferry. My brothers must have arrived. But as I open the text, I'm shocked to see it's not my brothers. It's Luke.

My heart races, as I read his text.

Luke: I've always loved this view, but now this view holds a whole new meaning.

What on earth is he talking about?

Me: Why's that?

Luke: It reminds me of you.

My cheeks heat at the thought of our time together. I've never jumped into such a physical relationship before. Just thinking about Luke sets my nerves on fire.

Me: In case I forgot to tell you, I had an amazing time this week.

Luke: Ditto. I hate that I don't know when I'll see you next.

Me: Hopefully, it'll be sooner than later.

Luke: Agreed.

I hear the distinctive crunch of gravel from my driveway, and I know my brothers have arrived. As much as I want to continue this conversation, I know I'll catch hell if either of my brothers catch wind of it.

Me: My brothers just arrived. Gotta go.

Luke: Have fun. I'll text you after the auction, if it's not too late.

Before I have a chance to respond, my front door bursts open. We've always just walked into this home, when my grandparents lived here. I smile when I realize some things will never change.

I quickly push my phone into my back pocket as I stand to greet my baby brother, Davis. Sure, he'd flip a gasket if he knew I called him my baby brother, but to me, that's how he'll always be. Being nine years older, even when he grows up and becomes a doctor, I'll always think of him as the baby.

"Hey, Dani." He reaches out to hug me. "Good to see you."

"How was the drive from Spokane?" I ask as he releases me, then turn to my brother Damien to give him some love as well. God, I've missed these guys. With my schedule and their classes, we don't see each other nearly enough.

"I made good time and can't wait to have two weeks without classes."

"Only our future doctor would take this many summer courses," Damien states dryly as he releases me from our hug.

"Don't be too hard on him, Dame," I chastise like any older sister would, but both of my brothers just chuckle at my poor attempt to be like Mom. "Did you hit much traffic from Seattle?" I ask.

As my eyes flit from one to the other, waiting for a response, I can't believe how much they resemble one another as they've gotten older. They could almost be twins, they look so much alike. Of course, each are in their typical summer wear—cargo shorts, sporting their college t-shirt logos, and Vans. Both have sandy-brown hair, dark-brown eyes, and sun-kissed skin. Davis's hair is cut shorter than usual, while Damien's is long on top and, while shaved on the sides, is nearly to his ears.

"Nah." Davis shrugs dismissively. "Traffic was light. The longest we stood still was waiting to board the ferry." Giving the timing of everything, I'm sure they must have crossed paths with Luke. Thank God, they didn't get the chance to meet him. I'd never hear the end of it. Both may be younger than me, but they've learned from my dad and Derek how to interrogate any guy I bring home.

"So... what have you been keeping yourself busy with?" Damien asks as he walks to the fridge and pulls it open to inspect the contents. "Obviously, it wasn't shopping. What the hell have you been eating? Ketchup on pickles?"

Shit. I'd forgotten to shop before they arrived, and I'll have to make a trip off the island to get enough to feed these two. The small mom and pop shop on the island has a few staples but not enough to cover what I will need for the week or so they're staying.

"If you're hungry, we can go to the cafe. They serve the best lunches." To sweeten the offer, I add, "My treat."

Both being full-time college students, I wouldn't dream of letting them pay, but I threw it out there to get their minds off the dilapidated state of my fridge. I really need to remember to shop when I write. But this week, I had an excuse. Eating nearly every meal with Luke kept me from needing to go off the island and stock up. Not all of us have a personal shopper like Luke. Evelyn was such a sweetheart when I met her. It is kind of Luke to employ her, so she can stay on the island to help her daughter.

"It beats the condiment special you have going on here," Damien mutters as he shuts the fridge. "I don't think I've ever seen a fridge in our family look so clean or bare."

"Oh, hush." I swat my hand in the air to dismiss his sarcasm. "Go unload your things then we'll grab a bite to eat. I'll stock up the fridge this afternoon."

By the time we finish eating, I realize the next ferry's due soon. Not wanting to venture out later, I convince my brothers to take a shopping trip to Tacoma. We stock up on all the things they will need during their short break from school.

The plan is for my parents and older brother Derek to come out next weekend and spend a few days together before they're forced to return to their real lives. For me, I plan to use every spare moment I can to stay on track with my editor. Three weeks will fly by and get out of hand if I don't make use of my downtime when I'm not spending time with my family.

Instead of staying in the car and working like I usually do on the commute back to the island, my brothers encourage me to get out and enjoy the hot July evening. The breeze feels refreshing, and I can't help but think of my trips with Luke out on his boat this week. Just as we get to the top of the ferry and find a place we can take in the view, I get a text notification.

I pull my phone from my pocket and can't help but smile.

Luke: Wish you were here. There's even a romance package with one of your books in the basket.

Me: Seriously???

I can't believe one of my books is at a charity auction. It's an honor to be represented. I wish I'd known. I would've created a basket and signed my entire series. I wonder who donated it?

An image comes through with an entire basket full of books. There must be at least twenty books in there. The basket includes a blanket, coffee, and gourmet chocolates. If I'd been there, I'd bid on that basket in a heartbeat. Most of my favorite authors are included. That's a real treat. Someone will be a hell of a lucky winner.

Luke: If I bid on it and win, will you sign it?

Me: You don't need to bid on that to get a signed copy. Rumor has it I know the author.

Luke: Hmmm... she's sexy as hell. Maybe I'll figure out a way to get a signed copy some other way.

This man... I roll my eyes as a light chuckle escapes. *Like he'd have to do much to get a simple autograph.*

Me: Do I need to be worried?

Luke: Absolutely. I've been told I'm ruthless when it comes to getting something I want.

Me: Promises. Promises.

Luke: It's going to be a really long week.

I sigh in agreement and look out at the water, thinking about how to respond. This man sure has made an impression.

"What are you grinning like a loon about?" Damien interrupts my thoughts.

"Um... It's nothing. Just a friend of mine found one of my books at a charity auction, and they were telling me about it."

"Seriously... You're going with that?" Davis pipes in. "I highly doubt you'd have that goofy look on your face over, *'just a friend.'*" The idiot makes actual air quotes with his fingers. What are we? Twelve?

"You're delusional," I dismiss. "You know, Doctor Davis, you might need to get out more."

"As if..." Davis starts, but Damien interrupts.

"You know, D, she's quite dismissive. Maybe you're on to something."

Both guys eye me speculatively, waiting for me to divulge whatever they think I'm hiding. This isn't my first rodeo with these nut jobs. The best defense is silence. I mask my poker face and simply raise my eyebrows with the sheer goal of outwaiting them. Finally, when they realize I'm not budging on this, Davis gives up and moves on to plans about kayaking in the morning.

With my crisis averted, we spend the evening watching movies and hanging out. Though I wouldn't be me without pulling out my laptop and writing while the movie plays in the background. I stay up later than my brothers, getting into a zone again. Partially hoping to hear from Luke, but no such luck. He's radio-silent the rest of the night.

12

LUKE

Waking up Sunday morning, I instinctually reach for Dani, but I find nothing but cool sheets in my grasp. The auction and dinner went later than I thought last night and as soon as I got home, I made the mistake of checking my email. Shit. I was supposed to text her when I got home. It hasn't even been one day, and I'm already fucking things up. *Way to go, Leighton.*

I reach to my bedside table and pick up my phone. Without thinking about the time, I shoot off a quick text to Dani.

Me: Good Morning. Hope you had fun with your brothers. Any plans for today?

Shit. It's not even six. Hopefully, she'll sleep through it or at least have her notifications turned off. Within seconds, I see three dots jumping.

Dani: The guys and I plan to go kayaking when it warms up.

Me: Did I wake you?

Dani: No. Couldn't sleep. Been writing for about an hour. Why are you up at this ungodly hour?

I can just imagine her eyeroll at my audacity. In my short time with her, I learned she's more of a night owl, or will often get up in the middle of the night to work if she can't sleep, then she'll happily sleep in until at least nine or ten.

Me: I always get up at this time. In fact, this is late for me. Usually I'm running by now.

Dani: Overachiever!

Me: Not really. Just have to find a way to get it all in. I prefer the open road, but sometimes I run on the treadmill and watch game footage.

Dani: Once again, if I'm running... look to see what's chasing me. Give me a bike or spin class any day.

Before I have a chance to reply, my phone rings.
"Hey, Luke." Her sexy morning voice slithers quietly through the line.
"Good morning, Danika." God, it's good to hear her voice.

As if she feels the same, a low sigh of relief can be heard. "Do you have to work today?"

"Yeah. With the start of the season, I'm back to working nearly 24/7 for the next few months. Where are you going kayaking?"

"Amsterdam Bay. We won't head out until the weather gets a bit warmer. Since Puget Sound never gets above fifty-three degrees, we'll wait until this afternoon."

"What are you doing this morning?" I ask with curiosity.

"Well..." She takes in a deep breath. "Since the guys are on break, I'll bet they won't show their faces until at least ten. They have always been notorious for sleeping in." Her light laugh makes me miss her more. *How does she do that?*

"What will you do while they're sleeping?" Her quiet sigh makes me wish I was with her.

"Oh, I plan to get my daily word count in and to edit some, if I can. Who knows how much time I'll actually get to write with the guys here this week. If I can get ahead, it'd be a relief."

Something in the way she says this makes me wonder if I was too much of a distraction. "Did I cause you to get behind this week?"

"Oh, no. I got plenty done. I just need to complete some edits and get a book to my editor by the end of the month. I'm on track for finishing it, but I always feel the pressure as the date looms closer."

"Ah... So, you work best under pressure," I tease.

She releases the sexiest laugh. "Busted."

My phone buzzes as my alarm goes off, reminding me I need to get moving if I'm going to meet Mike and Tony. We would've met yesterday but with the auction being scheduled, we rescheduled for this morning instead.

Dani must hear this because she asks, "Gotta go?"

I sigh defeatedly. "Yeah, but I'd rather stay and chat with you," I admit honestly.

"Go... do your thing. We'll catch up later." Dani's stern voice makes me think she could hold her own in my line of work, and I can't help but smile.

Sunday rolls into Monday with countless meetings, planning, and all the things necessary to get the season started right. I've been an assistant coach or have worked for the team for years but stepping into the head coach position takes things to a whole new level. The biggest difference is a shit-ton more meetings. I didn't get blindsided, but I completely understand why there's a Murphy's bed at my office. I refuse to use it because my condo's only ten minutes away from the stadium. Though, I may change my mind at some point.

I manage to both talk and text with Dani a few times throughout the day, but nothing compares to the real thing. I feel like a giant asshole for even considering a relationship at the start of the season. But for some reason, I can't make myself walk away either.

After our coach and coordinator meeting, I catch up on emails while waiting for my scheduled meeting with Campbell Beck. Now that I've had a chance to calm down and see how the story's played out over the week, I feel confident in how this meeting will go. I'm expecting him along with his agent, our GM, and Tanya Hart, the Rainier Renegades lead PR rep. Beck's the first to arrive. I know better than to talk about anything pertaining to this circumstance without everyone else in the room. But I stand to greet him anyway.

Cam walks into the room and immediately shakes my hand. Despite the current situation he's landed himself in, he holds his head high and as usual, is humble about his actions. "Thanks for coming in," I offer and gesture to a seat at the table across the room from my desk. Before he can respond, his agent, Pete Ward, and Tanya walk in together.

"Wish it were under different circumstances," Cam states quietly, so that only I can hear. I can't tell if he's upset we all have to be involved in this, or he's talking about his recent nuptials.

Before I can say anything in response, Tony enters the room and states, "Let's get started." He looks around the room for any objections before motioning to the conference table I have set up along one side of my office.

My assistant Harlow set up the conference table to make sure we had everything we would need. She's been a lifesaver since I stepped into this position. Since she was Ray's assistant for the past ten years, she knows the ins and outs of this business, and I couldn't imagine starting this season without her by my side.

When we're all seated, it's Cam who speaks first. I'd prepared to begin the meeting, but this doesn't surprise me. Cam's a straightforward guy and won't skate around any issues. It's part of the reason I respect him the way I do, despite his current situation.

"Before we begin, I'd like to apologize for having to take

this meeting in the first place. Yes, I married Hillary in Vegas. Yes. Drinking was involved and... Yes... social media took things to an entirely new level."

Ya think? The media got wind of this and made it a total shit show. It's been all they can do to keep it on the newsreel and contemplate just how much of a spectacle Campbell's made of his life, not to mention, our franchise. With this being Rainier's first season with me as head coach, and a few players still up in the air for how we will fill our roster in the next few weeks, we've been the talk of the league in more ways than we've wanted.

Cam's agent Pete starts to interrupt, but Campbell holds up his hand to keep the attention of the room. "Look. I know I could've handled things differently, and I'll take that responsibility." He pauses to take a breath and look around the room, gauging our reactions. He slowly shakes his head and looks me in the eye. "Look, sir..."

Tanya can't hold her tongue any longer. "Did you really think you could take a quick trip to Vegas and not have the world hear about it?"

"Son," Tony interrupts, "you know Mike runs a tight ship around here. As the owner, he doesn't approve of the Renegades' reputation being slung through the mud just a week before the preseason starts."

Pete interjects before anyone can say more, "If you'll give Cam a chance to explain, you'll see there's more to the story than what appeared on Hillary's social media feed."

Well, this oughta be good. I can't imagine what he can say that disputes what Hillary posted on her newsfeed. He appeared to be caught with his pants down, and her claims of him being off the market left little to the imagination.

Cam clears his throat. "Contrary to popular belief, Hillary and I have dated exclusively for the past two years, so she isn't just some fling. We've kept our relationship fairly quiet, except for personal friends and family so that she can have a life outside of being my significant other. We were tired of waiting for the right time and decided not to have a big fanfare wedding... So, we took a quick trip to Vegas. Unfortunately, we indulged in a bit of alcohol and might not have used our best judgement when it came to photo ops."

I feel my eyebrows raise on their own accord as I listen to his story. *Does he expect us to believe this shit?* As Cam locks eyes with mine, I can tell I haven't done a good job of schooling my features because he continues, "Yeah... Yeah... I know. That wasn't the best way to let the world know." *You can say that again.*

Cam shakes his head, and his features turn solemn. "Seriously, she thought she sent that photo to her best friends, instead of the world. Then my comment went viral about the fact I regret it was taken out of context."

"What was left off the recording that went viral was our conversation prior to it as well as my words afterward. Reporters bombarded us right outside the hotel. Hillary had asked if I have any regrets, and I told her yes because I wished we'd done it sooner... The part recorded was when I made a comment about how I wish I would've told my mama beforehand because she'd be hurt I didn't tell her before the world." He grimaces.

"And how did that go for you?" Tanya snarks. She's

typically very professional, but I can tell she thinks she has better things she could be doing than dealing with Beck's drama.

"Well..." He takes a deep breath. "Mama wasn't happy she found out the way she did, but I know she's happy for us."

Tanya doesn't say anything, but it's clear from the expression on her face she agrees with his mother. I know Mama would've had a conniption fit. She wouldn't care if I got married, but it'd definitely matter if she's the last to know. *God help Beck if his mother's anything like mine.*

Pete clears his throat to get the room's attention. "Campbell takes full responsibility for his actions. He's willing to go on the record to rectify this situation. You will also see he's made plans to volunteer as well as visit local hospitals with his wife. These were in place long before the trip to Vegas, the only difference is now they're married. He's never done these trips with cameras, and it will stay that way. Hillary's on board with no longer posting to social media on a whim, as well." Cam's face tightens at this comment. Obviously there have been words shared between them about this.

Pete continues, "Campbell's been nothing but a team player since he stepped foot in our stadium." He takes a moment to look at each of us in the room. Then he gathers some papers from his briefcase. "Here... Take a look at these. There is photo after photo of Cam working with underprivileged teens on their football skills, visiting sick children at the hospital, and pictures of Cam proposing to Hillary long before this trip to Vegas with a group of friends in the background."

"Just how do you propose we spin this?" Tanya asks the

room. "His video in Vegas and the social media frenzy Hillary's photos created already made this situation a different story."

Cam's eyes tighten as his lips form a flat line. I'm not sure his teeth will hold out if he continues to flex and grind them the way his jaw's ticking. He cuts a cold glance to Tanya, then to Pete. It's taking everything in his power not to unleash his anger at her. Pete shakes his head slightly as if to heed a warning of his own.

Instead of holding him back, I find myself letting a question fly out of my mouth without permission. Maybe it's my experience this week with Dani. Maybe it's something else entirely, but the words are out before I can think it through much further. "Do you love her?"

The entire room turns to gape, as if I've just grown three heads. Maybe I have lost my mind? But I can't see a man like Campbell Beck getting caught up in something like this, if his heart wasn't in it.

Simultaneously, Tanya and Cam respond to my question, "Do you expect us to say this whole fiasco is because he's young, dumb, and in love?" Tanya accuses.

Cam's eyes lock onto mine, and his expression leaves no room for argument. "Absofuckinglutely." The room quiets, and the tips of his ears darken. "Sorry for cursing. That wasn't my intent... But yes. I love her without a doubt. We were tired of waiting and wanted to be married before the crazy of the season starts."

Tony is the first to speak. "Well... that certainly changes everything."

"What do you mean?" Tanya quips. She's on the edge of her seat. Ready for battle.

"Maybe you haven't experienced this," Tony eyes Tanya who is all but rolling hers in disgust, "but that's how it was for me and my wife Margorie. I started dating her right after I was drafted, and I couldn't wait to marry her. It took us a year or two to get over the crazy of my schedule before we nailed down a date and were married. It's been twenty-two years this May. I still have no idea how she's managed to stay with me for this long. But I get where Beck's coming from. I would've eloped in a heartbeat, if Margorie had given me the chance."

To see Tony Marcelli talk about his wife this way is revealing. He's always kept his private life, private. I've never heard of how he and his wife started out, let alone watch him sympathize with players who scandalously elope to Vegas and become the talk of the league. This act alone seems to change the mood of the room. Pete relaxes in his chair. Tanya deflates slightly, and I realize there just might be more to life than football.

"I'm not young, or dumb," Campbell replies. "But I am in love. I sincerely apologize for any trouble my actions may have caused. I'm willing to do what it takes to get back in the team's good graces."

"I'm sure we can figure something out," I offer as I watch the others around me agree. Though Tanya's hesitant. I think she'll come around. "It's not like you've had any other indiscretions we've had to deal with. You've kept your nose clean, and you work hard. Just don't let your life off the field affect your work on the field, and I think we'll be good."

We continue to talk about the steps necessary to make this social media nightmare diffuse. Once Tanya's on board with how we should handle the story, everything falls into place.

There'll be a press conference this afternoon with both Cam and Hillary. Tanya will coach them in what they are to wear and say. Hopefully within the next few days, it'll all become a thing of the past, and the Becks can enjoy their status as newlyweds without any further complications.

By the time I get on the plane to Dallas, I'm as prepped for the game as I can be. My brain's fried, and I can hardly wait to get this first game under my belt as head coach. My coaching staff and I have gone over every possible scenario we can think of to outwit our opponents.

I typically would fly out with the team on Saturday, but I wanted to meet with a potential player we can pick up on our roster. He was scouted to play with Dallas, but rumor has it he might not be a good fit for them, since they already have a great kicker and a back-up ready, should they need it. With Reynolds being injured last year, I want to give him a chance to show he's recovered, but Mendoza might be worth looking into. I've booked a first-class flight to get some rest and maybe look over more footage.

As I briskly make my way through airport security and into the VIP lounge for my airline, I pass a bookstore and am taken back by the display in the window. There sitting front and center is Dani's latest book. I stop for a moment to take in the series title. I pull open my book app on my phone and quickly download the first book. The thought of Dani alone pulls the corners of my lips into a smile. *Damn, I miss her.*

I've made it a point to speak with Dani several times this

week. Each time we spoke, I desperately wanted to head out to the island to see her in person, but I just couldn't get away. The fact that her brothers were visiting didn't help much either. I can't believe I'm drawn to her as much as I am. This is the busiest time of my life. I don't have time to let my thoughts wander. Yet, I still find myself thinking about the sexy brunette with the wild and curly hair, beautiful blue eyes, and her sexy as hell freckles. *God. This woman just may be the death of me.*

Seeing her book on display makes me think of her sexy sass. She's so quick with her tongue, I never know what's going to come out of that sexy mouth of hers. Her entire body lights up when she gets on a roll with her books. Her sexy smile melts my heart every time I think about it. I love hearing her talk about characters as if they're living and breathing people sitting here with us in the room. I've never been that creative, and I can't help but be impressed by her ambition and drive.

Glancing at the display once again, I realize I'm not the only person who's fallen for her talent. She's made it on the top of the *New York Times* bestseller's list as well as *USA Today*. I haven't ever thought about those lists, but based upon the acclimations displayed, they are a sought-after list.

I quickly make my way to the lounge and find a place to charge my phone. If I want to check out what the rave is about, I'd better charge my damn phone. I open the app as I relax into the leather couch next to the charger and begin reading. Before I know it, my flight's being called, and I need to get my ass in gear if I'm going to make it on time. Holy shit. I don't remember ever being sucked into a book like this. I'll admit, this is my first romance novel, but there's enough action and suspense, I'm completely hooked on the first few chapters.

By the time I make my way on the plane, I send off a quick text to Dani to let her know I'm thinking of her.

Me: I might be reading the first book in your latest series.

A reply comes instantly, and my heart pulses in my chest.

Dani: Seriously???

Me: You didn't tell me you're a *New York Times* and *USA Today* bestseller.

I can picture her blushing as her modesty takes over. God, I wish I could see her face right now.

Dani: Well... it would be weird to bring it up in daily conversations.

Me: I can see that. Congratulations BTW. I'm on chapter three. Can't wait to read more. Though I do have some questions for you.

Dani: Questions? What kind of questions?

The flight attendant tells us it's time to turn off our phones for take-off and put them into airplane mode. I quickly shoot off one last text and can't help the grin that forms.

Me: Wouldn't you like to know. Listen. I gotta go. My
flight is taking off. I'll call you when I get to my hotel
room.

Before she can respond, the flight attendant walks by my
row, and I quickly put my phone in airplane mode. As soon as
we're in the air and beverages have been passed out, I get
myself settled with a soda and ponder the questions I could
ask Dani when I get to my hotel. Surprisingly, I find I want to
read more of her book. I open the app again before I can think
twice.

I knew Dani has a way with words, but this goes beyond
my imagination. I had no idea what I was in store for.

Holy shit! Some of these scenes are hot! My body reacts
just as if it were Dani and I instead of the main characters,
which isn't quite appropriate when you're on a crowded plane.
When a woman bumps my shoulder as she walks up the aisle,
I feel my cheeks heat at being brought back to reality. I glance
around and check to see if anyone is paying attention to me.
Not that they can tell what I'm reading, but I'd been so
completely entranced in Dani's world, I could have sworn I
was in the book itself. No wonder she's made the bestseller's
lists. After my pulse stops racing, and I realize no one's paying
me any attention, I settle back into the story and get lost in the
world she's created once again. One thing's for certain. This
woman can write.

13

DANI

THE WEEK WITH MY BROTHERS HAS FLOWN BY. I MANAGED TO finish another round of edits and make some headway on my latest work in progress. This was cause to celebrate and spend time with my brothers in true Fallon family fashion. We kayaked, binge-watched some of our favorite shows, and just spent time hanging out around our cabin. My older brother Derek and my parents made it out for a long weekend and will return home tomorrow morning, while my younger brothers will stay through next weekend.

Admittedly, a steady stream of texts and phone calls from Luke have also made my week memorable. They were thought provoking, flirty, and kept a smile on my face for hours. Don't even get me started on the scenes he inspired.

Unfortunately, my brothers completely noticed. They harassed me in their best brotherly brutality. Sometimes I swear they're still teenagers and can't let the fact I was talking with a guy go.

As my phone buzzes in my pocket, my heart races as I peek at the incoming text.

Luke: Busy?

Me: Not at all. Have you made it home?

Luke: Yeah. Just arrived.

Me: Do you have to work today?

Luke: Playing hooky.

Me: Everyone needs to sometime. Lol

Before he replies, there's a knock at my door. Knowing everyone in my family is already here and would never knock, I can't help but wonder about our unannounced visitor. *It's not like the island has many solicitors.* I pull open the door to greet our unexpected guest, and my jaw drops to the floor.

The most penetrating deep-blue eyes darken with delight as a sexy lopsided smile spreads across Luke's face. *Holy shit, he's here.* It takes a moment for my body to catch up with my brain as I register he's really standing before me.

His hand reaches out to run a finger along my cheek, sending an electric pulse soaring through my veins. "Dani," he says, almost guttural. I can't help myself. I launch myself into his arms.

Thank God, he catches me with ease. As I wrap my arms around him fiercely, I draw in a deep breath because he smells amazing. Clean citrus mixed with a scent that's entirely Luke. As I inhale a second time, *because the first wasn't enough*, I reach my hand to his face and pull him to me. It's as if I can't get close enough to him.

The second my lips touch his, it's as if all is right with the world. I hadn't realized just how much I missed him until this very moment. Hell. I write about these moments in books and could've sworn they were simply fiction. This never happens in real life. At least not to me.

I might have started this kiss, but Luke quickly takes control. As I wrap my legs around his waist, he takes one hand and guides me through a searing kiss that leaves me breathless. After all too short of time, I regretfully pull away to catch my breath. *Holy Hell. This man can kiss.*

"What... are you... doing... here?" I ask in ragged pants. I still can't believe he's here, in my living room.

He kisses me swiftly once more before answering my question, "Had to see you."

A throat is cleared from behind, and I hear Damien chuckle. Shit. I'd forgotten he'd been watching television with me. Everyone else was out back on the deck. "Don't mind me. I'll just leave you two alone. Apparently... you know this guy, right, Dani?"

Mortification doesn't even begin to describe my feelings. How could I forget I wasn't alone? I've never launched myself at any man... *Shit! My brother just witnessed everything.* And the bastard thinks it's appropriate to comment. Gah. He has some nerve. I quickly unhook my legs from Luke's waist as Luke helps settle me on the floor.

Before I can respond, Luke's body shakes with silent

laughter. When I make my eyes meet his, I see pure, unadulterated joy radiating from him. He smirks and says, "God, I sure hope she doesn't greet everyone like this." He waggles an eyebrow and waits for my response.

"What?" I stammer in disbelief. How could he think such a thing?

"Relax, Dani," Luke says as he tames a curl that has fallen in front of my face. "You have to admit. It *is* one hell of a way to be greeted. I don't think I've ever had anyone so eager to see me." Though his words would seem cocky coming out of anyone else's mouth, they feel almost humble from Luke.

I stare at him to see if my gut reaction is correct. When I realize his sincerity, I reach out for his hand and pull him into the living room so he can properly meet my brother.

"Damien, I'd like you to meet..."

But I don't get any further because Damien shouts, "Holy shit... Luke Leighton is kissing... *you*? When did you crawl out from the rock you live under and meet a guy like him?"

I see the tips of Luke's ears redden, and an unreadable expression fills his face. Fearing he's offended Luke, I'm about to lay into my brother for being such an ass when what he said sinks in. *What the fuck? How does Dame know Luke's name?* I haven't even introduced them.

"Wait..." I look between Luke and Damien. Damien seems to know Luke, but I can't say the same for Luke. Luke's expression is reserved and if I didn't know better, a flicker of guilt mixed with something else crosses his face, but it's quickly replaced when his eyes meet mine. "You know my brother?" I ask in disbelief. I know this is a small island, but seriously? How can my brother know him?

He shakes his head as he passes a glance at Damien. "I don't think we've met," he intercedes quietly.

Damien eyes me suspiciously as he crosses the room and reaches out his hand to greet Luke officially. "Sorry about that. It's not every day I react that way. I'm Damien. It's nice to meet you."

What the hell? Why is Damien shaking his hand repeatedly as if he's starstruck or something?

"Luke," he says in return. Watching their interaction goes beyond strange. They act like strangers, but clearly Damien knows him.

"Would somebody tell me what the fuck is going on?" I pipe in when neither of them says anything.

"I should be asking you the same question," Damien accuses. Then he darts an overprotective glance at Luke. Oh, geez. What the hell's he doing now? I'm the older sister. I don't need Dame going all alpha male, protective brother on me. I'm no longer in high school, and my virtue isn't in danger here.

"What the hell is that supposed to mean?" I scoff. Why would he be asking me what's going on. Obviously, I just greeted a guy I'm seeing. What's weird is Damien calling him by both his first and last name.

Damien smirks in only the way a brother can. "Just how long have you been seeing each other?"

I gasp in horrified shock. "What business is it of yours?" I spit out like a petulant teenager, but my brother's being a dick, and Luke doesn't deserve it.

Luke places a hand on my shoulder and against my will, my body instantly calms. *How the hell does he do that to me?* "It's okay, Dani." He steps around me because somehow during all this, I wound up between the two of them.

Damien raises an expectant eyebrow. I roll my eyes. He has some nerve.

"It's still new," Luke offers to Damien. "I had the afternoon off and decided to surprise Dani with a visit. Sorry if I've interrupted anything."

"You haven't interrupted anything," I blurt out. I love that he surprised me. I haven't been able to stop thinking about him since he left. Obviously, my traitorous body feels the same. I can't believe I attacked him in front of my brother though. I'll never hear the end of this.

"Nah, man. We're just hanging out. I have to admit, I'm a little surprised to see you myself. I had no idea you knew Dani. Shouldn't you be busy gearing up for the season though?"

"Like I told Dani, I just have the afternoon off. I'll be back at it tomorrow," Luke explains.

This is so strange. Why is Damien concerned about Luke's job? Is that where they know each other? I know Damien was doing an internship for part of the summer, but I didn't think it was in Tacoma. Before I can question it, the room fills with the rest of my family. Derek and Davis are in mid-conversation as they come in from the back deck, followed by my parents who are laughing about something.

When they spot Luke, everyone goes silent. My brothers and dad stare in disbelief. Fuck, it's not like I've never brought a guy home with me. What the hell's wrong with my family? Can they *not* act like I'm the hermit that never ventures out of her writing cave?

Thankfully, my mom's oblivious to their odd reactions, and

she's her normal self. "Oh, I didn't realize we had company." When she gets to Luke, she reaches out her hand. "I'm Daisy."

"I'm Luke." Luke's lips turn into a sexy smile, and my heart races. I can tell my mom isn't immune to him, either. The way her eyes light up at his greeting.

Davis and Derek exchange shocked expressions. Holy shit. *Can they act normal?* For fuck's sake, this is beyond ridiculous. It's like we've never had company before. Each of their eyes pivot to Luke, and their jaws drop as their eyes continue to bulge.

I'm about to introduce them to Luke when Derek finally finds actual words to come out of his mouth. Maybe there's hope for some form of normalcy yet. But sadly. I'm mistaken.

"Holy shit. What's Luke Leighton doing here?"

"What the hell?" I chastise, but suddenly it seems like I'm the only one who doesn't know Luke. I look to him, and he sheepishly glances at the floor for a split second before locking eyes with me. *Oh, shit. What isn't he telling me?*

"Wh... Why does everyone in my family seem to know you?" I whisper.

Suddenly, Luke's eyes tighten, and his posture stiffens. Luke's voice is filled with concern and a hint of regret. "Dani... I..."

"Who wouldn't recognize the youngest head coach in the league? You'd have to be living under a rock not to know Luke Leighton's going to lead the Rainier Renegades to victory this season. He's making league history," Derek announces to the room. "The bigger question is what's he doing in *our* living room?"

14

LUKE

Shit! Damn! Fuck! This isn't how I wanted Dani to learn I'm head coach, or meet her family for that matter. Since college, I've never been able to be *"just Luke,"* to anyone. Football was always associated with my name. Meeting Dani was such a breath of fresh air. Knowing she likes me for me and not my status, made my fucking world.

Her expression guts me. She obviously thinks I've been lying. Fuck! That was never my intent. Sure, I didn't tell her I'm head coach, but in all honesty, it never came up. She knows I work for the Rainier Renegades, and I travel with the team, but I haven't mentioned my specific job title. Regret fills every cell in my body. From the sudden mistrust in Dani's eyes, I know I need to rectify this. Right the fuck now. *But how?*

"God..." Dani's head shakes from side to side. "You must think I'm such a fool." Barely a whisper, her words knock the wind out of me, worse than a blindside tackle. This cannot be happening.

"Danika," I plead. *How can I explain this and not look like a complete ass?*

"I may not know much about football, but I'm guessing that being the youngest head coach in the league is kind of a big deal?" Her eyes narrow, and her lips purse as she waits for my response. Fuck, she's pissed.

Before I can say anything, her mother interrupts, "We'll... just... leave you two... alone." She ushers the rest of her family out of the room. Dani's brothers begin to protest, but their mom levels them with a single stare. Damn, I see where Dani gets it now. Only Dani's icy glare is directed entirely at me. Fuck. This is bad.

Once the room clears, Dani prompts me to continue, "Well..." Her narrowed eyes are nearly slits and her face stony. She's definitely learned a thing or two from her mom. God help her kids when she has them.

Where do I even begin? I'm not an idiot. Omitting facts is just as bad as lies, but I never intended to hide anything. I take a deep breath and go with the truth, hoping it will set me free.

"I'm sorry." At least my voice sounds confident, when the look in her eyes makes me anything but. "I never meant to keep anything from you. I told you my name. I told you who I work for. When you didn't recognize me, I just enjoyed the fact that I could be me, without any expectations."

Clearly this explanation doesn't cut it.

Her curly brown hair bobs as her chin cocks to the side and piercing-blue eyes continue boring into me. "Remember how I told you I played ball in college, was drafted, then started coaching when my knee took me out of the game?"

"Yes." Her response is short, but her eyes soften a fraction. I think. Well... at least I hope.

I stop contemplating her reaction and continue, "All that was entirely true. I didn't become the head coach until last spring, when Ray Carson retired." Her eyes widen a fraction, letting me know she believes me, to a point.

"Okay..." she draws out as if she's formulating her words. "But, why didn't you just tell me you were kind of a big deal?"

"Why didn't you tell me you were a best-selling author?" I hedge, reaching for strings and hoping she'll get my point.

The corners of her lips turn, and her face morphs from stony to shy. I know the instant she connects the dots. Her lips turn into the cutest O shape. If I was sure I've been forgiven, I'd kiss her expression right off her. She's so fucking adorable. But I can't, since I'm not entirely forgiven... yet.

"I'm not really one to brag about my accomplishments." Her defense is soft, her expression humble. This. Right here. Is why I like her so much.

"Neither do I. There are enough egos in my line of work. Sure, there are times I've let mine soar, but with you, I've never felt a need." I reach my hand up to brush a loose curl from her face and rest it on her shoulder as I caress her cheek with my thumb. She leans into it, and my heart races. "I just wanted to be me. I didn't have to show off or impress you. You didn't have any expectations or want anything from me. Except... well... orgasms," I tack on at the end to lighten the mood.

She blushes from her hairline into the depths of the loose tank she's wearing and maybe beyond. My intent met its mark. Her ocean-blue eyes fill with mirth, and a sexy smile spreads across her beautiful face. "You've spoiled me with multiples.

Of course, I have expectations, Leighton. You're a force to be reckoned with." My heart soars with her wicked sass. I know right then and there I've been forgiven.

I pull her close and lean in for a kiss and whisper across her lips, "Are you sure you can handle dating a football coach?"

Without giving her a chance to respond, I slant my lips over hers and kiss her for all I'm worth. Her touch lights my body on fire, the moment our lips meet. If I didn't know her family was nearby, likely listening, I have the reunion I'd been hoping for since I returned from Dallas. Hell, let's be real. I've been wanting this since I left in the first place.

When I realize I won't be able to control myself if I don't stop this now, I regretfully pull back. She feels as reluctant to put an end to our kissing, so I kiss her briefly a few more times before pulling back completely. Each of us pant out a few breaths before our breathing returns to normal.

Suddenly, a saucy grin lights up her face, and she taps the tip of my nose with her finger. "I think I can handle you being the coach, if you realize I know absolutely nothing about football."

A deep belly laugh erupts. I can't help it. Can she be anymore perfect? I don't think I'll have any troubles staying humble with her in my life.

Dani reaches for my hand and pulls me in the direction of her backyard. "Come on. Let's go introduce you properly, or I'll never hear the end of it."

I can just imagine what her family thinks already. I get here, she attacks me, we fight, and they leave the room. Fuck, Leighton. Way to make an impression. God, I hope they're at least fans of the Rainier Renegades or I'm really fucked.

***

As it turns out, I had little to worry about. Her family's laid back, just like her. We spend time on their back deck enjoying the beautiful August weather. Sure, her brothers and dad were eager to meet me, but they were almost more interested in my intentions with Dani than my status as coach as the afternoon wore on.

I'm relieved to find they're avid fans of the Rainier Renegades but typically watch from their TVs at home. I'm stoked when I make their day by inviting them to our home game next weekend. As soon as the idea hit, I sent a text to my assistant. I know I have some seats to use at my discretion each game but hardly use them. I wish I had more time to get a luxury box for them, but when Harlow assures me the seats are still great, I extend the invitation. Dani's younger brothers jump up and down. Literally. I had no fucking clue they'd react this way. Dani's embarrassed by their behavior, but I assure her it's fine.

"So…" her dad starts as we're finishing dinner that evening. "Dani's obviously not a sports fan. How on earth did you meet?"

"Dad!" Dani protests, but her brothers fill the air with laughter. I fall in right along with them.

"We met here, on Anderson Island." Not knowing what Dani wants to divulge, I stick with safe topics. Clearly, she's a private person, and I don't want to insert my foot into my mouth. Besides, we didn't meet that long ago, and I don't want her parents to get the wrong impression. As much as it started out as a potential fling, that's certainly not how I feel about her now.

"How'd you bump into her?" Her dad chuckles. "She hardly leaves the cabin with a deadline looming."

"Ha. Ha. Dad. I'll have you know... I was actually riding my bike when we met." Her cheeks blush, and everyone at the table knows her tells.

"And..." Davis prompts, knowing there must be more. Her blush is adorable, but she'd be a shit poker player.

Dani rolls her eyes and averts everyone's gaze. "And I... may have wrecked," she tacks on quietly at the end.

"Oh. My. God! That is classic Dani," Damien hoots.

"Seriously?" Derek asks with a bit of concern laced in his voice.

"Wait..." Davis all but shouts to the room. "Don't tell me... it was like one of your romance novels. Girl sees guy. Girl gets distracted... Girl crashes, and guy comes to the rescue."

Coming to Dani's rescue. "Nope. I witnessed the whole thing without her knowing. But..." I wink at Dani before continuing. "There may have been some rescuing involved. Especially where her bike's concerned. The rim was bent to hell and in desperate need of repair."

"Were you hurt?" Daisy asks, looking Dani over with care, as only a mother can.

Dani shakes off the attention. "Just a few scrapes."

"With the season starting, she's lucky you were here to help her. Do you stay here on the island year-round?" Trent asks casually.

He's fishing for more than just my schedule. It's been a long time since I've been under the scrutiny of a father, but you don't forget these things. "Uh... I have a place here and in Tacoma, near the stadium. I try to get out here as often as possible, but it's usually during the off season."

"Are you from around here? Originally, I mean?" Daisy asks with curiosity.

"No, ma'am. I'm from Tennessee. I went to college at Stanford and was drafted my senior year."

"I remember that," Trent mentions. Then apologetically asks, "How's the knee?"

Okay, so they really are football fans, if he's followed my career so close. Good to know. "It's great, but as you know, not good enough to continue playing."

"You've done well for yourself with Rainier. You'll be great as the head coach this season. Don't listen to what those idiotic announcers and analysts say. Keep your focus, and you'll make us all proud."

Holy shit. Trent sure has mastered a father pep talk. Damn. The man is good. I haven't had anyone be as blunt as this, other than Ray Carson himself. I had no idea those would be the words flying from his mouth with the way he started. I know I'm prepared for this job, but it's nice to have support from others as well. Not knowing what to say, I simply go with, "Thanks."

As Dani gets up to clear the plates from our meal, I offer to help.

"He does dishes, too?" Daisy asks in mock surprise. "Any way you can coach these guys to do that?" She pointedly looks to each of her sons before continuing, "If you have any advice for getting them to do their laundry while away at school, I'd think you're a miracle worker. God only knows why they bring home mounds each time they venture home. Don't you have washers and dryers on campus?" She looks pointedly at each of them, and the table erupts in laughter.

I can't help but roll my eyes. "Sorry. I was likely the same way. But I didn't live close enough to my mom to take advantage. Airlines only allow so much luggage."

"The advantages of living near home," Davis announces.

"Besides, Mom, if we didn't bring home our laundry, how else would you know we've missed you?" Damien teases as he stands to clear his own plate.

"Trust me..." Daisy shakes her head. "I don't need to know you've missed me so much."

Seeing Dani's family interact makes me miss my own.

15

DANI

MY FAMILY'S SHOCKED WHEN WE'RE SHOWN OUR SEATS FOR THE game. I hadn't thought much about it when we were ushered into the stadium. Never being a sports fanatic, I'd given little thought to seating. As long as we could see the field, I figured It was decent.

"Holy shit," Derek exhales as he sees our assigned seats. "We're in the front two rows on the forty-yard line."

"Ohmigod, Dani," Damien gushes. "I might just have a man crush on Luke. These. Seats. Are. Killer!"

"Do I need to be worried?" I tease.

"You know what I mean." Damien rolls his eyes. "You have to admit these are amazing."

I look around, nodding my head in agreement.

"I don't think I've ever been this close to the field." My dad's eyes are wide as he takes in the stadium.

"This will be so much fun to watch," Mom pipes in with enthusiasm.

"I can't wait to see Rainier stomp the Eagles," Davis comments as he takes a sip from his soda.

Just as we settle, the Rainier Renegades come out to the field from the tunnel, and the crowd goes wild. Everyone's on their feet. I'm thankful to be in the front row because I get a glimpse of Luke, and my excitement surges.

Hot damn! He's dressed in black slacks and a dark gray Rainier Renegades polo shirt. His muscles flex as he runs on with the team. He fills his slacks and shirt out so well, my mouth waters. *Holy hell. How can he look so hot?*

Luke's entirely focused on the game. He talks with a few members of the team and coaching staff as he walks to a spot almost in front of me on the sideline and puts on his headset. The Eagles are introduced to the stadium. There's a combination of cheers and boos around the stadium as they introduce each player. My focus stays on Luke. His back is to me, but as he holds a conversation with what looks like another coach, I can't tear my eyes away. Their exchange of words looks intense, and I'm riveted to my spot by their brief interaction. I haven't been to a live football game since high school, and let's face it, I was there to socialize, not watch the game. But as I take in this scene, it's like being transported to an entirely different universe. I can see the draw. The excitement is palpable, and the energy zings through the stadium.

Other than watching the players make the plays on the field, I've never considered all the intricacies that go into this sport. There's so much behind the scenes I never knew about. Before I know it, the players for the Rainier Renegades are introduced, the anthem is sung, the coin is tossed, and the kick-off takes place.

I may not know much, but I do know our team has the ball, and we keep making plays toward the end zone. Luke intensely talks into the headset as he paces along the sidelines. He must be making the right calls, because yards are gained, and the crowd's on its feet, cheering like crazy. I swear, our quarterback must have magic hands because every time he releases the ball into the air, one of the Renegades catches it, causing Luke to pump his fist in the air in celebration.

"Are you even watching the game?" Damien teases as he elbows me after a few plays, and my eyes continue to trace Luke's movements in my peripheral.

"Of course, I am," I scoff, somewhat defensive. "Why wouldn't I be?"

Dame shakes his head and laughs. "Dani..." He waits until I take my eyes off Luke and direct my gaze to him before continuing. "Your eyes have been glued to him. If I didn't know better, I'd bet you could map out his every move without a second thought."

Rolling my eyes, I try to avoid being caught. "We're about to score. Rainier is on the eighteen-yard line and... *If...* I'm not mistaken, we just got another first down."

"Okay... Okay... so you've been paying attention." Dame shakes his head. "But every time I glance your way, you're watching Luke, not the game."

I point down to Luke and more importantly, the man in nearly the same clothes next to him. "Do you see that guy down there?"

"Um... Dani? There's a lot of guys down there. Be more specific."

What a smartass. But I continue, ignoring the sarcasm dripping from him. "The one next to Luke. What the hell is he doing?"

Damien looks to the guy in question and shakes his head. Before he says anything, the crowd erupts in cheers as Rainier scores a touchdown. Of course, with my attention on Luke, I'd missed how it happened. When I watch the instant replay, my mouth drops. The guy leapt over another player and almost did an entire flip, landing on his feet as he finished in the end zone. *Holy shit. How did he do that? Talk about athleticism.*

"Let's see how the new kicker is..." Davis looks on with eagerness to the field. "I watched him play in college. Hope he's comfortable at the pro level. He'll either gain thousands of fans or have hecklers for a long time to come."

I can't imagine the pressure this guy must be under. At least I have an entire book for people to form an opinion of me, not thirty seconds to make or break it. My stomach clenches as the ball's snapped. Tension fills the stadium as it's caught and set into position. Gracefully, the kicker takes two steps and glides his foot through, connecting with the ball. It soars through the air, close to the left goal post. I'm so nervous, I bring my hands to my face. It takes everything I have not to cover my eyes. I'm on my tiptoes, anxiously awaiting the score, as if my height will keep the ball in the air longer.

This is why I don't like sports. I can't handle the stress. I'm not even playing, and my heart races like a greyhound at the track. After an agonizing second, the officials raise their arms to the sky, and the crowd celebrates.

Realization hits me like a ton of bricks. *This is only the first quarter. How the hell am I going to make it through the entire game?*

The score volleys between whoever takes the lead. If I thought watching the game was intense, watching Luke is nothing in comparison. His back is to me, but I've gotten plenty of glimpses of his profile as he paces up and down the field. His shoulders tense, his pace quickens with the intensity of the plays on the field, and his gaze never leaves the action.

Oddly enough, the thing I can't keep my eyes off of, is the handsy guy next to Luke. Instead of being able to watch the game, this man's focus is entirely on Luke. As Luke paces, this guy pulls him off the field, literally. He's kept Luke from running into officials, the players, and the other staff on the sidelines. It's almost comical to watch. This poor guy looks like he's dancing the tango the way he swoops in and saves Luke from potential disaster. Everyone else seems to give this guy a wide berth. He grabs Luke constantly, and Luke completely ignores him or is comfortable with it. I can't decipher which. Hell, in the three quarters of the game I've watched, I think this guy has touched Luke more than I have since we've met. *Do I need to be jealous?*

When the clock ticks down to the final seconds, I'm happy to know Luke's led his team to a victory. Rainier's up by a touchdown, and they have control of the ball for the last minute. The quarterback takes a knee, twice, and the game is over.

My family and I cheer right along with the rest of the crowd and sit to watch the post-game activity on the field. The look of pure joy radiates from Luke as he makes his way across the field to congratulate his players and other coaches. He interacts with players and coaches from the Eagles team, too. Pride soars through me as I see him celebrate his team's success.

Eventually, my family and I make our way out of the stadium and say goodbye before they exit the building. They each have long drives ahead of them, to be home for work or school in the morning. They insist I thank Luke again and tell him they look forward to seeing him again.

Instead of exiting the building with the rest of my family, I make my way to Luke's office. He had warned me it'll take some time before he can meet me, but I had assured him, I'd be fine. My parents had helped me drop off my car at Luke's building before the game, and we carpooled to the stadium. I handed off my laptop to Luke this morning, so I have something I can work on after taking a break from my writing schedule and enjoying the game. I was relieved to get to his loft before he had to leave for the stadium.

As I near his office, I'm approached by a middle-aged woman dressed professionally, compared to the fans in the stadium. She's wearing Rainier colors but pulls it off with a Navy-blue blouse paired with dark gray slacks. Her sleek brown hair lays on her shoulders, and her heels click along the concrete floors. She wears a friendly smile and stops to greet me. "Are you Danika Fallon?"

I nod once in affirmation. "Yes, I am."

"Hello." She reaches out her hand to shake mine. "I'm Harlow Ryan, Luke Leighton's personal assistant. He's asked me to show you around and get you comfortable while he finishes with the team."

"Oh," I say, a bit shocked. He never mentioned someone meeting me. "He didn't have to go to such trouble."

"It's no trouble." Her kind voice assures me. "I have to stay here until the dust settles from the game. Really. Showing you around isn't a problem. Trust me."

She leads me to what I presume is Luke's office and unlocks the door. She gestures for me to enter. "There's a bathroom off to the right and a fridge if you need anything to drink. I always keep a variety of things in this cupboard, too, if you want a snack."

Having just eaten before and during the game, I reply, "I'm good for now. But, thanks."

Harlow motions toward the door. "I'll be in my office across the hall should you need me." She walks to the door and stops. "For what it's worth, I've worked with Luke since he started here. I can't say I've ever seen him smile more."

What do I even say to that?

Thankfully, I don't have to say anything. She nods approvingly in a motherly way and slips out of the room, closing the door behind her.

Well... That was interesting.

Now that I'm alone in Luke's office, I take in the room around me. There's a full conference table off to one side that would easily sit ten people around it. Extra chairs line the wall behind it.

There's an inviting dark leather couch and loveseat in a sitting area around a large flat-screen TV encased in bookshelves that have a large set of shelves to the side. I walk closer to see some of the photos displayed. Some are of the stadium. Some are players on the field. There's one of Luke and what I assume are his family members, as they each share the same blue eyes, and the older man resembles Luke. His mother has similar dark hair, but her eyes sparkle a light-golden brown. Luke's sister is the perfect blend of her parents. She has her mother's lean stature with her father's distinct features.

Not wanting to invade Luke's privacy entirely, I force myself to stop reveling and get to work. As I turn to retrieve my laptop bag on Luke's desk, I notice his desk is dark, masculine, and a prominent feature in the expansive room. It's fairly tidy, with only a few folders in the corner in what appears to be an "in box." His high-back chair looks like it's made to withstand lots of hours of use.

Not wanting to invade his space, I set myself up at the conference table. I choose a spot where I can admire the City of Tacoma from the window as well as watch for anyone entering the room. Not sure why, but I don't like having my back to any door. It might have something to do with my brothers always sneaking up on me, but who really knows; maybe I watched too many scary movies as a kid. All I know is I've had this habit for as long as I can remember.

Unpacking my laptop, I spread out the notebook I use as my book bible and place one of my various pens next to it. I fire up my trusty machine and open my latest work in progress. I start my ritual of rereading the last scene written to make sure I stay with the flow of things. As I reach the end of what I've written, words pour freely. My fingers fly across the keyboard, and I'm deep into the zone, until I hear the door snick open.

My breath catches, and my eyes gravitate to the man with

the sexiest smile known to womankind. He glides effortlessly to meet me.

"Hey there, Coach," I tease. "Nice game."

"The game's the last thing on my mind right now, Danika." He wraps his arms around me and pulls me close to his body. He smells even better this close. My mouth waters, and I'm dying to kiss him.

"I can get on board with that." He leaves me breathless.

He closes the distance between our lips and sears me with the most toe-curling kiss I've ever experienced. *Football, smootball.* The game quickly becomes the furthest thing from my mind.

16

LUKE

WALKING IN, SEEING DANI COMFORTABLE IN MY SPACE, MAKES the high from our victory pale in comparison. The way her eyes eat me up as I walk through the room to meet her, makes me wish we were anywhere but my office.

I welcome her with a kiss that feels like the walls could go up in flames, and they'd have nothing on us. *Fuck! This woman drives me wild.* Just as things really get heated, there's a knock on the door.

Dani and I pull away, panting. I take a moment to smooth Dani's hair and adjust myself before saying, "Come in." *Damn, my voice sounds gravelly.* I quickly clear my throat just as the door opens.

Harlow's head pops around the door, thankfully oblivious to what she's just interrupted. "Don't forget I'll be out of the office until Thursday. If you need anything, feel free to call."

"Enjoy your time with your daughter and new grandbaby. I can manage things while you're gone," I assure her.

She gives me a knowing quirk of her eyebrow. Christ. She knows I rely on her a lot before away games, but I can't begrudge her this time with her daughter. That's just not my style. "If you say so..." She shakes her head. "Seriously, I've trained an intern to fill in on some of the tasks necessary for the week. But I'm only a phone call away."

Rolling my eyes, I grimace. "I won't call you, even if the building sets fire. Go! Spend time with your family. That's an order. If we weren't finalizing our roster before traveling to New York, I wouldn't bother having you come in all week."

Harlow starts to speak, but I cut her off with a smirk. "You may be a vital part of our team, but I'm sure we'll find a way to manage without you." I love giving Harlow a hard time. She always teases me that I'm just eight years older than her daughter, so I'm more like a son than anything.

"Yeah... Yeah... Leighton. I'll believe it when I see it."

I sigh. There's no arguing with Harlow Ryan. She's ruthless. Instead, I offer, "Give Ginny my congratulations and be sure to shoot a text of your new granddaughter when she arrives."

With that, Harlow beams. I know she's eager to be a grandma. It kills her having her family live almost an hour away. If she had it her way, they'd move in with her. But I don't think Ginny's husband would approve. She turns and almost exits the room but hesitates.

"It was nice meeting you, Danika," Harlow tacks on just as she's about to walk through the door.

"You, too," Dani chirps in.

"I hope to see a lot more of you." She pointedly looks in my direction, letting me know she approves. She winks then quickly hustles out the door, letting it slip closed behind her. *Leave it to Harlow to always to have the last word.*

"Uh... do you bring many girls here?" Dani asks apprehensively.

I shake my head adamantly. "Besides my mom and sister, you're the *only* one."

"Uh..." She hesitates and appears to choose her words carefully. "Why would Harlow want to make sure you bring me around then?"

"Who knows?" Without a conscious thought, I reach out to caress Dani's cheek. For some reason, I need to touch her. "But given the fact you're the first I've brought around since I started working for the Rainier Renegades, she must know you're special."

Dani sighs audibly as she brushes her cheek against my palm.

That sigh alone has me wanting her just as much as before. "What do you say to getting out of here?"

Her face fills with a cheeky grin. "I thought you'd never ask."

The game day traffic has dispersed by the time we get to my Mercedes in the players' parking lot. I quickly maneuver my way through town and arrive at my loft in minutes. Dani's unusually quiet during the ride, though she hasn't let go of my hand. The ride is fairly short, so I don't put too much weight into it. I pull into my parking garage, and we make our way to the elevator to my loft.

Earlier, we met in the parking garage when she dropped off her car because her family hit traffic before the game, so this is the first time Dani's in my home. I'm a bit nervous. It's not like it's a bachelor pad or anything, but I bought this when I first started working for Rainier and never felt the need to upgrade. It's a two-bedroom loft with brick walls and a fantastic view of the city and Puget Sound in the distance. I'm curious as to what she'll think of it.

"Everything okay?" I ask as we ride up the elevator. She's been holding my hand since we left the car, but she's got a far-off look I can't quite place.

"Oh..." She finally comes back from wherever she's been and gives me an apologetic shrug. "Lost in my head. Sorry. This would make a great scene in a book."

"What?" My voice fills with mischief. "You wanna write a story about a guy who's dying to touch his woman. He's waited nearly two weeks to and can't wait to rip her clothes off?"

Dani's eyebrows raise to her hairline. Her voice deepens to a sexy as sin tone, prompting me to continue. "Tell me more about this story of yours."

Fuck. I am so on board with this game. Could this elevator go any slower? The energy's almost electrifying as numerous thoughts drift through my mind. *Where to begin... Where to begin?*

"Well," I nearly growl. "First, he pins her against the nearest flat surface. He strips her of her clothes."

"Cliché," she deadpans, but her eyes twinkle with delight.

"Hey, now... sexy romance author. What do *you* propose we do?"

"Well..." she says, building suspense.

But I'm left with a cliffhanger.

The elevator dings, and the doors finally open. I quickly pull her out and make my way to one of the two doors available on the floor. My keys are in the lock and as soon as we're inside, I slam the door shut, flip the lock on the deadbolt, and prompt Dani to continue. My mind runs wild, and I can only imagine what she's contemplating. Having read her book, I know firsthand the complexities of her vivid imagination.

I clear my throat in an attempt to calm my thoughts. *Don't get ahead of yourself, Leighton. Take this at her pace.* "Ummm..." I draw out. "You were saying?"

The corners of her eyes crease, and there's a glimpse of deviousness. *What the hell is she up to?*

Before I can take another breath, Dani reaches for me. Instead of sliding her hands around my waist, as I anticipate, she reaches directly for my belt. She smiles coyly as her superiorly skilled fingers have my belt removed as well as my fly undone within seconds. She reaches in and cups my balls through my briefs, making me groan in satisfaction. *Holy mother fucking hell. This feels incredible. Her fingers flex and run along the underside of my shaft.*

Her other hand pushes at my pants and boxer briefs, and my brain finally catches onto her intent. I quickly toe off my shoes and push my pants to the floor. While Dani drops to her knees and focuses her attention on my cock, I swiftly pull my shirt over my head with one hand, while the other fists her hair at the base of her neck.

Another loud groan involuntarily pulls from my chest. "Holy fuck. What are you doing to me?" She fondles my balls as she traces the head of my cock with her wicked tongue.

With her other hand, her finger traces the veins along my shaft and *motherfucker*... if that doesn't turn me on further. She has the perfect combination of soft hands, firm touch, and movement that's right, causing my knees to go weak and eyes to roll back in my fucking head.

I'm not some young, inexperienced teen who finishes off with a stiff wind blowing in his direction. But fuck, if she doesn't stop soon, I will explode.

"Danika," I grunt out in warning. My body stiffens. Holy fuck. I need her to stop. After spending nearly two weeks apart, I need to end with her.

She peers up through dark lashes. Her deep-blue eyes glint in a way that tells me she knows exactly what she's doing. *The Vixen.* Before my next heartbeat, her mouth encloses around my cock as her hand fists what she can't take in. She simultaneously pumps her fist and moves her mouth along my shaft, coming up to just beneath the crown of my head before plummeting down to meet her fist. Over and over. The sensation is indescribable. The feeling too good, too strong, and too erotic.

"Fuck..." I growl. Damn, her perfect mouth knows just what to do. She feels spectacular. "Holy fucking shit... Yeah... Right there. This feels amazing..." In a slur of ecstasy, coherent thought quickly evades me. All I can process is my balls dropping and the tingling sensation quickly moving up my spine.

"So close..." I heed in warning, giving her time to release my cock.

She locks eyes with me and shakes her head, telling me she wants to do this. If I didn't know better, me warning her off only spurs her on. It feels as if she doubles down on her effort and before I know it, the tingling sensation that started at the base of my spine spreads throughout my entire body. Liquid heat sears every cell within me, and it takes everything in my power to remain upright.

Fuck knows what comes out of my mouth as I have the most intense release I've ever experienced. It goes on and on. The sexy woman kneeling before me milks me for all I'm worth and when I finally stop spasming, she releases me with a sly grin, wipes at the corner of her mouth, and says, "How'd you like that version of the story?"

I chuckle at her feign innocence. *Like she doesn't know she just rocked my world.* "I should know better than to compete with a romance writer."

"I not only have the imagination, but I have mad skills... If I do say so myself." Her triumphant smirk melts my heart.

I look her over with care and realize one thing must be rectified. "For some reason, you're fully clothed... and I'm standing here in only my socks."

I swoop down and lift her effortlessly in my arms, and she gasps in surprise. When she catches her breath, her sassy mouth sparks me even further. "Well... that certainly won't do."

It's late when Dani and I make it out to the kitchen to refuel. The sun has set, and the city lights shimmer in the distance. My pride soars when I notice Dani's blissed-out expression. It's a look I hope she wears a lot in our future. The thought alone has my blood tingling and desire resurfacing. Fuck! I've lost track of how many times I just made her come. God only knows how I recover so quickly when it comes to her. This woman drives me insane.

She's sexy wearing one of my t-shirts, with her curly hair barely contained in a top knot. I'm sure if she'd left it down, it'd take on a life of its own. I fucking love her massive corkscrew curls that flit in every direction as she takes her pleasure from me. Her flawless makeup-free face glows from the aftermath of our lovemaking.

Dani reaches for a grape from the fruit bowl on my counter and pops it into her mouth, while I walk to the fridge to see what's available to cook. We could order takeout, but most restaurants are likely closed with it being Sunday. Besides, there's plenty to eat here. My housekeeper comes weekly and also does my grocery shopping. God knows, I don't have the time.

As Dani climbs onto the barstool at my kitchen counter, my eyes greedily follow the movement of her sexy legs. She props one foot on the stool next to her, and I enjoy how my t-shirt creeps higher on her toned thigh. Her stomach growls, and I force myself to focus on the task at hand.

Christ, Leighton. It's not like she's going anywhere. Get the girl some food.

Trying to keep my mind from returning to the bedroom, I interrupt the silence, "So, what'd you think of the game?"

Her beautiful face lights up with an amused expression. "It was more entertaining than I imagined." Her expression turns pensive as she decides how to say what's on her mind. I've seen this look before. She does it when she's writing and trying to figure out a scene in her books. It's adorable to watch.

"Well... we pulled off a great win. I couldn't be happier with some of the new players on the team. I was a bit worried in the third quarter, but our recruiting staff has done a great job. I think we'll gel together by the time we finish the pre-season. I'm damn proud of a few of our recent additions to the team. We have two weeks to cut our roster."

Dani raises an eyebrow, appearing confused by my statement, so I continue, "Due to league regulations, we still have about twenty to cut to before the season officially starts." I take in a deep breath, and the weight of it all settles in. "Until I stepped into this position, I didn't know just how much influence I have over these men and their careers."

"Yeah, I'm sure you'll have a great season, if the games are anything like today. My brothers were saying you didn't have your regular players in the game."

Knowing football isn't really her thing, it warms my heart to see she's trying to understand the sport. "Yeah... I'm giving those on the roster bubble a chance to prove their worth and determine if they're a good fit for the team. With next week being our third game of the preseason, we have some serious decisions to make. I can only keep fifty-three players on the roster and currently, there are seventy."

"Cutting players must suck." Dani pulls off another grape, and I start throwing things into a bowl for omelets. It might not be the most gourmet food I cook, but it's quick and easy.

"There's so much involved when making these decisions. I'm glad our GM—Uh, general manager, owner, and I see eye to eye on most things, so it shouldn't be too difficult when the time comes." I pour my concoction into the pan and listen to it sizzle.

"There is one position on the team I have a question about..." As I glance in Dani's direction, I see her face flush, and I wonder what's going on in that beautiful mind of hers.

"Really?" I ask, hoping she'll fill me in on her sudden change in mood. "I'm happy to explain anything. Just ask."

"Well..." She plays with the grape in her hand and ducks her chin, as if she's suddenly embarrassed.

"You can ask me anything, Dani, you know that," I prompt to assure her.

"There's this one guy..." she drags out almost sing-song like. *What in the hell is she so nervous about?*

"You'll have to be more specific. *A lot* of guys are on the field," I tease.

"Well, there's one in particular... I'm not quite sure his role. It was all I could focus on for a while. Especially when the game got tense."

"Okay..." I draw out and attempt to be patient as I wait for her to continue. "What does he do? Maybe I can help you figure out his position."

"I notice... you... um... really get into the game when plays are made."

Okay. That's unexpected. I thought she was talking about one of the players. What does this have to do with me? I don't recall getting out of control or anything. Maybe it was too much for her. "Yeah. I get a little intense, as I'm sure you've noticed. Did that freak you out?"

She adamantly shakes her head. "Oh, no. That's not what I

meant at all. I thought you were sexy as hell in your coaching zone."

I roll my eyes. "I'd hardly consider making calls, sexy."

Dani smirks as if I'm being ridiculous. "Trust me, you are. I have to admit, I even got a little jealous." Her expression now dubious, leaves me more confused.

What the fuck is she talking about?

"Why would you be jealous?"

"Um... I have to admit, I probably watched you more than I watched the actual game."

Okay. This boosts my ego, and I feel the corners of my mouth pull up as I fight off a smile, but I'm still not following her line of thought.

"That guy I'm talking about... It appears his sole job was to get handsy with you. What exactly is his role on the team? I mean... I think he's groped you more than I have, since we've met. Is this something I should be jealous of? Or at the very least, can I apply for the job myself?"

A deep belly laugh erupts from me. Fuck. She's hilarious. I don't think I've ever heard it described this way before. Leave it to Dani to describe the situation with flair. Of course, she's talking about Sean Peters, our "get back" coach.

"That's Sean Peters," I say once I've recovered the ability to breathe. "No..." I gasp in a deep breath. "He wasn't getting handsy with me; you have nothing to be worried about. His wife and children keep him happy. To us, he's called the 'get back coach' because his job is to keep our team from being fined. If I don't pay attention and walk into the field, it could cost us a huge penalty. I'm not willing to take the risk."

"But doesn't it get annoying being pulled in the opposite

direction on a regular basis? I would've decked the guy for getting into my personal space," Dani admits with a shrug.

"Honestly, I'm so into the game, I don't even notice."

She plops another grape into her mouth and innocently asks, "Can I apply for that job? I want the excuse of having to touch you all day."

I chuckle. "There's no way I could concentrate with you touching me at any point during the game. I barely remember my own name when you're touching me, let alone our next play."

"Seriously?" Dani asks, disbelief written clearly across her features.

"As a heart attack. You're the ultimate distraction. I wouldn't get a call right if you were there pulling me back from the field."

I plate our omelets and hand Dani hers. She takes a bite and moans in appreciation. "Highly doubtful... Oh, this is so good."

"Trust me, Dani, you're quite the distraction," I practically growl as I look her over once again. She would be such a distraction. All I would think about is stripping her naked and having my way with her.

17

DANI

TEASING LUKE IS DEFINITELY BECOMING ONE OF MY FAVORITE pastimes. His laugh sends electric jolts to every sensory spot in my body. Between the amazing sex, his cooking, and his beautiful homes, he might never get rid of me. After cooking me a delicious midnight snack, we make our way to his sitting area in the open floor plan of his loft, and I can't help but be impressed with the gorgeous view of Tacoma from his floor-to-ceiling windows. Of course, there's a ginormous television along one wall, surrounded by comfortable dark-leather couches, like his home on Anderson Island, but Luke's loft is more modern with exposed brick and hardwood floors.

As I've become well acquainted earlier this evening, his bedroom's off the living room with a comfortable king-sized bed, a master bathroom suite with a waterfall shower I could live in. I haven't used it yet, but I'm intrigued. It might also be something I need to put into a book some time. The sex that could be done in there alone could fill up pages. He's mentioned there's an office with a spare bed, so I assume it's the other door off the living room.

As I tuck my legs under me and curl up onto the couch, Luke plops down beside me. He pulls me against his chest, and I instinctively take in a deep breath. He smells delicious with the perfect mixture of pheromones and masculine cologne. I seriously wish I could bottle this scent to take with me when I leave. I didn't know I would miss his smell of all things while he's gone. I trace my fingers along the planes of his chest, and his body tenses.

"Ticklish?"

"Just caught me off guard." He pulls me closer and sighs. When I glance up to his face, his expression's pensive.

"What's on your mind?"

He takes in a deep breath and releases it slowly. "Just wondering how others do this."

"Cuddle?" I tease in an attempt to lighten the mood.

"No, smartass. I meant how do they juggle a relationship and this job."

"Who is this *They* you speak of?"

Luke lets out a deep breath and his body relaxes which is confusing. Where's he going with this? "Normally after a game, I immediately start watching film to review. I spend countless hours prepping for our coaches meetings and work around the clock."

I stiffen and start to pull away. "Am I keeping you?"

He immediately pulls me back to where I'd been resting my head on his chest. "No. Not at all. I don't have to be anywhere until noon tomorrow. I've cleared my schedule, and you're right where I want you to be. I'm just trying to figure out a way to see you more often."

"I can always come to the city," I suggest. "I know you can't make it out to the island often. That is... if you want me."

"Don't doubt for one second, Dani, how much I want you. I just thought aloud, since I'm trying to figure out a way to spend more time with you. My travel schedule until January is chaotic, and I'm afraid I won't be what you need."

"Luke, I was perfectly content with my life before you came along." His body gets rigid and before he has a chance to say anything, I continue, "What I mean is... I didn't have much of a social life. I ate, slept, and wrote. Rinse and repeat. I enjoy your company. I don't have any expectations for you to change your life, just to fit me in it. As you know, if I get into a writing zone, I'm lost to everyone at nearly any given point in time. I'm a pretty independent person. My family hates it. Heck. You might, too, eventually."

"Doubtful." He grimaces. "We have two back-to-back road games, then a Thursday game. I should have the weekend off. Are you busy the last weekend of September?"

I groan. Of course, he picks the *one* weekend I scheduled a book signing. "I'm attending a book signing in Seattle all day Saturday. But I'm free Sunday? Want to get together then? I can cancel my hotel reservation. I'd planned to get together with Damien. But I could meet up with him Friday instead."

"What do you say to me joining you in Seattle? We could go to Pike Place and hang out on Sunday."

"I'd love that. But I might upgrade my room. I have a cheap room, not wanting to waste the money."

"Where's your signing being held?" Luke asks in interest.

"Sexy in Seattle is at the downtown Hilton. Though, I'm not staying there because I like to stay closer to Damien in the University district."

"Would you be opposed to staying at the Hilton? We could make a weekend out of it," he hedges.

Like I'd turn that down. The convenience alone as well as time with him. Even though I'm suddenly feel giddy at the thought of having more time with him, I somehow keep my features free from emotion. "I think I can manage."

"Good, I'll make arrangements in the morning, when I get to my office."

"Are you sure you can handle that? Your secretary's off for the week," I remind him with a bit of sass. I can't help myself. Then remorse sets in for being such a pain in the ass. He's the friggin' head coach of a major football team; he doesn't have time to make hotel reservations for us. I quickly add, "I can do it if you're busy."

"Danika, you have little faith in me." His voice is light and full of feign hurt. "I can be trusted to get a great hotel room in Seattle for the weekend. I'm not helpless. I may have a secretary that acts as a personal assistant at times, but I'm not an invalid when it comes to making travel plans." He nuzzles into my neck and kisses it softly.

"Okay. Okay. I believe you." I laugh lightly. "I'll be heading to Seattle on Friday. Just let me know where I should go."

"If you're free Thursday evening, wanna go to the game?"

"It would be such a hardship to watch you in your element. I don't know. Hmmm... sexy man... totally focused, pacing the sidelines..." I pretend to weigh out my options with my arms. "Or sit at home alone... decisions, decisions..." A smile forms on my lips, and I scrunch up my nose, pretending I might not be interested.

"Oh, you're such a little shit." He reaches to my side and tickles me. I burst out in laughter.

"Okay... Okay," I gasp. "I'll go to the game."

He relinquishes his hold on me but keeps me close to him on the couch. It's as if he can't stand to not be touching me. As if I'm going to complain. "Do you want to invite anyone? I can get as many tickets as you'd like."

"Uh..." I try to think. I don't really know anyone besides my brother who'd appreciate the tickets.

"Mind if I invite Damien? Everyone else lives hours away. He can come and still make it back to class on Friday."

"Would you prefer to have seats like before, or do you want to go into the owner's box?"

"Uh... I'd feel weird being in the owner's box. If it's not too much trouble, any seats would be fine. They can even be in the nosebleed section."

"Dani," Luke chastises. "I'm not putting you in the nosebleeds. Besides, how will you keep your eye on Sean from way up there! He gets pretty handsy, as you know."

I shake my head. "I'm never going to live that down, am I?"

"I can't wait to tell Sean. He'll laugh his ass off. In fact, why don't you plan on coming to the game early? I'll introduce you to more than Harlow. I think Damien will get a kick out of meeting some of the players, too. Unlike some people..." He smirks, and I can't help the eyeroll that naturally develops. "Damien follows the game and is a genuine fan."

I shrug. He has me there. "He'll be ecstatic. Before he left earlier, he was going on and on about how much he loved being at the game in person."

"I'll make the arrangements tomorrow," he yawns, and his exhaustion from today's activities is evident. "What do you say to going back to bed?"

I reach up and pull him in for a quick kiss. "I can be persuaded to do that, too."

The next morning, I'm woken to soft lips dragging against my neck. Luke spoons me from behind. His fingertips skim over my stomach, rib cage, and trace around my nipple. A moan escapes as I arch my back in appreciation. His hard cock greets me as it presses against my ass.

"Well, good morning to you," I murmur.

"God, you feel so good," Luke groans in satisfaction as he glides his fingers to my inner thigh. He traces the planes of my flesh but doesn't touch me where I want him most. I push back against him, and he takes the hint and finds his way to my center to circle my now throbbing clit.

"Luke..." I cry out when I can't take it anymore. I press back into him, and he lifts my leg over his thigh to gain better access with his fingers.

An animalistic groan rips from my body because I need more. I press into his lap, and I want nothing more than to have him inside me. This very instant. "Need you."

Luke's groan in my ear sets my senses on fire. "Condom..."

"Wait," I beg as I shamelessly rub against him. Feeling his

cock somehow lengthen beneath me, my desire only heightens. "I have an IUD. I'm clean."

"Best words I've ever fucking heard," he growls in my ear. "I've never gone without, and I can't fucking wait to feel you ride my cock in this position."

Wordlessly, he lifts my leg higher on his thigh and lines his cock up to my entrance. Without a second's hesitation, he pushes through my slickness and bottoms out against a sensitive spot I never knew existed deep inside my body. I gasp as I rasp out, "Again... Harder... Right there..." Holy fucking shit. My body's a live wire, waiting to explode. It doesn't take long before the combination of him strumming my clit like a friggin' guitar and his magical cock has me seeing stars. My body tightens as I spiral higher and higher, chasing the orgasm I know is coming. I arch into him with every thrust and cry out in ecstasy when I finally fall over the edge, pulsing like I've never experienced.

Luke continues pumping into me, never slowing his pace as I experience wave after wave of sensation. Soon, his body goes rigid as my body clenches around him as I feel him find his release, triggering another onslaught of tremors throughout my body.

As we come down from our euphoric high, all I hear is our ragged breaths fighting to regain control. They eventually settle, and I feel Luke pull out. I cry out at the loss, but I know it's inevitable. With his arms wrapped around me, Luke nuzzles into my neck and states, "This is the best fucking wakeup I've ever experienced."

I can't say I disagree.

18

LUKE

As I drive to the stadium for my meeting at noon, my thoughts linger on Danika. She's the most sensual woman I've ever experienced. It's harder than I thought to leave her at my house and come to work. I convinced her to stay until this morning, assuring her she'd have plenty of time to write yesterday because I wouldn't be home until at least eight. Knowing I have a full day ahead of me, and I'll pay for my time off this morning later this evening, I wouldn't have traded a second with Dani.

By the time I get to the office, it's nearly eleven. If Harlow had been at her desk as I whisked into my office, I know her eyebrows would have been at her hairline. I'm always here by seven, and I've already worked out. I'm predictable as the tide, and I chuckle aloud at the thought of changing my schedule on Harlow. She'd have a heyday.

Normally, I've responded to my emails by now, so when I boot up my laptop, I'm inundated with unopened messages.

Harlow typically filters through some to answer anything pressing, so her absence and my tardiness is more than noticed.

Before I unbury myself from the mound of impending emails, I pull up the Hilton to make a reservation for my weekend in Seattle. I spare no expense and reserve a suite for our weekend away. I also reach out to the ticket office and reserve two tickets to have available at Will Call for Dani and Damien. The poor woman who took my call, nearly swallowed her tongue when she realized she was speaking to me directly. It's unprecedented for me to call, and she let me know this. After getting the tickets taken care of, she politely thanks me and offers to help anytime I'm in need. I make a mental note of her name and remind myself to have Harlow reach out and thank her when she returns.

By the time I arrive at our coaches meeting just before noon, I feel unprepared. I've never stepped foot into a meeting without watching through the game tape at least once. Fuck. I need to figure out how to balance everything, since I'm obviously not walking away from Dani anytime soon. The timing might suck, but since I've never felt the way I do toward her, I know it's not something that comes around often. *Why couldn't we have met during the off season?*

"Hey, Luke," Tyrell Yates, the defensive coordinator, greets. He holds the door open for me, and we walk through together. "Great game yesterday, wasn't it?"

"Absolutely." I nod in agreement. "What'd you think of Reynolds' performance?" Brandon Reynolds is our kicker. He's returning from an injury and did one hell of a job in yesterday's game, but that's not what special teams' coaches are consistently saying in practice. "Have you heard from Mendoza?"

"He's on fire. I've spoken with him before the game in Dallas, so if we want to make the offer, we need to do it now. Time's a tickin'." No shit, we have until midnight to make a trade offer. My gut says we should get both on the roster, but I'm not sure. If Reynolds returns like I hope he will, it will be a costly choice, should we keep them both.

"Let's talk with everyone else, then make the decision before leaving the room." He nods in agreement as I take a seat at the table in the conference room.

As soon as everyone arrives, I stand to congratulate us on our second win. We discuss the players on the bubble, the game yesterday, and how we want to run practice this afternoon. We're an efficient group, so we're done with our team meeting with plenty of time to spare.

By the time I get home that evening, it's nearly eight. Entering my bedroom, I'm assaulted by Dani's perfume. I take in a deep breath and relive the memories from last night and this morning. Damn, I miss her. We've texted a few times today, but nothing compares to having her here in person. She had to meet her grandparents to help them find something they'd left in the garage this afternoon, or I might have convinced her to stay a bit longer. Though it seems selfish to have her stay here all day, when I can't spend any time with her.

My phone buzzes, and my face lights up when I see a text notification from Dani. Without even bothering to respond, I immediately hit dial.

"Hey, Luke." Her breathless words make me wonder what she's doing.

"Did you find what your grandparents wanted?"

"Yeah. I'm just rearranging a few things in the garage now."

"We can talk when you're finished," I offer, not wanting to put her out.

Her giggle makes my lips quirk. "I just finished. They left about an hour ago, so I'm good. Who knew they'd be busier now that they're officially retired. They want to get to my parents' tonight, so they didn't stay like I expected."

"Get any writing in today?" I ask as I settle onto my couch. Having eaten at the cafeteria this evening, my only plans for tonight include talking to her and watching our next opponents' game from this weekend.

"I hit two thousand words. I wrote while waiting for the ferry and a bit before my grandparents arrived. I'll write more tonight." I can't even imagine writing that much in a week, let alone a few hours.

"You're a rockstar. I made our hotel reservations and got your seats for the game in two weeks. I'll text you the information."

"I can't wait," she says with excitement but then sighs, setting my senses go on alert.

"What's up?" My attempt at nonchalance is reached, though I feel anything but.

"With you traveling for the next two weeks to Philly, then Atlanta, I'll miss you."

Her words make my heart soar, but my stomach sinks at the reality of my life as a coach. "I know... I wish I could make it out to the island to visit you, but my schedule's pretty tight."

A thought hits me. She knows she's welcome, right? Fuck. Have I ever actually said the words? I haven't ever wanted to before. So maybe I haven't. Shit. "You know, you're welcome here anytime. But... I have to warn you, I'm not home much."

"Luke," she chides. "You don't have to entertain me."

"I have to watch film in the evening and prep for the next day... but God, it was incredible waking up with you in my bed." Just the thought of her lingering perfume makes me miss her more. Christ. How does she have this effect on me?

Wait. That sounds like I just want a booty call. Shit.

Before she can reply, I rectify the situation immediately. "You know..." *How do I put this?* "I love hanging out with you."

Love? Did I really go there?

"I love hanging out with you." She sighs.

"You did say you could write from anywhere..." I point out, and a smile forms on my face. Fuck. I don't want to wait three weeks to see her. "We don't leave until Saturday... What would it take to convince you to spend a few days here?"

"Luke, I just left today. Are you sure you want me back so soon?" Of course, I want her back. I wish she'd never left.

"If you didn't need to meet your grandparents this afternoon, I would've asked you to stay earlier," I admit.

"Okay..." she hesitates. Not wanting to pressure her, I wait impatiently for her response.

Just when I think she's never going to respond, she makes my entire fucking week.

"Is tomorrow too soon?"

Waking up with Dani has its advantages. Let's just say I may have skipped my morning workout a couple of times this week because getting out of bed was the last thing I wanted to do. But I managed to make it into my office by eight each morning. Knowing she'd be there when I returned, left a lingering smile on my face. People may have noticed, but they were smart enough to not say anything.

Thursday morning, I run into Campbell Beck in the players' parking lot. "Hey, Beck, how's married life treating you?"

Beck's massive grin makes his thoughts evident. "Not bad. Not bad at all."

I can't help but chuckle. The man's been light on his feet all week and ever since his press conference, nothing seems to touch him. "I'm glad everything worked out for you and Hillary."

"No kidding. I never thought the fans would be so crazy. Now that Hillary's completely in the spotlight, people have come out of the woodwork to comment on everything she does. If I didn't know she loved me so much, I'd worry she'd hightail it out of here."

"She obviously loves you," I point out. "Why else would she have stayed with you for all these years?"

Campbell shakes his head as he holds the door to the training facility for me. "That's one of the reasons we kept things on the downlow for so long before deciding enough was enough and just getting married."

"Well, you certainly know how to jump into things head first."

"Don't I know it." He shakes his head, but his goofy grin

175

tells me he doesn't have any regrets. "Just wait 'till it happens to you."

Until I met Dani, I'd be denying this until the ends of the earth. But… maybe he has some merit. But it's not like I'm the star player or anything. "No one cares about the coach, Beck. I'm sure I'll be fine."

Beck stops walking and eyes me suspiciously. Just when I think he's about to say something, he shakes his head and continues walking. *What was that all about?*

Before I can say anything, Tanner Reid, our defensive end, joins us. He's a senior member of the team, playing for Rainier longer than I've been around. He's a practical jokester and smacks Beck on the back in greeting. "Mornin', fellas. What's shakin'?" His deep Southern drawl comes out. I'm not sure what it is about the guy, but he always seems genuinely happy.

"Just telling Coach about the finer points of married life."

Reid's mouth drops in surprise. "Dude. I've never seen him date. Why ya pushing that on him? Aren't you jumpin' the gun?"

"Just encouraging him to find happiness, like me." Beck pats his chest and although he's clearly joking, it's obvious there's truth in his words.

Reid coughs into his fist. "More like joining the circus. You keep the press focused on you. I'm happy over here in my quiet life."

"Whatever, man." Beck brushes Reid off. "You're jealous you haven't found someone worth laying it all down for."

We reach the end of the hall, and the guys turn toward the locker room. They continue their conversation, and I make my way to my office. I can't help but smile at the way

Beck wants his happiness to spread to his friends. His teammates love to give him shit about it, but ever since he's held his press conference, things have died down for him and Hillary.

When I reach my office, the intern Harlow trained to take over in her absence is at her desk. He has the phone in one hand and hastily takes notes with the other. He appears to have things under control, so I make my way to my desk and start up my computer for the day. I'd checked emails earlier from home, while Dani was still sleeping, so I shouldn't be too far behind.

Just the thought of getting ready while Dani slept brings a smile to my face. Though glancing at the curve of her back as she sprawled out on the bed made me want to rejoin her, I couldn't be more thankful for her visit again this week.

We've fallen into a bit of a routine. I try to be home early enough so we can eat dinner together. She's typically deep into her manuscript when I arrive, so I either cook or pick up something on my way home. We eat, then each go back to work in one form or another. She with her laptop, me watching film or responding to emails on the couch. It may not be romantic, but it works for us. After another hour or two of work, we find ourselves somehow distracted by one another in the most glorious of ways, and those distractions lead us to making love into the wee hours of the morning. Rinse and Repeat. I may not be living on much sleep, but I sure as fuck am happy.

Tonight, as I settle into the comforts of my couch, laptop in hand, I glance to Dani. To my surprise, her face is scrunched up, and serious confusion crosses her features as she taps something out on her laptop. "Dani?" I ask in an attempt to get her attention.

No response. Just frantic typing and pure concentration. *What the hell is she writing that has her looking like that?*

"Danika," I say a bit louder, but it does the trick.

She glances up in surprise at my breaking her absolute concentration. "What?"

"Everything okay? You seem confused..." I trail off, not knowing what to say.

She shrugs and tries to brush it off, but the sudden heat in her cheeks makes me realize this isn't something I'm willing to let go. Calling her on her BS, I raise an eyebrow. "What's going on?" Obviously, my BS meter's on high alert, so she'd better not try to slide something past me.

Her eyes dart everywhere but at me. *What the hell is going on?*

I attempt to be patient, but the longer I wait, the longer my mind reels out of control. She won't look at me. Is her blush actually going deeper? Finally, after what feels like a billion years, she clears her throat and swallows before finally looking me in the eye. Her curly hair bobs around her face in a barely controlled bun, and a smile lights up her face.

"I'm trying to write a scene."

"That's a given..." I deadpan.

"Maybe you can help? I don't know. It seems weird... You have your own work to finish tonight. I don't want to bother you."

"You can talk to me about anything."

"Even if it involves a sexy scene in my book?"

My interest piques. "Really?" I waggle my eyebrows. "I'm sure I can be of help. What do you need?"

"Well, I need to know if what's going on in my head can actually happen in real life. I have a hot and sexy build up, but now that I think of the practicalities, I'm sure she'd end up with a concussion or worse, fall and actually break something..." Before she can continue, she bursts out laughing.

If I thought my interest was piqued before, now I can't wait to find out what's going on in that beautiful and sexy mind of hers. "You know... he's not doing it right, if concussions are an option."

She shakes her head as if I've lost all my marbles. "I know..." comes out in a laugh. "I want it to be a realistic scene, but my imagination might be getting ahead of practicality."

"Okay... so lay it on me. What are you imagining that *might* cause bodily harm?"

Dani cocks her head to the side and bites on her bottom lip for a moment. I reach out and pull it free as she quietly asks, "You sure you wanna hear this?"

I sigh in frustration. "Obviously I do, or I wouldn't offer. Out with it already. The suspense is killing me."

Dani sets her laptop on the coffee table and turns to face me. "Okay... So... the couple I'm writing about, met recently. They've had combustible chemistry from the start, but every time something's about to happen, they get interrupted. When they finally get together, they end up in her apartment alone for the first time. She's in the kitchen cooking breakfast in just one of his t-shirts and a pair of underwear, thinking she's alone. He comes up behind her and as she finishes making her breakfast, he stands there watching her from the entry to the kitchen, until she notices him. He's fresh from the shower and wearing nothing but a pair of gym shorts. There's some conversation, and they work their way around to the other side of the bar. Since he knows they're alone, he closes the distance between them and kisses her. She's much shorter than he, so he sets her on the counter of the bar to make up for the height difference. Eventually, he skims her underwear down her legs and decides he wants to kiss her there. The height difference makes it too high for him to kneel and too low for him to simply lean over. He reaches under her ass and lifts her to his shoulders and pivots to have her lean against the wall as he perfectly positions himself to ravage her."

Dani takes a deep breath, then looks to me, still focused on her thoughts. "So... do you think it's possible to move from the counter to the wall without dropping her? Would it even be physically possible to experience oral from that position?"

Being a man of action, I simply stand and say, "Get up."

"What?" she asks in disbelief, her eyes wide, and her mouth gaping.

"Get up. The only way you'll know is if we try it." I reach for her hand and pull her to her feet. I briskly tug her to the kitchen and hoist her up on the counter.

As soon as I have her on the counter, I bend to get her into position. She giggles and bats at my shoulders. "Luke... You don't need to do this. We could have just talked it through logistically."

"I'm more of a method actor," I tease, causing her to full belly laugh. I reach under her ass and hoist her in the air to my full height. I pivot to step toward the wall, and Dani wobbles. Fuck, I almost drop her. When I get her to the wall, there's no fucking way I'd have any access in this position. "Uh... you'll need to move back a bit."

I lean her back against the wall and go to take a step back to give myself space. Unfortunately, at that exact moment, Dani shifts on her own accord, and I hear a loud smack against the wall as her body suddenly drops between my chest and the wall. Her legs are still over my shoulders from the knees down, and her face is suddenly eye level with mine. Laughter pours from her, and her body begins to shake.

"Um... that didn't go quite as planned." I chuckle.

"You think?" she pants between fits of laughter, as I try to figure out how to get out of this position without dropping her.

Not being one to give up, I suggest, "Wanna try that again? I'm sure we can get it right next time." I hold onto her shoulders as she lets her legs fall off my shoulders.

As Dani rubs the back of her head, she contemplates my suggestion.

"Okay, Leighton. Let's do this." She stands in front of the countertop, and I reach to lift her. She gets her legs into position, and I stand to pivot.

Fuck. Once again, there's no room to maneuver any which way. Sure, my face is in direct contact with what would be her pussy, but as she's fully dressed, this doesn't have the same effect. Just as I'm about to lean her against the wall, Dani smacks her head against it. Fuck. Fuck. Fuck.

"Oof." I instantly try to step back away from the wall. Her body slides between myself and the wall, and she's once again at eye level. The expression on her face has me bursting into laughter, and she quickly follows suit.

"Epic... Fail!" she spits out between gasps of air, and all I can do is nod my head in agreement.

She reaches up to rub her head, and guilt spreads through me. "Are you okay?"

"I'll live. But let's chalk that up to a position I never want to be put into again. Either I'm not limber enough, or it's entirely impossible. Either way, it loses its sexiness, don't ya think?"

"Kind of does take the spontaneity out of it, doesn't it? You might want to consider rewriting that scene in your book." I release her legs and help her slide her body down mine.

"No kidding." But her eyes suddenly darken with desire. "What do you say to helping me figure out another position instead?" She traces her finger down my chest and pulls at my belt buckle.

"I think I could happily oblige, Miss Charlotte Ann. Anything for the sake of research."

DANI

On Thursday, I have my car loaded for my book signing and my weekend with Luke. I'm just about to pull into the line at the ferry terminal when I get a phone call from my friend Stacey Gardner. She's meeting me at the hotel tomorrow morning to be my lifesaver and personal assistant for the book signing. We've done countless meet and greets as well as signings together, so she knows the drill and keeps me in check.

Eagerly, I hit accept on the call and shout out with enthusiasm, "Hey, You! I can't wait to see you tomorrow!"

"Ugg," she moans and sounds like death warmed over. "I'm so sorry, Dani."

"What's wrong, Stacey?" Uh-oh, this isn't good. Stacey's one of the most positive people I know and has more energy than the energizer bunny on a caffeine high.

A low groan escapes from her before she has a chance to explain. "Uh... I can't get off the bathroom floor... I think I have food poisoning or the flu. It came on so suddenly. There's no way I can get to Seattle to help you tomorrow." Stacey lives in Bellingham and has been my best friend since college. She always helps me with big events. I typically fly her out and together, we crush them. She's practically my right hand and handles the logistics of the day for me.

"It's okay, Stacey. I'll figure something out. I have time. I'm on my way to Tacoma today. I'm catching a Rainier Renegades game this evening, then I'm on my way to Seattle. I have time to set up. You just focus on getting well."

"Uh... Dani, when did you start watching football? What aren't you telling me?" Shit. She's known me for years and even on her deathbed, this isn't something she'd let slip by her.

"Very recently..." I admit. "I'm..." I hesitate, wondering what to say. Then a thought hits me, and I continue, "I'm going to the game with Damien." There. That bit of information might make her back off. Things are going so well with Luke, but I don't want Stacey to read too much into it. Besides, with her puking her guts out, the last thing she needs to think about is the state of my love life.

"When I'm not dying on my bathroom floor, you're going to tell me," Stacey warns. "You've never liked sports. Damien could have front-row tickets on the fifty-yard line, and you'd pass up the opportunity. What gives?"

"You spend your time worrying about getting better, Stace." The line for the ferry starts to move. "Look, I'm about to board the ferry. I promise I'll fill you in on everything once you're feeling better."

"Oh, Danika Fallon," comes out in a deep frog-like voice. "You know you can't blow this off so easily. I know you.

184

Something's up. As soon as I get my energy back, you can bet your ass I'll be getting answers."

Stacey knows how to make me laugh, even when she sounds seconds away from death. "I'm sure you will. Look, Stace, I'm the next car in line to board the ferry. Get better, and we'll catch up."

"Sorry for leaving you in the lurch." Stacey's guilt is evident in her voice. We'd been looking forward to catching up this weekend. "I'll call you when I come back to the land of the living."

"I wouldn't expect anything less," I tease. "Get well, Stace. Love you."

We hang up the call just as I'm being directed onto the ferry. I park my car and decide to stay put for the twenty-minute ride to the mainland. I need to pull up my contact information for the book signing tomorrow. Stacey typically deals with the small details of the day. I know I can do it on my own, but I'll need to get there earlier than anticipated to set things up.

Damien arrives at Luke's loft shortly after I do. I invite him up as I take care of the few last-minute things to get ready for the game. I asked him to meet me, so we can ride to the stadium together, then I'll ride home with Luke.

When he knocks on the door, I let him in and rush to the bathroom in Luke's room to finish getting ready. "I'll be right out. I forgot my sweatshirt and jacket in my suitcase. Make yourself at home."

When I return from Luke's bedroom, I find Damien enjoying the floor-to-ceiling view of Tacoma. "Did you hit any traffic on the way down from Seattle?"

"Not much. Thanks again for inviting me." He turns to face me with a smile on his face. He's dressed in Rainier Renegade gear. He takes off his team hat to run his hand through his hair before replacing it and adjusting it to fit perfectly. He has an oversized jersey with a sweatshirt on underneath. "You must really like Luke, if you're being subjected to football so soon."

"The game's growing on me. I know a lot more about the team since the last game. Besides, I love watching Luke in his element. He's so intense, and his love for the game's contagious."

"Holy shit. You really like him, don't you?" Damien's eyes are wide and filled with amusement.

There's no use denying it. "Yeah, I do, Dame. He's something special."

"I knew he was something special when he subjected himself to our entire family for that day out on the island," Damien teases. "No guy would do that, unless he's really interested. Not to mention, getting our entire family tickets to the game. I know he's the head coach and can pull some strings, but if you weren't special to him, I doubt he'd even bother."

I can't say what Luke would do for someone else. But Damien has a point. "Yeah, he's pretty fantastic."

"I love that his place is still humble. Luke's not pretentious or anything. He's a great guy for you, Dan. You could've done a lot worse."

"Geesh, Dame. Such a vote of confidence."

"Seriously, Dan. I love you, and I just want you happy. You haven't dated anyone I've heard about since Chris. I like Luke and hope things work out for the two of you."

"Awe, thanks, Dame." I walk over and extend my arms for a hug. He pulls me in and pats my back after a few seconds.

"Anytime, Dan. Anytime."

Watching the game's just as intense as last time. I have to admit, I watched Luke more than the players out on the field. He's wearing a gray Rainier Renegades sweatshirt over a pair of black dress pants. It fits his broad shoulders like a glove. When he first walked onto the field with the team, I practically salivated on the spot. Damien and I cheer on the team and love that they've kept the lead throughout the game.

Now that I know Sean Peters' job, I can't help but laugh at the intensity of his focus on Luke. He successfully keeps Luke from receiving any penalties. As the game became closer in score, his job was much more difficult. Luke paces down the sideline with his play sheet covering his face as he adamantly speaks into his headset. I'm not sure what he says, but with the next play, the crowd's on its feet cheering as the quarterback throws to a receiver in the endzone. Touchdown!

Damien and I are on our feet instantly. Jumping up and down and high-fiving the crowd around us. For the briefest of moments, Luke glances in my direction, flashes a crooked smile, and winks. My heart nearly combusts. It's like the entire stadium empties, and it's just the two of us. I continue staring long after he breaks eye contact and refocuses on the game. *Damn, that man does something to me.*

Damien heads out as soon as the game's over, to get back to Seattle for classes early tomorrow morning. He makes me promise to thank Luke as he gives me one last hug. I make my way to Luke's office and once again, Harlow greets me.

"Hey, Danika. The door's open. Make yourself at home."

"Thanks. How's that grandbaby of yours?" I ask as I get closer.

"Oh, she's just precious. I got there in plenty of time to see her birth. My daughter Ginny was such a trooper. She was in labor for ten hours before Annalise decided to make her arrival in the world."

"Do you have any photos? I'd love to see her," I eagerly ask.

Harlow whips out her phone and enters her passcode. Within seconds, she's swiping through the photos to get one of her first granddaughter. "Here she is, swaddled like a burrito." She chuckles with pride as the cutest baby fills the screen. Annalise has the chubbiest cheeks with the tiniest fingers popping out near her chin. Her eyes are closed, but she couldn't be more precious.

"She's adorable, Harlow. Congratulations." I'm not sure what it is about babies, but they always make my heart mushy. There's no way I'm ready for them yet, but maybe someday... if the time is right.

We spend the next few minutes ogling over baby pictures. I can't believe how cute she is. Harlow takes her role as grandma seriously and can't say enough good things about her newest family member. She's showing me how long her skinny little legs are when Luke enters the room, taking me by surprise.

"She sure is a precious little lady, Harlow."

"Ohmigod, Luke. Did you see her with the little pigtail?" I squeal in delight. I take the phone from Harlow to flip it in his direction. His face lights up with the sexiest smile. My ovaries explode with how much joy he takes from seeing this baby.

"She's absolutely adorable," Luke agrees. "Will you get to see her this weekend?"

Harlow nods emphatically. "Yeah, I'm taking off as soon as we're done here. I'll be back first thing Monday."

"Well, don't let us stop you. You have a baby to hold," I gush, causing us all to laugh.

"She's right, Harlow," Luke agrees. "Anything that needs to be done can wait until Monday. Enjoy your weekend."

As soon as we say our goodbyes to Harlow, Luke places his hand on my hip and pulls me in closer to him. "Hey, You..." His low and rough voice sends butterflies to my belly.

"Hey, yourself." My voice is breathless as my face is mere inches away from his. "Great game, Coach."

"Thanks. The best part was watching you cheer us on. I don't think I've ever seen anyone sexier in Rainier gear." His eyes heat as his lips inch closer.

His breath, warm and minty, has my body tingling in anticipation. The moment our lips meet, I lose track of every thought. I feel consumed by all that is Luke. His hand sweeps down my back and rests at the base, pulling me tighter. Our bodies are flush against one another, and I can feel his warmth everywhere. His other hand moves to the back of my neck and guides our kiss in the perfect combination of sweet and seductively sensual. This man is lethal. With my sudden burst of desire, I'm seconds from forgetting we are at his place of work, and pushing him behind the closed door of his office.

A door shutting in the distance has us pulling up short. I'm practically panting as I fight for control of my breath. Luke smirks, but his eyes smolder. *Holy fuck. How does he do that?*

He leans down and gives me one last quick kiss before straightening to his full height. "We should probably get on the road to Seattle."

"Shoot," I gasp, remembering my dilemma with Stacey. "I forgot to tell you. I have to be there early Saturday morning. Like super early. My assistant has the flu and isn't able to help me set up. I'll see if I can get into the convention room to do some of it tomorrow night. It's been so long since I've gone solo to one of these events, I feel a bit out of sorts."

"What can I do to help?" Luke offers.

"I could sure use some help with the totes of books I have stacked in my trunk." I squeeze his biceps for emphasis. "These could come in handy," I tease.

Luke's eyes roll as he shakes his head. He looks at me as if I've lost my mind. "I'm sure they can manage to do some heaving lifting..." comes out humorless. "But seriously, what do you need done?"

Realizing he's serious, I roll over the list of things I've been creating in my mind. "I could use some help setting up as well as taking down the booth."

"Done. Anything else?"

"Um..." I contemplate what Stacey typically does when another thought hits me. "God, I hope my fans don't get pissed they're waiting too long in line. Stacey usually runs the credit cards and chats them up, while I personalize and sign books," I groan, already seeing the entire day being an epic fail. My worst fear is pissing off fans. "It's going to take forever to do both." I shake my head, look up to the sky, and pray things will work out.

"Dani?" Luke gets my attention by placing a hand on my shoulder. Immediately, my eyes are redirected to his. He holds my gaze, and I feel myself instantly calm. I take a deep breath, and my shoulders inch down from my ears.

"Yes?"

"It's been awhile since I've worked retail, but I'm sure I can figure out how to run the credit cards. I majored in business, so I can also give change, should they pay in cash. I've even been known to charm a few people in my time... trust me." His playful smile tells me he's charmed the pants off a few women in his time. God knows if he lays on his charm like he does with me, there'll be a riot on our hands. Luke's quite the charmer. His deep-blue eyes crinkle at the corners as if he can read my mind, and a shit-eating grin forms on his face.

Fuck, this man's impossible. "Are you sure you want to spend your day off helping me sell books?" I ask, trying to let him off the hook.

His features turn stern as if he's making a call on the field. "Danika, I wouldn't have volunteered if I didn't want to." Then they lighten considerably. "I'd rather spend the day with you than sightsee alone in Seattle or be cooped up in another hotel room alone. Besides, you've seen me in my element; it's only fair I get to see you in yours."

I contemplate this for a moment. But it's useless to pretend I'm going to say anything other than yes. "We may have to ugly you up a bit... or we might have a riot on our hands." I reach in and mess up his hair playfully.

This earns me another eyeroll. "Whatever you say, Dani,"

he says in a tone leaving little to my imagination. *He thinks I'm nuts.*

Thanks to Luke's persuasion, we wake up in Seattle on Friday morning with an entirely free day ahead of us. Of course, waking up with Luke is quickly becoming my new favorite way to start the day. His roaming fingers skim my body and play it like the finest fiddle. He knows how to get me hot and bothered in mere seconds, to the point I'm practically begging for him to slide inside me.

I lift my leg to his outer thigh, feeling more than ready for him. With a well-practiced move, he glides right inside me. His tongue traces the shell of my ear, and his warm breath turns me on even further as his fingers strum my clit. I let out a moan as he whispers, "You feel so good, Danika." The deep timbre of his voice sends vibrations through my body. "So tight..." He nips on my neck. "So perfect," he practically growls as he picks up his pace.

I feel myself climbing toward ecstasy. As I get closer and closer, I suddenly feel a great sense of loss as Luke pulls out. I cry out in frustration, but I'm quickly changing my tune when I feel him turn my body and lay on his back to pull me on top of him.

"Needed to see your beautiful face." I quickly climb him like a tree and place him at my entrance. His hands grasp my hips and pull me on top of him. "You're so beautiful when you come."

He guides my hips up and down, and I place my hands on

his chest for balance. This new angle has me reaching for the stars in no time. "Oh... Luke. So good." His large hand sprawls across my hips, and his thumb quickly finds my clit. A new wave of sensation overpowers me, and I quickly find myself tingling from head to toe. "Oh... Fuck..." My entire body convulses. A slur of words escapes my mouth, and for all I know, I could be speaking in tongues. *This man knows how to rock my fucking world.*

"You rock mine, Danika. Every. Fucking Time..." are the last words I hear before he thrusts into me one last time and falls over the cliff himself. I fall forward and collapse onto his chest, panting for dear life.

God, if I'm dying... this is surely the way I want to go!

LUKE

I finally convince Danika to leave the hotel room around noon. Since she admits she hasn't been a tourist in forever, I'm eager to show her what I've planned for the evening. I must admit I had a bit of help from Harlow with the reservations, but that's only because I'd been prepping for this week's game, and she volunteered once I mentioned going to Seattle.

Instead of driving, we walk to Pike Place Market. Though I'll admit I haven't been here since I started working for the Rainier Renegades, I've always loved this place. Where else can you go to watch fish be thrown, see the oldest Starbucks, and the infamous Seattle Gum Wall. Let's not forget the Pike Place Chowder. That stuff has me coming back for more every time I visit the vicinity.

As we walk through the market, Dani lights up when she sees trinkets and handmade jewelry. She insists we stop to look at it. She's not really what I'd call high maintenance, as she wears little makeup or accessories. But I do notice the styles she picks. They're sleek, simple but still hold your attention. I can't help but grin when I notice they're just like her.

Dani picks up a necklace and inspects it before replacing it. "Did you know that you can't sell in this market unless it's your first place of business?"

"What do you mean?" I ask. I've never given it much thought, but now I'm curious.

"While researching, I found many famous businesses started here, then branched out. But famous businesses can't be in the market if they didn't start here. For one of my books, I did some research on local markets as a job for one of my main characters. I came across that tidbit and thought it was odd. Apparently, they want you to get your start from here, not have commercialized vendors. It keeps things local."

"I'll bet you've come across some interesting information when you research," I say as I pick up a necklace that's caught my eye. It has the same shade of stone as Dani's eyes. It has a simple silver chain and is the shape of a tear drop. The gem's held in place by a smooth loop-like setting. When it catches Dani's attention, she gasps.

"That's beautiful." She reaches out and strokes the stone and my decision is made.

I motion to the man standing behind the table. "We'll take this."

The look of pure shock on Dani's face is evident. "What... You don't have to do that."

"It doesn't seem fair to leave it here." The words come out of my mouth before I give it any thought. *When did I become the guy who buys jewelry?* I don't think I've ever bought it for

195

anyone except my mom. But there's just something about it that won't let me walk away. Maybe it reminds me so much of her. Fuck, I have no idea. But I'm not questioning it now. I'm usually a "go with your gut" type of guy. And my gut is speaking loud and clear. This is meant for Dani.

"Did you see the matching bracelet here?" The clerk does his job with due diligence, that's for sure. It's the same color of stone, replicated in smaller portions set in the same sleek silver setting.

I look to Dani, whose eyes have gone wide. I'm not sure if it's from shock or annoyance. But once again, I go with my gut. They're a perfect match. "We'll take it."

"Luke," Dani admonishes. "What. Are. You. Doing?" in a low tone, trying not to draw attention from the crowd around us.

I simply shrug and show her a devilish grin. "What does it look like?"

"Seriously, I don't need this," she protests.

"No, you don't *need* this. But I think you'd look even more stunning wearing it."

Dani lets out a sigh in defeat, and I can't help but roll my eyes. "What do you have against me buying this for you?"

"It's nothing... really. I'm just not used to anyone doing that sort of thing. You don't need to spend money on me."

True to form, she wants nothing from me but my time. God, I love that about her. It's so refreshing to just be liked for me and not my status or money. "Danika." I quirk an eyebrow in her direction until I have her full attention. "It's not a big deal. I'd like you to have something to remember this weekend by. That's all."

Her cheeks blush that beautiful shade of pink, and I can tell her mind immediately went to somewhere it shouldn't. "Oh, I have plenty to remember this trip already. I have a memory like a steel vault. I think there'll be plenty I reminisce about after we get home." Her eyes darken, and my body heats. But since we're in public, I quickly plant a chaste kiss on her lips then turn to the vendor.

I hand the man my card and give him my full attention. He nods in appreciation and runs it in an instant. When he notices my name, I catch his eyes widen as he stares at me critically. I'm wearing jeans, a black hoodie, and a baseball cap to blend in. His eyes narrow as he hands me back the card. "Thank you, Mr. Leighton. Hope you have a great afternoon." He places my purchases in a black velvet pouch and hands them to me. "Let's keep up that winning streak," he says in a much quieter tone, to keep from gaining attraction of the crowd.

"Thanks, we will." I quickly grab the purchase and guide Danika through the crowd to get lost from his view.

"Does that happen often?" Dani asks when we're out of earshot.

"Do I buy beautiful girls jewelry?" I tease.

This earns me an exaggerated sigh and a brush of her hands on my arm. "No... do you get recognized often?"

"Um..." I take in her question and give it some thought. Sure, I get recognized and unless I'm near the football team, people usually don't make a big deal about it. "I wouldn't say it happens a lot, but in the past few months, since I've taken over as head coach, it's definitely happened more often. But I'm just the coach. No one's interested in the likes of me."

"I'm not sure how I'd handle that," Dani responds still in thought. She bites her bottom lip and has a far-off look in her eyes.

I've witnessed it before but still don't know how to respond, so I ask for clarification. "Don't people recognize you as an author?"

"Yes, but only at book conventions. And even then, it's by my pen name. I'd never get called by my real name by a complete stranger. Anonymity has its perks. I can go out in public looking like a scrub and never be thought of twice. I sit in coffee shops and other places where inspiration hits and write for hours on end and never get a second glance." She shakes her head and sighs dramatically once again. "It's crazy enough at book signings. Charlotte Ann gets enough attention at those."

"I can relate. When I was initially drafted, I had a bit of a following from college, but it died down once I was no longer playing. I'd much rather just keep my head down and do my job without having a random stranger spectate on my latest decision for the team. I never had this much attention as a coach before I took this position. Everyone blamed or applauded Ray if they had an opinion about the team. It's much different being in the hot seat this season."

"That must be a lot of pressure to always perform," Dani surmises.

"It's not that, necessarily. I'm just not used to random strangers inserting their opinions so much."

Dani bumps my hip as she takes my hand to walk through the shops downstairs in the marketplace. "Well, you aren't a sore sight for the eyes, that's for sure. I must admit, I may have watched you more than the game yesterday. You're sexy as hell when you're focused."

Did she really just say that? She can't be serious. I quickly dismiss it by muttering "Whatever you say, Dani." Letting her know I think she's being utterly absurd.

One of my fondest memories of the day will be when I doubled over in laughter as she bends down to hug Rachel the Pig, the mascot of Pike Place, like it isn't a big deal. I have my phone out and quickly capture the moment. The pure joy radiating from Dani is infectious. Of course, she takes it upon herself to fill me in on Rachel's backstory, which prompts me to pull out my wallet and fill the famous pig with cash. Who can deny contributing to such a good cause? But this prompts more impromptu photoshoots for each of us as we enjoy our adventure.

When we finish up with Pike Place Market, Dani and I make our way to the Seattle Center. We share many laughs as she picks out ridiculous things I should try on, or stops to pose for a selfie at one of the tourist attractions.

When we get to the base of the Space Needle, I casually walk Dani toward the line. "Wanna take a ride?"

"Don't we need tickets?"

I tap my phone. "Already taken care of. Come on. Let's go."

The wait is short and as Dani and I step into the elevator, we pick a spot where our view won't be obstructed as we ascend the Needle. I step closely behind Dani and can feel her body tremble slightly. "You okay?" I whisper so only she can hear.

"Yeah... Not really a huge fan of heights, but I've always

wanted to come up to see the view. Especially since it's been remodeled."

Fuck. I hadn't even thought she might be afraid of heights. I'm such a dumb fuck. It's too late now, since we're already soaring high above the skyline of Seattle. I lean in and wrap my arms around her from behind. Doing my best to distract her, I whisper, "Fun fact. I think you're one of the most incredible people I know. Those butterflies you're feeling right now? Well, they have nothing on how I feel when you walk in the room."

Her gasp is audible as her arms clamp down around mine, causing me to hold her tighter. I don't give her a chance to say anything before I continue, "I'm completely falling for you."

She quickly turns to face me, her eyes wide and searching mine. "Are you serious?"

"Absolutely." I keep my eyes locked on hers to leave zero doubts. The elevator stops, and I quickly pull her through the door to a place away from the vast windows to have a bit more privacy, if you can call it that. "I probably should've found a different way to tell you, but I didn't want to go another moment without you knowing. Feeling you tremble and knowing I'd put you in this position..."

Dani reaches up to my face and runs her palm along my cheek and interrupts my ramble, "Oh, Luke..." she sighs. For a moment, we stare into each other's eyes. My feelings are reflected like a mirror. Words don't have to be expressed, to know she clearly feels the same. Relief washes over me in an instant. Not being one to put myself out there often, I'm not even sure what came over me.

She guides my neck to bring my face closer to hers as she

steps onto her tiptoes to close the distance between us. The moment our lips meet, I want to lose all control. I want to sweep her into my arms and take her to a place with more privacy. But when I hear a loud man grumbling about *getting a room*, I slow my pace and level of intensity.

I reluctantly pull back and reach for Dani's hand. "Come on, let's get something to eat and enjoy the view from the restaurant."

It takes about an hour for the room to rotate and see the entire view from below. I'm relieved to know Dani isn't as nervous being further away from the window. With each passing minute, she noticeably relaxes. Not having planned a date like this in forever, I'm glad I didn't fuck up completely. I know she's adventurous, but heights never came up before now.

As we finish our meal, Dani shocks me when she suddenly stands and says, "Let's go to the observation deck."

Even as she reaches for my hand, I can't help but ask, "Are you sure?"

With her head held high and the confidence of a champion, she dons the sexiest smile and simply states, "I'm not giving up this experience with you by being scared."

If I wasn't already falling for her, she would've had me right there. I eagerly stand, ready to follow her anywhere.

LUKE

HOLY SHIT. I THOUGHT FOOTBALL FANS WERE CRAZED, BUT THEY have nothing on the romance industry. Dani and I were in the conference center before seven, setting up her booth to open at nine. Her booth sits between two lively women I'll never soon forget. One is set to give out condoms and small bottles of alcohol by the dozens, while the other sports a graphic tee that reads, "I love Guns and Buns." She writes military romance, and her fans loved to tease her about her obsession with describing the perfect ass in her books. Her name is Shay Ketring, and her personality is bigger than life. She and Dani have known each other for some time and have a great time catching up as they get ready. It's going to be one hell of a day, should their constant laughter have anything to do with it.

Of course, Dani insists I call her Charlotte, since that's what everyone in the room knows her as. It's easier said than done, but so far, I'm managing. She has totes of books under the table, merchandise, and what she calls swag available for fans to purchase. She's given me a rundown on what to expect, but I completely underestimated the intensity of the crowds. To help model the product, I'm wearing her Charlotte's Cove baseball hat to remind fans of her reader's group, and I sport a black t-shirt with her logo and catchphrase on it. "Charlotte's Cove ~ Melting hearts one reader at a time."

As a professional athlete, and head coach, I have been to several meet and greets in my career. But this is nothing compared to what Dani, or should I say Charlotte, endures. My fan-based activities usually only last an hour, max. Today, the doors open at nine and stay open until four. I have no idea what to expect, but from the sounds of it, Dani will be busy all day.

Last night, when we returned to the hotel, she gave me a rundown of how to look up pre-ordered books from her website, how to use the credit card machine on her phone, and a cheat sheet for her product pricing. She was adamant about making sure I knew ways to help keep her line moving, should people get stacked up. Along with her product she plans to sell, she also has bowls of chocolate, pens, and other swag to give away to her fans. There are bookmarks with her book series and reader's group. Dani's a great strategist when it comes to marketing. She has QR codes on the back of everything to take them to her website to purchase things they don't find here.

Just as the doors are about to open, and Dani slips off to use the restroom, Dani's phone rings. I see the name Stacey flash across the screen, so I answer, "D..." Shit, I almost outed her. "Uh... Charlotte Ann's phone, Luke speaking."

"Uh... is Charlotte available?" Her voice is stinted, full of confusion.

"She'll be right back. She stepped away for a moment. Can I take a message?"

"This is Stacey. I was checking to see how things were going. Are you helping her today at the reader's weekend?"

"Yep." I pop the p, and a smile forms on my face. "As best as I'm able. She gave me the rundown last night, and I feel prepared," I encourage, knowing Stacey is Dani's usual assistant.

"That's good..." she draws out. "Can I ask you for a favor?"

"Sure. What's up?" I offer, knowing it must be important if she's calling right now.

"Dani will kill me if she knows I said this... But can you make sure she eats? I always make sure she has plenty to eat and drink. She will let herself get stuck at the table all day and won't take a break unless it's a dire bathroom emergency." She takes a deep breath and continues, "If it gets slow, can you please pick up the food yourself or have someone from the hotel deliver it? I can text you the contact I have at the hotel."

Stacey takes another deep breath, and I use this as an opportunity to interject, "Of course. I'll take care of her. Don't worry about a thing. You just focus on getting better."

"Wait... she told you about me? Of course, she did. You wouldn't have to be there otherwise. But I know nothing about you. Wait... How exactly do *you* know Dani?"

Not wanting to disclose too much information given my location, as well as feed Stacey with more info than necessary, I opt with, "I'm a friend of hers, and I'll take good care of her. Don't worry."

I glance up and see Dani walking up the aisle in a pair of

dark skinny jeans and a green top with the shoulders cut out. Her smile's infectious, and I can't wait to get more time alone with her tonight. "Stacey, she's here now. I'll let her answer your questions."

I hand the phone to Danika as she mouths, "Stacey?" in disbelief.

"Hey, Stace, what's up?" I can hear words coming through the phone, but I can't make them out. They sound like they're going a million miles a minute. Dani rolls her eyes, attempts to interject a few times, but is defeated. Finally, she gets the chance to talk, and her cheeks pink as her lips twitch at something that was said. *God, what was said to make her look like that?*

Finally, Dani interrupts, "Look, Stace. I have it covered. Luke's a good friend. I'll fill you in later... The doors are about to open... You focus on getting well. We'll catch up later." A few more seconds of silence. "Love you, too, Stace. Next time, I expect you to be here."

She gets off the phone, shaking her head. "I swear, it's like she thinks I don't remember what needs to be done. Sure, she's been in charge for the last couple of years at these things, but I'm not incompetent."

"Stacey's just looking out for you," I encourage.

Danika shakes her head and locks her eyes onto mine, her expression enduring. "In case I forget to tell you, I really appreciate you being here today," she whispers.

I place a hand on her hip, pulling her close, so that only she can hear, "There's no place I'd rather be." I lean in and brush a quick kiss on her lips. Then I pull pack to push a corkscrew curl out of her face. The main doors open, and I hear the crowd in the lobby enter. I lift an eyebrow and simply ask, "You ready to kick some ass?"

Dani chortles, "Ohmigod, you are such a coach."

The first two fans to make it to Dani's booth are ecstatic to say the least. I almost jump out of my skin with the high-pitched squeals. *Holy shit, these women can scream.* Dani gracefully walks around the table to gleefully hug them. Trying to be helpful, I offer to take their photo while they chat Dani up like there's no tomorrow. They each pre-ordered her latest book from her website, so I don't have to run the card machine. By the time I check them off the list Dani had given me, there are more people to greet Dani.

"OMG, I can't believe I'm meeting Charlotte Ann," a woman in her early forties practically shouts as she approaches the booth with a friend. Of course, Dani goes around the table to hug her. Once they've taken a photo together, courtesy of me again, the woman's attention is drawn to me. "Oh my. You're a hottie," she boldly states. *What the hell do I say to that?*

Her friend pipes in, "Can we take a picture with the two of you? We know Charlotte has a fantastic imagination, but now we definitely know where she gets her inspiration. You're like a book boyfriend coming to life." She giggles at the end as if she might have the audacity to be embarrassed.

Holy fucking shit. These women have balls. Eyes wide, I look to Dani. Of course, she laughs it off with a shrug. "Well, he certainly leaves an impression."

"Oh, honey, you are one lucky woman," the first woman teases.

Still feeling odd, I take the attention off me by stating, "I'm the lucky one." Not wanting to disappoint her fans, I pose with Dani and her fans, then help them with some merchandise purchase as Dani greets the next person at the table.

For the next couple of hours, there's a steady stream of people at Dani's booth. I'm completely impressed by the way she greets each fan with genuine enthusiasm. If they purchase a book or bring one from home, she takes the time to give each person a personalized message in the books she signs. She also chats them up, takes a photo if they're bold enough to ask, and she flirts shamelessly with me if I happen to catch their attention.

Who the hell am I kidding? I draw a lot of attention being her assistant for the entire day. Which means I've resorted to calling her a nickname because I jokingly said her name reminds me of drinking sweet tea from home between fans. She thought it was hilarious and now instead of almost outing her, I simply call her Sugar.

When there's a lull in the crowd just before noon, I quickly run to the restroom and grab a bite for Dani and me to eat back at the booth. When I return, Dani is, of course, with another fan. As soon as she gets a break, I encourage her to use the restroom, figuring I could hold down the fort until she returns.

I. Was. Wrong.

What the hell had I been thinking? The second, and I mean the second Dani exits the room, no exaggeration, all hell breaks loose. It starts with a simple question.

A woman in her mid-twenties comes up to the table with a friend about her age. She's dressed in a pair of skinny jeans and a flowy pink top. Her energy radiates from her as she approaches. "Ohmigod! Are you the cover model for Charlotte's latest book? I swear you look familiar."

She picks up the book in question and eyes me and then the book, holding it up for comparison. The cover has a faceless man from the chin down, with a hairless, eight pack boldly on display. My abs look nothing like his.

I attempt to laugh it off by picking up her book and displaying it next to my abs as I lift up my shirt to show the obvious difference. For starters, my chest isn't waxed. I do have some ink, but it's not displayed on that book. I'm not an ape or anything, but I do have some chest hair and a definite hair heading south from my abdomen. "Sorry to disappoint. But it's not me." I drop my shirt and shrug with a shit-eating grin, hoping they'll let it drop.

She eyes me suspiciously, but doesn't seem convinced. "I swear I know you from somewhere."

Her friend steps forward, and her eyes go wide. Her mouth opens to say something, then closes. She looks from me to her friend, her mouth gaping. As she draws the attention of her friend, she points in my direction. "He... Uh... Isn't the cover model. But I'm pretty sure you might recognize him."

It's then I take notice of her shirt. Fuck. Fuck. Fuck. There in the center of her shirt is the logo I wear almost daily. Yep. She's a Rainier Renegades fan. Her wide eyes take me in, and it's only a matter of time before I'm outed.

"Listen," I begin, and her friend gasps.

Thankfully, Dani interrupts by saying, "Thank you so much for waiting for me."

Dani's fans are excited, but instead of the accolades being only about her, the first woman reaches out to her other friend and jumps up and down. She freaking jumps up and down. I can't make this shit up. "Ohmigod! Ohmigod! It's Charlotte Ann *and* Luke Leighton."

The friend who recognizes me doesn't disappoint. "It's *The Luke Leighton*! Only the hottest coach in the league! And he's helping Charlotte Ann!" She turns to us. "Can we take a picture with the two of you? This has to be the best. Day. Ever!"

Dani pulls out her best smile and wraps an arm around the closest woman. "Here, why don't you stand here, and I'll take the photo."

"Can you be in it, too?" the Rainier Renegades fan practically begs.

Dani, never being one to disappoint a fan, steps to me and wraps her arm around my waist. "Sure. Hey, Shay, can you take our photo?" Thank God, Shay happens to be between fans at the moment.

She steps up and takes the photo. We've been helping her throughout the day, so I'm sure she thinks nothing of it. When she's done, the Rainier Renegades fan continues to look questioningly between Dani and me. "Wait..." and my stomach drops to the floor. Her eyes scrutinize my hand still on Dani's waist. "Are you guys dating?"

"Shelby," the first friend scolds. "That's none of our business... Besides, if it keeps Charlotte writing hot as hell books, who are we to complain?"

I look to Dani who looks as if she's just been caught with her hand in the cookie jar. Fuck. I have no fucking clue as to how to proceed. Just yesterday, she was talking about loving her anonymity.

The Rainier Renegades fan misinterprets Dani's expression and jokingly states, "Well, if you're not dating, can I volunteer as tribute?"

Dani's spine straightens, and her chest pushes out. Unsure as to what she'll say, I wait and watch. Dani steps closer to me as if her ass is on fire, placing a hand on my chest. "Oh, he *is* most definitely taken." Holy shit. *Is she jealous?*

The girl she's directed the statement to just steps forward and hugs her. She fucking hugs her, and it's as if I've been sent to an alternate universe. There is zero cattiness and nothing but excitement displayed. "I'm so happy for you, Charlotte. You deserve all the happiness in the world."

Well, that was unexpected.

The Rainier fan reaches out and pats me on the arm. "You have one hell of a woman here. Treat her right." She winks at Dani, and Dani all but rolls her eyes.

"Oh, he does." The words come out of Dani's mouth as if she's forgotten I'm standing right here.

"Your fans are going to flip their lids when they realize you've been hiding out with Luke Leighton," the Rainier fan whispers so only the few of us can hear. "We'll all be wondering which character you write about is most like him," she teases as she rolls her eyes in my direction.

"Well..." Dani pretends to think over something. "You never know." Her beautiful smile lights up my world and if she's happy with this, I guess it's okay.

Within a minute or two, another fan makes their way to

Dani's booth. The two fans who recognized me quickly depart and say their goodbyes. I feel my phone buzz in my pocket, but I ignore it. It's too loud in here, and Dani needs my assistance. Besides, there's a steady line for the remainder of the afternoon. Whatever it is can wait.

22

DANI

LUKE. IS. A. SAINT. HE HANDLES THE DEMANDS OF THE DAY LIKE a champ and never complains once about the obvious ogling my tenacious fans display. He's so graceful under pressure and doesn't show an ounce of stress the entire day. As we pack up for the evening, I count my blessings. It was an amazing day and having him here was better than I could imagine.

I nearly died when the first two women recognized him. There were a few others afterward, but nothing as boisterous as the first ones. When I think back to the events of the day, I'm relieved it's over.

As I relax because the doors have officially closed, it hits me. *Holy shit! Did I stake a claim to him publicly?* I quickly recall the turn of events. Shit. I think I did. I'm not even sure what came over me. I just knew I didn't want that woman to think she had a chance with him. *Not that I could blame her.* But to boldly claim Luke as mine? Damn, my green-eyed monster must have been bearing its horns. What the hell came over me?

"You okay?" Luke breaks me from the thoughts spinning in my head.

"Yeah," I sigh as exhaustion sets in. I typically have a day or two of complete downtime to decompress from these events. "I'm just thinking about the fans." *Well, that's sort of the truth.*

His deep voice chortles as he states, "I thought I'd seen crazed fans in football, but they have nothing on the romance industry." He shakes his head at some memory and reaches to pull me close. "Thank you for showing me your world. I had no freaking clue what to expect, but this was really something."

"Ha... I threw you into the deep end. Thanks for being able to swim so effortlessly." I reach in and caress his cheek. His deep-blue eyes darken.

"What do you say we get this packed up and get out of here?" His suggestion comes out low and gravelly, setting my nerves on fire.

"I like that idea very much." I reach up on my tiptoes to close the distance between us, giving him a quick kiss.

Of course, I get carried away, and he remembers where we are. He pulls back with a sexy as sin smile and promises, "Later."

I playfully groan. "If you insist."

By the time we make it back to our room, I'm completely exhausted. Luke must see it on my face because he insists I rest while he orders room service. I plop down on the couch, putting my feet on the coffee table. I hear Luke speaking, but my brain is too tired to decipher the words. As soon as he's done, he joins me on the couch.

"Wanna watch a movie?" he suggests as he pulls me closer. His sexy scent still makes my body tremble, but I simply don't have any gas left in the tank. I inhale deeply and relax into him more. I'm sure this is the last thing he wants to do in our romantic suite, but this is what he's going to get.

"You pick. I'm not sure I'll last long." I snuggle closer and wrap an arm around his waist. The warmth of his body and his steady heartbeat does me in. When a knock at the door startles me, I bolt upright in a useless attempt to hide my slumber.

Luke brings back a tray of food that smells delicious. I snacked at the conference between chatting with fans, but I didn't eat much. He lifts the tray, and my mouth salivates. "Mmmm..." I moan in anticipation.

Luke smiles in appreciation. "There's plenty here. I wasn't sure what you wanted, so I got a bit of everything."

There's a large charcuterie platter with an assortment of meats, cheese, and fruit. He also ordered strawberry rhubarb cobbler, a French dip sandwich large enough for the two of us, and two large iced teas.

"We won't have to leave the room until check out tomorrow with this much food," I tease.

He pulls a sexy smirk and rolls his eyes. Damn, those dark-blue eyes drive me wild. "I'm pretty sure we'll need more by tomorrow. Come on, let's dig in."

He hands me an empty plate, and I fill it with ease. I take my first bite, and my stomach growls loud enough for him to clearly hear, causing us both to chuckle. "I'm so sorry. I didn't realize I was this hungry."

"Nothing to apologize for, *Sugar.*" Luke's eyes crinkle at the corner, and I laugh.

"God, I can't believe you decided to call me *that* of all things today."

"What can I say? You remind me of my favorite sweet tea. Strong with the perfect blend of sweetness. It's like you were made for me. Besides, I almost called you Dani more times than I can count, so I had to think of something."

I cock an eyebrow at the ease of his words. "Are you sure you're not a romance writer in disguise?"

"Hardly," he deadpans. "I'm just a guy who knows what he likes."

"That you do," I say before taking another bite of the French dip. As I finish chewing, I continue, "You were quite the charmer out there today. I swear half the people in line wanted to get a closer look at you. If you ever decide to give up your coaching gig, I'm sure you'd make bank as a model."

Luke groans. "Oh, please... I'm just a regular guy."

"Uh... Luke..." I wait until I have his full attention. "You're anything but a regular guy."

"Whatever you say, Danika. If anyone should be on the cover of books, it would be you. Not me."

"Oh, you're a charmer, Luke Leighton. A real charmer." I dismiss his words and dig back into the food in front of me.

"Are you still up for a movie?" Luke asks as he finishes his sandwich and reaches for a piece of cheese.

"Sure. But I'm warning you, it might be a snooze fest

instead. I absolutely love meeting my fans. I wouldn't be here without them, but book signings always wipe me out."

He nods his head in agreement. "I can imagine." Then he reaches out and pats my thigh beside him. "I just want to be here with you. I don't care what we do."

That. Right there is why I'm falling for this man. He knows how to say just the right thing, and I know without a doubt he's sincere. I love that he can take me hot and heavy as well as simply enjoy the quiet times we share.

Within a few minutes, our meal is devoured, and Luke covers what we'll save for later. We snuggle into the couch, and he orders a movie to watch. His steady breaths and the scent of everything that is uniquely him pulls me under in record time. I don't even fight it.

I awake sometime later to the ringing of a phone and groggily hear Luke answer.

"Hey, Tanya, to what do I owe this pleasure?" His tone is thick with sarcasm but drastically changes to one of concern. "What? Seriously? Give me a second." This has me instantly alert. I sit up, and Luke gives me an apologetic smile. "I have to pull up my laptop. Hold on."

It's déjà vu. I'm immediately brought back to that night at his house. What the hell has another player done now?

As Luke bolts off the couch to grab his laptop from the bedroom, my phone buzzes in my pocket. I pull it out, see it's Stacey, and immediately answer. I don't even get a "Hello," out before she ambushes me.

"Luke Freaking Leighton was your assistant today?" Her tone is high on the verge of screeching. *What the hell is she freaking out about?* Didn't she know this? They spoke for quite a bit. She mentioned his name... or I thought she had.

"What's going on, Stace? Why are you freaking out about who my assistant was?" Clearly, I'm not firing on all cylinders and am unable to connect the dots.

"You don't know?" she asks incredulously. "Ohmigod. I thought you knew."

"Know what?" Of course, I know who Luke is. I get that she didn't, but what's the big deal?

"You haven't been on social media, have you?" she accuses, instead of making it a question.

"You know how signing days are. I'm exhausted. We got back to the hotel, and I fell asleep while Luke watched a movie."

"You're at a hotel with Luke Leighton? I thought you were on a dating hiatus. When the fuck did you meet a man like Luke Leighton?" she quizzes me like only a best friend can do.

"Why do you keep calling him by his whole name?"

Stacey groans loudly into the phone. "Grrr... Danika Marie Fallon. You have some explaining to do. I want *all* the details... NOW!"

"Geesh, Stace. I've dated people before. Why are you freaking out about this?"

Stacey takes a deep breath, and I can picture her fortifying herself to speak clearly. Her hand is likely on her hip and her chin jetting out. "Are you sitting down?"

"Uh... I am. But why do I need to be sitting?" What the fuck is she about to tell me? The hairs on the back of my neck tingle. Whatever she's about to say, it's not going to be good. I can tell from the tone of her voice.

"It's made the national news..." she whispers.

"Come again?" What the hell is she talking about?

"Luke Leighton Being Romance Writer Charlotte Ann's Boy Toy."

I nearly choke on my own spit, and my mouth drops open wide.

No. I didn't hear that correctly. I couldn't have. "Wh... What?" I sputter.

"Oh, yeah. It's literally on every news broadcast and every sports and entertainment channel."

"What is?" My mind's still reeling.

Thankfully, I don't have to wait for Stacey to continue, "There's a photo of him lifting up his shirt to show off his abs and one of the two of you with your arms around each other, holding your book."

"Holy shit," I say in disbelief.

"So, I gotta ask, Dan. Are you really dating Luke?"

"Uh... yeah," I admit, still mystified.

Stacey's tone turns to teasing, "I gotta say, it sucks that I had to hear it from the entertainment industry first. Here I was, flipping through channels and see your face flash across the screen. I immediately flipped back to the channel. Then couldn't believe you've been holding out on the fact you're dating one of the hottest men in America."

Only Stacey could get me to laugh at this situation. "He *is* pretty hot, Stace. But why the fuck are we making national news?"

"Uh..." Her tone tells me it should be obvious. "Have you seen him lately? I know you live under a rock out on that island and live in your book world, but to the rest of us mere mortals, he's kind of a big thing."

Of course, he's a big thing. I haven't had anyone affect me like this... ever. How do I even begin to explain this to Stacey? She of all people knows me. She knows my past and also why I likely wouldn't have said anything about him yet.

When I don't say anything in response, she feels the need to continue, "He's the youngest friggin coach in the league, single, and hot as hell. You have to know the rest of the world would take notice, if he's off the market. They're all speculating why would he spend his weekend at a book conference? You have to mean a hell of a lot for him to subject himself to countless women likely objectifying him each time they walk past. Come on. I've been to enough of these to know any hot guy gets attention behind the booth."

"Some women mistook him for one of my cover models," I finally whisper, realizing how this could've gotten out of control. Remembering the scene I stumbled upon when I returned to my table. "He jokingly tried to show them he wasn't." Fuck. That's when I remember my bold statement. "Shit. That's when I publicly claimed he was mine, too."

"Hell, yes!" Stacey practically shouts into my ear. "You go, girl. I'd be claiming that man as mine if I were you, too." Leave it to Stacey to encourage this.

"He said no one would notice the coach," I mumble, still trying to let reality sink in.

"Does that man eat a big ole' helping of humble pie on a regular basis? Geesh... People notice him, Dan. He's just taken over as head coach for the team that *won* the championship game last year. Of course, he's noticed. Add in the fact he's single and sexy as hell... I don't think there's a woman in the country that hasn't suddenly become a Rainier Renegades fan just to watch him."

"Ha... funny you should mention that," I tell her about my experience at the game where I watched him more than the plays on the field. She's gasping for air with laughter when I get to the point where I asked him about Sean Peters' position on the team.

"Wait. He got you to go to football *games*, as in more than one?" Stacey asks in disbelief. "How on earth did you even meet him?"

"Well... for your information, I met him on that island of mine. I uh... kind of... went over the handlebars of my bike... and he happened to rescue me. I had no idea who he was, other than a hot guy who had to witness it all."

"Only you... You big, dopey, romance writer. You're the only person on the planet who wouldn't have a clue who Luke Leighton was."

"You know I don't watch sports..." I say in defense.

Stacey's grin can be heard through the phone. "I know. But this *is* Luke Leighton we're talking about. Even the old lady in accounting has mentioned Luke to me last time I went to drop something off."

Not sure if she's exaggerating, I dismiss it. Then a thought comes to me. "Wait. You said... he was my 'boy toy?'"

"Uh... you caught that, did you?" Stacey suddenly goes quiet, leaving me on pins and needles. So, I prompt, "What else is being said, Stace?"

"Well," she draws out. "I guess it depends on which channel you turn to. The local news lead with, 'Sorry to disappoint you, ladies, but it appears Luke Leighton's off the market.' The sports channels are debating whether you're going to be a distraction for him, now that he seems to be dating. And the entertainment channels are playing up the romance card and teasing you'll continue to have quite an imagination, now that you have him as inspiration."

"You gotta be fucking with me, Stace." Thank God, I don't have to have a filter where she's concerned.

When she doesn't reply, I groan loudly, "Seriously?" They're talking about Luke being inspiration for my books?" This cannot be happening. Fuck! Not everyone knows I even write romance, but with my picture out there for the world to see connected with my pen name, it's only going to be a matter of time before people connect the dots.

This brings on a whole new set of problems.

Just as I'm about to say more, Luke opens the door to the bedroom and solemnly steps out. This does not look good. "Uh, Stace. I gotta call you back."

"Okay, but this doesn't mean I'm going to drop this. You have lots to tell me, Dan. I'm not letting it go," she warns as only a best friend can.

"I know. I will. I promise. We'll talk soon."

With that, I end the call and look to Luke, who's keeping his distance from me. Fuck. This isn't good.

23

LUKE

GETTING A CALL FROM TANYA WAS THE LAST THING I EXPECTED. But my job never ends. I pick it up and jokingly state, "Hey, Tanya, to what do I owe this pleasure?"

"Luke, I think we have a problem." Her tone cuts through me. It's not one I've ever experienced personally, but I've witnessed it plenty with guys from the team. Shit, whatever this is, it must be directed at me personally. "Are you aware you're making headlines on every news outlet, SportsCenter, and entertainment show?"

"What?" No fucking way. "Seriously? Give me a second. I have to pull up my laptop." I stand and walk to the bedroom where my laptop is stored for our stay. "Hold on."

It takes for fucking ever for it to boot up. Not being able to wait to find out for myself, I demand, "Give me the lowdown."

Tanya sighs, clearly exasperated. "Are you by any chance dating Charlotte Ann, the *New York Times* best-selling romance author?"

"Uh... yeah. What's going on?" Clearly confused with what Dani has to do anything.

"Did you or did you not pose for a photo of you exposing your abs earlier today at a romance convention?" she states as if I'm suddenly on trial.

"No... I... Fuck. I joked around, trying to demonstrate I wasn't the cover model. But I didn't think there'd been any photos."

"Oh," Tanya chortles, "there were definitely photos. You know better than this. In fact, they've gone viral."

"When you say viral..." I trail off, trying to think of the ramifications.

"Let's just say you're the talk of the town. It's apparently big news that Luke Leighton is no longer *on* the market. That is, if the rumors are true."

"What the hell are you talking about? No one's ever cared about who I've dated before. I'm the friggin coach, not a star player. I haven't been in the spotlight since I was drafted my first year. You know that."

"Luke," Tanya chides. "Are you really this dense?"

I take a moment to calm myself when I reach my favorite news site. There I am, flashing a shit-eating grin across the page with Dani, or should I say Charlotte, at my side. Her arm is around my waist, and we're posing with her newest release. That isn't what infuriates me though. It's the caption at the bottom of the photo. *Leighton scores with New York Times bestseller.*

"Luke, are you there?" I hear through the phone. My fist clenches at my side as I try to stay calm. I take a breath or two to steady my thoughts and control my sudden frustration.

"I'm here..." I mumble as I click on the next photo. It's a similar pose but with a different caption. *Are Luke Leighton's bachelor days gone?* But the next photo takes the cake. It's of me lifting my shirt and holding Dani's book, the caption reads, *Is Luke Leighton leaving for modeling career?*

"Jesus Christ. These people will stop at nothing to sell a story," I mumble more to myself than to Tanya.

"Ah, I see you've gotten online. How do you want to roll this? I think we should get your side of the story out there, so we can put a rest to the rumors."

How do I want to roll this? What the fuck am I supposed to say to that?

"Uh... I gotta ask," Tanya asks sheepishly. "You've never been known to date or be a player, so is she the real deal or just something to pass the time?"

"Are you fucking kidding me?" I practically growl. "Since when did my private life become something you need to get out in front of?"

"Um... Luke, you *are* the head coach for the team that just won the championship. You're also the youngest coach in history, and no offense, you're attractive and most importantly, single. The minute the media sniffs out you're dating *anyone,* it would be big news. Add the fact that you're peddling books at a romance conference, and this story is spreading like wildfire."

"What do I need to do?" I ask, realizing she's right.

"Well," she starts but hesitates. "Uh... this is personal, but how serious are you about this... Charlotte Ann?"

"I'm completely fucking serious," I say before I give it any thought. Dani is everything to me. But she wanted her anonymity. Fuck, is this going to out her?

"Okay, then. I think this can wait until Monday, since we don't play tomorrow. The story might blow over with it being game day. Let's meet with Mike and Tony to all be on the same page, first thing."

"Since when did the head coach's personal life become a thing for PR to handle?" This is fucking ridiculous.

"Since he's gone viral," she deadpans. "I'll see you Monday, Luke."

Shaking my head, I can't believe my life has come to this. I'm just about to say goodbye when Tanya pipes in, "Oh, and, Luke... if Charlotte is a pen name, you may want to warn her. I can't see the media letting this go. Since she's famous in her world, now that your paths have crossed, I doubt it will be kept a secret for long."

"That's what I was afraid of," I mumble. Fuck. How could I be so careless? Her privacy is everything. How the hell am I going to tell her this?

"Good luck," Tanya wishes me before getting off the phone.

After disconnecting the call, I take a moment to gather my thoughts. Leaning my head into my hands, I sit on the edge of the bed and sigh heavily. Dani and I are having the best weekend. How he fuck do I go out there and break this news to her?

Time to man up, Leighton. I sigh as I stand and walk to the door. She's going to hate me. I've fucked up royally.

24

DANI

I STAND AND WALK TO LUKE. HIS FACE IS SO FULL OF GUILT, IT
nearly kills me. What the hell could be wrong? When the
silence stretches longer than I can handle, I blurt out, "What's
wrong?"

"Uh..." he hesitates then continues, "that was Tanya on the
phone, the head of PR for the Rainier Renegades. Apparently,
we've made the news."

I groan at the audacity of it all but thank God he already
knows. "Uh... I know. Stacey just called."

With that, his face perks up, slightly. But not nearly
enough for me to feel comfortable about what comes next. Did
he not want it to be known that we're dating? Damn. I
shouldn't have outed us publicly.

"I'm so sorry, Dani," he says in a blur. "I didn't mean for
this to happen."

Shit. I shouldn't have let him come to my book
signing. This is all my fault. "It was bound to happen

eventually." I bow my head, waiting for the worst to happen.

When he's quiet for way too long, I glance up to meet his eyes. They're scrutinizing my every move. "What do you mean?" he questions.

"I shouldn't have had you come to the signing. You're a bigger deal than you let on." I shrug as if it should be self-explanatory. I mean, come on, look at him. And even me, who knows nothing about football, knows the head coach is still a big deal. I pace in front of him as I try to figure out what to say to make him realize I didn't intend to out us like I did.

"Uh... you didn't *let* me do anything." He steps closer to me, placing a hand on my shoulder to get me to stop. "I chose to be there with you, Dani."

"I know, but I let the green-eyed monster loose and was the one who outed us publicly."

"Green-eyed monster?" he asks, confusion clearly written across his face.

I let out a huff of air more forcefully than I intend. "Luke, I'm the one who couldn't let that woman even *think* you were available."

He laughs. He fucking laughs. What the fuck is he laughing about? This isn't funny.

"Danika, that was one of the sexiest things I've ever seen. You'd better damn well be staking claim because you can bet your ass I'd do the same, if the situation was reversed."

I hear his words, but it still doesn't explain why he was so grief stricken when he entered the room. "Then... what are you so upset about? Why did you apologize?"

"Tanya says there's a good chance your real name will get

leaked if the press stays on this story for long. They're relentless when they think there's a story. If I hadn't been so careless today, by trying to prove I wasn't on the cover of your book, there likely never would have been a story."

"Uh... according to Stacey, you're a pretty big deal on your own, Luke. I don't think flashing your sexy abs had anything to do with it. Though, I'm sure it didn't help. I apparently have been living under a rock because I was one of the only people on the planet who didn't know who you were."

"Jesus, Dani. I swear, I'm not that big of a deal. The press hardly has anything to do with me. Their attention goes to the players. Not me."

"Oh, Luke. Stacey isn't even a sports fan. But she assures me you're the sexiest coach in the league." I smirk. Even a blind person would see the sexiness Luke exudes. It's in both his looks and actions. Who else would volunteer on one of his few days off in the entire season to go to a book signing and be ogled by women without complaint. "There's no point in denying it."

Rolling his eyes. "If you say so..." It's obvious he disagrees, but he continues, "But that's not the point. Anonymity is important to you, and I just fucking blew your cover."

Could this man be any sexier? Here he is, being mocked all over the media and he's worried about me. I don't think I could've fallen harder for him than in this very instant. "Luke... the minute our photos went viral, I knew it was a possibility."

"But are you okay with it?" His deep-blue eyes pierce through to my heart.

"Let's take it a day at a time. I don't think I could have

stopped myself from claiming you, if I'd tried. Besides, according to Stacey, the sheer act of you being at the signing with me, was enough cause for speculation about your intentions."

"Let's be clear right now. I have every intention of being with you," he boldly states as he brushes a piece of hair from my face. "I don't give a fuck what the media or my PR team says. I wouldn't have traded today with you, for anything."

I cock my head to the side, wondering if I've heard him correctly. *Did he just say his PR team would be on this?* Thank God, he can read me like a book, because I don't have to prompt him before he continues, "About that... I have a meeting with the owner and general manager of the franchise first thing Monday morning. They want to get behind the story and control it the best they can. *Apparently,* they don't think this is a story that will blow over on its own. Since this has everything to do with you, I think it might be a good idea you attend it with me."

"They want me at this meeting?" Why? I'm nobody in comparison to him, and I have nothing to do with the team.

"I want you at this meeting. I'm not making any decisions that concern you without your voice being heard."

"Okay then," I agree since he's left little room for argument. Luke's relief flows through him, and I instantly relax. Whatever will be, will be. No sense in worrying about it now.

Luke reaches for my hand and pulls me in the direction of the bedroom. "Now that that's settled, what do you say we spend the rest of our time here in this bubble of bliss, forgetting about the world beyond us?"

"I can't think of anything better."

Our blissful bubble lasts until we enter the lobby to exit the hotel. Hand in hand, we exit the lobby to a commotion outside the main entrance. Someone screams Luke's name and immediately I'm aware of the mass of people that have gathered not far from the entrance. Security is keeping them at bay, but it doesn't keep them from noticing our presence.

A man in a suit steps close to get our attention. "If you'll excuse me, Mr. Leighton. I'm Darren Markus, head of security. I think it might be best if you follow me."

Wide eyed, I look to Luke for guidance. He nods, and we follow Darren through a set of double doors and away from the mass of people waiting outside. Once we're alone in a hallway with Darren, Luke speaks. "I'm sorry. I had no idea this would happen."

"It's quite fine, Mr. Leighton. We respect the privacy of our guests and took the proper precautions when your situation was brought to our attention. As a rule, we keep the press and any loitering fans out of the lobby when instances like this occur. I assume your car is with the valet service? If you'll come right this way, we can bring your car here to avoid anyone noticing you. If you'll give me your ticket, I'll be happy to get it for you.

"Thanks. I appreciate your help. I've never had the press bother me before. I had no idea this would happen."

"I'm a huge fan of the Rainier Renegades, and I'm happy to assist you in any way I can," Darren offers.

Luke gives him his ticket, and the car is brought to us in minutes. This must be a shortcut to the parking garage because our things are loaded into the trunk, and we are on our way before anyone has the faintest idea we've even left the building. We take a side-street exit from the parking garage and are on in the hustle and bustle of Seattle city traffic within minutes.

As we make our way to the freeway, my mind reels with what we've just experienced. Having read too many books, I also suggest, "You may want to take the scenic route to your loft. God forbid someone follow us." Though I'm joking, Luke can sense the hint of truth.

"No kidding." Luke reaches his hand to mine and holds it on his lap. "I have the perfect place in mind."

It turns out, Luke knows every back road from Seattle to Tacoma. We zoom down side streets, zigging and zagging our way to his loft. We opt not to stop anywhere, in fear of being recognized, and we make our way into his home within the hour. He points out some of his favorite places as we get closer to his home. It sheds a light on who Luke is, when he's not coaching. It's obvious he loves local businesses and does his best to support them when he can. He mentions that he'll send Darren some tickets to a game as a personal thank you for helping us avoid the crowds, and my heart soars. Luke is possibly one of the kindest people I know. I open up to him and let him know I am nervous about going with him to the meeting tomorrow. I don't want to be a burden to him or the franchise, and Luke being Luke, assures me everything will be okay. I just hope he's right.

25

LUKE

As soon as I got home last night, I texted both Mike and Tony, letting them know my thoughts on including Danika at our meeting, since this concerned her, too. They agree and expect her in our meeting this morning. I can tell Dani's nervous, so I try to distract her and keep us in our bubble for as long as we can.

Needing to stick to my usual routine, Dani and I are up and out the door a little after six. Harlow greets us as we approach my office. "Morning, Luke. Danika, it's a pleasure to see you today."

"I wish it were under different circumstances," Dani admits, though she says it with strength and determination.

Harlow nervously laughs. "I can see that. But things have a way of working out. I'm sure the two of you will get through this just fine." Then Harlow pats Dani on the shoulder. "Don't worry, dear. Your secret's safe with me. By the way, I'm a huge fan of your work. I had no idea you were Charlotte Ann."

"Thank you, Harlow. That's kind of you to say." Dani's shoulders relax a bit, and I loosen up as well.

Harlow always knows just what to say. She turns her attention to me and winks before saying, "Luke, you have a talented lady here. Treat her right." I shake my head.

"Thanks, Harlow, you know I will. You should've seen her in action this weekend with her fans," I state honestly. "This woman's a force to be reckoned with. She makes our hour-long meet and greets look like child's play. She was at it for hours on end and never broke a sweat."

"From what I saw on television, you have yourself quite the fan base as well, Luke." Instantly, I feel my ears heat and roll my eyes in disagreement.

But Dani adds her two cents before I can brush it off, "Maybe if he wasn't such a hot commodity, we wouldn't be in this mess." I can tell from the tone of her voice she's teasing, but with the instant nodding of Harlow's head, I see she might have a point.

"Luke's a talented coach, but let's face it, he's easy on the eyes. The women at that book conference were bound to notice him." Harlow then looks to me. "No offense."

"How the hell am I supposed to take that?" I ask honestly. Seriously?

Harlow swats her hand in the air dismissively. "Oh, Luke," she states just like my mama would say, *Bless Your Heart*. I don't miss the tone. I'm not being a dumbass. I seriously don't know what I did that caused such a shitstorm in the media. I was just being helpful. Sure, I could have kept my shirt down, but it was the only way I could prove I wasn't the cover model. I look nothing like that guy. *Obviously.*

"Luke," Dani catches my attention, "she didn't mean to offend you. But no one's blind in this room." *Like that's supposed to help the situation.*

I drop the subject and to Harlow, I ask, "Did Mike or Tanya happen to mention where our meeting is this morning? I haven't checked my email yet and want to make sure we're on time."

"They'll be in Mike's office at seven thirty," she states, getting the point I want to drop the subject.

"Thanks. I'm going to get things set up for the coaches meeting and delegate some things I wanted to cover with the offensive line, since I'm unable to attend the meeting this morning."

I walk toward my office, and Dani follows. "Mind if I set up shop at your conference table?"

"Not at all. Make yourself at home. Sorry, but I have to get a few things done before the coaches meeting that starts in twenty minutes," I offer as I start up my laptop and pull up the list of things I'd created last night before going to bed, while Dani got some words in.

"No problem. You don't need to entertain me, Luke. I know you have a job to do." She pulls out a notebook and her laptop. Sets some pens on the table and settles in to get to work, while I do the same.

I focus my attention on adding some things to my list and making sure there's enough details in my instructions so the other coaches can easily lead the meeting I'm missing. After I finish that, I shoot off a few emails and respond to the giant pile stacked in my inbox.

Soon there's a knock at my open door, and I glance up to

see Tyrell Yates, our defensive coordinator entering the room. He greets me with, "Hey, Casanova. I hear you're moonlighting as a model these days."

"You can't always believe what you see on TV," I deadpan.

"So... You're not dating the sexy romance novelist?"

I glance at Dani who covers her mouth, doing her best not to laugh at the ridiculousness of Tyrell. He's been a good friend for years, but he's been known to have a one-track mind and doesn't pay attention to my glance at the conference table.

Tyrell walks to my desk, his back now completely to Dani. "So, what's the deal, Romeo? Are you dating this girl or not?" He runs a palm over his chin and looks to the ceiling, as if he's suddenly in deep thought. Whatever it is he's thinking, he's concentrating harder than necessary. Completely entertained by this, I remain silent.

Tyrell mistakes my silence for a denial and looks me square in the eyes. "Okay, hotshot. Tell me this. If you're *not* dating her, can you help me get her number?" His eyes waggle, baiting me for a response.

And I don't disappoint. I bolt out of my chair and stand to lean over my desk. The thought of Dani dating anyone but me makes my blood boil. "Uh... that would be a hard no."

A mischievous grin forms on his face, and he taps his chin, pretending to think. "Is that a hard no, as in you're not dating her, or a no as in you're not helping me get her number?"

The jackass has the audacity to look innocent, but the twinkle in his eye tells me something more. I lean forward and practically grit out a response through clenched teeth, "That would be a no, as in you're not going to date her. Ever."

Still feigning innocence, his grin widens. "Now why would you say a thing like that?"

"Because she's *not* available," I blurt out in a rush.

He shrugs. He fucking shrugs. "Does that go for just me, or everyone?"

"Everyone," I spit out. *What the fuck is he doing?* He's my friend. Or at least he's supposed to be. Why is he acting as if he's going to make a move on her?

"Good." Tyrell smirks.

"What?" I ask, suddenly confused.

"Good. Because you need to go into that meeting you're about to have and claim her as such. Don't back down and don't take shit from anyone. The minute I saw you on TV, at a romance conference of all things, I knew she had to be something special."

"Okay..." I draw out, still not following where he's going with this.

"You get your ass into that meeting and make them spin things the way you want them. Claim her as yours and don't let anyone take that away from you."

Dani then clears her throat. Shit. For a second, I'd forgotten she was in the room. Tyrell and I both turn our attention to the sound. Her face is flushed, obvious embarrassment written all over her face. Fuck. I can't do anything right.

I clear my throat to swallow my emotions. "Um... Tyrell, this is..." Fuck, who do I call her? Dani? Charlotte? "Um... my girlfriend..." I look to Dani, hoping for guidance.

She stands and closes the distance between her and Tyrell, reaching out her hand to shake it. "Thanks for the support. I'm

Dani Fallon, but most of the world now knows me as Charlotte Ann."

Tyrell's eyebrows pinch together in confusion and he looks to me. I jump in to clarify. "Her author name's Charlotte Ann. She's hoping to keep her anonymity, but who knows how long that will last. *Apparently*, dating me might cause her to lose it."

I walk around my desk to stand next to her. She reaches out to take my hand. "We'll figure it out." Her assuring touch calms me instantly. It's like she has magical fingers that cast a spell on me at the simplest of grazes.

We're interrupted by Harlow on the intercom. "Luke... You have ten minutes to be in Mike's office. Do you need me to drop anything at the coaches meeting?"

"I'm good. Thanks. Tyrell's here. He can handle things."

I take a few minutes to walk Tyrell through what he'll need for the meeting. He's on board with my suggestions and will pass them along to the team. It's not long before he leaves, and Dani and I are off to our own meeting.

We walk hand in hand to Mike's office. She's unusually silent. Knowing her as I do, I can tell she's nervous because neither of us know what to expect. I feel a bit apprehensive as this is the first time a personal relationship has spilled into my professional life. But Tyrell's right. If we have a united front, we'll get through it. I squeeze Dani's hand in hopes of building her confidence and mine.

As we approach the door, I feel a bit like being sent to the principal's office back in high school, when I'd participated in the senior prank and moved his car into the main hallway entrance of the school. If Dani weren't holding my hand, I'd feel worse.

We arrive to an open door. Mike sits at the center of his large conference table. Tony is to his right, and Tanya is to his left. This leaves the chairs across from them available to Dani and me. Once again, it feels like we're in the hot seats.

As we enter the room, both Mike and Tony stand to greet Dani. Before I take a seat, I announce, "This is Danika Fallon, also known as Charlotte Ann." They each greet her, shake her hand, and proceed to sit.

Mike's the first to break the silence. "Before we begin, can you give us the backstory between the two of you? I assume you didn't just meet at this book conference?" He looks between the two of us and waits for a response.

I draw in a deep breath, relieved he wants the whole picture, not just what made the headlines. "No, sir. We've been dating awhile." I clear my throat to rid my gravelly voice and continue in a much more normal tone. "We met before the season began and when her assistant got the flu, I volunteered to help. I had no idea my presence would make national news."

Tony lets out a light laugh. "I can't imagine you did." Then he looks to Dani. "Do you typically make the front page when you attend book signings?"

Danika huffs, "Hardly. If I'm being honest, I didn't even know Luke was a household name when we met. I typically stay out of the spotlight and only have a small following under my author name, in comparison."

"You didn't know who he was?" Tanya asks in disbelief.

I quickly clarify, "Nope." I chuckle at the memory. "She didn't have a clue until her brothers pointed it out when I showed up at her door one evening."

"You gotta be kidding," Mike chortles, shaking his head in disbelief.

Dani's shoulders reach her ears as she shrugs sheepishly. "What can I say, I'm a book girl. Sports and TV were never my thing. I knew he worked for the Rainier Renegades but had no idea what he did. At first, I thought maybe he was a vendor or something that traveled with the team. He was always wearing their logo on his clothes."

Mike lets out a hoot that fills the room, then he slaps his leg. "You gotta be kidding me. This is priceless. Our head coach suddenly finds a love interest. A romance writer at that. And she didn't know who he was? Since Ray Carson retired and we announced Luke as his replacement, his mug has been plastered all over the place." His deep belly laugh lightens the mood in the room. "I can't believe it."

"It's true," I offer. "It was such a relief to not have anyone know who I am, besides just Luke."

"I can imagine," Tony commiserates. "I don't know what I'd do if I had to start dating while in the public eye."

"This brings us back to the reason we're here." Mike's loud voice booms. "Luke, you've always kept your nose clean and out of the media. I had Tanya look back, and it's obvious this is the first relationship you've taken public."

"Yes, sir, it is," I agree.

"So, how do you want to spin this?" Tanya asks the room. "There are a few issues at hand. First, there's the fact the media's in a frenzy about Luke no longer being single." *Why the fuck do people care who I date? It's not like I'm a player or anything.* I'm about to say something, but she continues, "Second, he was photographed in a compromising position, selling a brand that isn't the Rainier Renegades." This comment has me sitting straighter. Tension rolls off me in waves, but Tanya's oblivious because her next point rolls off her tongue, "Third, he's dating a woman who also has a pseudo name and will likely be outed due to his exposure."

I glance to Dani, and she's sitting rigid in her chair, mirroring me. I can tell she wants to say something but is biting her lip, literally. Fuck. I have to fix this. "First of all, I can't help that the media has shown an interest in my social life. I've never dated anyone serious, so it was never an issue."

Tanya looks as if she's chomping at the bit to say something, but I press on to the point I'm most pissed about. "We have players who are sponsored and sell something that isn't the Rainier Renegades, so you can't tell me that's the issue here. I was helping a friend. Simple as that. The photo was taken out of context. I was joking around with her fans who thought I *was* the cover model. Believe it or not, it was my attempt at setting them straight. That's all." My temper ebbs as I continue, "It *wasn't* a compromising position by any means. Our players on this team wear a hell of a lot less for the promotional things they do." *I showed a peek of my abs for fuck's sake. It's not like I was fucking someone in public or making lewd suggestions.*

I force myself to take in a deep breath and calm myself before continuing. When Dani reaches out to place a hand on my thigh under the table, I feel my muscles loosen slightly. Feeling a bit calmer, I continue, "When the picture was taken, the fans in front of me didn't even recognize me as Luke Leighton, head coach. That didn't happen until later."

"Luke," Tanya chides. "You had to know you'd be recognized being at an event like that."

My brows reach my forehead as my eyes widen in response. "I had no idea this would happen. It's *never* happened in my entire career as a pro athlete or coach. Why would this be any different?"

I don't give Tanya a chance to respond. I'm on a roll now. God help her if she wants to make this more than it is. "Though..." I hesitate to formulate my response appropriately. "If I had to do it again, I'd be there in an instant to help Dani. She was stuck in the lurch, and that's what friends do." I see everyone at the table nod in agreement, so I continue, "I might not have raised my shirt to prove it wasn't me, but that's my lesson to learn."

"We're back to my original question. How do we want to spin this? You know it's going to be brought up until it's been addressed."

Everyone's quiet for a moment as we process her question.

That's the million-dollar question. Fuck, what can we do? Suddenly, it comes to me. "What if..." I start but take a minute to figure out the ramifications of my idea. Damn. It might work. I've seen it work in the past for others.

"What, Luke?" Mike prompts, leaning his elbows on the table.

I look to Dani to gauge her response. "What if we grant *one* joint interview? Set the record straight and agree to not talk about our relationship publicly again."

Thankfully, Dani nods in agreement. "I can live with that."

Tanya looks to Dani and eyes her speculatively. "But who

will she be? Danika Fallon or Charlotte Ann?" Tanya points
out. And fuck, if she doesn't have a point.

I stare into Danika's wide ocean-blue eyes. A curl has
sprung loose from her ponytail, and she pushes it behind her
ear. God, I hate that I've put her into this position. In a low
voice, I quietly ask, "What would you prefer?"

As I've seen her do before, she closes her eyes to think for a
moment. After a few breaths, she opens her eyes and inhales a
long, slow breath. "I haven't spoken with my publicist about
this, but I'm pretty sure she'd say I need to be Charlotte Ann
publicly, for now." I nod to show her support, then she looks to
the room for approval.

"I'd give you the same advice, if you were my client. I'd get
ahead of the story about you dating the famous Luke Leighton
here." She points in my direction, and I want to groan. *Why of
all things, do people care about my social life?* I knew this was a
possibility, when I took over as head coach, but there's gotta be
bigger stories than me.

"Good point," Tony pipes in.

Tanya nods in agreement. "It'll be a bigger story, if you out
her anonymity at this point. If the story comes out on its own
later, you'll have to deal with it. But it's my understanding,
most authors have a pseudo name, so her fans won't mind.
Most respect their privacy and move on."

"So... we're in agreement," Mike retakes control of the
meeting. "They'll take a joint interview with one press outlet,
and we'll make a press statement to coordinate with it."

As I look around the room, I see nods in agreement. Relief
washes through me, and I feel Dani's hand relax on my thigh.
Knowing she's not as stressed makes it so I can relax even

further myself. I fucking hate that I put her in this position to begin with.

"If that's all," Mike stands and gathers the pad of paper he had in front of him, "I have another meeting across town, so I'll be on my way." He turns his attention to Danika. "It was a pleasure to meet you. Thanks for coming in today."

"Sorry to meet you under these circumstances, but it's a pleasure to meet you, too." Dani shakes his outstretched hand.

"Thanks for being here. My wife's a huge fan, and I'm happy to be able to tell her everything's worked out."

"Wow. Thank you. Please tell her thank you for the support. I'll be sure to send my upcoming book in with Luke, when it's about to publish."

"Wow. Thank you. I can't wait to surprise her with it. Apparently, she's read all your books and is an avid fan." Mike rocks back on his heels while stuffing his hands into his pockets, as if he's embarrassed to reveal he's spoken about Dani to his wife.

"Maybe one day I'll meet her," Dani says with grace, and Mike visibly relaxes. *And I think I just fell harder for her.* God, she's so giving.

Mike smiles wide, and appreciation shines through. "Thank you." He pats her on the arm and pivots toward the door to exit.

Tanya and Tony say their goodbyes, then Tanya, Dani, and I decide when to set up the interview. When Tanya says she's going to work her magic to get an interview scheduled later this morning, I bring Dani back to my office to wait. I must say, now that there's a plan in place, my walk is a lot lighter, and I certainly can breathe easier.

26

DANI

I'M STILL NERVOUS AS HELL AFTER OUR MEETING WITH LUKE'S bosses and his PR rep. We not only have to hold an interview, but it's going to be an exclusive, which will likely make the national news. Fuck. That alone makes my belly flip, and I'm not sure I'll be able to keep my breakfast down at this rate. Luke may not think he's that big of a deal, but obviously, the world thinks otherwise. I should've known better than to think this gorgeous man who's doing everything he can to lessen my burden wouldn't have caught the media's attention. *Though, in my defense, I had no idea who he was until I after I'd already started to fall for him.*

"You okay?" Luke's deep voice is filled with concern as he looks up from his desk. Tanya couldn't schedule the interview until noon. To make things easier, I decide to stay and work from his office, while he conducts meetings and goes about his business. I typically can write from anywhere, but unlike Luke, who appears laser focused, I can't hold on to even one of the million thoughts flying through my head.

Luke's been in and out of his office multiple times. The man attends more meetings than I can comprehend. He's been out on the field with practice, met with multiple coaches, and has spent a considerable amount of time at his desk as it gets closer to the time of our interview. I had no idea what went into his job, other than standing on the sidelines making calls into his headset. My admiration for him grows as I get firsthand knowledge of the intricacies of his daily routine.

Of course, this does little help to my wondering brain at the moment.

I'd been staring off into space, apparently focused on him. His voice snaps me out of my revelry. Shit. I'd been staring and hadn't realized. Not knowing what to say, as a million thoughts flash through my brain like several freight trains wildly out of control, I opt to bite on my lip until I can think of an appropriate thing to say.

No. I'm certainly *not* all right. Sure, I've done interviews before but never at this level. My nerves are a tightly bound string, waiting to snap. I don't want to say anything and look like a fool, yet I don't want to sit there like a jackass and not say anything either. *What the fuck am I supposed to do?*

Luke stands, and it registers he's coming to me at his conference room table, when he prompts, "Talk to me."

His eyes scrutinize my every move, and his face reveals nothing of how he's feeling. He's cool as a cucumber, while I'm freaking the fuck out over what we're about to do.

Logically, I know conducting an exclusive interview will

likely give the media what they want and get them to back off a bit. But I've never held an interview of this caliber. Luke assured me he knows the journalist conducting the interview. We've opted to stay and hold the meeting here in his office, rather than the team's press conference room, to keep the focus off the Rainier Renegades. After some discussion with Tanya when she returned, she felt it would be more comfortable and relaxed keeping our interview informal and in a casual setting, like his seating area with the couches, than to sit behind a desk with the franchise logo displayed in the background.

Luke reaches for my hand that has been frozen above my keyboard for the longest time. "Come on. Let's go for a walk."

I glance at the clock, and panic sets in further. "We've only got an hour until the interview."

"Let me show you one of my favorite places." Luke's deep-blue eyes shine as the corners crease from the sexy smile, now fully on display. *Damn, with a look like that, I'd gladly follow him anywhere.*

The moment I stand, and he clasps my hand in his to lead me out the door, my heartrate slows. Somehow, the anxiety that had been paralyzing my thoughts just moments ago, loosens its hold on my body. With each step we take away from his office, or the scene of my impending doom on camera, I feel as if I can breathe easier.

When we finally get out of the executive offices, I get up the nerve to ask, "Where are we going?"

"You'll see." The excitement on his face is like a kid at Christmas. Obviously, the place he wants to show me is special. I can't imagine what it might be here at the stadium. Maybe the field? But the team's still practicing, if I heard correctly from his brief conversation with Harlow when he returned last. When he leads me up a ramp instead of down, I'm at a complete loss.

We walk at a leisurely pace through a series of corridors. Luke walks as if he doesn't have a care in the world, or a full agenda for his day. *If only I could be so calm and collected.*

When we get to the end of a corridor and a door marked, *Authorized Personnel Only*, I raise an eyebrow in his direction. Of course, he only shrugs and pulls out his key to open the damn door. I mentally slap myself for expecting an answer because as I've gotten to know Luke, one thing's for sure—that man's locked up like a vault when he has a secret to keep. When he leads me to another door that opens to the outside, I'm shocked to find there's a lookout of the city before us. Mount Rainier's off to the right and city with the Sound in the distance is to our left.

"Come on." Luke pulls me in the direction of a small bench I hadn't noticed. "Let's sit and take a load off."

"Wow. This view is amazing. I had no idea where we were going."

Luke's sly grin tells me that was the point. His deep voice makes my belly flip, but it has nothing to do with nerves. "That was kind of the point." He pulls my body close to him, placing a hand on my hip.

I swat at the air between us. "Geesh. You could've just told me."

"It would've ruined it." Now he places a finger under my chin and guides my face to look him directly in the eyes. "Now... tell me what's got you all worked up."

Ugg, where do I even begin? "I don't know..." I trail off as I gather my thoughts. Fuck. I'm articulate and precise in my writing, but when it comes to describing my feelings at this moment, I'm all over the place.

"Danika, I can't help you if I don't know what's going through that beautiful mind of yours. Are you okay with doing the interview? You've been quiet since our meeting this morning and each time I enter my office again, you've been lost in your own world. At first, I thought you were caught up in writing your story. But then you'd stop writing entirely for endless amounts of time. This isn't like you... what's going on?"

"I'm..." I look to the sky in hopes words will find me. But no such luck.

"You're what?" he calmly probes. The sincerity in his gaze has my heart stopping. I need to figure out how I'm feeling, so I can put him out of his misery. I owe him that.

"I'm... nervous," I whisper. After a long pause, I continue, "I've never done an interview of this caliber. I don't want to come off looking like an ass, or worse, an attention whore who's only after her five minutes of fame, for claiming *the Luke Leighton* as her own."

He laughs. The fucker laughs. Here I am, baring my heart, and he thinks I'm just overreacting. What the actual fuck? I'm about to tell him off, when he interrupts, "Dani," he pleads. "Please stop putting me on a fucking pedestal. I'm just Luke. I'm just an ordinary guy who'd do anything to spend time with his girl, including going to a reading conference and subjecting myself to pervy women."

"Luke..." I chastise. "*Ordinary guys* don't have to conduct interviews to set their social lives straight. *Ordinary guys* also don't need to explain to the world that they're '*off the market*.'" I use air quotes to drive my point home. "Ordinary guys can date, and it doesn't make the national news."

Luke's face heats, and I can tell I've hit the nail on the head. "Danika." His voice is gravelly and filled with concern. "What are you saying?" A flash of pain crosses his features before his face turns stony, and his expression becomes unreadable.

My stomach plummets to my toes. Fuck, he's misreading my reaction. "Luke..." I start but still can't find the words. I inhale slowly and will myself to find the words to convey my message. "Luke," I try again but with more clarity this time. "I'm nervous about the interview."

"If you'd prefer I do it solo, say the word, and it's done." His face is still unreadable, but almost apprehensive, like he's not sure about something. As I stare into his eyes, a glint of hurt crosses his features.

"Luke, all I'm saying is that you're a bit bigger than you let on. The entire country seems to know your name... I feel like the biggest idiot in the country because I didn't have a clue as to who you were."

He reaches out to brush a wayward curl from my face, and as his thumb brushes my cheek, I lean into it. "Danika, I'm still just Luke. Nothing about me is different."

"I know..." I plea, trying to figure out how to get him to understand. "It's not really about who you are..." I trail off.

"Then what is it?" He locks eyes with mine until I cave.

"I've never done an interview of this caliber. I'm afraid I'm going to fuck it up. The world's going to think I'm the biggest idiot, or worse, hate me for taking you off the market."

"I highly doubt anyone will care that I'm off the market for long. I just happen to be the youngest coach in the league, who's single. I'm new to this position, so people are skeptical. The Rainier Renegades are coming off a championship season and so far, looking quite promising for another ring this season." He's quiet for a moment, then as if another thought hits him, he waggles his eyebrows and continues in a teasing tone, "Besides, if you weren't a sexy as hell romance novelist, it might have blown over with no attention from the press."

"Uh, I wasn't the one with my abs on display for the world to see, mister. I think you may want to look in the mirror for the sudden attention." I poke the abs in question, and he flexes instinctively. "Damn, these are hard as stone."

"Dani," he chastises. "I'm being serious. We both drew the attention because in our own worlds, people pay attention. The question is... can you handle it? Do you want to continue to see how things go, knowing we'll be in the public eye, until our five minutes of fame are over, or do you want me to do the interview solo and downplay our relationship?"

My heart stutters at the thought. My stomach once again plummets, and my body's clearly telling me this isn't what it wants. "No!" I shout out a bit more forcefully than I expect. There's no fucking way I want the world to think he's available. "I don't want you to do the interview alone. I'm just nervous and trying to process the severity of this situation."

Luke leans in, and his warm breath sends shivers down my spine, all the way to my fingers and toes. "Good, because I want you there by my side." He inches closer to me before continuing, "I wouldn't do this for anyone but you. I'll take your lead on how you want the world knowing about our relationship, but I really would prefer to do it with you by my side."

He closes the distance and kisses my response away. His lips graze mine, and a fire ignites. It's a tender and loving kiss. The type of kiss that tells me we can conquer the world together. I reach for his inky black hair and run my fingers through it as we get lost in one another. Neither of us take it to the next level, but as he kisses the life out of me, he also kisses away the worry and stress of the day. This. Right here. Is where I want to be and what I need most of all. *How does this man know me better than I know myself?*

When he breaks the kiss, he pulls back to look me squarely in the eyes. "What can I do to make the interview go smoother for you?"

My heart melts right here on the spot. I know I can make it through whatever the interviewer throws at me, if I have him by my side.

27

LUKE

FOR AS NERVOUS AS DANI WAS A MERE HOUR AGO, SHE'S handling our interview with ease. She effortlessly slips into her author role as Charlotte Ann and completely charms Cara Bretz and her crew. Before I know it, we've revealed how we met and how I came to the rescue last weekend when her personal assistant came down with the flu.

Cara's been interviewing players on the team for years, so not much surprises her. But she nearly loses it when Dani shakes her head and plainly states, "I had no idea who Luke was."

"Seriously?" Cara asks, her pitch rising. She looks to me, and all I can do is shrug in defense.

"I told her my name, and that I worked for the Rainier Renegades. It's not my fault she didn't put two and two together."

Dani shakes her head and laughs at the memory.

"Seriously, Luke showed up to my house one afternoon to surprise me, while my brothers were visiting. At first, I thought their reaction to him was just typical brother stuff. You know, eyes bugging out over the fact I had company, never leaving the room, and staring like I'd never had a man over to the house. It was beyond ridiculous. It got to the point where I was about to rip my brothers a new one, for acting like idiots. I hadn't even had the chance to introduce them, and their reaction was completely obnoxious." She laughs it off and lowers her voice to a conspiratorial whisper, "I'm sure you know how brothers can be. I have three, and each are extremely protective."

Cara nods in agreement. "I sure do. It doesn't matter how old I get, they always think they have a say in my life."

"Exactly!" Dani exclaims as if it should be obvious. "Well, that's what I thought they were doing. But boy, was I wrong."

"What do you mean?" Cara prompts, and I shake my head at the embarrassing memory. I mean, seriously, I'm no one special.

Dani continues, laughter close to emerging, "It wasn't until my brother asked what 'Luke Leighton' was doing in our living room, that I caught on to *this guy*," She points to me and winks. "Was more than what he let on."

"You're kidding?" Cara clarifies. "You had no idea you were dating the youngest coach in the league, not to mention, the most eligible bachelor in Tacoma."

Christ. *She really had to go there?* This is getting beyond ridiculous. I dismiss her statement the best I can by waving a hand and shaking it off, while forcing myself not to roll my eyes. Damn, it's so fucking hard not letting my instincts come into play. But, if I've learned anything over the years, it's important not to react to ridiculous hype. This is beyond infuriating. In an attempt to divert the attention off me, I suggest, "There's plenty of eligible bachelors in Tacoma. I'm nothing to get this worked up about. Besides, the tables were turned when we were in front of her fans at the book signing. Hardly anyone even recognized me for most of the day."

"Oh, Luke," Cara says in the same tone my mama would bless my heart. It's not missed on me, that she doesn't believe the line I'm feeding her. "But they did notice you, or I wouldn't have the privilege of meeting with you today."

"You could say that again," Dani spews but then covers her mouth as if she hadn't meant to say her thought aloud. Her cheeks flash crimson as she quickly schools her features, to make it appear as if she'd meant to drop that bomb. *Damn, she's adorable. Though she'd be shit at poker.*

Thank God, Cara moves this interview in another direction. "So... Charlotte, I have to admit, I'm a huge fan of your work. I was excited to get to do this interview with you because not only am I a fan of Luke's, but I've read every one of your books. I'm dying for your next release to hit the shelves soon. Anything you want share with your superfans like me, to give them a sneak peek?"

In a well-practiced speech I've heard dozens of times over the weekend, Dani excitedly tells Cara how this may be the best book she's written. She claims, if she goes into too many details, she'll spoil the experience. But she continues to win Cara over when she ends with, "Trust me, you're going to want to read this for yourself."

"I have no doubt I will." Cara reaches out and pats Danika on the arm. Then she turns her laser-focused attention on me. "So... Luke, any predictions for the season? You're off to a great start, but will you be able to bring the Rainier Renegades back to reclaim the championship title?"

"That's the goal, Cara. But for now, we'll just focus on one game at a time. We have some great momentum going. Our focus is continuing to make improvements each week and do our best to outplay the other team. That's all I can ask for from the team and so far, each week, they've risen to the challenge."

When I leave little room for discussion, Cara thanks us once again for allowing her this exclusive interview. She wishes us the best of luck and lets us know it will likely air on this evening's news.

As Cara and her crew leave the office, I see Danika visibly deflate, as if a huge weight has been lifted. When the door clicks shut, she looks to me with hopeful eyes. "Did I do okay?"

"You were fantastic, Danika." I pull her close and hug her fiercely. "I'm so proud of you. I know you were nervous, but I think we nailed it." I take in a deep breath and let myself relax into her. My mouth waters, she smells almost edible. A subtle vanilla mixed with amber, yet something entirely all Danika, too.

"I sure hope so. I've never been on the evening news or in any interview of this caliber. I should probably warn my parents. They do watch the news on a regular basis."

I slowly exhale again, knowing the realization is true. "Yeah, you might want to do that." I squeeze her tight once more.

"I still can't believe we're making headlines."

"You and me both. I had no idea this would blow up so big. But enough about that. What do you say we grab some lunch?"

After letting Dani take my car back to my loft, I return to my office to get some work done, before I must be at the special teams meeting in an hour. Sure, I managed to do some things this morning out of necessity, but the interview hadn't been far from my mind. My stress level's decreased, especially since I plan to spend the evening with Dani, before she heads back to the island for a few days.

Walking into my office, I practically jump out of my fucking skin when the lights flicker on. There standing near my desk is a life-sized dark figure. Dark hair, blue eyes, and half-dressed. My heart pounds in my throat as I take a breath to steady myself. Thank God, it's not real, or I would've swung a punch out of instinct, in defense.

Fuck. They got me good.

From the corner of my eye, I spot more over by my conference table. *What the actual fuck?* There're at least ten life-sized cardboard cutouts throughout my office. Each have my face, but the shirtless body of the model from Dani's latest book, with abs fully on display. Someone did one hell of a Photoshop job. If I didn't know better, I'd say it was me, holding Dani's latest book, the one with the model's face cut off just above the mouth.

As I pivot around my office, my mouth drops in astonishment. Holy shit! There are also posters on the wall, with me—the actual me—from the conference this weekend.

There I am, on full display, lifting my shirt to show the comparison, as I hold Dani's book next to my stomach, with a shit-eating grin on my face. Someone went to great lengths to pull off this prank. These fuckers are good.

Shaking my head, I walk to Harlow's office. She must've seen or heard something. But to my surprise, she's nowhere to be found. Glancing at my watch, I know she's likely at lunch herself. Convenient. Very Convenient.

Not knowing what else to do, I return to my office and attempt to gather the things I need for the special teams meeting. Sitting at my desk, it's creepy as fuck. I feel like I'm being watched by the replicas of myself propped around the room. What am I even going to do with this many of them? Who the hell wants this many life-sized cutouts of themselves with a Photoshopped body? I sure as hell don't.

Whipping out my phone, I take a few photos of the displays, left untouched, and send them in a quick text to Dani.

Immediately, she responds.

Dani: Are you serious?

Me: WTF do I do with them???

Dani: Um... wanna be my new promo material? Lol

Laugh aloud, I do. *What a shit.* God, she knows how to make me laugh. Shaking my head, I contemplate my response. But before I can respond, another text arrives.

Dani: Sorry. Not Sorry – you'd make great promotional. Sexy as hell. Women would go wild. But please know, I'm totally joking.

Me: Oh, I'm laughing. I can't concentrate with all these faces staring at myself. It's really unnerving. Creepy as fuck, too.

Dani: I can't imagine.

Me: Though if they were life-sized cutouts of you, I'd appreciate them more.

Dani: Oh please... you're ridiculous.

No. Not at all, but I'll let that slide. I type quickly tap out another question.

Me: Getting any words written?

Knowing Dani's been back to my place for less than an hour, it's highly doubtful, but she's determined to finish this next book.

Dani: Not yet. I stopped to get my caffeine fix. About to get started. Shouldn't you be working?

Me: I'm trying – but I'm staring at myself, and it's distracting. Thank God, my meeting starts soon, and I won't have to sit here much longer.

Dani: Can I have at least one cutout?

Me: Depends. Will you be focusing on my face or your cover model's body?

Dani: You're hysterical.

She doesn't answer, yet I'm the one who's hysterical. Great.

Dani: Of course, it's for you... silly. Plus – it would be a great souvenir from the weekend. Though it's not likely something I'll soon forget.

I glance to my watch and tap out one last message.

Me: Got to run. Get your word count in, and I'll text you when I'm on my way home.

Dani: Don't forget to bring that home. I'm dying to see it in person.

A second later, one last text comes through.

Dani: Will it even fit in an Uber?

Me: Smartass.

Dani: Always – Get to work. I have words to write, mister.

Chuckling aloud, I stuff my phone into my pocket, grab my

laptop, and make my way to my meeting. Relieved the worst is behind me regarding unsolicited attention. But you know what they say about those who assume things...

LUKE

THE SPECIAL TEAMS MEETING GOES SMOOTH, AND I'M RELIEVED to get things back to business. I'm no longer distracted by the events of this weekend, and my steps feel lighter as I make my way to the offense meeting.

As I walk in, the room's fuller than I expect, causing the hairs on the back of my neck to rise. Members of my defense are in their typical section for a full team meeting. What the fuck? Confused, I look to my defensive coordinator and wonder. *Did I mess up the agenda for the day?* Tyrell Yates' face is impassive, and I'm unable to get a read. Spotting Brandon Reynolds at the front of the room, he smiles and simply shrugs, like I have things wrong.

Another peculiar fact about this situation is *everyone* is here, early for that matter and in their seats. I typically arrive before the majority of the team, to set up and prepare for our meetings. It appears as if my entire roster is present. To make matters worse, now that my presence is known, the room goes silent.

"Hey… uh… anyone want to tell me what's going on?" I glance to my assistant coaches and make eye contact with my captains of the team. Nothing. No one will clue me in. What the fuck is going on?

Finally, someone speaks up, "Coach?"

I look to see who finally has the balls to speak up. I'm relieved to see it's Campbell Beck. He's always been straightforward and a leader of the team. He'll set me straight. Our schedule's like clockwork, and there's no way I've messed up this meeting.

"Beck? You know what's going on?" I ask, making my way toward him. He's always been upfront with me and God knows, I don't need anymore surprises today. As head coach, I'm rarely left out of the loop, and it feels quite unnerving.

Why the hell is everyone so silent? This place usually takes a 'call to order' to get things started, and you can hear a pin drop at the moment. Well, a sneaker squeak would be more accurate. *What the hell are they up to?*

"Uh…" Beck clears his throat. "I guess we're all here to see if the rumors are true?"

This causes some snickers throughout the room, but with a look from Beck, they quickly cease. *Okay, this is interesting.*

Not following where the fuck he's going with this, I eye Beck speculatively, waiting for further explanation.

Beck stands and looks around the room as he rocks back on his feet. He slowly takes in a big breath, making me even more nervous, if that's possible. Shit. I really don't need anything else to go wrong today. If the entire team's here, something major must have happened, while I've been dealing with my own media shitstorm. I glance around looking for a clue, but still nothing.

Beck's large frame rocks twice more onto his heels before he finally speaks, "Since you missed our team meeting, and everyone wanted to be in the know..." He looks around the room, and I swear, everyone nods in my direction. "The coaches said it was okay if we joined in this one. Hope that's fine with you..."

I nod in agreement. I'm always for us being on the same page as the team, but what does this have to do with me? Before I can say anything, Beck continues, "Well..." He looks to the ceiling, then back to me as if he doesn't know how to work what he's about to say. Christ. Could it be that bad? Finally, he spits out his thought. "It seems you made the news this weekend..."

No shit. I had to have a friggin' interview because of it. But what business is it of the teams? Or the worlds for that matter? I'm just a coach, not a star player or anything. "Yes, it appears I did," I vaguely agree, not wanting to spur on any further reactions.

This time, Trent Montoya, one of the team captains, pipes in, "Will you be leaving us soon for a new career?"

"Uh... I just started this job. Where'd you get that idea?"

Trent's composure breaks for a split second, and a flit of mischievousness flashes quickly before it's schooled. "Well..." He clears his throat. "We're under the impression you're taking a different career path in the near future."

"This is news to me," I deadpan, waiting for the real explanation.

Someone hollers from the back of the room. "So... you're not planning to switch careers to modeling?"

I raise an eyebrow at the smartass speaking out. "Um... that would be a hard no."

"But, Coach, you have a huge following on social media already. You could make bank if you keep this up."

With this, everyone in the room. And I mean, Every. Single. Person pulls out an eight-by-ten photo of me—the real me. The one where my shirt's lifted and Dani's book is next to me in comparison.

Mother fucker. These bastards are taking this prank to an entirely new level. I do my damnedest to keep a straight face. But when I make eye contact with Sean Peters who's leaning against the wall with a knowing smirk, I fucking lose it. Laughter erupts from me and throughout the room. Tears spring to my eyes as I double over to catch my breath. When I finally think I can stand to face the team through watery eyes, the crowd settles.

Another smartass from the back of the room shouts out, "Can I get your autograph?"

Before I can respond, another person yells, "My wife loves Charlotte. Can I get her autograph, too?"

Not wanting to speak for Dani, I search the room looking for the culprit, as I ask the room, "Which one of you redecorated my office?" I seriously want to know how they pulled it off. The person who orchestrated it had impeccable timing.

At this point, not one single person in the room makes eye contact with me. The bastards are good, I'll give them that. They look to the floor, the ceiling, the photo in front of them.

Each has a smirk or a gleam in his eyes. They know who the guilty party is, but they're a united front, for the moment. Well, they're a team, that's for sure.

Hell, I don't even blame them. As far as pranks go, this was fucking brilliant. In my younger days, I would've been involved as well, so I can't blame them. "Maybe the better question is, what the hell am I going to do with all these photos and life-sized cutouts?"

"I'm sure we could find a use for them!" someone shouts out.

"Target practice for our accuracy?" someone from the crowd suggests.

"Sure, can't use it as an online dating profile. Charlotte wouldn't approve."

"Hey, now," I chastise and glare around the room. My social life shouldn't be a team conversation. But hell, I just had to do an interview to set the record straight. "Not that I've had an online profile, but no, I don't think she will."

This causes more laughter from the room.

"Are you endorsing books now?" comes from the back of the room. Another guy thinks he's a real joker. This time, it's Darius Wittacker, our defensive end. His smile's wide as he points to the photo in his hand. "Cuz, I gotta say, Coach... you're damn sexy in this shot." His eyebrows waggle, and the room erupts in laughter... again.

Geez... will this ever end?

Andre Adams, our starting quarterback, pipes in, "Maybe you could model for Calvin Klein, if the book deals don't come through?"

I have to set the story straight. They'll hear it soon enough, so I might as well fill them in on how my impromptu media shitstorm came to life. Maybe it will get them to back off.

"Nope." I pop the 'p' at the end to make my point clear. "Sorry to disappoint. I'm not switching careers. D..." Shit, I almost outed her. "There's not much to it. Charlotte's personal assistant got the flu. I helped her out. Simple as that."

Leaving little room for discussion, I look from person to person around the room. Once again, they remain quiet. To drive my point home, I state, "I can't imagine any of you having a close friend in need and not helping them out, if you could."

Nods can be seen around the room, but of course, some smartass can't keep his mouth shut. He just has to get one last jab in about my newfound relationship. Fuck, it's not like I was a monk. I just haven't had anyone caught in the media's attention.

"Hey, Coach, is dating a romance author all that it's cracked up to be?"

Hell yes, it is. But there's no way I'm publicly commenting about it. First, I have way too much respect for Dani to allow commentary in any way that can be construed as derogatory. Second, it's none of their fucking business.

I level Jackson, our defensive lineman, who's been known to always run his mouth, with a glare that tells him and everyone else in the room I won't be commenting on my sex life, ever. "*Romance authors* are hard-working individuals who put their heart and soul into their work. They probably work harder than you or I when it comes to effort into their job. Sure, it may not be physical, but they pore over every detail. So much more goes into writing a book than you'll ever know. I'm not sure what you're *insinuating*," I emphasize to drive my point home, "but I'm sure you mean that as a rhetorical question, right?"

I draw in a quick breath and wait for the expected jab to come my way, but as I look around the room, mouths snap shut. Apparently, they realize Jackson's just had his ass handed to him and don't want to get in line for a helping of their own.

As no one dares to speak another word about Danika, I bring us back to our original business at hand. "Last I checked, we're due to have an offensive strategy meeting." I look around the members of our D-Line. "Unless you're wanting me to switch up the roster, I'd suggest we get down to business."

"You heard what he said," Tyrell calls to the room. "I want to see you running defensive drills in ten."

With that, half the room empties, and we settle into our regularly scheduled meeting with the offense. We spend the next hour focusing on strategies to strengthen our game. We also talk about some of our pitfalls from last game as well as what we need to tighten up before next Sunday. Thankfully, no one has the nerve to mention Danika to me for the remainder of the afternoon.

29

DANI

Knowing I haven't been home in a week, I drop by the grocery store on my way to the island. Maybe I'm feeling self-conscious, maybe I'm just being paranoid, but it feels like I'm being watched. Not in a creepy way, but just that eyes are on me. But when I look around, no one's even paying attention.

Maybe it's just the hype of the interview that has me on pins and needles. As much as I didn't want to see it, I couldn't help but tune into the broadcast when it went live. Luke and I both squirmed in our seats as we snuggled on the couch to watch, since neither of us like watching ourselves on TV.

Sure, he has way more experience in dealing with the press and media, but it was cute watching him fidget when his closeup flashed across the screen. Damn, just recalling the memory, the man's good looking. Though if I'm being completely biased, he's far better looking in real life. As far as the interview itself went, it was portrayed as best as we could have hoped.

Since the segment ended, I turned off my phone and stayed off my social media accounts. I'll deal with it later today, when I get home. Before the interview, I popped into my fan group and updated them about my weekend, as well as thanked them for coming out to visit this weekend in Seattle. I mentioned going into my writing cave and won't be resurfacing for a few days. I've been known to do this. Hopefully, by the time I hop back onto social media, things will have died down.

I grab the last few items on my list and make my way to the checkout counter. As I place my items on the conveyer belt, I can't help but gasp.

Holy. Fucking. Shit. There for all the world to see is my face plastered next to Luke, taking up the entire cover of an entertainment magazine. As much as I want to grab one for a souvenir, I look around and hope I'm not noticed.

Shit. I'm not wearing anything concealing. I look almost exactly as I do on the magazine. Except, thank God, I'm not wearing the same clothes. There's no line at this time in the morning, so I take the opportunity to slip a few magazines onto the conveyer belt as the woman who's about my mother's age scans my items.

She had said hello, but I was too busy looking at myself on the magazine to give her much of a response. As she scans my final items, I make my way to the debit card reader to finalize my purchase. Just when I think I've escaped being noticed, the kind woman on the other side of the counter makes eye contact.

"You two are such a beautiful couple. I'm a huge fan of you

both, and I wish you the best of luck. I can't wait for your next release either, Charlotte."

Well... That's unexpected. I've never had a complete stranger feel the need to comment at the grocery store. My face heats, and I glance around to see if I've caught anyone else's attention. Thank God, no one's around. "Thank you." I clear my throat as I straighten my spine. I might as well own it. She's a fan after all. "My next book should be out by the end of next month. I'm glad you're enjoying them."

"Oh, I've read everything you've written. My daughter got me hooked right after you released your first book." Interesting. You never know who you'll meet out in the wild. I'm *so* not used to being recognized in public. It feels as if I've entered another universe.

"Wow." Once again, I'm at a loss for words. "Thank you so much."

The woman whose nametag reads Jackie, lowers her voice and stage-whispers, "I'm so happy you're happy with Luke Leighton. He's been the talk of the town since his arrival to the Rainier Renegades." She raises an eyebrow and partially covers her mouth so that only I can hear her next words. In a conspiratorial voice, she adds, "I must admit, I've become a bigger fan since his arrival. That man is *definitely* not hard to look at. You know what I'm sayin'..." Yes. Yes, I do know what she's saying. I've been caught staring a time or two, and I'm woman enough to admit it.

"Yes, I do." I nod in agreement. Who am I to deny the truth? But not wanting her to think I'm all about his looks, I add, "He's a wonderful man, inside and out."

"He sure is." She nods emphatically. "That interview you

two did last night was just spectacular. He's such a nice young man, helping you the way he did. I would've loved to seen him in action."

"He's amazing, that's for sure."

Another customer joins us in line, and panic sets it. I don't want another impromptu press situation and thankfully, Jackie reads my worry well and hurries the end of my purchase along. "Thank you for coming in today. I sure hope to see you again soon. Next time, you bring that man of yours in. I'm so happy the two of you are together, Charlotte. I wish you the best of luck."

"I'll keep that in mind, Jackie. Thanks again." I gather my bags quickly and walk to my car. I'm not sure how I feel about complete strangers talking about my personal life as if they've known me forever. On one hand, it was amazing to be recognized. On the other, it's absolutely terrifying.

It's late when Luke finally has the chance to call. I didn't know how much I'd missed him until I hear his warm greeting.

"Hey, Danika," he exhales heavily, and I can picture him relaxing onto his couch after a long day at work. "It's so good to finally get to talk to you." My heart squeezes, and the tension in my body releases with those simple words.

His voice is a welcomed relief after a long day without him. Who knew I could get this attached to being around him so quickly.

"You, too." I release a heavy breath and find myself instinctively relaxing into my oversized armchair as well. "Did

271

I really just leave you this morning? It feels like days have gone by, rather than mere hours."

A soft grunt comes through the phone, and a smile forms on my face. "No kidding. I'd give anything to have kept you here. But since you insisted on returning home so you could work and meet with your agent, I can't say I blame you." I can picture him with a wry smile and smirk forming on his beautiful face. When he tacks on, "Though I would've been perfectly fine letting you use my loft as a meeting place."

"Luke," I admonish. "You know she and her husband are coming to the island to stay at an Air B&B. They've had this trip planned for a while. The whole point of our meeting at the island is so they can be on vacation afterward and not be in a big city. They're getting their first break from their kids since they've been married. They deserve every moment of peace they can get."

"But isn't she a book publisher, too? Why haven't you gone with her company and published traditionally?"

"Uh..." This is such a long story. Where do I even begin? "She's the best in the business for getting book deals into movies. She knows I prefer to be an independent publisher but loves to help indie authors as much as she can. Her business thrives on both. Sam wants what's best for me. Though if she gets this movie deal we've been working on, her commission will be more than worth her while, dealing with an indie like me."

"Makes sense." I can picture Luke shrugging off my explanation in agreement. "Any word on how that deal's going?"

I sigh. I haven't had my hopes up too high over this, since I know it's a longshot. I know I have a big enough following, but I'm not sure Hollywood execs want my story. "I haven't heard anything yet. I hope she'll have more to say when we meet tomorrow."

"Well, I'm sure it will go well. From what I've read, you're pretty talented."

"Luke... You've read *one* book. For all you know, the rest of my books could suck." When I hear Luke suck in a quick breath and before he can say anything, I stop myself from letting self-doubt creep in. It has no business occupying my thoughts, so I take in a deep breath and change my course. "But thank you for the vote of confidence, it means a lot."

"I... uh, happen to be onto book two now, for your information." I can see the smile play across his lips as his admission is saucily stated.

"Seriously? Since when do you have time to read? You've been in non-stop meetings and traveling with the team."

His voice lowers, "Well, I picked it up this evening to read before bed. Since *you're* not here to keep me occupied, maybe your words will."

That is the sweetest thing ever. Leave it to Luke to melt my heart further. "If it makes you feel any better, I'd rather be there."

Another heavy exhale is heard through the phone. "I know. But it made sense for you to head home for the time being. We're traveling to Boston and staying back East until we play in Nashville the following week."

"I know..." I groan into the phone. The thought of being without him makes my heart ache. *When did this man become so important to me?* To lighten the mood, I tack on, "Adulting sucks, doesn't it?"

Chuckling, Luke agrees, "Yes. It does. But speaking of adulting, do you have plans for the week after next?"

"Uh…" I mentally play through my schedule. "Not that I know of."

"What would you say to coming to our game in Nashville?"

Not looking forward to being away from him for nearly two weeks, I jump at the chance. "Sure. Just let me know when, and I'll make arrangements." I think aloud. I've traveled quite a bit, so it shouldn't hit my pocketbook too hard. "I should have enough air miles to make the trip affordable."

"Danika." Luke stops my rambling. "I'm taking care of the arrangements right now." Now that I've stopped talking, I can hear him tapping away on his computer. "Want a window or aisle seat?" Holy shit, this man's efficient. I should've known better than to doubt him.

"Uh, window." Who wants to be bumped every five minutes? "But you don't have to do this," I assure him. "I can get my own ticket, Luke."

"Already done. I'll arrange for a rental so you can come and go as you please. I'll just need some of your information."

I give him what he needs and within minutes, I'm apparently traveling to Nashville. My heart thumps out of my chest with the thought of spending more time with him. After being with him this week, I know his schedule's grueling. How the man even made the time to spend with me was impressive. I guess I should be grateful.

"I hope you don't mind, but Mama will kill me if we don't stay with her, at least one night. After talking to her this afternoon, she insisted I do everything necessary to get you to visit her ASAP."

"Wait... You've been talking with your mom about me?"

"Uh... the interview yesterday wasn't just for local affiliates. It's a nationally syndicated show. I called and gave my family warning that we're dating, or I'd never hear the end of it. Trust me. Mama may be tiny, but she knows where to hide a body, if need be. I wasn't about to tell the world we're dating, before I told her."

As he talks about his mother, his Southern drawl slips out a bit. It's fucking adorable and sexy as hell. I hadn't heard it much before now. "And... she's okay with you bringing me home?"

"Oh, Danika, you have no idea." He chuckles as if I should know better. "In her mind, we're already getting married and ready to bring her grandbabies."

"Seriously?" I ask in disbelief. That's not at all scary. *Yeah, right.*

Though, it's not hard to picture having beautiful, dark-haired, blue-eyed babies that resemble Luke. He's a handsome man and is bound to make gorgeous babies. Who *wouldn't* want to be the mother of his children? Throw in the fact he's the kindest man I know? Yeah...

"Dani?" Luke's voice interrupts me from my rambling thoughts.

What the fuck? Why am I thinking about babies? We just started dating, for crying aloud. But butterflies make their presence known in my belly, and my denial's evident. Fuck. I'm so screwed when it comes to this man.

275

"Did you hear what I said?" Luke asks, clearly expecting an answer to an unknown question.

Hell no, I didn't. I'm too busy fantasizing about babies with beautiful blue eyes to have heard a word. Shit. I really need to get it together. "Uh, sorry. No, I didn't."

"Mama wants to spend the day with you while I'm at practice with the team. Since we're staying on the East Coast, I've arranged for us to practice a few times that week. I don't want to put any pressure on you, so if you'd rather not go, please feel free to say so." For the first time, Luke's confidence waivers. I can tell it's important to him for me to meet his mother. Hell, he's already met most of my family. It's the least I can do.

"It shouldn't be a problem, Luke. If they're anything like you. I'm sure I'll love your family."

Did I just say love? Yep. I think I did.

I hear a smile in his tone as he says, "I'm sure they'll love you, too."

We spend the next half hour talking about our day. When I hear his voice become groggy, I suggest getting off the phone. I get to sleep in tomorrow. He, on the other hand, must be at the stadium before seven. God knows how this man has lived off the little sleep he's gotten in the past few days. I know I'm beat, and I've done only a fraction of what he has.

As Sam and her new husband Enzo exit the car, she squeals with delight. "I have the best news for you, Dani!" She rushes to greet me by embracing me with a hug.

This could only mean one thing. "What's that?" I ask with excitement as she releases me from an enthusiastic hug.

"You did it! Your book's being made into a movie. I just got off the phone with the producer and by the end of the day, I should have a contract for you to look over."

"Are you kidding me?" This cannot be happening. This is just as good as waking up to finding my book had reached number one on the national bestseller's list.

"No, not at all," Sam assures me as she steps back. "I told you good things would happen if we just waited. They called this morning. I'd planned to put out another feeler, but it turns out I didn't have to. They want to work with you and from the sounds of it, you'll be able to name your terms."

"Holy shit. This is happening..." I say in disbelief.

"Sounds about right to me," Enzo says. "Congratulations!" He reaches out his hand to mine. "I'm Enzo. It's nice to officially meet you, Dani."

"Oh." Sam bats her hand in the air. "Where are my manners? Dani, this is Enzo. Enzo, Dani." Causing Enzo and I both to chuckle at her embarrassment.

"Nice to meet you, Enzo. Have you been to Anderson Island before?"

"No, but I'm looking forward to our first night away from the family. I know they're in good hands with my parents, so Samantha and I will get a good night's sleep for a change."

"To be fair, I might just pass out as soon as we get to the Air B&B. I don't think I've slept well since before we were married."

Enzo looks to Sam as if she's set the sun and the moon in the sky. I could only hope to have someone look at me that way. "I'm fine with anything, beautiful. You know that. I do hope we get to do more than sleep on this vacation though. We haven't been kid-free in nearly a year."

"Oh, don't remind me," Sam tsks. "Besides our wedding, I think we were in Germany before that. And that was far too eventful for my liking."

"Hey, neither of us knew how that would turn out." He places his hand on his chin and pretends to think something over. "If I remember correctly, you thought it was just the flu. Hmmm... I'm sure glad you were wrong."

"Hey, it turned out to be a blessing." She sighs. "But it doesn't mean I'm not exhausted."

"Do you have kids of your own, Dani?" Enzo asks.

"Oh, no." I shake my head. "I'm not ready for them yet."

"Honey, you know Dani's also known as Charlotte Ann, right? My client who's dating Luke Leighton, the head coach of the Rainier Renegades."

"Oh, right." Enzo shakes his head in acknowledgement, then explains, "I've been out of town on a job until yesterday, but Samantha mentioned something about it."

"Yeah, it's still kind of new." I shrug off. I've been working with Sam for the past couple of years. She typically doesn't work with clients like me who are independently published, but after reading my books, she wants to help me bring them to film.

"No judgement here, trust me," Enzo assures me with a warm smile. I can see why Sam's so happy with him.

"Let's go inside and work out some possible terms you want in your contract, Dani. Then we'll get out of your hair and head to the rental house. I can't wait to see if it's as cute as the online photos showed."

"As long as the bed's comfortable, I'm sure it'll be fine," Enzo teases. "A full night's sleep has been unheard of in our house."

It doesn't take long for Sam and me to hammer out the possible terms we want. She has the standard contract written and just wants to clarify a few things for when the producers contact her. Hopefully, all will go my way, and I'll have a movie deal in the next few weeks.

Before they can even pull out of my driveway, I'm dialing Luke. Energy bursts through me like fireworks on the Fourth of July. I can't wait to share this news with him.

It's torture waiting for him to pick up. Just as I think it's about to go to voicemail, I hear a rough, "Hello," come through the line. "Everything okay, Danika?" His words are clipped, filled with concern. Shit. He's probably in the middle of a meeting or practice. But I'm just too excited, and this news can't wait.

"Yes!" I practically squeal. "I did it, Luke! It's really happening!"

"What's happening?" he quickly asks, his voice still filled with concern. I can picture him starting to pace, like he does when he takes business calls and doesn't know if the news is good or bad.

I take a deep breath to steady my nerves. Who knew I'd get so worked up over this. "My book's getting picked up for a movie deal. You know, the one I told you about."

"Seriously?" he asks with shock filling his tone. "That's incredible. I knew you could do it. I really enjoyed that book."

His confidence and support fill my heart to the brim. "I'm so excited. I'll know more about the details later this week, but Sam seems to think it's a done deal."

"I'm so proud of you, Danika. When you get out to Nashville next week, we'll have to celebrate."

"Yes, we will!" I boast into the phone, still riding the high. "I've never been to Nashville. Will you be able to get away from the team and show me around?"

"I'm sure I can manage something. But Mama will likely show you all around before I get the chance. I will carve out some time each day to do something special with you."

"Luke, I don't want to keep you from your work." He's so busy as it is, there's no way I want to be a burden.

"Danika, if you're in town, I want to spend as much time with you as possible. Besides, my day's usually done earlier when we're on the road. We don't stay back East often, and the practice facilities are only available for so much of the day. The team still gets their workouts in, but our meetings are cut a little shorter. Since I'm from that area, I'd planned to spend time with my family as well."

"Are you sure you want me to come?" I ask hesitantly. Sure, I want to see him and meet his family, but I don't want to take any time away from them spending time together.

"Absolutely. I had no idea how much I wanted you there until I spent last night alone in my big empty bed."

"So... you just want me there to warm your bed," I tease, then chew on my lower lip to keep from saying anything else. Shit, why did I say that? I'm sure I know the answer to this accusation, but now that I've said it aloud, I need to hear his words.

"Danika." All humor is gone in an instant. "I want you in my life both in and out of the bedroom. Yes, having you in my bed's a huge bonus, but I want to show you around my hometown and spend time with you." *You should know that,* is heavily implied in his meaning with his last statement. And God, does it feel good to hear it.

"Me, too," I whisper honestly. "I feel the same way."

"Good." I hear some noise in the background then Luke says, "Listen. I need to get back to practice."

"Go," I urge, then tack on, "Sorry to interrupt. I was just so excited about my news, I didn't think about interrupting your work."

"You can call anytime, Danika. If I'm able, I'll answer. Congratulations on the movie deal. I can't wait to hear more when I get home."

"Thanks." I end the call with excitement still buzzing throughout my body.

30

LUKE

As I get off the plane in Nashville, I power up my phone, and notifications blow up my phone. I have a few texts from Harlow, Mama, my sister, and of course Dani. I ignore everyone for a moment and click open Dani's messages.

> Dani: Hope you had a great flight. I can't wait to see you tomorrow. What's your mom's favorite color?

I quickly tap out a response, telling Dani her favorite color is purple. There's no response after a few moments, so I click into my other messages and answer Harlow's questions first, as they are the easiest to get out of the way.

When I tap onto my sister Marie's message, my eyes bug out.

> Marie: I'm coming to town this weekend, with Becca. Tell me everything about Danika before I get there.

Be prepared to be ambushed, is the unwritten message. Becca's been Marie's best friend since middle school. She's outspoken, to the point of obnoxious at times, if you don't know her well. You never have to guess what she's thinking because the woman has zero filter. It's the one thing you can always count on, like clockwork. Becca and I have a history of either being friendly or at each other's throats because we're both competitive, though it's done out of love. She's like another older sister, and I can hear the hounding now. Somehow, I have to warn Dani. Becca's a bull in a china shop when she's on a mission, and it's clear from Marie's message—their sights are set on Danika.

I quickly tap out a response to Marie, knowing she'll send a follow-up soon.

Me: I'll call you when I get to my hotel. No need to send in the pitbull. Geesh, I'll tell you what you want. But I think you'll like her.

While I wait for a response, Brandon Reynolds comes up to me. "You staying with the team at the hotel, or with your parents?"

Brandon's known me for years. I do the best to stay with my family for at least a night, if we're in Nashville. I used to have to stay with the team, in my early years, but ever since Mike got word of my family living so close to the team's hotel, he insisted I stay with them instead, knowing I could be back to the hotel as soon as possible, if there was ever a problem.

"I'll be staying with them. Dani's coming out to meet them tomorrow."

283

"Dani?" Brandon asks apprehensively as an eyebrow raises in my direction.

Shit. I hadn't meant for her real name to come out. But Brandon's one of my closest friends here on the team. We go back a long way, and I know he won't say anything about her real name, to anyone. "Uh… Charlotte Ann is the pen name she uses as an author, to keep her anonymity."

Brandon nods in understanding. "Makes sense. Don't a lot of authors do that? Have a pen name, I mean."

"Some do," I admit. "But for now, can we keep her real name between us?"

Brandon nods. "You won't hear anything from me. Hell, I'd bet there were times this past week, you wish you had a pseudo name. You've been so popular in the news this past week, I can't imagine what it's like to go out in public. Just the social media platforms alone would scare the bejezus out of me."

"No kidding. Who the fuck cares if I'm dating? It's not like it's going to affect my performance as a coach."

"Leighton…" Brandon shakes his head as if I should know better. "You're the youngest coach in the league. Of course, eyes are gonna be on you. Add the fact that you're *easy on the eyes*, as the trend on Twitter says, and you're bound to draw attention, now that you're suddenly off the market."

"Fuck, Brand. Don't be ridiculous. I'm still just me. I wake up each day and do the best I can. How many coaches in the league have families? I'm not a lost unicorn or anything. I put on my pants just like everyone else, one leg at a time. Why the fuck do people care about my social life?"

Brandon smirks as his eyes roll to the back of his head, like

I should know better. "I hate to break it to you, man, but you have your own personal fanbase, especially with women, since you've become head coach. I know your avoid social media like the plague, but according to my wife, fans are devastated you're off the market."

"Christ," I mutter.

Brandon shrugs and levels me with a stare, the way Tyrell once had. "But tell me this, is the hype worth being with her?"

"Without a doubt," flies from my lips without any thought.

"Good to hear. Just stay the course, and I'm sure you'll be yesterday's news soon enough. She must be pretty important for you to bring her home to meet the family."

What can I say. "Yeah, she is. For the first time in forever, football isn't my only priority. Thank God, she's patient and flexible because my schedule during the season is insane, as you know."

"Don't I know it. I'm thankful my wife's understanding and isn't the jealous type. She knows I don't want anyone but her. Being on the road isn't easy when you're in a relationship, but if it's meant to be with Dani, I know it'll work out for you."

I simply nod in agreement when others from the team approach. I'm not about to open the opportunity for discussion about Dani again. Brandon and I grab our luggage and make our way to the charter bus and load with the rest of the team.

Though we pulled off a win in Boston, this past week has been hell being away from Dani. We tried to talk every day, but it wasn't enough for me. Somehow, she's burrowed her way into my life with little effort, and I'm beginning to see she's not something I want to let go of anytime soon.

After a coaches meeting to confirm the agenda for tomorrow, I text my dad to let him know I'm ready to be picked up. I'd call for a car, but I'm not sure I want people to know where my parents live. Thankfully, our property is gated, but I'm not willing to risk it with the added hype this week. Besides, Dani will be here in the morning. I don't want the media to get wind of anything.

I can't help but shake my head when Dad pulls up in his beat-up pickup he uses as a work truck around the farm. *The man has a brand-new luxury Ford F250 crew cab, but chooses this to drive into town tonight?* I can't believe he won't let his favorite truck go.

He spots me and grins widely. Before he can put the truck in park, I throw my luggage into the bed of the truck and climb into the passenger side. It smells like I remember— peppermint and his trademark aftershave. "Hey, Pops. Thanks for coming to get me."

"Anytime, son. You know that," he says in his Tennessee drawl. His deep laugh lines show as he shakes his head before pulling out into traffic. "So when will we meet this girl of yours? There must be something special about her, to have you bringing her all this way."

"No sense in denying it, Pops. I really like Danika."

Pops hums as he switches lanes and gets onto the highway. I'm not sure how to take it, but he's never been one to mince words. Whatever's on his mind will come out soon enough. In the meantime, I just lean my head back and relax from the day. Thoughts of today's plays as well as Dani flicker through my mind as the truck weaves in and out of traffic.

When we've made it out to the outskirts of town, Pops finally speaks up.

"Tell me, Luke, is this girl you're bringing home a flash in the pan, or someone you wanna hitch your ride to, for the long term?" Pops, being a rancher his entire life, has little time to beat around the bush.

I take in a deep breath and wonder how to put words to my thoughts. Pops has always been the one person I can confide my darkest fears with. As I slowly exhale, I go with the truth. "The kind you hitch your ride to and never let go. But if I'm being honest, the timing sucks. I couldn't be busier with my new job as head coach. With the season barely getting started, I know I won't have the time needed to put into a relationship she deserves."

Pops glances in my direction then returns his focus to the road. "Seems to me," he begins slowly, as if he's choosing his words carefully, and knowing Pops, he is. "If she's as special as you claim, you'll figure it out. As far as the kind of relationship she deserves, don't ya think any girl you commit to needs to accept the lifestyle you live?

You aren't changing careers anytime soon, are ya?"

"Uh, I just got this job. Why would I leave?" He knows as well as I do, I've worked my ass off my entire career to get where I am. Why would he even ask that?

As we enter the driveway and have to wait for the gate to open, Pops turns to pin me with a smirk. "That's what I thought. So..." He takes a deep breath, "if she means something to you, figure out a way to make it work. Despite all the hoopla with the media, just seeing the way you looked at her, I knew she's special."

Seriously? "You could see that... on TV?" Surely, he's mistaken.

"Luke, I may be old, but I'm not blind. Why the heck do you think your mama's so worked up over this? She's been singing Dani's praises since the second she saw that interview. We've never seen you look at anyone like that."

"What way did I look at her?"

Pops grunts, as if he's irritated. Which doesn't help. I have no fucking clue what I looked like in that interview. Why would Mama get worked up over it?

"Son, answer this instead. Maybe you'll figure it out for yourself. Since high school, have you ever brought a girl home to meet us? As in... you've made a special trip across the country to get her here?"

"Dad, Tennessee's been on the schedule all year. This isn't a special trip."

"Don't be dense with me, son."

"Never, sir."

Pops' face clearly reads, *I told you so*, but he's gracious enough not to say it. "That's right. Your mother's plannin' the day with this bell of yours because she's special. Don't let a silly thing like your job get in the way of being with the woman you love."

Love. Why would he throw out a word like that? He knows we just started dating.

Love. Is that what I feel? Sure, I think about her all the time, when I'm not working, of course. Just being around her makes me feel as if I've found something I never knew I'd been missing.

Fuck, I do love her. Just thinking about Danika makes my

heart race and my blood flow quicker. I never thought I'd fall so fast, without realizing it. But I have. There's no other way to describe how I feel toward Danika.

Silently, I revel in my thoughts as Pops steers his truck up the winding driveway. When we pull into the garage, Mama's waiting at the door with wide arms and a loving smile. As soon as I'm within reach, she hugs me in a way only my mother can. She may be tiny, but her intensity has never weakened in my lifetime. Clearly, it's been too long since my last visit. Her hug nearly takes my breath away.

She whispers, "So good to see you," as she releases me.

"Good to see you, too, Mama."

"Have you eaten? You're looking so thin."

I scoff. It's what we do. I'm six-three and over two-hundred pounds. I look anything but thin. But Mama doesn't know how to have visitors without stuffing them full of food. She leads us into the kitchen where she has a pot roast with all the fixings dished up on a plate for me.

"You didn't have to do this."

She gives me a look that says, *Of course she did*, she's my mama.

I want to argue since I ate with the team, but I know better. If I turn down food, I'll never hear the end of it. She motions for me to sit at the barstool as she dishes up a plate for my dad as well.

"We were just about to sit down when you texted. I figured we could wait and enjoy it with you."

As I take my first bite, my mouth explodes with flavor. Even though it's been waiting, it's perfectly cooked and still tender. My stomach growls, and Mama pats my arm knowingly. As I finish chewing, I add, "Thanks, Mama. This is fantastic."

Of course, I'm at practice when Dani's flight comes in. I've rented a car for her while she's here, as Danika insisted on driving herself to my parents. She didn't want to put them out any further. Between plays, I keep glancing at my phone to see if she's arrived. I wish I could've picked her up, but duty calls. We only get the practice field for so much of the day, and we need to make every second count if we're going to beat Tennessee on Sunday.

I blow my whistle after another play is made and shout. "Watch the gap, Clarke. You can't let them slip by you."

Clarke nods, and I yell, "Again."

We practice all the new plays we plan to pull against Tennessee until I know our team has them engrained in their DNA. Then I finally call it quits for the day, knowing we'll have another practice tomorrow to take care of any last-minute changes we want to make. So far, I have to say the O-line looks good. I think we'll be able to pull off a win, if all goes as planned. Our defense is ready, too. I feel confident we're doing what it takes to prepare to be our best.

As we wrap up practice, I pull out my phone to text Pops I'll be ready for a ride soon, when I see another notification arrive.

My heart soars with a mixture of relief and anticipation when I see the sender's name. A breath I didn't know I'd been holding throughout the day releases, and I instantly feel my body relax. It's been one hell of a week without her. Sure, it's been great visiting my parents and working with the team, but it feels as if a part of me has been missing.

Dani: My flight was delayed. Just getting rental car now.

My fingers fly over my keys as an inspiration hits me.

Me: Want to pick me up from practice?

Dani: Sure. I'd rather meet your parents with you, than alone. Send me the address.

I send the address, and she replies letting me know she's at the counter dealing with paperwork. Knowing she won't reply for a while, I send off one last text.

Me: Can't wait to see you. You won't believe how much I've missed you.

31

DANI

THE MINUTE I SEE LUKE WAITING BY THE CURB OF THE PRACTICE center, my heart races. I can't believe I've missed him this much. Though we talk every day, there's something to be said about seeing him in person. I'm still a block away, because I'm stuck at a light, but it gives me a chance to get my fill of his sexiness.

He's leaning against the building with one foot propped against the wall, looking into his phone. His inky black hair hangs forward and looks as if he's run his hands through it a lot during practice. While watching their last game—yes, he's made me a fan—I noticed when the game got intense, it's one of his trademark moves.

He's wearing dark jeans that cover his muscular thighs perfectly and a navy hoodie that fits like a glove over his muscular chest. Damn. This scene. Right here, might need to be in a future book... If only I could write.

Since he left a week ago, I've hardly gotten any words

written in my latest book. I'm not sure what's gotten into me. I never get writer's block, or if I stumble, I'm usually able to write myself out of the block. Maybe it's the stress of the movie deal. Maybe it's the fact I miss him. I have no freaking clue. My mojo's off, and I need it back, as soon as possible. My next book won't write itself.

The light turns green, and I roll down the passenger window as I pull up to the curb beside him. "Hey, sexy, can I offer you a ride?" I suggestively waggle my eyebrows once I've gotten his attention.

"Not sure my girlfriend would approve." He sighs. "She's a sexy author with a vivid imagination. She might not approve of me getting in the car with a hot woman, such as yourself."

"Flattery will get you everywhere, Luke Leighton. Get in, and let's go meet your parents. I'm nervous enough as it is, I don't want to keep them waiting."

"If you insist. Though there are a thousand hotels we could stop at along the way. I'm just not sure I can wait to have my way with you until bedtime."

"Tisk, tisk." I shake my finger at him. "Your girlfriend won't approve of such behavior," I tease.

He reaches in to give me a welcoming kiss, but of course, I can't help myself. I kiss him senseless. Well, at least until I hear a horn honk near us and someone shout, "Get a room!"

I pull back embarrassed. I'd lost track of our surroundings. I should know better, especially after the media fiasco.

But Luke's grin is contagious. "God, I've missed you."

His hand reaches for the base of my neck and pulls me close once more. This kiss is a lot more controlled but just as panty melting. When he ends the kiss, he pulls me in for a tight hug. God, this man smells delicious. His sexy scent invades my senses, and I just want to be alone with him.

Luke's gravelly voice fills the car once we right ourselves. "We should probably get to my parents' before I decide staying at the nearest hotel is the better option."

"That does sound tempting," I admit. But I know better. I turn on my blinker and merge into traffic. "Lead the way, Luke. Lead the way."

Of course, we go to his parents'. His mother welcomes me with open arms, literally. From the moment she sees me in the driveway, she rushes out the door, arms spread wide, and pulls me into the tightest hug I've ever experienced. Thank God, Luke warned me, or I might not have been able to breathe. He told me the trick was to hug her just as fierce, and I'd survive.

"My, you're even better looking in person, Danika," she gushes, causing my face to heat and me to stammer on my words as I thank her. She asks about my flight and about Luke's day with the team. She must've been one of his biggest fans growing up because the way she talks about football is like the way Sandra Bullock portrayed the mom in that movie The Blind Side. This woman keeps Luke on his toes and makes him justify his decisions, like nobody I've ever seen. And I think I fall for her, too, right in that moment.

Eventually, she states, "Let's get you two inside. I have supper ready."

"Thank you, Mrs. Leighton. I haven't eaten since before I

got on the plane this morning," I admit as we walk through the door.

"Oh, none of that Mrs. Leighton business. I love my mother-in-law, but every time I hear that name, I look around for her. Please, darlin', call me Mona."

Walking into the kitchen, I'm blown away by the smell of a roast cooking. My mouth waters, and I can't wait to try what she's fixed.

"Mama, it smells great." He pats his stomach like he's just as eager to eat. Then he adds, "Thanks for making my favorite."

"Like you'd ever have to ask." She shakes her head and walks behind the kitchen island to the stove, where a giant roast with all the fixings are still in the roasting pan, waiting to be served.

An older version of Luke walks into the room, and Mona asks, "Ken, Honey? Are you ready to cut that roast for us?" Her Southern drawl is slight but still pronounced. Her friendly attitude puts me at ease, and my nerves begin to settle. Not having to meet anyone's parents in years, I hadn't realized how worried I was about meeting Luke's until I feel my muscles relax.

"Ah, you must be the Danika?" Since his wife has already put him to work, he nods from the other side of the counter in my direction. "It's a pleasure to finally meet you. I've heard great things."

"Oh, gosh," I stammer. "Don't believe everything you hear."

"I tend to wait and make my own judgements." His eyebrow cocks, just like Luke's when he's teasing, and the family resemblance is even more predominant. Luke will age well, if he's anything like his dad. And doesn't that make the butterflies in my belly flop, but for an entirely new reason.

"Good to know." I laugh in agreement and to cover the thoughts flying through my head.

"Any word on when Marie will get here?" Luke asks his parents. "She said she's coming with Becca."

"Well... let's see..." Mona looks to her watch. "She said Conner has a big project at work due on Monday, I expect her and Becca to arrive anytime. I actually thought you were them when you pulled up. Oh..." she suddenly gasps, "with the two of them coming, the two of you will need to stay in your old room, if that's okay with you, Danika."

I glance nervously to Luke. What am I supposed to say? It feels like a red flashing sign shouts to the room, telling everyone our intentions if we sleep in the same room. Not that I'm complaining about spending the night with Luke, but should I really tell his mother this?

Thankfully, Luke responds before I have to. "Sounds great. I'll just grab her things from the car and go wash up for supper. Want me to call Marie to see when we can expect her?"

"Good. That'll give us a chance to get to know Danika better." And as comfortable as I once was, I can't control the fact that my heart skips a beat. Sure. His parents seem nice enough, welcoming even, but to be left on my own with them, does make me a little nervous.

Luke looks to me and silently asks if I'm okay with this arrangement. My heart pings, and my stomach flutters at the thought of him taking the time to make sure I'm all right. I nod that I'm fine and ask, "What can I do to help?"

"Oh, darlin'," Ken dismisses. "You're only a guest for the first time in this house. I'd take advantage of it, if I were you. After that, you'll be pitching in, just like the rest of us."

Putting me back at ease in an instant, I can see where Luke gets his charm. His dark-blue eyes twinkle and wide smile are so much like Luke's, it's crazy. I take in a deep breath to focus my thoughts. *Geesh. What has gotten into me?* "Okay, if you insist. But I'm from a big family; I'm not used to just sitting around and being waited on."

"Oh, don't get too used to it," Ken teases. "From the sounds of it, you'll be back soon enough, then we'll put you to work. Sit. Relax. Can I offer you a glass of wine?"

Feeling dehydrated from the flight, I suggest, "I'll just take some water, thanks."

Within seconds, Mona takes a glass from the cupboard and fills it with ice. "Is there anything else I can get you, honey?"

"I'm good, thanks." I take a moment to look around the kitchen. It's open and inviting. The color tones are yellow with splashes of red in the art and accents she has decorating her home.

"You mentioned you have a big family?" Mona prompts, and I need little invitation to tell her about my parents and brothers. I quickly fill her in, much like I did with Luke when we first met. Just as I'm telling her how Damien's finishing his senior year at the University of Washington as a civil engineer, Luke returns, placing his hand at the small of my back as he stands beside me at the island that separates his parents and myself. I'm not sure how he does it, but that simple touch sends a tingle up my spine and calms me at the same time.

"Pops, you'd get a kick out of Damien. He's a hard worker and has a good head on his shoulders."

Ken nods in agreement, but I add, "Davis is the brains of the family, wanting to be a doctor and all."

Luke nods. "True, but I think brains run in the family You have a tremendous way with words, Danika."

Why is he bringing this up now? We're not here to talk about me. "Oh, Luke," I stammer awkwardly, not knowing what to say.

"Well, I'm hooked," his mother adds to my surprise. "I picked up one of your books after your interview, to know what the hype is about, and I think I'm on book three or four of your first series. I absolutely love them."

Holy shit. His mother's read my books... and likes them. Don't get me wrong, I'm proud of my work. But knowing she's read the hot sex scenes, and can still look me straight in the eye, is something. Don't even get me started on the fact she probably knows I'm likely fantasizing doing said things to her son... Fuck, is it hot in here? I push a lock of my hair out of my face as I gulp my water and nearly down the rest of my glass in an instant.

Finally, when I have my wits about me, I remember my manners. "Thank you. I've enjoyed writing them."

"I absolutely love Rhonda and Cameron," Mona boasts. "They cracked me up with their constant bickering. I love enemies to lovers stories."

"Their fights were spectacular," Luke interjects.

"Am I the only one in the room that hasn't read your books, Danika? If so, then I need to change that. I don't like to be left out of the loop."

Oh, God. Please, no. I want to be able to look him in the eye and not know he's read my books. I never prepared myself for this. I wouldn't want my dad reading my books, and I certainly don't want Ken to read them.

Thank God, Mona interjects, "Since you typically stick to non-fiction, these might not be up your alley, Ken."

"What's not up his alley?" a woman who resembles Mona asks as she enters the room with a tall, blond woman right on her heels. There's no doubt who Marie is, that's for sure. Luke's family has predominant genes. Every single one of them is gorgeous and confident in their own skin.

"Oof," Mona quickly dismisses the thought. "Your father says he might start reading romance novels. As much as I love them, I really don't think he'd appreciate them the way we do."

"I don't know," Luke interjects. "I've enjoyed them. But then again, I have a thing for the author." He pulls me close from the side and grazes a kiss on the top of my head. "Marie, Becca, this is Danika. AKA – Charlotte Ann. But we'll keep that part between us."

"Nice to meet you." Marie holds out her hand to shake mine. "I've been dying to meet the woman who's captured Luke's attention. Huh... I can't say I've ever said that before. Until you, his life's been rather private."

Uh... how do I take that? He's certainly more famous than me. Sure. I'm known in my author world, but until meeting Luke, no one recognizes me outside of the book world. Now I get recognized at grocery stores... never planned on that happening.

Thankfully, I don't have to say anything because Luke says it for me, "Well, Marie... I've never had anyone worth going public for. Not that either of us planned the shitstorm with the media. That took on a life of its own." He laughs lightly then adds, "I had no idea helping Dani would get so much attention."

"It wasn't that bad, Luke." Marie sighs. "Though, I never thought your abs would go viral... Your face maybe... *but having my friends going gaga over my brother's sex appeal?* That's just weird." Marie makes a face as if she's sucked on something sour, and I school my features to not show my reaction. I'd probably feel the same, if one of my brothers had that happen to them, but damn, she's hilarious. It's evident she loves her brother, but she can give him a run for his money, that's for sure.

"Gee, thanks." Luke rolls his eyes dramatically then deadpans, "When do you leave, again?"

"Oh, hush." Marie bats the air between them. "You know you love me."

"That doesn't mean I have to like you," flies off Luke's tongue before anyone bats an eye.

I cover my mouth in my best attempt to stifle a laugh, but when Ken grumbles, "Children... company," I lose it.

Through laughter, I manage, "Don't stop on my account."

"Or mine." Becca giggles. "This is getting good."

"Becca," Luke growls. "Don't encourage her."

Becca's eyes roll as she shakes her head. "Luke, I've known you all for years. When has anyone been able to stop Marie?"

"True." Luke shrugs. "She's a force to be reckoned with, especially when she gets on a roll."

Becca places a finger on her chin as if she's contemplating her response. "True." She nods in agreement. "It's like raking leaves in a hurricane. You might as well let her say her peace, because there'll be no stopping her."

"Uh... I'm standing right here," Marie interjects, hands pressed to her hips defensively.

Mona steps between them with a plate filled with roast. "That's enough, you two. Let's eat supper and call it a truce." When she places the food on the table, she turns to Luke. "Luke, baby. I love you more than chocolate, but please stop showing the goods for the world to see. The girls at my book club were having a heyday. I had to walk out with my ears plugged because some things are just plain wrong for a mother to hear."

"Christ," Luke grumbles as his face reddens. "I so didn't need to know that."

Humble Luke's adorable. We walk to the table, and I reach out to squeeze his hand for support. Then I whisper so only he can hear, "I don't mind seeing the goods."

He bends down to brush a kiss to my cheek as he pulls out a chair for me. Then whispers, "Promises, promises."

My heartrate spikes as my cheeks heat. Maybe I should have taken him up on the offer of staying in a hotel?

32

DANI

AFTER DROPPING LUKE OFF AT THE PRACTICE FACILITY EARLY THIS morning, I take a few minutes to find a local coffeeshop on my phone to slip into and get some work done before I meet Mona, Marie, and Becca for lunch. They're showing me around Nashville this afternoon, but I have to get some words written before I can enjoy the sights.

It's barely seven in the morning when I settle into a table to write. There are a few people visiting in the corner and a line of three to four people at the counter, while I quickly go through my routine of getting ready to write. My music is set, earbuds adjusted, and notebook's set up next to my computer, while I wait for my order to be delivered.

Needing to get into the flow with my words, I quickly scan the previous chapter and make a few adjustments here and there to help with editing later. When I get to the point where there are no more words written on the paper, my order's delivered to my table.

"Here ya go, hun." An energetic woman who sounds as if she's been injected with more than her daily dose of caffeine bops to my table. "Is there anything else I can get for you?"

"I'm good, thanks." I nod in appreciation as I take my drink and breakfast sandwich from her.

I assume she'll just bop along to another customer as I glance to my laptop. But from the corner of my eye, I see her shift her weight from foot to foot and oddly remain standing next to me. Lifting my head to see what's keeping her, I notice her face is flushed, and her eyes are wider than when she arrived. *What the hell is wrong with her? Why is she just standing there?* The place is filling up, and other customers surely need their orders.

"Uh..." I finally break the silence. "Is something wrong?" I ask when curiosity gets the better of me.

"You're... You're Charlotte Ann..." she says, barely above a whisper.

Flattered and shocked to be recognized outside of Washington, I reply, "I am."

"Ohmigod." Her voice raises slightly, but not enough for others to notice her enthusiasm. "I'm a huge fan. Are you sittin' down to write, here in our café?"

I smile graciously, not wanting to make a big deal. "That's the plan." I eye my laptop, hoping she'll take the hint. But she just stares in my direction and bites on her lower lip. She lives near Nashville; surely, she's seen famous people before?

I glance around and am relieved to not be drawing further attention.

"Wow, this is amazing." She stares for a moment longer then shakes her head as if to clear her thoughts. "This may sound crazy, but I actually have your latest book in my bag. Would it be too much to have you sign it?"

Holy shit, a true fan out in the wild. I've never had someone approach me out of the blue before and ask for my signature. This is surreal. I stare at her and revel in my thoughts for longer than I should before her raised eyebrows draw my attention. Shit. Don't be a dumbass, Dani. Answer her. "Uh, yeah. Sure. Just bring it out when you have a chance."

"Ohmigosh!" the young waitress practically squeals, as her long, brown ponytail swishes in both directions from her body bouncing with excitement.

"Jennifer," a woman from behind the counter demands her attention. "I need you to take this order out."

Before Jennifer returns to work, she whispers, "Thank you so much. I'll bring it out on my next break."

I sigh, relieved she's not making a huge deal out of this. "I'll be here."

When she leaves, I do my best to get back to writing, but it's of little use. I can't for the life of me get my words to flow onto the page. I type a sentence or two, realize they're utter shit, erase them, then try again.

Before I know it, thirty minutes have gone by, and I barely have a paragraph written. *This fucking sucks*, I internally groan. I have a bit of time before my next book is due, but each day, I need to meet the goals I've set for myself, or I'm fucked when my deadline approaches. In the past week or two, my brain's been shit for getting words written. *What is wrong with me? This never happens.*

Glancing at my watch, I realize I still have an hour before

I'm to meet Luke's family. I slowly inhale to clear my mind, but it feels as if a million thoughts are exploding at once, and not one of them will help me write this scene. Closing my eyes, I do my best to focus on my breathing for a minute or two, to re-center my focus.

Of course, Jennifer uses this time to approach me again. "Is this a bad time?" she whispers.

Opening my eyes, I see she's nervous, but she has no need to be. "No." I might as well visit with her. To cover for my rudeness, I add, "I'm just stuck in a scene. Sorry. Please, take a seat."

"No worries. I can't imagine what it's like to be inside your head," Jennifer states in awe.

Rolling my eyes at the plethora of thoughts that are jumbled at the moment. "It's not all it's cracked up to be, trust me. I'm a hot mess at the moment," I admit.

"Are you working on Rowan and Callie's story?" she probes.

Yep, she's a true fan. And relief washes through me. For some reason, it's easier to talk with people who really like my books. She must follow me on social media, because I've only mentioned their names a few times.

"Yes, I'm writing a scene that'll give away some major plot points if we discuss it too much, but for some reason, they're deciding to be difficult at the moment," I grumble.

"Well, if they're anything like your other characters, I'm sure their story will unfold as time goes on. Just give yourself time and relax. From the sounds of it, that's how your process works, right?"

I state the obvious. "I take it you're in my fan group."

Jennifer's smile widens. "Yeah, I have been for years. I don't think I've introduced myself. I'm Jennifer." She reaches out her hand. "It's a pleasure to meet you in person, Charlotte."

Now that she says her name, and I look closer at her, I recognize her as being one of my fans from the beginning. "Wow, Jennifer, it's a pleasure to meet you, too. Have you always lived around Nashville?"

"Yep, born and raised. My cousin went to school with Luke Leighton. I'm so happy the two of you are together." Seriously, the world keeps getting smaller and smaller.

At first, I think it might be awkward to talk with Jennifer, but I quickly find that isn't the case. She tells me she's finishing her bachelor's at Middle Tennessee State University in Murfreesboro this spring. We discuss what she'll do after graduation, since her major is in communications and minor is marketing. We also discuss our love for all things in the book industry. Our conversation quickly turns to our favorite authors. We both wholeheartedly agree we love books that have amazing characters, combustible chemistry, and enough suspense to keep us burning through the pages.

When her break is over, she asks, "Do you mind taking a selfie with me? This just totally made my day."

"Of course not!" I notice we get some looks from surrounding customers, but I try not to think about it. I pull out my phone as well and after we're done, I post in my reader's group, it was so nice to meet her and wish her the best of luck in school.

By the time I settle into writing some more, my alarm signals, telling me it's time to leave. Shit. I don't want to be late to meet his family. They probably already think I'm a freak for leaving so early to get some writing done. Well, I attempted to write, but no such luck. I quickly gather my things and head to the car. I guess I'll have to make it up later. Who needs sleep, right?

When I arrive, the girls are dressed and waiting to play tour guide. They let me drop off my things then rush me out to the car. I'd arrived earlier than expected, but Mona insists we get started if we're to see everything I want to today. After finding a place to park near the Country Music Hall of Fame, Becca suggests we walk down Broadway first. I'm in awe of the amount of people here on a weekday. As we walk along the street, music can be heard everywhere. It has a magical feel as we bop along between the shops and bars. When the music hits us, we stop into several bars along the way to enjoy the atmosphere.

When Marie suggests we stop for some lunch, we all pile into a crowded bar and sit at one of the high-top tables to enjoy the performance on stage. The band takes requests and from what I can tell, they play just about every genre out there. When we walked in, they were playing an old Merle Haggard song, then they switched it up to Luke Bryan.

Becca calls out, "Play some Taylor Swift," as a joke and sure enough, they break into "Shake it off," like it was something they play daily. It's impressive how they can switch gears so fast.

Mona, Marie, and Becca are easy to get along with. The fear I'd had is put to rest, and I quickly find myself swaying to the music and singing along to the songs I know in my mind. The atmosphere's something I've never experienced. The crowd in the bar is filled with humor, and everyone just wants to have a good time.

After we finish our lunch, Mona suggests, "The Grand Ole' Opry is on the next block, let's go in there."

We quickly purchase our tickets, and my heart races as I eagerly wait to see the museum and the stage itself. I've watched performances over the years, and I'm eager to see what it really looks like.

"Oh my goodness, can you believe Dolly Parton is that tiny?" Marie points out a petite costume display Dolly once wore. She's much shorter and skinnier than I could have ever imagined. Down to her beautifully designed shoes, Dolly Parton has class and style.

When we walk into the auditorium itself for the Opry stage, I'm blown away at how quaint it feels. From television, you can never tell how big the hall is, but it's much smaller than I expect. The acoustics must be amazing to see a live show.

Mona settles in beside me and mentions, "I remember a time when Luke and Marie would put on shows in our living room."

"Really?" I ask in disbelief. "Luke never mentioned anything about being musical."

"That's only because I made him," Marie pipes in. "He plays the guitar better than me, but obviously, he loved football more."

Surely, I've heard her wrong. "Luke plays the guitar?" I've never seen one at his house.

Marie nods. "Yeah, you should have him play sometime. He's got a great voice, too."

Why did I not know this? Is there anything the man can't do?

"I think I still have his old guitar at the house." Mona looks as if she's trying to remember something. "I'm not sure he's played much since college. He claims he hasn't had the time."

"Now, I'm intrigued," I admit.

"Oh, make sure you have him play 'Lovebug' by George Strait. It was his 'go-to' song to get the ladies back in the day." Becca giggles.

"I doubt he had trouble getting girls," I deadpan. But inside, I'm curious.

"Do you remember the time he entered that talent show contest and played that for the girl he'd been crushing on?" Becca asks.

"Ohmigod, yes!" Marie gushes. "The poor boy thought he'd impress her, but she only had eyes for Bobby Jacobs."

Marie adds, "I felt so bad for him. But I have to say, he got a lot of attention from others after that. Then when he made the team as a varsity starter his freshman year, all the girls came out of the woodwork, including that Sarah. I was glad to see he was over her by then. I don't remember him playing guitar much after football took over his life."

I'm dying to know more, but Becca changes the subject by pointing out another display on the far side of the room. and we rush off to see it. I can't wait to confront Luke about his musical abilities when I see him next.

By the time we get back to Luke's parents, I'm burnt out. My feet ache, and I know more about country music than I ever expected. I've always had a wide taste for music, but I didn't know how influential it was until I went to the Country

Music Hall of Fame and my walk through Nashville. I could've spent days there, rather than mere hours.

My favorite part about the day was getting to know tidbits about Luke and his family. I was filled in on many family stories as they reminisced throughout the day. Even Becca had funny stories to share and felt no need to hold back her thoughts on Luke throughout the day.

When I walk into his parents' living room, my energy returns at the sight of Luke and his dad, watching what looks like a game tape. My pulse races, and I pick up my pace to close the distance between us.

"There you are," Luke announces as he turns off the television and stands to wrap me in a hug. "I hope you're still talking to me after hearing God knows what from these two." He gestures to Marie and Becca, who suddenly look as if they're the cat who's eaten the canary and won't make eye contact with anyone.

"Oh, it wasn't that bad," I offer.

"Are you tired, or would you be up for a little tour from me?" Luke's eyes fill with delight and even if I have to drag myself, I know without a doubt, I'd follow him anywhere.

LUKE

"WHAT DO YOU HAVE IN MIND?" DANI LOOKED TIRED WHEN SHE entered the room, but a newfound energy has replaced it. Secretly, I hope it has something to do with me.

"It's a surprise. Grab your coat and purse, and I'll meet you in the kitchen."

Dani seems hesitant but does as I ask. I know she's not one to wait for surprises. She's like a kid in a candy shop who hates waiting for a treat. As soon as she leaves the room, I turn to Pops with a knowing grin.

"You'll tell Ma and the girls we'll be back late, and not to wait up."

"You just enjoy your night with Danika. I'll handle everything here." Pops grins widely but doesn't say anymore.

When Dani returns to the kitchen, I usher her out the door before anyone has a chance to stop us. When we reach the car, her body trembles with giddy excitement. "Where are we going?"

"Not gonna tell. So, stop asking." I smirk as I hold the door open for her.

She reaches up to her tiptoes and brushes a kiss to my lips. "You're lucky I like you, or I just might have to thump you." She pretends to scowl, and my smile carries me around to the other side of the car.

As we travel to the other side of town, I ask about her day. She gushes with excitement about all the things my family showed her. I can tell she enjoyed herself. But when I ask how her book is coming along, her expression turns dark.

"Uh... not very well. I haven't been able to write for the better part of a week or more. It's really frustrating."

This is news to me. A week is an eternity to her. Concerned, I ask, "What changed?"

Dani shrugs and looks out the window. "Not sure. I write a lot, but when I go back to re-read any of it, I end up deleting it all. Nothing flows as it should. I hope I get out of this funk soon. It really sucks having daily word counts of crap filling the pages."

"I'm sure it's not that bad." In an effort to comfort her, I reach out to place my hand on her thigh, giving it a light squeeze. "Anything I can do to help?"

Her heavy sigh tells me no, and her words confirm it. "I wish. I just need to get out of my own head and stop doubting myself. In the meantime, I'll just keep writing."

Not knowing what else to say, I squeeze her thigh once more. When she places her hand over mine, I know things will be okay. With her simple touch, I feel her muscles loosen. Her head falls back to the headrest, and she takes another calming breath. I wish there was something I could do for her. Maybe this surprise will help.

About thirty minutes later, I pull off the highway to drive down a dark well-known street. Dani eyes me quizzically but knows better than to ask. When we reach our destination, she raises an eyebrow.

"You've brought me to a bar? What's so special, you needed to keep it a surprise?"

"You'll see." I smirk as I exit the car and quickly make my way to the other side to help her out.

Placing my hand on the small of her back, I lead her into the bar. As the door opens, the music gets louder. The lights are dim, and the smell of alcohol permeates the air. This was one of my favorite hangouts back in college. There's live music a few nights a week and occasionally, someone big will just come in to hang out for a set or two. I just brought her here so I could spend time with her outside of the media and my family's attention.

I guide her to a booth and offer to help her with her jacket. She slides into the seat, and I sit on the opposite side. Instead of looking at me, she takes in the room. There's a busy bartender mixing drinks, a crowd at the stage dancing to the music, and patrons fill the tables in the center of the room as well as booths along the side. It's just like I remember.

Before I can ask Dani what she thinks, I hear, "Luke Leighton, is that you?"

Dani's instantly on edge as I turn to see Sandy, the owner of the bar, fast approaching with a wide grin. "What on earth are you doin' in this neck of the woods? I thought you'd be staying with the team while you're in town."

"Hey, Sandy. It's good to see you. I'm with the team during the day, but I'm staying with my parents."

"I saw on television that you're finally off the market. Boy, the girls around here were sad to see that happen." She then turns to Danika. "Hello, Charlotte. I'm Sandy. I run this joint." She points over her shoulder to the bar. "If there's anything you need, don't hesitate to ask." She focuses her attention back to us. "I'm happy for the two of you. Don't listen to a word the media says, girl. This guy is one of the best men around."

"You've known Luke long?" Dani asks, curiosity filling her features.

"Since he was knee-high to a grasshopper. Back in the day, his folks were neighbors of mine. I'm a couple of years older than his sister. But we knew each other."

"What she's too kind to tell you is that I used to play for her dad, so I was always around, pestering her and her friends."

"Oh, Luke." Sandy shakes her head. "You were always one of the good ones. I'm just so happy to see you. I can't believe you're all the way out in Tacoma and made your dream come true. You know I'm a die-hard fan of Tennessee, but when we're not playing the Rainier Renegades, I'm a huge fan."

"Thanks, Sandy. Be sure to tell your folks hello for me."

"I will." She then pulls out a menu from her apron. "Just let me know when you're ready to order. Ya'll are in for a treat tonight. Nick Conners from the band Riser is here for the evening. I've begged him to play a set for us, reminding him I was one of the few who gave him his chance when he started years ago. He's from your neck of the woods, out in Portland, but he's played here quite a few times over the years."

"I've been to a few of Riser's shows," I announce. "The band's amazing. But what's he doing here on his own?"

"Oh, I'm sure he came to get away from it all, but I called in a favor. Besides, he's only gonna play a few songs. It's not like it'll be a full set or anything."

I nod in understanding. Something tells me, Sandy will get anything she sets her mind to. "Can I have an IPA? You pick what you think is best." I trust Sandy implicitly. She's never steered me wrong when it came to good beer. I turn to Dani, "What would you like?"

Dani's face lights up. "I'll have what he's having. I'm ready to try something new."

"Okay, folks, be right up." Sandy sashays to the bar as quickly as she arrived.

"So, what's the real reason you brought me here?" Dani asks.

"I knew you could use a break. You've been with my family all day, and I, as much as you, are a people person. You need your downtime, too." Her eyebrow raises as if she knows I haven't spilled it all. "Besides, I wanted to take you out and knew this place would be safe from the media. Sandy values her customers' privacy."

"Okay..." Dani draws out as if something else is on her mind. "Will this include dancing?"

Dancing had been the last thing on my mind, so I answer truthfully, "It wasn't in the plan, but if that's what you'd like to do, I won't object." The thought of Dani swaying to the music, my hands on her hips and watching her let loose, does something to me. My pulse races, and my jeans tighten. Hell, if this woman wanted me to dance all night, I'd happily oblige.

"Don't you have an early morning?" she asks, reminding me of reality. Christ, I sure as hell do, but I know she needs time with just the two of us. Besides, we currently can't go out on a date at home, without being bombarded.

"Who needs sleep?" I tease to lighten the mood, knowing I'll have to put an end to tonight's activities sooner than I would want. Beggars can't be choosers. I'll take what time I can get with the gorgeous woman across from me.

Dani leans forward onto the table, "Yeah, right." She knows me better, but at least she plays along. "What do you say to getting out on that dance floor, letting off some steam, then heading home early, so you can be fresh for the game tomorrow?"

Could this woman be anymore perfect for me?

Sandy comes back with our beer before we can get out of the booth to dance. "Here ya go," she says in her typical chipper fashion. "Can I get you anything from the kitchen?"

"No, thanks, Sandy," I reply. "We're good for now."

Before heading to the dance floor, Dani and I take a moment to taste the drinks Sandy brought. It tastes cold and refreshing as it slides down my throat. When I look up to see Dani licking her bottom lip, I want to haul her home, rather than the dance floor.

She takes another drink, and my body heats as I watch her lick her lip again. Of course, she catches me watching. "You ready to dance?"

"Sure." I stand from my side of the booth and offer her my hand. As we make our way onto the dance floor, I'm grateful to have other people already enjoying the music being played. It's a song I'm unfamiliar with, but the tempo's upbeat, and I easily find the rhythm.

The best part about this scenario is watching Dani move. She sways freely to the beat, causing my blood to set on fire. She turns her back to me and watches the musicians perform, while I step closer to her, in an attempt to hide my erection. I keep a slight gap between us, so she doesn't find the evidence of my attraction herself. Damn, even in jeans and a simple top, this woman does something to me. She's wearing a simple pair of black flats, making her fit perfectly under my chin.

The band switches songs and slows to a basic two-step beat. Dani instinctively turns to face me, wrapping her hands around my neck. I pull her close for the briefest of kisses, before settling my left hand at her hip and gripping her right hand in my mine. I lead her around the dance floor, practicing moves I'd learned years ago. Mama would've tanned my hide if I didn't learn to properly dance as a boy. I can't help but grin when I remember the way Mama taught me. Dani picks up the rhythm instantly, and we make our way around the floor with ease. Occasionally, I push her out for a spin or try to change up the moves to keep her on her toes, but Dani being Dani, keeps up with ease.

All too soon, the song ends, and the band announces they're taking a short break, and Nick Conners from Riser will be honoring us with his presence this evening between their set. Dani pulls me back to the booth, while we wait for Nick to set up.

"I'm starving," she announces when we return to the table. "Are the burgers good here?"

"The best," I eagerly reply, remembering the savory taste of

Sandy's special sauce. It's been years since I've been here, but my mouth waters at the thought alone. I motion for Sandy's attention and quickly place an order, including her famous hand-made curly fries.

After we finish our meal, Dani drags me out onto the dance floor for a couple more songs. I have to admit, it's nowhere near a hardship having Dani in my arms. Her soft skin on mine, delicious scent, and sexy movements make me want to stay on the dance floor for an eternity. But eventually, reality gets the better of me, and we agree it's time to leave.

Once settled into the car, Dani suddenly gasps, drawing my immediate attention.

"What is it?" I frantically say, dying to know what's wrong. The sheer panic alone shaves years off my life. I wait for her to reply, but nothing is said. *Good God, woman! Why won't you tell me what's the matter?*

When the vehicle stops at a light, I finally see the cause of her sudden noise. She's in the zone. She says nothing as she pulls out her phone and begins to type frantically. It appears as if her mojo has returned, and this trip did more for her than I ever could have hoped for.

34

DANI

THE NEXT MORNING, WORDS ARE STILL FLOWING. I WROTE MOST of the night, but for some reason, despite my little sleep, waking up in Luke's arms has made all the difference.

Luke has left for the stadium, and I'm going to ride with his family to the game this afternoon. In the meantime, I've locked myself away in his room and pour my story onto the pages. I've shut off my phone, internet, and anything that can distract me. I had asked Luke's mother when I saw her earlier to interrupt me about an hour before we leave for the stadium. She was gracious and immediately understood my request.

By the time she arrives, I've written more today than I have in the last two weeks. My characters are now talking clearly in my head, and the world they live in has become crystal clear. With nearly six thousand words written in a single morning, I gladly take the much-needed break when Mona knocks on the door.

We make it to the stadium with plenty of time to spare. I

laugh and joke with everyone as we wait for the game to start. Despite the fact we're the only ones around us proudly wearing Rainier Renegades gear, we couldn't be happier rooting for our team. According to Ken, Tennessee's been a strong rival for years, so this should be an interesting game.

Whatever high I'd been riding from getting my mojo back, quickly disappears by the end of the first quarter. After our quarterback threw an interception with three minutes to go in the quarter, it went downhill from there. Tennessee ran it back for a touchdown. Then one of our better receivers gets pulled from the game for a possible concussion due to an illegal tackle, which got one of one of the guys from Tennessee ejected. Thank God, I had Mona here to explain everything to me because I had no freaking clue what everyone had been so upset about.

I watch the game on the edge of my seat, but of course, Luke draws my attention more. By half-time, his hair appears as if he's about to rip it out. It stands up on end, from his hands frequently running through it. When the team returns to the locker room, I can only imagine what Luke's going to say. His parents remain hopeful we'll be able to pull it off, but his sister and Becca remain skeptical.

My eyes whip to theirs, when Becca casually states, "I guess Luke's attention has been focused elsewhere."

"Excuse me?" I ask for clarification. Has she not been watching him nearly rip his hair out over the plays that aren't coming together? Luke's working his ass off for this team. It's the players who can't pull them off.

"I'm just saying, maybe he should've spent the evening with the team, rather than out clubbing last night?" Becca states as if it should explain everything. "They obviously weren't ready for Tennessee."

"Luke wasn't out clubbing," I spit out, standing immediately taller as I come to his defense. No one knows we went out last night, and we only danced to a few songs. It was a hole-in-the wall bar, not a dance club.

Becca pulls out her phone and shows me an image. Shit. It does indeed appear as if he's in a nightclub, as all you can see is us with the band behind us. We're embraced and dancing to a slow song, from the looks of it. "It's not what it looks like," I protest. "Luke was home before nine. We simply went out to dinner and danced when the band began to play."

"We know that," Mona says, coming to my defense, and I couldn't appreciate her more. "Luke's just having a bad game. That's all." She looks pointedly to Becca.

"Have you seen what's being said about the two of you?" Becca asks, but I can't quite read her intent. She doesn't appear to be malicious, but I can't quite tell if she's being genuinely concerned either.

"I don't pay attention," I admit. Luke and Tanya had warned me to stay off social media, unless it was something I typically do. I haven't been on any troll sites or read any gossip, since we made the front page a few weeks ago.

"Well..." Becca scrolls through her phone and stops to read something. "Is it true one of your books just got a movie deal?"

I nod, acknowledging the truth of that comment. What can I say, it's true.

"Really, Dani?" Mona asks, shock written all over her face. "That's amazing! I'm so happy for you."

But Becca ignores Mona and continues reading aloud,

"According to this site, the only reason you got that deal was your newfound fame by dating Luke."

What. The. Fuck? My mouth drops open, and I immediately hear Mona chastise Becca, but I'm not sure what else is said. I'm too busy lost in my own head. I've had this movie deal in the works since before I met Luke. Sam and I had been putting out feelers for a while. There's no way that's true. I start to feel some relief, but then another thought hits me.

There's no way it's true, unless... Shit. Maybe she's right. I didn't find out about the deal until after we made the national news and had our joint interview. Would the Hollywood execs really give me a movie deal based on the guy I'm dating? Surely not.

The thought of not getting the movie deal on my own merit makes my stomach turn. I immediately jump to my feet and rush to a bathroom. I push through the crowd and barely make it to the toilet in time, before I'm relieving myself of the contents of my stomach. I wretch over and over, until I am doing nothing but dry-heaving into the toilet.

When I think I'm finished, I flush and make my way to the sink. I quickly wash my hands and bring some water to my mouth to get rid of the horrid taste. I can't imagine that comment being true, but I can't be certain I got it on my own either.

I glance to the woman in my reflection, and I barely recognize her. My face is red and splotchy, my eyes are bloodshot, and my hair springs out in all directions from the ponytail it's falling out from.

I'm startled when the door slams open, and Mona briskly

walks into the bathroom. She immediately halts when she sees me. "Are you okay, darlin'?"

I half-moan a response. "I don't think so. I'm gonna catch an Uber back to your place." There's no way I can walk back in and watch Luke's team play right now. Especially if the media catches wind of where I'm sitting and sees me looking like this.

"Give me a minute, and I'll go with you." Mona reaches out to tame a lost curl by pushing it behind my ear.

There's no way I'm up for company, so I shake my head. "No. You go back with your family. I'll be fine on my own. I just need the code to your gate, and I should be fine."

Mona looks hesitant and unsure of what to do. She contemplates her decision for almost an eternity before she asks, "Are you sure? It wouldn't be any trouble to take you home."

I straighten my spine and say with more confidence than I feel, "Positive. I just want to get out of here before anyone sees me. If you're with me, it'll draw more attention."

Her mouth opens to argue, but she must think better of it. It quickly snaps shut. "If you insist..."

I can tell it pains her to let me go, but really, it's for the best. I nod to make it sound more forceful. "I insist. I'm just feeling under the weather. Please tell Luke after the game. I'll see him at home."

Mona still looks as if she doesn't want to leave me. But eventually, she concedes. She steps forward and embraces me with a well-needed hug. "I'll see you later. If you need anything, please call."

"I will," I lie for the first time to her. The lie feels bitter on my tongue, but it's necessary. I need to get the hell out of here, and I don't want anyone fussing over me.

She quickly tells me the code, and I give her one last hug. As I walk out of the stadium, I pull open the app from my phone to order a car. It should be here in six minutes. I have just enough time to walk to the corner of the parking lot. When I finally drive away, I glance one more time at the stadium, and unshed tears stream down my face.

The entire ride, I contemplate my choices, but I come to only one decision. There's no way I can have a career on my own *and* be with Luke. I can't let his fame dictate my future. I also can't sit around and be a distraction to him. We obviously shouldn't be together.

Look at the game today; it's the perfect example of why it won't work. It's best I get out now, before I fail miserably down the road. I wipe the tears from my face the best I can with my Rainier Renegade jersey. It's scratchy but does the trick.

We haven't even said, 'I love you' to one another, so I owe it to both of us to take myself out of the equation before either of us get hurt any further. I was happy with my life before meeting Luke, I'll be fine afterward.

But that's not true, a quiet voice in my head reminds me, and my heart squeezes. *It's what has to be done,* I scold myself, over and over, until I can make myself believe it's true.

By the time I've made it to Luke's parents' home, my mind is made up. I ask the driver to stay as I dart into the house. I quickly gather my things and make it out to the car in record time.

When I get in, the driver asks, "Where to?"

"Take me to the airport, please."

35

LUKE

Whoever said 'It doesn't matter if you win or lose, it's how you play the game,' is a fucking liar. Losing sucks! There are no ifs, ands, or buts about it. It fucking sucks. No one can tell me otherwise.

We were outplayed on the field today, plain and simple. I made some good calls, my team made some great plays, but at the end of the day, it wasn't enough to get the job done. With this being the first loss of our season, it's a particularly hard blow to the team's ego.

But I truly believe we'll get back out there and kick ass in our next game. I told my team as much during our post-game meeting. We'll stay in a hotel tonight and return to Tacoma tomorrow. I'll stay with my family and leave with the team, bright and early in the morning.

Though all I want to do is lose myself in Dani, I force myself to be present and focused in the post-game press interviews. I have to say, it's a lot easier having these interviews when you've won. Losing sucks. Plain and simple. But I've been trained enough to know how to spin it as an experience to learn from. I do believe the words I say, but it doesn't mean my gut isn't churning.

At one point, one of the asshat reporters asks about my time here in Nashville with Dani. I refused to comment, just like I promised in the one and only interview Dani and I did together, and quickly steered the interview back to the game. I could tell other reporters wanted to ask more, but I wasn't having it. They even mentioned me being out on the town, but I cut it short with I went to dinner and was home before curfew, which I was—leaving zero room for more commentary.

By the time I'm done with obligations for the afternoon, I'm more than ready to head to my parents' home. We'd agreed I'd meet them at their place, but as I look around, I secretly had hoped Dani would've stayed to ride back with me.

The one good thing about being one of the last to leave the stadium, is that traffic's light. My parents know to give me space to clear my head after I've lost a game, so I'm relieved I'll be able to spend more time with Dani before flying out at the crack of dawn tomorrow. Knowing she'll be in my arms will make the world right again.

When I enter the kitchen, I see my parents sitting at the table, drinking a cup of coffee. Marie, Becca, and Dani are nowhere to be found.

"Hey," I greet them as I remove my jacket. "Where's Dani?"

"We hoped you knew." My mother's voice fills with concern. "At first, we thought she'd stayed to wait for you at the stadium, but when we got home, we noticed her things were gone."

"What do you mean, her things were gone? She doesn't fly out until tomorrow." Clearly, I didn't hear them right. Then another thought hits me. "Didn't she ride home with you?"

"Well... honey." Mama worries her hands like she does when she must deliver bad news.

Instantly, I'm on alert. "What's going on, Pops?" Maybe he'll give me a straight answer. He's never been one to beat around the bush.

"Son, Danika left during half-time. She got sick and wasn't feeling well." Pops' voice sounds huskier than usual.

"She got sick?" Okay, that makes sense. Of course, she'd come home if she got sick. "Why didn't you come with her?"

"She was upset, and I followed her into the bathroom," Mama starts to explain.

"Wait..." I interrupt. "What was she upset over?" My voice raises as my anxiety grows. What the fuck was wrong with Danika? What aren't my parents telling me?

"I'm... not exactly sure."

Becca and Marie choose that moment to come in. Becca's eyes are red-rimmed and looks as if she's been crying, and Marie isn't much further behind her. "I'm pretty sure I know." She looks pointedly to Becca as if she's waiting for her to fill me in.

"What is it?" I spit out. Why the fuck won't my family tell me what's going on? If Dani's sick, I need to find her and make sure everything's okay.

"Well..." Becca starts, then looks to the ceiling as if it

somehow has the answer written on it. "I may have said something to upset Danika."

"Ya, think?" Marie's snarky attitude takes me by surprise.

Becca looks to me with pleading eyes, "I'm so sorry, Luke. I never meant any harm."

"What. Did. You. Do?" I spit out each word as if it is its own sentence. "Somebody had better tell me what's going on..." I practically growl.

"Well, I made some smartass comment about how you should've been with the team last night and not out clubbing, because of how the team was playing today..." She takes a deep breath and rambles on, "And... Danika may have taken offense to it."

"What? We weren't out clubbing."

"That's not all, Becca. Tell him the rest," Marie demands. My sister's voice is stern, leaving little room for interpretation, letting Becca know it's time to cut the shit.

What else could she have possibly said? I've loved Becca like a sister for years, but if she doesn't fucking spit it out soon, I can't be held liable for my response.

"I also may have... insinuated that the only reason she got her movie deal with her book, was because she's dating you." All of it comes out in a rush.

"Come again?" I ask for clarification because clearly, I didn't hear her right. There's no fucking way Dani's movie deal had anything to do with her dating me.

Marie interjects, in what I assume is an attempt to keep me from killing her friend. "She told Dani about what fans were saying online about her getting a movie deal. According to the site, it was only offered because of her recent notoriety."

"You gotta be fucking with me?" I ask in disbelief to everyone in the room. Surely, this is the time where someone cracks a smile and fills me in on this sick joke they're playing.

"I'm afraid not, Luke." Mama stands to place her hand on my shoulder. I brush her off as heat radiates from my body, and she steps away.

"What happened next?" I grit through my teeth, knowing if I relax my jaw, I'm likely to tell them all exactly where to go and how to get there, in no uncertain terms.

"There's not much to tell. Dani suddenly looked as if she were about to be sick, and she bolted from the stadium." The scene Marie describes makes my heart wrench. What the fuck is wrong with Becca for telling her that bullshit? Why the hell would Dani even believe it? Surely, she knows better. *Doesn't she?*

"I followed her into the bathroom. She'd just exited a stall, but it was evident she'd just been ill. She convinced me I should stay and watch the rest of the game... And that she wanted me to tell you, she'd see you at home..." Mama's eyes suddenly go round as saucers, "Wait, you don't think she meant home... as on Anderson Island, do you?"

I reach to my pocket and pull out my phone to call her. Fuck, it doesn't even ring. It goes straight to voicemail, so I hang up.

"Well, with her things gone, I'm afraid she might." Pops' usual voice of reason does nothing for me now.

I frantically hit redial on my phone. This time, when it goes directly to voicemail, I wait and leave a message. "Danika. Please call me back. I need to talk to you."

"What do I do now?" I ask myself aloud, not expecting an answer.

But of course, Pops being Pops, he answers it for me, "You wait until tomorrow morning. You fly home with the team, and you go get your girl."

He makes it sound so simple. If only it was.

Mama reaches out her hand in an attempt to soothingly rub my back. "Don't worry, Luke. Danika knows you love her. You'll get this sorted out."

My first response is to agree with her because I know without a doubt in my mind, that I love Danika. *But fuck... she doesn't.*

What the fuck am I going to do now?

DANI

By the skin of my teeth, I manage to catch a red-eye flight. It's now a little after six, and I've been up for nearly twenty-four hours. Of course, Luke had bought me first-class tickets for the way out, but on the way home, the only seat available is in the center seat, of coach. Just my luck.

I can't sleep a wink on the flight home. My thoughts whirl like a merry-go-round and never let up. I can't stop worrying about ruining Luke's career by being a distraction or having this be the end of mine because I can't seem to write lately. And of course, I can't stop thinking about how much it actually hurts to walk away. Without a doubt, I love this man enough to walk away. It's what's best for us. Or at least I'm trying to convince myself of that. Just the thought of never seeing him again, hurts so fucking much. It's difficult to breathe, and it feels as if I might crumble to pieces at any minute.

The weather in Washington matches my mood. Dark and

dreary. Rain falls in buckets, and the wind howls as I take an Uber to the ferry terminal. Knowing I don't want to pay for the driver to wait for the ferry, I hop out and wait inside the building after buying my ticket online. Thank God my bag's waterproof, because my computer would be toast by the time I walk home from the terminal when I get to the island. It's only a mile or so, so it shouldn't be too bad.

Boy, I am wrong. It takes every ounce of energy to walk from the ferry. By the time I make it home, I'm completely soaked to the bone. My clothes stick to my body, and my hair looks as if I've taken an outdoor shower. I protect my computer bag as much as I can, to be safe. I flop my things in the entry and lock the door behind me.

Once I've rid myself of my wet clothes, I walk straight to the shower, in hopes of warming up as soon as possible. I hadn't been prepared to walk any distance, and my teeth chatter as I adjust the temperature of the water.

As the water cascades over me, I warm up. Eventually, my chattering stops. By this time, I'm so weak and exhausted, I slide down the tile and sit on my shower floor. I lose track of all time sitting on the shower floor. Fortunately, my mind's numb from sheer exhaustion. I can do little but merely exist.

When the water cools, I force myself to get out. My arms and legs feel like lead weights attached to my body as I stand. They barely want to do more than just hang. I force them to find a towel and dry off. I slump to my bedroom, with my hair wrapped in a towel and grab the first pair of clean underwear and pajamas I can find. I slip them on, only to plop onto my bed.

Knowing my brush is in my suitcase, I dig it out and

quickly pull it through my hair, or I'll regret it later. As I unzip my suitcase, I see Luke's t-shirt from the day before. In my haste to leave, I must've picked it up by mistake.

On instinct, I pull it to my nose and inhale. It smells just like him. The realization of how much I miss him makes my heart break once again. How does it even have enough pieces left to shatter again? Instantly, I know I've made a huge mistake. *God. What did I do?* A fresh batch of tears fall freely down.

Exhausted, I fall back onto my pillow with his shirt clenched in my hand. I'm not sure how long I stay that way before I feel a chill. I haphazardly worm my way under the blankets and snuggle with Luke's shirt. I take another deep breath, inhaling his scent. There's nothing I can do about anything, now. Sleep. I need sleep. Somehow, I'll find a way to make this better. I just have to...

When I wake up, it's dark, and I'm disoriented. It feels like I've slept for hours, and with it being fall in the Pacific Northwest, it's to be expected. I reach to turn on my bedside light, and nothing. *What the hell?*

More alert, I stumble out of bed and try the switch on the wall. Nothing. Of course, I flip it back and forth just to double, triple, and quadruple check. Fuck, the power's out. I try to remember where I've left my phone and instantly return to my bedside to check the time and use it as a flashlight.

Feeling around with my fingers, I finally find it. I press the button to activate it and sure enough—it's dead. *Why don't I ever fucking charge my phone? I should know better. Especially living on the island for the winter.*

It's then I hear the wind whip through the trees with a low

howl. I should've expected this with the way the storm was when I arrived this morning. Though, in my defense, I'd been a bit distracted.

Instantly, my memories flood back. *Shit... Luke... How do I get a hold of him? I need to apologize and beg him to take me back.* I rush to my dresser and fumble around in the dark to find clothes. I need to get to him. *Maybe he'll come here to the island.* If not, I'll go to his loft in the city. Either way, I'm going to camp out until I make him see me. He has to hear me out. Hopefully, he'll forgive me.

God, do I need him to forgive me. I overreacted and just left, without even giving him a chance.

Fuck. I wish now more than ever I hadn't disconnected my grandparents' landline. I could at least call Luke. Shit... No, I can't.

For fuck's sake, Danika, you don't even know his number. Without your phone, you won't be able to call. God, I'm such an idiot.

I rush to my dresser. I throw on the first pair of pants, sweats I think, and fumble in my drawer for a shirt. In the next drawer, I find what I think is my favorite oversized-sweatshirt. Not caring that they may look hideous together, I grab a pair of socks and fumble in my closet for what I hope are a matching pair of shoes. As I slip my feet in, they feel as if they're at least on the right foot.

Grabbing my keys and purse from the table next to the living room, I make my way to the garage.

Shit! With the power out, I can't drive my car since it's stuck in the garage. Not having been on the island during the winter before, I'm obviously unprepared.

I feel my way along the car and open it. The light from inside illuminates the garage, enough for me to get my bearings. I sit in the car and turn the key just to get enough to get the clock to illuminate. Christ, it's already nearly seven. I've slept the day away. The good news is, Luke should be in Washington by now. His flight was due in earlier this afternoon.

Think, Danika. Think. How can you get to Luke?

I have no fucking clue, but one thing's for certain. I need to find him. I think through my options, but no matter what I choose, it won't be simple.

I remember my grandpa once saying how he had to dismantle the garage door, but as I look up at the opener, I immediately rule that out. It's too freaking complicated. There are some flashlights and headlamps in the camping gear... Maybe I can walk? The wind chooses this moment to pick up and bat some branches against the house, causing me to shiver. The thought of roughing the elements twice in one day has me cringing. Fuck. It's nasty out there.

From the corner of my eye, I see my bicycle. It's less than a couple miles to Luke's. At least if I ride my bike, I can get out of the storm sooner than later. Walking to the bike, I fondly remember the day Luke brought me a replacement tire. The look on his face when he arrived that afternoon, melted my heart. His bright-blue eyes and boyish grin knocked away at the wall I'd been holding in place for years. If he hadn't done that, I'm sure my life would be vastly different.

My heart aches at the realization of what I've thrown away. My insecurities and the fact that I gave a fuck about others' opinions, might as well have been the death of me. *Fuck... what have I done?* I need to fix this. Now!

Without another second of thought, I leap out of the car to search for either a headlamp or flashlight. There's no way I'm literally willing to kill myself by traveling down a dark road in a storm. I do have some brain cells left after the last twenty-four hours, even if I didn't use them in Nashville, I sure as hell plan on using them now.

If I could kiss my grandparents, I would the second I find a working headlamp. Thanks to their obsessively organized garage, I find one within a few minutes. I use the light from the dome of the car to secure my helmet and maneuver my bike to the door of the garage. Upon opening the side door, the breeze hits me like a hurricane. Fuck, it's really coming down out there.

Using the headlamp, I rush back into the living room to get a sturdy jacket that will hopefully make me look less like a drowned rat when I finally do find Luke.

It doesn't take long to rush out the door and head to where I pray to God, Luke is. As the rain pelts my face, I pump harder and harder down the narrow road. In the back of my mind, I know there's a good chance he won't be here.

But I have to try. If he's not here, hopefully the ferry's running, and I can take a cab from the mainland to his loft. Maybe Evelyn will be at Luke's and can help me figure out a way to get a hold of him. This thought alone puts some pep into my pump, and I peddle with all my heart, hoping to find Luke as soon as possible.

As I enter his gravel driveway, I'm disappointed to find his property completely dark. The gravel turns to complete mud, and eventually, I can't pump much further. I jump off my bike and push it to his door. I run up the steps and in what's sure to be a futile attempt, I pound on the door. I wait for what seems like an eternity... nothing. I knock again, just for good measure, but again. No such luck... Fuck! Where is he?

3 7

LUKE

THE CHARTERED FLIGHT HOME MUST BE THE LONGEST FUCKING
flight I've ever been on. Since last night, if I called Danika
once, I've called her at least a hundred times. Every fucking
time, it goes straight to voicemail. I've left so many fucking
messages, her voicemail now says it's full. Why the fuck isn't
she answering? Is she just being stubborn? Or has something
happened to her? Not knowing is absolutely hell. Of course,
being on a plane means I can't call anymore, so I'm back to
fucking waiting.

Fuck, Leighton, get it together, I scold myself. She's likely just
forgot to charge her phone. *But what if she hasn't? What if she
didn't even make it home, and she's stuck in a fucking airport
somewhere between here and Nashville?*

Somehow, I'm physically present in all the coaches
meetings we typically hold on the plane, but my brain can
only focus on Dani. I almost feel sorry for Tyrell and Brandon.

They've had to repeat themselves often. Eventually, they figure out something's wrong. But of course, as the annoying bastard I am, I don't reveal anything. It's none of their fucking business why I'm a train wreck. *How could I explain it, even if I did open up? I have no fucking clue what's going on.*

Eventually, they leave me to my own devices for the last hour or so of the trip, which is a huge relief. Unfortunately, I can't concentrate for shit. But at least I'm not annoying the fuck out of anyone but myself.

My biggest conundrum throughout this entire thing, is the fact I can't figure out Danika's headspace. I really thought everything was good between us. She hit it off with my parents, and I get along with hers. Sure, I've been busy with the team, but I never once thought she never had a problem with it. She's the type of girl I can go out and do things with, as well as sit back, relax, and enjoy the silence. She's also the first girl I've actually allowed to know the real me, beyond the surface. *What the hell happened to make her flee like that?*

I've analyzed the conversation between Becca and Danika to the point where I feel my only option is ripping my hair out. On the surface, what Becca said wasn't horrible... she could have been a lot worse, with as blunt as she typically is. Danika's got pretty thick skin, if how she's handled everything from the media so far tells me anything... So, what's the underlying issue?

Knowing the island is likely the only place Danika will go, as soon as it's humanly possible, I get off the plane and practically run to my car. I'm sure some people called after me, at this point, my give a fuck is well beyond broken. I zip out of the parking lot and find the fastest route. Of course, with the weather being shitty, traffic's hell on the interstate. It takes twice as long to arrive at the ferry terminal.

Just as I pull down the hill, I see the ferry pull out of the docks. Fuck! Could my luck get any worse? Now I have to wait for almost an hour for it to return and load again.

Waiting's the last thing I need. My concentration's shit, so there's no use in trying to get any work done, like I typically do while waiting for the ferry. Tapping my hand aimlessly on the steering wheel, my nerves fray. Just when I'm about to lose my mind, I give up and call my parents. Pops is probably the only person who can bring me back from this preverbal ledge I'm dangling from.

True to form, Pops cuts to the chase when he answers, "Have you worked things out yet?"

I sigh heavily, and my heart drops to my stomach. "No," I groan. "I haven't been able to reach her all day. It's killing me, Pops."

"Where are you now?" he calmly asks as if my world hasn't just fallen apart.

"I'm waiting to board the ferry. I can't believe how messed up this is. What the fuck had her high-tailing it out of town like her ass was on fire?"

"Uh..." he hesitates, "I'm afraid you'll have to find that one out from her." As worked up as I've been today, it's a relief to hear rational thoughts for a change. I love that Pops is a no-nonsense man.

"I know," I agree, and the noose around my chest lightens a hair.

"Not to rub salt in your wounds, but your mama and I really liked her. I sure hope you're able to work it out." My heart pangs at the thought of failure, causing me to instantly sit up straight. *Hell no! Failure isn't an option. I haven't felt this way about anyone, ever. I'm not giving up yet. Christ, but she left. Am I the only one feeling this?*

With my silence, he takes it upon himself to put things into perspective. "You know, son, if it's any consolation, I'm certain Dani fancies you, as much as you do her. I saw the way she looked at you. A girl who looks at a man like that, has her heart on the line."

"That's just it, Pops. I've shown her how I feel, but I don't think I've ever said the words." As soon as the words are out, my stomach turns to stone. But I continue, "With as much as she has on her plate, if she doesn't think I'm all in, why would she stick around?" Even I can hear the desperation in my voice, but at this point, I don't fucking care. I just need to find Dani and make this right.

"Seems to me, the answer's simple."

As I let what he says sink in, my mind races, and I stare out into the Sound. I gasp when I see what's before me. How had I not noticed this? Instead of seeing the island, with sporadic lights spread throughout, it's mysteriously dark. With the raging storm outside, it's evident the power's gone out. Fuck, can this day get any worse?

At least I have a generator, but does Dani? Is this why she hasn't returned my calls? Will she even be home, once I get there? With each passing second, my nerves get wound tighter and tighter.

"Luke?" I hear Pops call for a second time. "What is it?"

"The storm took out the power to the island. I'm so fucking preoccupied, I hadn't even noticed it. Maybe that's why Dani isn't answering her phone?" I wonder more to myself than expecting an actual answer.

"Just calm down, Luke. There's nothing you can do until you get there. There's no sense in wasting your energy worrying."

Yeah, those words are far easier said than done. But I'm not about to argue with Pops, I know better. Besides, as much as I hate to admit it, he's right.

"I know, Pops," I quietly say in defeat. I need to get my shit together.

"It will all work out the way it's meant to be, Luke. Have a little faith."

"Yeah. I know," I admit. One way or another, it will work out as it's supposed to. "Uh, Listen, Pops, I gotta go. The ferry's unloading, and I need to drive on board. Give Mama my love, and I'll call you tomorrow."

"Love you, Luke."

"Love you, too," I say as I hang up the phone.

My nerves are frayed by the time I drive off the ferry nearly forty minutes later. Without hesitation, I beeline it to Dani's. It's dark, but I still get out to knock on the door. As I run up the steps, I'm pelted with rain. With strong winds, it's coming at me from all directions, and I hardly think an inch of me is dry when I make it up the steps. As I pound on the door, I'm not sure what's louder, the wind or my heart beating out of my chest.

Nothing.

I pound again and out of desperation, I holler, "Danika, are you there?"

There's still nothing. Just the trees blowing hard and rain hitting the siding of the house. Obviously, she's not here. But where could she be? "Fuck," I grumble in defeat and stomp back to my car. I can't catch any breaks today.

Knowing the storm could have dropped some tree limbs, I carefully maneuver my way back to my house at the end of the island. My wipers turned on as high as possible, are still no match for this vicious storm. *Shit, it's nasty out here.*

As I pull into my driveway, movement from my deck catches my attention as my headlights sweep the area. What the fuck is someone doing out here in this storm? Are they breaking in?

Instead of pulling into the garage, I park, directing my light onto the deck to inspect it further. To assess the situation, I stay in the car before jumping into action. The person on the porch is drenched as water rolls off them. They're dressed in a bright red jacket with an oversized hood, purple sweats, one bright-blue sneaker and the other dark purple. The face is hidden by an arm blocking the light so I can't discern if it's male or female. The form looks easily smaller than mine, so I should be able to take them on with little effort. I turn off the engine but keep my lights on to illuminate the porch, giving me another moment to decide what I should do. They don't look threatening. Could they be homeless looking for a warm place to stay? *I can't really blame them if they are.* At the same moment, my eyes spot the familiar wheels of a bicycle propped against the deck and... holy shit, she's here?

I must be fucking hallucinating. There's no way she'd risk

being out here in this fucking weather. Would she? I'm frozen in place as I scrutinize the figure on my deck. After all the shit I've gone through in the past twenty-four hours, I can't allow myself to hope. But when the figure lowers the arm and a lock of curls flies out from under the hood. I'm flying out of my car in an instant.

"What are you doing?" I shout over the wind as the rain pelts my face as I bound up the steps.

Something is said, but lightning flashes across the sky and thunder booms seconds later.

It dawns on me she must have ridden through this storm to get here. Worry sets in, and my protective instincts take over. "What the fuck were you thinking? You could've been killed." My voice is more menacing and gruffer than my intent.

I make quick work at the lock on my door and quickly usher her inside, leaving the door open and zero room for argument. Once I get her inside, she takes off the hood of her coat, and her trademark hair springs in every direction.

Dani starts to say something, but I quickly interrupt, "Why are you out in this storm on a fucking bicycle of all things? There's no power on the entire island, and it's dark as fuck outside."

To stop the constant dripping on the floor, Dani takes off her coat, and I take it from her to hang it on the coat rack by the door. Underneath, she has a lime-green hooded sweatshirt. I pause for a moment to take in her entire ensemble. Dani's typically put together well, but it's like she's been dressed by a color-blind clown going to the circus.

"What happened to you?" I ask in wonder as I reach for a

blanket on the couch to hand it to her. She eagerly accepts it and wraps it around her body.

"Ohmigod, Luke. I'm so glad you're here," she stammers, though I'm not sure if she's talking to me or herself now. "I don't know what I'd do if you hadn't shown up." Dani shifts her weight from foot to foot and worries her hands wrapped at the ends of the blanket, waiting for my response.

Instantly, I lock eyes with her. She still hasn't answered my question, and her look of sheer desperation hasn't made any of my worries go away. "What's going on?"

"Shit..." She bites on her lower lip and looks anywhere but at me. "I think I've made a mistake."

"Mistake?" What the hell is she talking about?

"I shouldn't have come here." She glances to the door and winces when another bolt of lightning streaks across the sky.

There's no way she should be out in this weather. "Why did you ride your bike here?" It had to be important, to risk riding in this weather.

"I... Uh... Obviously fucked this up." Through the shadows from the light illuminating my entry, I see her face fall dramatically, and my stomach turns to stone and drops to the floor. "I'm so sorry."

Fuck. This is bad. She's seconds away from fleeing... again. I can't let her go. Especially in a thunderstorm. She turns to grab her coat. "Stay," I practically shout. I've been on edge since yesterday and after finally getting to see her beautiful, though distressed face, I can't let her bolt again. At least not without knowing why.

"But... But..." she stammers. Fuck! I can't tell if she's crying or if it's from the rain, but her eyes are glistening.

"Danika." I take a step closer. "What's going on? Why'd you risk your life to be here?"

"I... I..." Her eyes are wide, and she takes in a deep breath, before releasing it all at once. "I needed to see you."

But why would she ride her bike in the fucking dark? The thought of losing her makes my blood go cold. I want nothing more than to wrap her in my arms, but I need to be sure I'm welcomed. "Why?"

"Shit." She looks to the ceiling. "I'm already too late."

Too late? Too late for what? "What..." I begin, but I'm cut off.

"Obviously, you don't want me here." She drops the blanket and reaches for her jacket.

"Like hell I don't," I call out louder than I expect. "I've been going out of my fucking mind since you left. Why the fuck haven't you answered your phone?"

Eyes wide, she sputters, "I... I was on the plane, then it... died."

"I've left you messages for the past two days. I've been an asshole to everyone within earshot, all because you didn't charge your phone? Why did you even leave to begin with?" This all comes gushing out like the floodgates on my thoughts have been lifted.

Danika shakes her beautiful head, and curls bounce in every direction. "I'm so stupid."

"No," I forcefully disagree. "You're not stupid. What's going on in that beautifully brilliant mind of yours, Danika? Talk to me," I plead.

"I got stuck in my head. I let all my fears, doubts, and speculations fill up my headspace. I... I... just reacted."

When she shakes her head in disgust, I'm not having that.

"Danika." I wait until her eyes focus on mine. "If you have a problem with me, talk to me. I'm pretty dense at times and have no clue if I've fucked up." Hell, I still don't know what I did to piss her off and make her leave.

She gasps. "Oh, Luke. You didn't do anything wrong. I just freaked out because I thought I was ruining your career by being a distraction. Since you were losing, and I've been sucking at my word counts lately, I foolishly thought we were a bad mix... and..." She takes a deep breath and closes her eyes before blurting out the rest, "I... I thought I should end it before I fell even harder for you... So, when Becca mentioned I only got my movie deal from your notoriety, I fully let myself freak out. And when given the chance, I ran."

Holy shit. What do I tackle first? I run through each of her points as I determine which is the most pertinent. Might as well go in order. "First, you had nothing to do with the loss. We were outplayed on the field, and it's as simple as that. We'll bounce back and adjust as we continue the season."

"But..." she interrupts.

But I persist, holding up a hand to stop her. "Second, if you're having a difficult time, I need to know this. If you can't tell, I'm not a mind reader, so I'd appreciate it if you'd fill me in." This brings a smile to her face, and my heart soars. "Third, you're a brilliant writer. You got that movie deal on your own. Any fool who'd tell you different... is just that, a fool."

"I know, but..."

"No buts," I forcefully continue controlling the conversation. "And as for falling for me... well... that's fucking

347

spectacular because I'd hate to think I'd fallen head over heels in love with you, alone." I grin like a loon as I wait for it to sink in. *I'm not going anywhere, and if she thinks I'm going to let her go, she's got another thing coming.*

Her mouth forms an 'O' as her eyes go wide. "You... you love me... too?"

Relief radiates throughout my body. Who knew those few simple words could change my entire world. "Fuck yeah, I do." Without giving her a second to react, I step forward and crash my lips on hers. Her face is cold, but her breath is warm.

Her sudden gasp allows me to taste her with my tongue. Fuck, she's delicious. Her hands wrap around my neck, and I pull her body to mine, leaving no space between us. As I devour her with my mouth and run my hand along her back, the other guides our kiss at the base of her neck. As consuming as our kiss is, eventually, I feel her clothes soak mine, causing me to break the kiss.

When I do, Danika rocks my entire world with her declaration, "I love you, Luke Leighton. Please forgive me."

"Nothing to forgive, Danika," I reassure her. I brush a kiss against her once again, roaming my hands to her ass. The dampness brings me back to reality. "What do you say I go turn on the generator and get some lights in here?"

"You have a generator?" she asks in disbelief.

"Living out here, of course I do." I pull her close once more, simply to feel that she's here. When I release her, I take in her outfit once again. "When I get the lights on, I need to know about this outfit you're sporting."

She looks down to inspect herself and even in the near darkness, I see her flush. "Ohmigod, I'm a hot mess! In my defense, I dressed in the dark and rushed over here after waking up from taking the redeye last night."

"I'll take you hot mess and all," I growl, bending down to give her a reassuring kiss. "I love all of you, Danika. Not just the pretty parts. Though, those *are* pretty nice."

A big gust of wind comes through the door, causing her to shiver. Fuck, I need to get moving. "Take off your wet things here, and I'll start the generator. No need for you to get sick on top of everything else." With that, I turn and rush to the shop to get the lights back on.

When I return, I'm soaked. Having only stopped to turn off the lights to my car, I can't imagine how Dani must feel after trekking here from her house. She must be soaked to the bone. I'm sure it's pure adrenaline that's keeping her from shivering at the moment. It's cold in here, so we must've lost electricity sometime earlier today.

When I return, she's taken off her shoes, sweatshirt, and is about to peel off her pants. She hadn't made much progress, but she gasps, when I turn on the light. I wince at her discomfort, "Sorry."

"It's a relief to have electricity," she says, peeling off the purple sweats that stick to every inch of her legs. She's standing in my living room with nothing but her underwear and a thin tank top, leaving nothing to the imagination.

"Need help with anything?" I step closer, wrapping my arms around her. I kiss the top of her head. "God, I've missed you." Her closeness makes everything right again, and the worries of the past two days quickly fade into the past.

"I've missed you, too." She wraps her arms around me. "I never should have left the way I did."

When I feel her shiver again, I suggest, "Let's get you into something warmer."

The temptress that she is seductively says, "I have something else in mind for how to warm me up." This immediately gets my blood pumping and awakens my body.

Without another word, she takes my hand and leads me to my bedroom.

DANI

As I lead Luke into the bedroom, my worries from the day melt away. Relief washes over me, and a newfound confidence guides Luke into the bedroom. Don't get me wrong, I've always been one to ask what I wish for, but knowing he loves me makes my heart nearly burst out of my chest. I want nothing more than to show him how I feel.

I lead him to the bed and turn on the lamp from the bedside table. As soon as I illuminate the room, I turn to make fast work at removing his clothes. It's not fair that I'm standing here in my underwear and tank top, while he remains fully dressed. This simply won't do.

As soon as he sees me go for his belt, he quickly toes off his shoes. Just when I've released his belt, he pushes my hands away to rid himself of his jeans. He must be as desperate as I am to be together, because he doesn't waste any time. He pulls off his boxers in one swift move and reaches for the hem of my tank. Within seconds, we're both completely naked. His lips press down onto mine, and I wrap my hands around his neck as I press my body to his.

The heat from his body sears my soul, igniting a flame I wonder if I'll be able to control. Needing to be closer, I push him toward the bed. When he falls backward, bringing me with him, laughter erupts from both of us.

"In a hurry?" he teases.

"Yes," I pant out breathily. "Need you." I sigh as I climb on top of his muscular body. As soon as I'm astride his thighs, he pulls me down for a toe-curling kiss. His fingers find my core, and he strokes me in just the right spot, that has me writhing with need instantly.

"Fuck the foreplay," I moan. "I want you inside of me."

"Not... Gonna... Complain," he grunts as I grab a hold of his more than ready cock. As soon as I line us up, his desperate hands on my hips guide me onto him, rougher than usual.

I take a minute to adjust, while he thumbs my clit with one hand and rolls my nipple with the other. As soon as I feel I'm ready to move, I let loose with everything I have. I abandon all thought and simply feel every part of Luke.

His dark hooded eyes look at me with such need and admiration. I can't help but fall deeper in love with him. When we find the perfect rhythm, he lets out a moan that tells me he's enjoying every single second of this experience. My ignited flames become an inferno, turning me on beyond my wildest belief.

"Oh, God, Luke," I pant as I find the best possible rhythm.

Just when I think I have total power over this man and am about to make him beg for his release, he places his hands upon my hips and tops me from the bottom. The power of our thrusts causes me to brace myself against his chest, holding on for dear life as we both race to orgasmic bliss. When I feel my body tremble, I moan in appreciation.

Luke, knowing me as well as he does, is only spurred on further. He bends to take my nipple in his mouth as he thrusts deeply in and out of me in the perfect motion. My body climbs, my muscles tighten, I cry out as wave after wave of my orgasm rolls through me.

"God, Danika. You're so beautiful," Luke practically grunts as he brushes a lock of hair from my face. Luke continues pumping into me until he's milked each and every wave of ecstasy from me.

He lets out a guttural curse when he stills deep inside me, and his orgasm sets off miniature waves of pleasure inside me. When he can't hold himself upright any longer, he collapses on top of me. His breath's ragged, and his body radiates heat. After thinking I've lost him, it's the best possible feeling in the world.

After a few moments, he rolls onto his back, still panting, in an effort to catch his breath. His head rolls toward mine as his hand cups my face. "Don't. Ever. Leave me again. I love you so much, and I don't know what I'd do without you."

Feeling the exact same way, I simply reply with an impish grin, "Same goes for you."

His beautiful laughter fills the room. "I think I can live with that. You have yourself a deal."

EPILOGUE

Luke

Three years later...

ASKING DANIKA TO MARRY ME WAS THE SIMPLEST DECISION I'VE ever made. Finding time in our busy schedules to have a wedding is a different story. Coaching football and her movie deals—yes, I said deals because three of her books are now being made into movies—have made it difficult to schedule. I've begged her to elope more than once, but both of our parents would've had our hides if we'd done that. Besides, we want to share our nuptials with our closest friends and family and wouldn't have it any other way.

Watching her walk down the aisle this afternoon is one of the happiest moments of my life. With each step she glides toward me on her father's arm, I'm in awe she's choosing to be with me for the rest of her life. Aside from the day I found her on my doorstep in the pouring rain, I don't think I've ever had such a reaction to her. Her beauty makes me breathless and whether she's in a beautiful gown like today, or looking hideous in a disarray of assorted clothes, she's still just as beautiful. It takes everything in my power to not rush down the aisle and haul her into my arms.

When her father finally places her hand in mine, a tingle runs through my spine, and pure joy washes through me. I whisper, "I love you," and she repeats my favorite words and practically mirrors my feelings. She squeezes my hand as the minister begins the ceremony.

Words are spoken, vows are made, but my entire focus is on her beautiful face. When the minister says the words I've been dying to hear, I kiss my bride for all she's worth, not giving a fuck who's there to witness it. I love this woman, and I'm not holding back any longer. Cheers erupt from the crowd, along with a few people clearing their throats and comments, like "Get a room," when it apparently becomes uncomfortable for them to watch. But when I pull away from Danika, her beautiful face lights up with delight.

"I love you, Luke Leighton," she whispers for only me to hear.

"I love you, Mrs. Leighton. You've made me the happiest man alive." I quickly peck her once more before we are introduced as 'Mr. and Mrs. Leighton' to the ecstatic crowd.

We chose to be married during my off week before the season starts, on what we consider to be our anniversary. My family's flown in, and we've invited a few of our close friends and immediate family to help us celebrate. Pops and Mama couldn't welcome Danika into our family fast enough. They love her as much as I do and have made her feel just as welcomed.

As we make our way to the reception being held at the Tacoma Glass Museum, I can't help but think of how much my life has changed since Danika's accident on the island. She's flipped my world upside down, and I wouldn't have it any other way.

To our relief, it turns out she didn't need to worry about her losing her anonymity. Her fans wholeheartedly accepted her using a pen name, which she will continue to do now that we're married. Our close friends know us as Luke and Danika, but most of the world still calls her Charlotte Ann.

"What are you thinking about so hard over there, Mr. Leighton?" Danika asks as she draws me out of my own thoughts.

"Just reminiscing on some of my fondest memories with you, Mrs. Leighton." *God, I love hearing that.* The fact she's officially a part of my family makes me smile even wider.

"I have a few of my own," she teases. "And if you're lucky, when we're alone, I'll share them with you."

"Do we really need to show up at the reception? I'm sure everyone will be fine without us and can enjoy the food and open bar. I'd rather direct the limo driver to our hotel room."

"Luke Leighton!" she pretends to scold. "Your mama would kick your ass from here to next Sunday if we didn't show up. Not to mention, my family would likely hunt us down. God knows, we don't need my pesky brothers butting their noses in where it doesn't belong."

"Speaking of brothers..." I raise an eyebrow, and my curiosity sets in. "How long has Damien been dating Vanessa?

He looks at her the way I look at you. I'm sure he's fallen for her, even if he won't admit it to anyone." Damien's always been focused and kept his personal life private to my knowledge. "It's interesting he'd choose our wedding to bring a woman and her child for the long weekend."

"No kidding, and her daughter's adorable. I never thought I'd see him settle down, but if I had to guess, I'd say he's heading that way in a hurry."

"I'd say so," Danika agrees. "It's funny, I always thought I'd be a parent before him, but clearly things between him and Vanessa are serious, if he's bringing both of them to the wedding."

"Well, I couldn't be happier for them," I admit. "Though I can't wait to be a father."

"Someday." She smiles as I reach over to place my hand on Danika's flat stomach, and she rests hers on mine. She's no longer on birth control, and I hope we get news that she's pregnant sooner than later. I can't wait to have our baby growing inside this beautiful woman. The thought alone makes me giddy.

I never pictured myself as a family man, but after meeting Danika, there's no way I'd picture my life otherwise. I thank God every day since she crashed into my life. She's turned it upside down in all the best ways possible. She's a force to be reckoned with, but I never doubt my decision to make the call and ask to see her again. *Hands down, best decision. Ever!*

We arrive at the museum, and our close friends and family who've arrived before us greet us. As we get out of the limo, I pull Danika into my arms and kiss her breathless. "God, I love you, Danika," I whisper as I pull apart from her all too soon.

"I love you, too, Luke." She takes my hand and guides me through the glass sculptures at the entrance. We stop for a few photos along the way, and her laughter fills the air.

Just as we're entering the reception area, Dani rocks my world in a way that only she can when she reaches up and cups my ear, to whisper the words I never expected to hear on my wedding day.

"By the way, Luke, we won't have to wait for someday." Confused by her train of thought, I cock an eyebrow in her direction, encouraging her to continue. "By the time the season's over, you'll be a dad."

My mouth drops to the floor, and I feel as if my eyes are about to pop out of my head. "Are you kidding me?" I ask in disbelief. There's no way I'm getting married and finding out I'm to be a father on the same day. I haven't felt this excited since the Rainier Renegades finally won the championship game with me as head coach last season.

"Surprise! We're having a baby! I'm due at the end of April."

Filled with emotion, I fling my arms around her and lift her to my height. I twirl her around in a circle, and she squeals with delight. "You've just made me the happiest man, ever! Thank you so much, Danika!"

I feel her arms pat at my shoulders. "Put me down, Luke." She laughs joyfully.

Crap. That might not be good for her or the baby. It would suck if I made her sick on our wedding day. Instantly, I place her on her feet and drop to my knees, where I whisper to her still-flat belly, "I can't wait for you, little one. I'm going to be the proudest papa you've ever seen. You just wait!"

"Aww, Luke." Dani sighs as she leans onto her toes to close the distance between us.

We turn to face the crowd that's now gone silent upon our entry. Shit. I hadn't even realized we'd drawn their attention. But fuck it! I'm too damn happy to care.

I shout to the room, my voice barely containing my excitement. "This is my year! First, Dani's now my wife. And this beautiful woman beside me just told me I'm going to be a dad!"

Cheers and applause erupt from the room. Dani's a bright shade of pink when I look down to gaze in her eyes, but instead of drawing into me, her larger than life personality explodes throughout the room. "Damn straight! Let's get this party started!"

The End

Want more of the Fallon family? Damien and Derek each have their own stand alone stories in Damien and The Boy Upstairs. Begin reading today!
https://amandashelley.com/books-by-amanda-shelley-2/

ACKNOWLEDGMENTS

First, I want to thank you, the reader, blogger, and reviewer for reading this book. There are plenty to choose from, and I want you to know I appreciate you choosing mine to spend time with. Hopefully, you've enjoyed Dani and Luke as much as I have. I'd love to hear from you. You can find me on social media or at www.amandashelley.com. If you care to share your thoughts on this book with other book lovers, please feel free to leave a review at any of the retail sites or on Goodreads and BookBub.

I'd like to thank Amy Queau at QDesign Covers and Premades for creating the incredible cover for this book. You took my vision and brought it to life! You are brilliant, and I absolutely love working with you!

To my editor, Susan Soares at SJS Editorial Services, thank you for working with me. I appreciate your time and feedback. You are amazing to work with. This book would not be what it is today without you.

To Julie Deaton at Deaton Author Services, thanks for making my book pretty. I appreciate knowing your proofreading is exquisite, and my worries become less. Your eagle eyes are spectacular, and I don't know what I'd do without you.

To Mickel Yantz, thank you for designing my Rainier Renegade logo for chapter images. Little did you know as a graphic designer, you'd be talking plot and inadvertently beta reading at times. I can't wait to work with you for swag in the near future.

Cara, thank you for your support from the beginning. Your willingness to beta read is priceless. Thanks for always being willing to talk plot, give honest feedback, and choosing the best adventures in my stories. Life would certainly be different without you in it.

To the people who have supported me along the way, I'm humbly grateful to have you in my life. Whether you've read my books, asked me about my progress, listened to me talk about my fictional characters as if they're a part of my family, plotted with me or been my cheerleader, I truly appreciate your continued support. Please know it has not gone unnoticed.

Last but certainly not least, to my four beautiful girls, who have had to wait patiently when I said, "Just one more minute," when I obviously meant a lot more than one. I appreciate your support more than you'll ever know. I love you more than words can express. You are the reason I continue to strive and reach for my goals each and every day.

ABOUT THE AUTHOR

Amanda Shelley loves falling into a book to experience new worlds. As an avid reader and writer, sharing worlds of her own creation is a passion that inspired her to become an author. She writes contemporary romance about characters who are strong and sexy with a twist of sass.

When not writing, Amanda enjoys time with her family, playing chauffeur, chef and being an enthusiastic fan for her children. Keeping up with them keeps her alert and grounded in reality. She enjoys long car rides, chai lattes and popping her SUV into four-wheel drive for adventures anywhere.

Amanda loves hearing from readers. Be sure sign up for her newsletter and follow her on social media. Join her reader's group Amanda's Army of Readers to talk about her books and stay up to date on her latest information.

Website: www.amandashelley.com
Readers group: https://www.facebook.com/
groups/AmandasArmyofReaders/
Newsletter: https://bit.ly/3iyENe6
Goodreads: https://www.goodreads.com/author/show/
19713563.Amanda_Shelley

facebook.com/authoramandashelley

twitter.com/AmandShelley

instagram.com/authoramandashelley

amazon.com/author/amandashelley

bookbub.com/profile/amanda-shelley

ALSO BY AMANDA SHELLEY

If you enjoyed this book, you will be happy to discover Amanda Shelley primarily writes in one world. For a complete list of the series reading order as well as a chronological time line, please visit: https://amandashelley.com/reading-order/

Coming Soon

Kiss & Tell

What could go wrong when the good girl gets stuck with the bad boy? After all, it's just chemistry...

This limited edition collection takes readers on a whirlwind through new adult college romances where the good girl is stuck with the bad boy and she's not happy about it, until their chemistry together makes her question everything she thought she knew about him.

My contribution is Zander: A Perfectly Independent Series Novella

Zander's known for being a player both on and off the court. When his name shows up as my next client, my heart stalls and not in a good way. There's no way I'll survive the semester with him. I just don't have the patience.

However, when I need help, Zander makes a proposal I can't refuse. He'll be my fake date to my best friend's wedding so I don't have to face my ex and his new girlfriend alone.

The weekend goes off without a hitch as we effortlessly pretend to have the time of our lives.

All is perfect... until I realize my feelings for Zander are no longer an act.

What will I do when our arrangement comes to an end?

Preorder now! Proceeds go to St. Judes Research Hospital
Universal: Books2read.com/kissNtell
Add to TBR: https://tinyurl.com/axdrp2ps
Bookbub: https://tinyurl.com/vz5ckjux

The Vegas Pitch

This pitch could make or break my career.

Not only will it set a personal record for the biggest account I've ever landed, but it could set my newfound company three years ahead of schedule for expansion.

Thank god I've got Nate Barringer on my team.

Even though I had my reservations hiring the sexiest man I've ever laid eyes on - he more than meets my expectations with his hard work and determination. Together, we've formed a solid team and play off each other perfectly.

As we wait for the final verdict, I begrudgingly take Nate up on his offer for a night on the town. After all, this is Vegas and I need to let the chips fall where they may.

Imagine my surprise when I wake up the next morning to find we've not only won the campaign, but I'm apparently married to the man I've only ever let myself fantasize about.

The kicker of it all - he has no intentions of letting me go.

But what will it mean once we leave Vegas?

https://amandashelley.com/books-by-amanda-shelley-2/

Now Available

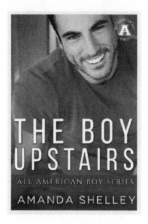

The Boy Upstairs

I ran into Derek while trying to escape the neighbor from hell. Instantly, we hit it off. Since he's only here for three months and the microbrewery leaves me little time for commitments, it's the perfect setup for a fling.

He's adventurous, challenges me, and he just gets me from the inside out.

With our expiration date quickly approaching, I'm left to wonder... Will my heart ever be the same without the boy upstairs?

https://amandashelley.com/books-by-amanda-shelley-2/

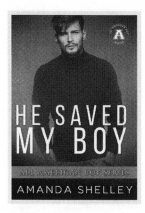

He Saved My Boy

Davis is the first guy to catch my attention since... hell, I don't even know.

Instantly, he makes me think and feel things I've forgotten existed. It has been forever since I put my needs first, so I take the chance and let him light me up from the inside out.

Our night is the kind that will ruin me for all others.

But then I get the dreaded call.

I rush out without a second glance, knowing I'll likely never see him again.

My son will always come first—Always.

Imagine my surprise when Davis walks in, and I find he's the only one who can save my boy.

This cannot be happening—*I guess it's time to pull up my big girl panties and see what happens.*

https://amandashelley.com/books-by-amanda-shelley-2/

Drew: Book One of the Perfectly Independent Series

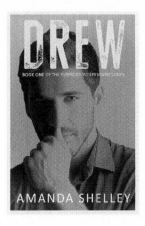

Drew: Book One of the Perfectly Independent Series
Abby

My heart races, palms sweat and knees go weak.

I've never seen anyone like Drew in a science lab. He's made me a firm believer in chemistry existing outside a textbook. Until his ego shows up. Nope – No thank you. Moving on. I mean... who has an entourage in college?

When our professor announces we'll be stuck as lab partners, I nearly lose my mind – I'm certain my dreams of becoming a doctor will go up in smoke with a distraction like him around.

Drew

I don't date during the season.

The number of trolls who venture into the arena simply to chase jerseys is unbelievable. In fact, I typically distance myself from the social side of being a college athlete because I have my eye on something bigger than our next D-1 championship.

I've taken painstaking measures to avoid distractions – at all costs. This plan has worked perfectly until Abby shows up at my door.

Gone is the *plain studious girl* I left in lab the day before. Left in her place is the intriguing woman I want to know better. Here I thought she wouldn't be a distraction – yeah right... I am so screwed.

Abby's gorgeous and there's nothing plain about her.

I am this close to having it all. If I let Abby in, will my perfectly laid out plans disappear?

https://amandashelley.com/books-by-amanda-shelley-2/

Vince: Book Two of the Perfectly Independent Series

It's funny how one night can change everything.

Family comes first. I knew that. I knew there would be sacrifices and we are so close to having it all. I knew because I had the perfectly laid out plan to make it happen.

That is until she walked in and knocked my world on its ass.

Sydney's strong, sexy, independent – possibly more than I can handle. She's everything I've ever wanted, but my reality and the secret I'm harboring, might have her running in the other direction.

Will it all go up in flames if I take a chance on her?

I guess I'm about to find out.

https://amandashelley.com/books-by-amanda-shelley-2/

Damien: Book Three of the Perfectly Independent Series

Beautiful girls are not hard to find at Columbia River University.

The coeds on campus are great to look at but I was over that scene after graduation three years ago.

These days, outside of being part of the largest civil engineering job on campus, all I'm searching for is a decent meal and some peace and quiet. It's why I'm happy to have found what I consider a hidden gem in the diner I frequent. All I need to do is finish this job and move on to the next by year's end.

Should be easy enough. Only when Vanessa walks up with a sexy smile and a mouth full of sass, she does more than take my order. She completely takes my breath away.

Next thing I know, I'm here every morning, making every excuse to dine with this intriguing woman. Not only is she smart and sexy, but she's laser focused on reaching the goals she's set for herself.

The more I get to know her, the more I'm convinced she's the one. I just have to find a way to get her to deviate from her perfectly laid plans and take a chance on me.

https://amandashelley.com/books-by-amanda-shelley-2/

Resilience: Book One of Resilience Duet

Resolution: Book Two of Resilience Duet

Samantha never saw Enzo coming.

As the dust settles from her divorce, her life is full. She doesn't have time for distractions. She's too busy running her own company and checking off numerous items from her kids' demanding schedule to have a life of her own.

Then he walks into her kitchen with his breathtaking green eyes and a mischievous grin. He's there to surprise his father - her contractor, but his presence makes everything off kilter. Enzo's perfectly content with his adventurous life as an elite rescue pilot, until a harmless prank turns on him. Instead of surprising his father, he finds his world thrown off course by the beautiful woman with a sexy smile, wicked sass and the mouthwatering ability to keep him on his toes.

With his limited time on leave, is she worth the risk to his heart?

https://amandashelley.com/books-by-amanda-shelley-2/

Collide: A Sweet Romance

Falling head over heels was the last thing I expected.
Literally.
Coffee is everywhere – and more than my ego is bruised.
When the handsome stranger I plowed into calls me by name,
mortification sinks in.
He rushes off to class. I run home to change, hoping to forget
the whole incident.
If only I could be so lucky.
I quickly find it's a small world and Gavin Wallace is
completely unavoidable. Everywhere I turn he's there. In my
classes. Hanging with my friends.
I've got his full attention and I have to admit, I like it a lot more
than I should.

https://amandashelley.com/books-by-amanda-shelley-2/

Made in the USA
Middletown, DE
07 November 2022